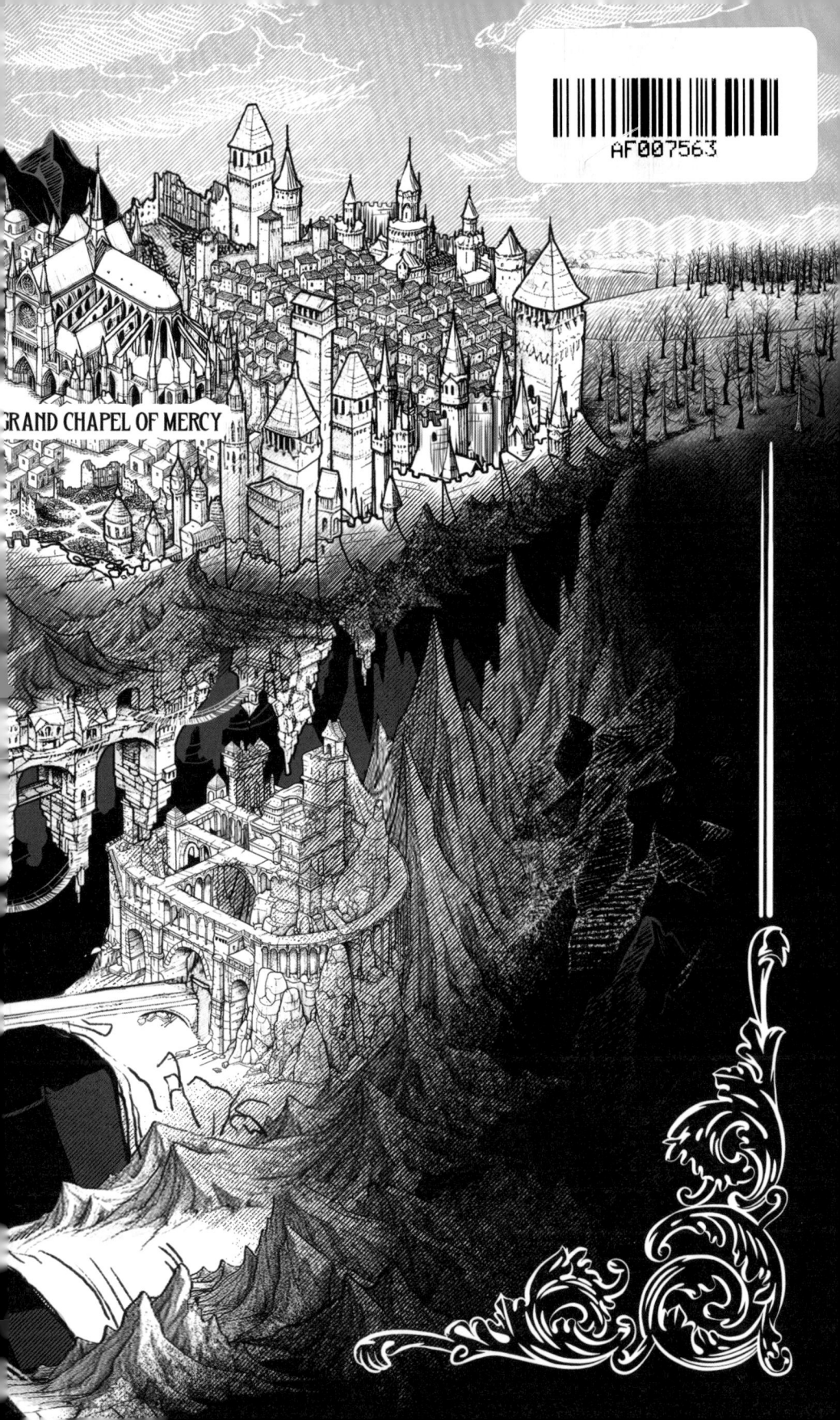

DRAGON CURSED

BY ELISE KOVA

Arcana Academy
Arcana Academy
Prince of Swords

Dragon Cursed
Dragon Cursed

Married to Magic Novels
A Deal with the Elf King
A Dance with the Fae Prince
A Duel with the Vampire Lord
A Duet with the Siren Duke
A Dawn with the Wolf Knight

Air Awakens Universe

Air Awakens Series
Air Awakens
Fire Falling
Earth's End
Water's Wrath
Crystal Crowned

Vortex Chronicles
Vortex Visions
Chosen Champion
Failed Future
Sovereign Sacrifice
Crystal Caged

Golden Guard Trilogy
The Crown's Dog
The Prince's Rogue
The Farmer's War

A Trial of Sorcerers
A Trial of Sorcerers
A Hunt of Shadows
A Tournament of Crowns
An Heir of Frost
A Queen of Ice

The Loom Saga
The Alchemists of Loom
The Dragons of Nova
The Rebels of Gold

ELISE KOVA

DRAGON CURSED

HODDERSCAPE

First published in the United States in 2026 by Entangled Publishing, LLC
First published in Great Britain in 2026 by Hodderscape
An imprint of Hodder & Stoughton Limited
An Hachette UK company

The authorised representative in the EEA is Hachette Ireland, 8 Castlecourt Centre, Dublin 15, D15 XTP3, Ireland (email: info@hbgi.ie)

1

Copyright © Elise Kova 2026

The right of Elise Kova to be identified as the Author of the Work has been asserted by her in accordance with the Copyright, Designs and Patents Act 1988.

Cover design © Marcela Bolivar 2025
Map illustration © Elizabeth Turner Stokes

All rights reserved. No part of this publication may be reproduced, stored in a retrieval system, or transmitted, in any form or by any means without the prior written permission of the publisher, nor be otherwise circulated in any form of binding or cover other than that in which it is published and without a similar condition being imposed on the subsequent purchaser.

All characters in this publication are fictitious and any resemblance to real persons, living or dead, is purely coincidental.

A CIP catalogue record for this title is available from the British Library

Hardback ISBN 9781399740029
Trade Paperback ISBN 9781399740036
ebook ISBN 9781399740043

Printed and bound in Great Britain by Clays Ltd, Elcograf S.p.A.

Hodder & Stoughton policy is to use papers that are natural, renewable and recyclable products and made from wood grown in sustainable forests. The logging and manufacturing processes are expected to conform to the environmental regulations of the country of origin.

Hodder & Stoughton Limited
Carmelite House
50 Victoria Embankment
London EC4Y 0DZ

www.hodderscape.co.uk

for my little dragon

Dragon Cursed is a pulse-pounding young adult romance set in the ruthless city of Vinguard, where dragon hunters reign supreme. The story features elements that might not be suitable for all readers, including torture, violence, death, injury, grief, starvation, hallucinations, imprisonment, common phobias such as bugs and falling, and other similarily intense scenes and themes. Readers who may be sensitive to these elements, please take note.

Boots strike the cobblestone in the alleyway, as sharp to my ears as a dagger being pulled across a whetstone. I press my shoulder into the corner of the building and peer down the narrow squeeze that leads to the alcove where I'm frozen, holding my breath. This is going to be one of two people, and I just hope it's—

My eyes catch on the flap of a dragon-blood red cloak, and I suck back into the shadows, praying he didn't see.

Dragon-burned hells. I *knew* he was following.

I strain my ears as the footsteps disappear. But then they return, slower, more purposeful. The crunch of gravel in the tight passage between buildings has me sucking in a breath. There's nowhere to run.

Pulling myself as tight to the wall as I can, I shut my eyes and lock my muscles into complete stillness, but the footsteps draw ever closer. And as I feel the cool wisp of shadow fall across my face, I know:

I'm so incredibly, impossibly screwed.

Opening my eyes, I expect to see Lucan's towering form. Instead, I'm met with a familiar emerald gaze set against freckled cheeks above the biggest grin.

"Surprise," Saipha whispers.

"Oh, thank Valor." I yank her closer to me, pulling her from view right as the other footsteps cross the alleyway. *Again.*

We wait to speak until he's gone.

"Sorry I'm late. I think you know why," Saipha whispers.

"Because the hound the vicar sends after me was sniffing around your ankles?" I say dryly. "He see you?"

"*Pffft*," she scoffs. "He's not good enough to see me if I don't want him to." But I notice how Saipha doesn't lower her hood. It's the same sandy gray as the stone all of Vinguard is constructed from. Like me, she's dressed to blend in. Her eyes drift to the heavy wooden door over my left shoulder. "Isola, is that what I think it is?"

"Yep." My turn to grin. "I found it."

A way in. Or, more accurately, a way *up*.

"How do you keep finding these?" She's shocked but absolutely delighted. I can tell by the way she shifts her weight from foot to foot, trying not to bounce up and down like she did when we were kids and I agreed to play her favorite game: Mercy Knight and dragon.

I was always the dragon.

"I'm stuck under the Grand Chapel of Mercy more days than not," I say. "The library is full of ancient maps of Vinguard." And those maps show where all the old watchtowers are—towers that have long since been mortared together into a massive wall that now rings Vinguard.

"But those without the gilding can't access the library," she says reflexively. Then immediately blanches as I lock eyes with her. I wave a hand in front of my *two* golden irises, the only matching set in Vinguard. Saipha folds her arms, glancing away, mumbling, "Point taken. I still didn't think the vicar would let you into the library, since you're not a full citizen yet."

"He doesn't. Not on my own, at least. But I do it anyway." As if to underscore my point, I push on the door we're also very much not allowed to enter.

The wood is ancient, hollowed by insects and hundreds of years of weathering. It splits apart at the heavy iron bars that help give it structure, crumbling with a heavy *clang* that feels more ominous than the bells on the wall.

We both freeze.

My chest squeezes, heart skipping a beat.

Saipha slowly leans back, glancing down the shadow-crossed gap between the buildings back to the alleyway.

"Any sign of him?" I whisper.

She shakes her head. Without another word, we step inside quickly, having had the same thought at the same time: *Let's not stand at the scene of the crime.*

There's a tiny room—a landing, really, at the base of a spiral stair. The air is stale and thick with age. But the small hairs at my temples catch on the slightest of winds. With the door open, there's a cross-breeze. That means there's an opening somewhere above.

Saipha taps my shoulder and holds out a lantern.

I resist the urge to tease her about stealing her father's lantern—property of a Mercy Knight—and press my thumb into the lower corner where two lines emerge from behind a plate. Etherlight flows from the soles of my feet, up through my body, and into the pads of my fingers. As the lantern flares to life, a faint golden glow illuminates the ancient stair that's quickly swallowed by the darkness above.

Saipha pushes past me, taking the lead, as she always does. Just like a Mercy Knight would.

As soon as she's two steps ahead, I rub my palm on my thigh and stop suppressing a shiver. It rips through me with a wave of hot nausea that's gone as quickly as it came. *It's getting worse.* Gritting my teeth, I shake my head and start up before she notices me falling behind. But I can't stop myself from massaging the scar on my chest, where it feels like my heart is trying to beat through bone and skin.

"So how'd you manage to get out of training today? I'd think the vicar would be having you run every drill one more time before the Tribunal," Saipha says once we're about one floor up and it's clear we haven't been followed. "Don't tell me you tried to barter with Lucan again?"

"Of course not. He can go suck a dragon talon." I more than learned my lesson with that. Just thinking of that day has my hands balling into fists. But I force myself to relax. *It doesn't matter now.* At least that's the lie I tell myself. "I said I was sick."

"And Vicar Darius bought that?"

"Clearly not completely, since he sent Lucan after me. But Callon is at work. As is Marie. And I'm sure Father is still locked in his workshop." As he has been for weeks. "So it's not like anyone is home to rat me out."

"How's your father handling you leaving tomorrow?"

"Fine." I shrug. "Seemed a bit emotional earlier when I brought up going to Mum's tonight."

"I can't imagine master artificer, architect of dragon-slaying weapons, *the* man who knows how to draw Etherlight, Kassin Thaz being 'a bit emotional.'"

"My father would be flattered you've paid such attention to his accolades." I'm not sure if it's the mention of Etherlight that has my scar itching...or the mention of dragon-slaying weapons. *Will one of those soon be pointed at me?*

I change the subject before Saipha picks up on my dark thoughts. Or asks about Mum. "What about your parents?"

"Mom's been fine, overall. Though I'm convinced she's trying to fatten me up. I've been getting an extra portion every night." Saipha pauses on a landing, catching her breath and glancing down another dark passage. Without consultation, she continues heading up. "Dad's a weepy mess."

Laughter distracts me from the itching. "The Marius Celest? The man with five confirmed kills under his crossbow? *Weepy?*"

"Now who's keeping track of the accolades?" Saipha grins over her shoulder. I roll my eyes. "And you know, Dad's all soft inside. He's scary for dragons, not people."

And for dragon cursed, I stop myself from saying. But any Mercy Knight would kill a dragon cursed on sight. *Will it be him?* I stare at Saipha's back, stomach churning, throat so tight I can barely draw labored breaths. The question that's kept me up every night for weeks returns. The one that's usually gone with the dawn, but today, I can't seem to banish it. Not when there's so little time left.

Will it be you *who kills me, Saipha?*

"Pause." Saipha holds out a hand and passes the lantern back to me. "Listen."

There's a soft *whooshing* sound coming from above. "Too irregular to be dragon wings," I whisper.

"We'd hear the bells if it was a dragon. Snuff the light."

I do.

The worn stone steps ahead are outlined in a cold light. Faint but undeniable. I can barely see the look of excitement Saipha shoots me in the near-total darkness. But I know it's there, because I return it.

She begins taking the steps two at a time, and I follow. Heart pounding. Hoping, *hoping* this is what I think it is. I can get what I need, then get to Mum's. Tonight's the night I'll ask the question I've been wanting to for months yet have been too afraid to voice. Too afraid for years to even let myself think about. And then—

"Talon and fang, Isola!" Saipha calls to me right as I round the bend, harsh light nearly blinding me after our dark ascent.

I skid to a stop, Saipha's arm like an iron bar bracing me, keeping me from careening off the ledge and tumbling down the sheer wall to my death. Wind batters my face, carrying a putrid yet sweet zing of the scourge that's slowly ending our world.

I've found what I came here for.

2

Something big—a yellow dragon would be my guess, based on the size and depth of the gouge—has torn a chunk out of the wall. Rubble is littered across the stone landing at our feet, spilling from the collapsed stairwell above us. But all I can focus on is the opening.

It's as if one of the Creed's scrolls has tumbled off its shelf and unfurled before me, painstaking drawings now rendered in living color.

To my left, the Nightgale Mountains loom larger than ever against a gray sky already beginning to darken with night. I can see them in full—down to the foothills at their base—when all I've ever beheld before has been their snow-capped spires carving the sky like a jagged saw from over the wall. Barren earth stretches between them and a distant forest of blackened, skeletal trees, rising from a red haze tangling around their corpses.

"Is that what I think it is?" Saipha's words are tight with horror.

"The scourge." I've never seen it active before. It's only ever lived in Mum's stories and the Creed's warnings.

"*No.*" Saipha turns away, covering her nose and mouth. "We shouldn't be here. We need to leave."

"Mercy Knights walk the ramparts above us. If it wasn't safe at this distance, all of Vinguard would be dead," I say to her back, eyes never leaving the jagged opening in the wall. My breath catches as I take in just how much scourge dust is here.

This is better than I could've hoped.

"Mercy Knights have been through the Tribunal. They know they're not dragon cursed. This is why the wall exists, Isola—to keep that *out*. We shouldn't be breathing it."

I almost, *almost* tell her that everything the Creed has told her is wrong at best. A lie at worst. The Creed says that dragons are creatures of Ethershade—the *wrong* half of Ether, the deadly kind. That they are born of the scourge. And to be cursed is to be susceptible to Ethershade to the point that *you* turn into one of the vicious, mindless beasts.

Except...to tell her that the Creed is wrong would be treason. So I keep my mouth shut, even though it kills me a little to see my friend so afraid.

Saipha, between the two of us, I'm the one who should be scared.

"Why don't you see if you can find a way up?" I suggest.

"We should go back *down*, Isola."

I need her to not look at me for just a little bit longer. My hand is in my pocket, Mum's sample jar in my grasp. I push a bit. "This is the last chance we're going to have at this."

"Only for three weeks, then we'll be Mercy Knights, and we'll walk the ramparts with our gildings and without fear," she says, glancing over her shoulder.

"Assuming we get into Mercy."

"Like we're not getting into Mercy." Saipha scoffs.

"Please? We could break our highest climb record if we go a little bit farther. Let's just check if there's any other way," I beg.

"Fine, fine. But if I turn into a dragon because of Ethershade exposure, I'm eating you first," Saipha grumbles and starts for one of the large chunks of rubble.

I take my chance.

Holding the small jar up to a narrow ledge of stone, I sweep a whole bunch of dust into the jar. *To beat it, we must first understand it*, I hear Mum saying with a note of pride as I do. She's going to be ecstatic. This is more than I've ever been able to get before. Maybe enough for her to actually find a cure for the curse.

It's a foolish hope, I know. Even if this much scourge dust is what she's missing to finish her research on the curse, there's no chance she'd make a cure before the night is over. But, as I cork the small vial and stare at it for half a heartbeat, I feel lighter than I have in weeks.

For a second, I can almost ignore the little beetles that skitter under my skin and the thrumming in the back of my mind that threatens to grow into a pain that could make me want to split my skull in two.

"Are you going to help me or just stand there?" Saipha grumbles, straightening away from her inspection. I shove the jar in my pocket and turn, trying not to look as guilty as I am. Her brow furrows. "What do you have?"

What do I say? *What do I say?* I swallow hard and force myself to appear calm as I search for a response she'll accept. There's no excuse for touching anything on the outside of the wall.

"I—"

I'm interrupted by the sudden toll of bells. Dozens of them. All at the same time. They reverberate so loudly, the wall itself vibrates with every frantic toll.

Dragon attack.

A string of foul curses races off Saipha's tongue faster than a Mercy Knight can fire a crossbow bolt.

A vast shadow sweeps across the opening, blotting out the sun. The air itself seems colder to the point that I wonder if it's a blue dragon. Then, with a roar as our only warning, the dragon lands on the wall right above us.

I'm thrown off balance, arms pinwheeling.

"Isola!" Saipha shouts and lunges for me as the wall around us cracks and groans—threatening to give in under the weight of the beast. Her hand closes around mine.

I lean at an unnatural angle, half out of the wall, the world slowing for a second as I catch a glimpse of a massive, emerald tail swaying above us. A haze of green follows its movements, emitting a faint, cloying scent that's wholly different from how the scourge on the breeze hit the back of my tongue earlier.

For a second, it's not a dragon I'm staring up at, but full gallows. My stomach churns, and a scream catches in my lungs. But I blink and it's gone. Green dragon haze causes hallucinations of the worst kind.

With a strength I could only imagine on my best day, Saipha throws her weight to yank me back inside. We land hard, but neither of us move. We don't make a sound other than the fall of our bodies. Both of us hold our breath, waiting. Wondering if this is it. If collapsed wall under dragon ass is how we go.

I never would've thought it, but being killed by one of my countrymen because I'm dragon cursed might be preferred. Who would've thought I would find a worse way to go than that? But that's life in Vinguard... Every day is learning a new way to survive. Hopefully.

"Fire!" a Mercy Knight shouts in the distance.

I wince as Etherlight flares across my senses as dozens of magically enhanced crossbows are fired at once.

The dragon roars, and there's a *whooshing* sound right before the wall above and around us rumbles, groans, and threatens to crumble. A putrid gust of air billows down to us. Another roar, this time farther than before. It must've taken flight.

I lock eyes with Saipha, both of us realizing it at the same time.

"Let's get out of here before we're a part of the wall forever." Saipha scrambles to her feet, passing me the lantern.

I quickly light it and hand it back. "Go."

We race down the staircase at an impossible speed. It's more like a controlled fall than running, and it's amazing we make it to the bottom without breaking any bones or face-planting.

A light misting of rain hits my cheeks as we emerge into the small alcove between buildings and the wall. *Of course it's raining. No wonder the dragon attacked.* The Earthtenders didn't forecast it. They're becoming more and more unreliable by the day as the world continues to rot.

No sooner have we stepped outside than the roar of the dragon echoes over Vinguard. The sharp *twang* of a massive ballista high on the wall is followed by a *zip* of the projectile through the air.

Saipha and I both suck in a breath.

She does it in anticipation for what might happen next.

I do it because the Etherlight released from the ballista hits me like a shock wave. All at once, my skin is too hot. Too tight. I press a palm against the wall for support.

The dragon roars triumphantly. A miss.

"Damn it, kill the monster already," Saipha snarls. It almost hides the slight quiver in her lip that betrays her fear.

As if in response, there's a thick, wet splattering sound followed immediately by a chorus of screams that overtakes the bells. Green dragons don't breathe fire. They spit an acid that can melt clay roof tiles like a salt cube in a rainstorm.

Poor souls didn't stand a chance. I'm cold all over, and not just from the faint rain that's finally beginning to soak through my clothes. So much death.

It's your fault, you fraud, a nasty voice in me whispers. *If you were truly Valor Reborn, you'd have killed the Elder Dragon and saved them by now.*

"Let's get a better look." Saipha grabs my hand, tugging me to the passage between the two buildings.

"A better look at what?"

"The dragon, of course." Ethershade is about the only thing Saipha fears. And I suspect even that won't give her pause after she's through the Tribunal and knows she's not cursed.

"Saipha, we shouldn't get in the way of the Mercy Knights."

"We're not going to get in the way. I want to see what they're doing. Maybe it'll help us in the Tribunal."

"They're not going to have us fighting dragons in the Tribunal," I mumble. But she doesn't hear me; she's already side-stepping between the buildings.

I glance back at the alcove that leads into that forgotten tower lost within the stone and mortar of the wall. We should've waited out the attack in there. What was I thinking, coming out?

Yet, for as much as I want to retreat and wait, I follow Saipha. I wouldn't have the words to explain it to her if I didn't. Nor could I bear her disappointment if I tried.

We emerge into the alleyway as a rumble heralds the dragon landing again on a not-so-distant rooftop. Aboveground, Vinguard is a bit like a bowl—the center is its lowest point—so up by the wall, we can see most of the Upper City. My heart stops and falls into my stomach, where it's promptly dissolved by acid.

"Isola, isn't that where your—" Saipha starts.

"Mum," I finish, eyes so wide that they're stinging from the haze of dragon smoke that's pluming throughout the city.

The dragon is perched next to my mum's apartment. I can see its rooftop from here…dripping in sickly green acid.

4

I lurch.

Saipha throws her arms around me, nearly deafening me when she shouts right in my ear, "You can't!"

She thinks I'm going to run toward the dragon. My friend believes far too much in me. She has no idea that my knees have given out. That I'm pressing so hard against her arms because I can hardly hold myself upright.

The spinning in my head is threatening to turn the world upside down and my stomach inside out.

"Do you hear that?" Saipha points to Mercy Spire. It's an ominous, thorny structure of a hundred vantages for ballistae and crossbows. But the distant clicking and grinding emanating from it is something Vinguard has never heard before. "Just wait. They're going to fire it."

We both watch. Saipha still has the shine of anticipation in her eyes. Somehow, she's able to ignore all the risks—even the danger to her parents and older sister up on the wall. All she sees is the final kill. The thing that makes all the sacrifice worth it:

One less dragon in the world to spread Ethershade and suck up the Etherlight of our Font.

The dragon turns its head my way, emerald eyes luminescent in the waning light. Out of the whole city, for a breath, it feels as if it finds *me*.

In an instant, I'm no longer standing in a cage of Saipha's arms. I'm on a rooftop six years ago. It's not a green dragon staring me down, but a copper one, and I've no idea if this is a hallucination from the haze drifting through the city or one of my mind's favorite nightmares to torture me with.

Flames, hotter than I ever felt before. So hot the stone around me is starting to melt. Corpses. Destruction. Death. I'm surprised my eyes haven't boiled in their sockets as its massive snout emerges from the thick smoke.

The beast crawls forward. Eyes locked with mine. It reaches out a clawed hand, straight for my chest, as though it wants to play with its food before it—

A *bang* so loud it rattles the ancient foundations of Vinguard jolts me back to the present. A beam of light that could rival the sun shoots from Mercy Spire straight across Vinguard, striking the dragon where it's perched. The shot goes straight between its wings on its back and punches out through its chest, killing the monster instantly.

Saipha lets out a cheer with the rest of Vinguard, releasing me. Forgotten for a second, I sag against the wall at my back, breathing hard as wave after wave of Etherlight strikes me. The world suddenly seems too bright. Every color is blinding. I swear the raindrops on my skin evaporate into steam as I burn from the inside out.

My best friend turns back to me, and a raw, sharp terror cuts through me as I half expect her to scream and tell me my pupils have turned to slits.

But she doesn't. "Amazing, isn't it? I didn't believe it when my dad told me, but *damn*."

She doesn't notice. She doesn't see what's happening to me. Never has. *Probably because she doesn't want to. She can't admit it to herself—*that's the only reason I've ever come up with.

I lock eyes with the point on Mercy Spire where the shot originated. *A cannon*, Father had called it. His greatest work.

Good job, Father. I'd say you succeeded, I think as I push away from the wall. "It used a lot of Etherlight," I murmur.

"Worth it to kill the beasts."

"I'm going to check on Mum."

Saipha's expression falls from excitement and wonder to stern concern. "You can't."

"Saipha—"

"You know no one but Mercy Knights can be around a dragon carcass."

Yeah, that's exactly what I'm afraid of. "I must know if she's all right, Saipha."

"Her building is still standing."

"That doesn't mean anything, and you know it," I counter.

Saipha sighs and rakes her fingers through her shoulder-length red hair. "Fine, go on ahead. I'll find my father and send him your way. He can help you search."

"Thanks." I take a step backward.

"Watch out for the acid," Saipha says hastily. And, right as I'm about to turn, she adds, "And I'll see you tomorrow morning."

Time pauses, as if holding reverence for the heavy meaning behind her farewell. Tomorrow morning is the Convening—the start of the Tribunal. What could be my last day alive.

"See you in the morning," I murmur with a nod and begin to run.

When Vinguard couldn't build out, it built up. When it became too risky to build higher than two stories because dragons like to perch on the tallest buildings, it built in. The streets are mazelike, barely wide enough for one person in some places. They switch back on themselves, forming tunnels where houses have been built around and over them and turning into short bridges where they span rooftops.

Lucky for me, during a dragon attack everyone hides inside, so I can sprint at full speed without fear of running into anyone. Which is why it's almost insulting how unfair it is when out of this whole city of people, *he* emerges.

Lucan steps into view at the end of the street. I skid to a stop. His dragon-blood red curate robes are almost black when soaked with rain.

Why do you wear those? You're not even a real *curate*, I want to jab. He's eighteen, like me, and about to go into the Tribunal. He can't really be a curate of the Creed until after he has his gilding. I'm sure the robes are the vicar's doing, like the collar on a dog. A signal to everyone, making it clear who he belongs to. I, of all people, know how much Vicar Darius loves dressing up his pets.

Lucan dips his chin, scowl deepening. "I knew you were slinking about."

5

"Takes a slinker to know one," I quip back. *Should've given more thought to that. Not my finest work.* But I don't really have time to exchange verbal barbs with him.

Lucan steps forward. His thick eyebrows have a deep line between them. His dark-blond hair is turned brown when wet, though golden highlights still glint in the last of the twilight.

"What're you doing, Isola?"

Going to see if my mum is still breathing, I almost say. *Almost.* But then I remember how well that worked out for me last time.

The Creed hates Mum. The vicar has all but said he'll kill her himself if I step out of line. And Lucan is nothing if not an extension of his father.

"I was out to get some medicine when the dragon attacked. I'm going home." Lying is so easy when you don't care about the person you're lying to.

"Your home is in the opposite direction." He's close enough that I can see his eyes. They're a frustratingly beautiful shade of hazel, if I'm being honest. Well, if I'm being really honest, all of him is quite annoyingly attractive, given he's the spawn of the most evil man I know.

"Oh, is it?" I feign confusion as an excuse to take in my surroundings, stepping back in the process. "Weird, I must have gotten turned around."

"I can escort you home."

I'd rather walk with a silver dragon than you. "Such a generous offer, but not necessary."

"I think I should."

"Really, I'm fine. Thanks for your concern. See you tomorrow." Those last three words are ash on my tongue as I dart away down a side alley. Lucan shouts after me. I hear his footsteps hammering the cobblestones. But I have a solid head start, and after years of the vicar's training, I know *exactly* how his son is going to think.

I rip off my cloak, hanging it on a loose shutter before sprinting in the opposite direction. It might buy me only a second of him being fooled. But that's all I need.

Even though he probably knows where I'm going... The thought has me running faster still, my heart straining with every beat against the cage of scar tissue between my ribs.

I catch my breath at a crossroads. To the left is Mum's apartment. To the right is where the dragon fell.

One step left. Pause. "Damn it all." I turn right and run again.

I know where she's going to be because Mum, for all her brilliance, doesn't have a sensible bone in her body. She's as reckless as Saipha, but where Saipha is all the "good" kind of reckless—wanting to kill dragons and walk the wall before she's allowed—Mum is the "bad" kind of reckless. The kind that has her questioning the Creed, conducting illegal research that gets her kicked out of a guild, or—

Holding back a green dragon's jowls as she works to pry out a dragon fang.

"Mum." My voice fails to carry over the growing rain. I rush over. "Mum."

"Fascinating, very fascinating..." she mumbles.

"Mum!"

She jolts, and the dragon's jowls snap shut. Her eyes turn toward mine—one black, one gold. "Oh, hello, Isola."

"Don't 'oh, hello' me and smile like we're about to sit down for dinner." I gesture at the dragon carcass. The only reason my knees aren't completely jelly and I'm not frozen in shock is because of the gaping hole in its chest. My father might be a man of few words, but he certainly can speak loudly through his inventions. "What're you doing?"

"Researching." She pats her satchel.

"Oh, dragon-burned hells, Mum, taking dragon parts is one of the most illegal things in Vinguard." I know it's useless to tell her. She's lived here all her life as well, went through the Tribunal, worked in the Earthtender's guild, and lives under Creed rule. Mum knows every law, and I sometimes feel like she treats them as a checklist of what to break next.

"How am I supposed to know if I can't look?" She shrugs and turns back to the corpse. "It's rare for me to get to one this fresh. Usually the red capes are swirling by now."

"And they absolutely will be, any second." I grab her elbow, Lucan flashing across my mind. He's close, too. "We need to go."

"All right." She sighs as if I'm the one being utterly unreasonable. "One more thing."

"Not one-more-thing. *Now*." I tug her arm, all my careful plans for the night unraveling. My hope waning before my eyes. Even if I knew I couldn't be saved, I was hoping that maybe I could do *something*, in however short my life ends up being, to actually help Vinguard. Rather than lying as a beacon of false hope and then dying to a Mercy dagger.

"I need to check under the scales." She pulls back the scales in the opposite direction, like petting the fur on a cat the wrong way. "No sign of scourge dust... You know what this means? The dragon isn't making the scourge, so they are truly creatures of—"

"Explain it all to me back at your apartment." I tug hard enough this time that she takes a step away from the dragon. "We need to go because I actually have—"

The light of Mercy lanterns reflects off the wet streets, outlining the inky pool of dragon blood encircling Mum's boots. Even if we did run, they'd find us. Dragon blood stains worse than ink. Mum's boots would leave a trail and will be a damning crimson forever.

"Halt!"

I freeze.

"By the order of the Creed, you are—" A familiar silhouette walks forward, backlit by Mercy lanterns. Tiny lightning bolts dance around the silver pauldrons that cap his shoulders, highlighting hair a familiar shade of red. I remember the night Father etched sigils into the underside of that plate. "Oh, for Valor's sake. Isola?"

"Hi Marius," I greet Saipha's father with a weak smile. *Good job, Saipha. Your father managed to find Mum, all right.*

His eyes drop to Mum's boots. Our proximity. He sighs as heavily as I imagine my own father would, then says, "The law's the law. Arrest them."

Mum and I sit on opposite sides of a bleak holding room in one of the smaller towers that dot Vinguard. It's not part of the wall and, instead, is manned by Mercy Knights that didn't pass the tests to walk the ramparts, lending mid-city aid when a dragon lands—like this evening. It's also a place to hold prisoners until they can be judged by the Creed, enforcing the laws of Vinguard—also like this evening.

I shift. The shackles biting into my wrists are uncomfortable, but it's the stool that's currently the bane of my existence. The stone floor might be softer.

The only other thing that's a larger pain in my ass is right across from me... As soon as the thought crosses my mind, I look into the corner of the room, scolding myself. Mum's life hasn't been easy. And she means well, I know she does.

I sigh heavily. At least no one has discovered the jar of scourge dust in my pocket. Marius "spared Valor Reborn the indignity of a search." That's one thing going right since the wall.

"I'm sorry," Mum mumbles.

"It's fine." It's not. "I know why you did it."

"It's so hard, Isola, being so close to a breakthrough, yet also knowing you're running out of time." She tilts her head and rests it against the wall behind her, staring at the ceiling. "I hope you never feel this way."

"I know what it feels like to be running out of time," I murmur.

Fate was cruel in making the dragon attack me when I was twelve. Young enough to change my life forever. Old enough to remember what life was like before my eyes turned gold and the

Creed declared me Valor Reborn—the legendary Dragon Slayer returned, destined to kill the Elder Dragon and restore the balance of the world.

It's very poetic on paper. Stories often are, like they're trying to make up for how messy and ugly and complicated the real world is.

"What do you mean?" Mum's attention is solely on me. She heard how heavy the words were.

"I..." *I've felt like I'm cursed for years. Am I?* I can't ask her now. Valor Reborn and her mother taken in for questioning? If I was one of the Mercy Knights standing guard on the other side of the door, my ear would be glued to it. "The Tribunal is tomorrow."

The carved statues of knights that adorn the spires of the Grand Chapel of Mercy have more movement than Mum does at the mention of the Tribunal. "Don't—"

"Don't worry. I won't hesitate," I interrupt hastily and loudly, pinning her with a look and nodding my head toward the door.

She catches herself, and a spark of rage alights in her eyes that turns into an inferno when the door suddenly opens, revealing Vicar Darius.

Right on time.

The vicar doesn't walk; he glides with authority. In two long strides, his wiry, towering form is between us, staring down his daggerlike nose with judgment cast my way and outright loathing toward Mum. A frown tugs on his carefully trimmed mustache as his eyes—one blue and one gilded—rake over me in disappointment.

Expectedly, Lucan strides in after him and leans against the corner to the left of the door, farthest from me. I bet immediately after I gave him the slip, he went to the vicar. They were probably halfway here when the Mercy Knights found them to inform them of our capture.

I shouldn't be surprised but am when one more person walks in: Father. He's still dressed in his dragon-blood red robes as a high curate of the Creed. I wonder what official capacity he was acting in when the dragon attacked, because the circles under his eyes are darker than normal. The salt of his dark-brown hair seems more plentiful. He often burns the midnight oil for days on end in his laboratory. But this is something different...more than physical exhaustion, like something is weighing on his soul.

"Would you care to explain yourselves?" the vicar asks us both as soon as the door shuts. But his attention remains solely on me.

"I was just—"

"She was looking out for me," I say hastily. Whatever excuse Mum would think up isn't going to be as good as mine. I glance her way, trying to say, *Let me protect you*, with my eyes alone. I might not be the real Valor Reborn, but as long as the vicar thinks I am, I'll use it to shield the people I love. And I know exactly what the vicar wants to hear. "When the dragon landed, I felt a pull—almost like a draw of Etherlight—and I had to rush to attack it."

The vicar's eyes shine. No one else would notice it. But it reminds me of how a dragon regards its prey. With eager brutality. "And what of this pull of Etherlight now?"

"It faded when the dragon perished and the threat was gone." Do the words sound too much like a script? I've been kicking them around ever since Marius marched us here.

He clicks his tongue. "A shame. But you will have time in the Tribunal, and Mercy after, to hone your skills as our great slayer reborn. I'm sure it will come to you soon." He speaks as if he hasn't tried to wring the power from my bones every day for six years during our often brutal training sessions.

I hold up my wrists as he approaches, a heavy key in hand. As my shackles are unlocked, I ask, "My mum?"

There's a second of hesitation where I think he's about to refuse. In Vinguard, lawbreakers aren't kept long. If they're found guilty, they're sentenced to labor in the quarries of the Undercrust, excavating stone for the Mercy Knights to use to repair the wall. Or put to death.

And I know which one the vicar would choose for her.

But in the end, he turns to her and unlocks her shackles as well.

"In the future, your concern is unnecessary. Our savior has the skills to keep herself safe. Or the Creed and our Mercy Knights will protect her. You can rest easy," he says to her, voice ominously low. But what he means is, *Stay the hell away from the Creed's favorite symbol, you heretic; you're only alive because killing the mother of Valor Reborn would look bad.*

My hands ball into fists for just a split second. But as soon as they do, I feel eyes on me. My gaze drifts to Lucan's. He didn't miss it.

Going to tell on me for this, too? I ask with a look.

If Lucan sees it, he doesn't answer.

I start for the door, glancing at my father as I pass him. His tired expression doesn't change. Nor does he move for me for any kind of embrace. But his eyes are full of worry and compassion...at least for me. He shows Mum nothing.

It's been easier to accept as I've grown, but I still have a hard time *understanding* how he could love Mum for twenty years and then be a stranger to her. I know how difficult her personality is. But so did he when he proposed to her with a handmade ring, etched with a sigil that, to this day, Mum has kept to herself.

The rain has cleared when we emerge from the tower into a small square. The moon's a talon in the sky, its faint light glinting off a wet, dark city. It's late enough that the streetlights have been extinguished and shutters drawn to avoid attracting dragons.

Not that it does any good... The dragons attack whenever they please. More frequent year over year.

"I'm going to say goodbye to Mum," I announce to my father and Lucan, the edge of a challenge creeping into my words. Maybe it's because the vicar stayed back to talk with the Mercy Knights in the tower. I'm sure he's threatening them not to spread rumors about the Creed's precious Valor Reborn. The mere thought puts an angry edge in my voice. "I'll just be a moment."

Neither of them stops me as I stride across the square to where Mum waits at the street leading to her apartment.

"I'm sorry," she says again. "I really had been planning to give you a good dinner before the Convening."

"I know." I put my hand in my pocket, closing it around the jar as I position my body in a way that my father and Lucan can't see what I'm doing. Grabbing her wrist with my other hand, I place the jar in her palm and close her fingers around it. Her eyes widen and lips part slightly. Just the sight of the jar has a chill running down my spine as I remember the writhing, tightening feeling of the Ethershade *and* Etherlight compressing around me. "Wasn't a total waste of a night, though. I got this for you."

Mum's gaze darts to Father and Lucan before she quickly pockets it. "Isola…"

"I know it's why you ran to the dragon. Well, one of the reasons." I smile weakly. "Look, it might be too late for me, but please, complete your research, Mum. Try to figure out what the curse *really is* and how to end it."

"Too late for you?" she repeats faintly, brow furrowing. Her hand finds my cheek. "What do you mean, dear girl?"

"Mum, I… I'm not a child anymore." My throat is thick, and not from any magic in the air. Not from the scourge. "Most people don't need the tinctures to make their bodies feel right."

Her hand rests on her pocket where the jar is. But I know what's in both our minds is a different glass vessel—a small vial filled with the mysterious liquid only she can make for me. A remedy for the aches and shakes and sweats. Something that makes my mind and my heart a bit calmer. That allows me to be around sigils without wanting to peel off my skin.

"And I'm aware that the way I feel is not because I'm Valor Reborn. If I was, I'd be able to draw Etherlight without sigils by now." I stare at my toes and will my tears not to fall. I've cried enough nights over this, and it never made it better. I lift my chin and force a smile even though happiness is the last thing I feel. "Which means I'm cursed. Aren't I?"

Her entire face crumples. Lines fold at the corners of her mouth, between her brows, around her eyes. "Isola…"

"It's okay," I say quickly, the urge to comfort her winning out over my own terror. Even though we both know that if I am cursed, it'll mean my death. And soon. "I figured it out a while ago. You're making tinctures to help the side effects of it. Maybe I was so susceptible to the curse—whatever it is—that it came early. My eyes changed gold but just never went to slits? Maybe your tinctures really have kept the rest of the transformation at bay.

"But once I'm locked away in the monastery for the Tribunal, I won't get any more. So I'll probably change, then. But I still wanted to get you what I could today. Maybe it's too late for me for whatever cure you might find. But there are generations of children who need you, so please don't give up on your research. I… I wish I could've helped more, done more for you and all of Vinguard."

Without warning, she pulls me in close, clutching me like it's the last time she ever will. Like this is goodbye. I stare up at the talon moon as it blurs with tears I'm fighting so hard not to let fall.

"I will get you another tincture. I will not let them kill you," she whispers, words as strong and sharp as a Mercy dagger.

"But—" *The monastery is locked for three weeks during the Tribunal, and no aid can be given to those inside*, I don't have a chance to say.

"Have faith, Isola."

"You're not one to quote the Creed," I choke out with a weak laugh.

"Not in them. In yourself. You are so much stronger than you know. But they will do things to you in there…horrible things that should never be forgiven, and they'll tell you it's normal. Don't let them win."

"Isola." The vicar's stern tone is like an axe that cleaves us apart.

I hate that I pull away on instinct at the sound of his voice. Mum smiles sadly. I wasn't the only one fighting tears, and that makes it worse.

"Isola," Father echoes, far gentler. "You should rest before tomorrow."

I still look at Mum. She gives a slight nod. I don't want to speak. It feels like if I don't, then time won't continue. Tomorrow will never come. I'd be stuck here forever, but I'd be alive.

"I love you more than Etherlight." I finally whisper the first half of our goodbye.

"I love you more than *all* the Ether in the world," Mum finishes before stepping away into the dark streets of Vinguard.

It isn't until I'm walking back across the square that I realize she never actually answered my question—she never confirmed I was cursed. It'd probably be too cruel to expect her to. What mother could readily admit to their child that they're going to transform into a monster—that they're going to die?

"…and will it be ready tomorrow?" I barely hear the vicar ask Father as I approach. Lucan stands at a distance. Told to, I assume.

"It will," Father replies.

They silence as I approach. It's obvious they're talking about the Tribunal, so I don't ask. They won't tell me anyway. All I know is whatever my father made isn't going to be good for any of us who are about to be locked away for three weeks.

Father is as expressionless as ever as we walk home. Fortunately, the vicar and Lucan go their own way. At least if the Tribunal is good for just one thing, it's helping me avoid a scolding.

I murmur a soft, "Good night," to Father as we cross the threshold of our home. Everyone else is already asleep. But I know that even though I should rest, sleep will evade me.

As soon as the sun rises, the Convening will finally be upon me, and the Tribunal will begin.

7

The Tribunal has a uniform. It's a simple pair of dark-gray woolen trousers—sturdy and suitable for just about anything. A loose white shirt of a soft nettle fabric with long sleeves that I roll up to my elbows. The collar swoops, but not very low. And a leather jerkin over it with a wonderfully high collar. I won't have to put the upper part of my scar on display.

I admire myself. A new outfit in Vinguard is usually reserved for birthdays or other major life events. Resources are scarce here, and we are not a wasteful people. As Valor Reborn, I'm lucky enough to indulge in clothing more than most, but these pieces are different than what the vicar dresses me in. Even though the Tribunal is overseen by the Creed, and the vicar by extension, the clothes haven't been designed to make me stand out, so I know they aren't Vicar Darius's choice. These feel like *mine*...even if they're still a uniform.

If I'm going out, at least I'm not dying dressed up like his doll, I think bitterly. I'd rather go out naked if that'd been my only option. This is much better.

Lucan flashes across my thoughts, soaked to the bone in his heavy curate robes. He'll have a few weeks free of the vicar's decree, too. *Like that matters to him*. I scold myself for even allowing him to cross my mind. I'm sure Lucan *loves* wearing the Creed's uniform, given how much he relishes in wielding the vicar's power by extension.

There's a knock on the door.

"Isola?" It's Marie, my stepmother. I'm grateful it's not Father. I still have no idea what to say to him yet after last night.

"Come in."

She opens the door but doesn't enter. Marie's only been a part of my life for three years and is overly cautious of my boundaries as a result. It makes me like her even more, and she's already a pretty likable person to begin with.

"You look good." She forces a smile. I can tell because the edges of her eyes don't crease. She's worried for me.

"I look like every other supplicant." I assume. I've never seen the opening of the Tribunal. Only full citizens of Vinguard are allowed to witness Convening Day.

"Is that so bad?" The question is layered. Marie might not see *all* of me, but she sees enough. What she's really asking is, *Haven't you been trying to blend in every day since the attack?*

"It just is." I shrug and avoid saying anything more. Anything more would flirt a little too much with treason, and while she's not what I would call a zealot, she is faithful to the Creed.

"Would you like me to pin your hair?"

"I was going to leave it down." The vicar prefers my wild, raven curls tamed, so I wear them loose when the opportunity arises. Plus…it reminds me of Mum.

"You know I think down and loose suits you best." Marie's smile is more genuine now. "And it gives us a little more time at breakfast."

I follow her, but my toes snag on the threshold of the door. I memorize my room one last time—the way the motes of dust drift through the sunlight. The cool scent of the stone. The heavy pelt on my bed that was a birthday gift from Father two years ago. *Maybe Saipha can use it after I'm gone…* I wish I could ask Marie to give it to her, but that would mean admitting to believing I'm cursed. And I might as well say, *Kill me now. Mercy.*

Throat tightening around all the memories, I exhale them with a heavy sigh and bid my home goodbye.

"Good morning!" Marie's son, Callon, chimes from the stove as we enter the cramped kitchen. His coiled hair is a warmer shade of brown than Marie's, though hers has begun to silver and contrast against her dark-brown skin despite her hardly being middle aged. "Toast and button mushrooms. Something hearty before you're forced to live off Tribunal gruel for the next three weeks."

No sooner have I lifted my brows in surprise than Marie shushes him. "No details."

Citizens are sworn to secrecy about what they endured in the Tribunal. They say it's to prevent anyone from being able to hide the curse by having an advantage in the tests, but I think the Creed just loves keeping people ignorant and powerless.

"Saying the food's awful is hardly a hint that could give her an advantage." He rolls his eyes.

He heaps a portion worthy of two people onto my plate as I sit. My stepbrother, as of three years ago, is an apprentice to one of the best stone layers in the city. But I swear he should've been a chef.

I force myself to eat, though my nerves steal the food's taste.

"The Tribunal isn't so bad," Callon says reassuringly through bites of his breakfast. "They make everything about it super intimidating, but finding someone dragon cursed is *so* rare. The tests will push you, but they're also a chance to show off for guilds and find good mentors, so try to have fun with them."

"Callon," Marie scolds again.

"*Mom*, it's not cheating to tell her she'll be fine. Everything else, she already knows."

Marie sighs and pushes strands of hair that have fallen loose back into place. She's one for the letter of the law, which is part of why I think my father fell in love with her. He's a stickler like that, too.

Speaking of... Father strides into the room. He gives me a quick glance and simply says, "It is time to go."

"Now?" I shovel another chunk of oil-drizzled toast into my mouth. Callon took out the flaky salt this morning—no doubt just for me—and every bite crunches delightfully like thin sheets of frost shattering, so I leave nothing.

"You haven't even touched your breakfast," Callon says dejectedly to Father.

"There will be other mornings. Today is a special day, and we cannot be late." He's shepherding me up from the chair and out the door before I can even think of an objection or excuse to stall. Instinct tells me to grab my satchel before leaving the house. But not today. I'm allowed nothing but the clothes on my back.

"We'll meet you there," Marie says. Father gives her an appreciative look and ushers me out the door to one of the Creed's ghastly carriages. They're excessively ornate and utterly unnecessary in Vinguard. Very few roads are still wide enough for them—the space has been repurposed for housing—so it's much faster to walk everywhere. It's yet another thing that screams, *Look how different I am!* I hate it.

"Are you nervous?" Father asks when we're settled inside its stuffy, velvet interior.

"A little, if I'm being honest." I shift. It's the same carriage that transports me to my training with the vicar, but today it feels like I'm sitting on pins.

A flash of Etherlight, and the wheels begin to turn under us as the carriage moves forward. *What a waste of the power that keeps Vinguard safe.*

Father speaks with pride. "You'll be exceptional. You're Valor Reborn. This is the start of your true destiny. Last night was a sign."

"What if—" I don't get to finish my sentence. Father stops me by raising a hand. He knows what I'm about to say before I finish. *What if I'm not the hero you all think I am?*

"We've been over this." Father shakes his head. "You're always so ready to ask what if you're not. But what if you *are* Valor Reborn, Isola? Why not change your instinct to believe it could be true instead of fighting it?"

You'd love that, wouldn't you? I bite back from saying. Instead, I ask, "You don't think it's convenient how people were beginning to lose faith in the Creed and then, suddenly, they have their legendary warrior and all the legitimacy that comes with it?"

"Your eyes," he says, intending to silence me with the simple fact alone. His one golden eye shines, but I focus on the other. Before the attack, I had the same eyes as his remaining brown one.

"I was alone after the attack." The words are bitter and harsh. "With *them*. Unconscious. The vicar could've changed my eyes himself and told no one." The Creed, and the vicar specifically, oversees the gilding.

Father leans away, clearly shocked I'd even suggest it. "Granting connection to the Font through the gilding is something that only happens after the Tribunal—once they're certain that the curse isn't present."

"Vicar Darius makes his own rules."

"The gilding only makes *one* eye gold."

"The vicar keeps so much information locked away." What I've seen is only a quarter of it. "Who knows what he can do that he doesn't tell us about?"

"When did you become so jaded?" Father frowns. "Did your mother—"

I won't hear it. I hate it when Father acts like the vicar is everything when all that man has ever done is take from me. "If I'm jaded, maybe it's because you persuaded the council to keep me from her when I was just twelve." Following their divorce, I couldn't even see her whenever I wanted until this year when I turned eighteen. I'm clutching the jerkin over my chest now. Grasping at the remnants of the dull ache that only her tinctures can relieve. Tinctures I didn't get.

Dragon-burned hells, I hope she's got some at the Convening. I don't know how I'll survive the next three weeks if not.

Father's eyes grow cold and distant. Most people wouldn't be able to tell this apart from his usual stoic expression. But I can. "Your mother—*Valor bless her*—is a danger to herself. I know you don't want to believe me when I say it—"

"Then don't say it," I cut him off again. Our eyes catch, hold, and I exhale. "Just...don't."

For once, he obliges. Silence folds in, heavy but as brittle as the leaded glass that lines the old windows of the Grand Chapel of Mercy. It feels just as dangerous to shatter. Only the creak of the carriage dares to break it—wood groaning like bones under strain—as if even the wheels sense where they're carrying me. My scar itches, sharp and sudden, a phantom reminder of talons and fire.

With every turn of the wheels, the itching gets worse, as if to remind me that I am that much closer to my death.

8

I stare at the city through the small carriage window. In the distance, I catch a glimpse of Mercy Spire—the home of the Mercy Knights. It's the highest structure, taller than even the towers that rise from the wall. Like a sword stretching from the crust of the earth, point piercing the heavens. Every window is a vantage. Cannons poke out of freshly built turrets—a little lighter than the much older, dark-gray stone—giving the whole thing a thorny appearance.

At its foot is a building only opened to non-curates once per year: the monastery.

The carriage stops, and the swell of Etherlight that had surrounded us as it moved dissipates. A crowd has gathered. The Tribunal is a rite of passage—a source of pride and apprehension. Though I suspect with a sinking feeling in the pit of my stomach that all the commotion isn't just because of the hall reopening.

My fear is confirmed the moment I emerge from the carriage. Vicar Darius is already waiting. His clammy fingers clamp viselike around mine as he "helps" me down. There are murmurs and even some applause as surrounding gazes swing to me, single golden eyes glinting like a shimmering sea among natural colors. The vicar raises my hand as though I have carried out a great triumph by existing.

More applause.

This is the worst. I never thought I'd be yearning for the Tribunal to begin. I offer a tight smile. *Duty*, I remind myself and stand a little taller, *this is your duty.*

At least until the dragon within claims you.

My father emerges next, and they escort me to the end of the line of supplicants convening for the Tribunal. It looks like there are about thirty of us this time around. Children are few in a city besieged by dragons and scourge. Thank Valor, they didn't make a show of walking me to the front of the line.

"Good luck." The vicar drops my hand to allow Father to give me a final, tight embrace. Over his shoulder are Marie and Callon. I didn't notice their arrival. They must've left shortly after us and taken a more direct route on foot. The vicar adds, "Not that you need it."

"Thanks," I murmur as my father releases me, trying on a brave smile. It doesn't quite fit my face.

"I wish I could send you in there with something warmer." Marie squeezes both my hands. I return the gesture with a slight but appreciative smile. "Winter will be here before we know it."

I doubt they're going to supply us with anything warmer. Luckily, the Tribunal almost always ends before the first snow.

"She'll be fine." Callon steps forward, holding out his arms and pulling me into an embrace so tight I let out a wheeze. This isn't like him, but I realize why when my stepbrother whispers in my ear, "Red staircase, black dragon—"

He pauses, head turning slightly. A woman I don't recognize passes behind us, heading to hug a different supplicant, and he waits until they're gone to continue.

"—shield for food. A safe hiding place is behind the crossbow rack. Out the fourth-floor workshop window is good for hiding, too. The ledge is bigger than you think." The words are so hasty, they almost blend. When he pulls away, he wears a broad smile, as if he hasn't said anything at all.

I'm stunned. He risked telling me something about the Tribunal. It's been years since he went through it, and everything could've changed... Still, the gesture warms my heart, giving me some confidence that if I'm not cursed, maybe I'll be all right. It's a long shot, but I wouldn't be Vinguard-born if I didn't hope.

I smile as if nothing happened and say, "I'll miss you, too."

He gives a knowing nod.

I turn, naturally expecting to see Mum there. But next to Callon is an almost purposefully vacant spot. My head whips around as I search for any sign of her. There's no way she's not here... She wouldn't miss this. Not after what happened last night. My throat tightens. *She said she'd get me a tincture.* I was certain she'd be here. I'm about to be locked away for three weeks. It's now or never.

As I search, my attention lands on the vicar. He's still hovering close by. His golden eye glows like the light of the Font deep below the Upper City. The expectation is apparent on his face, and I'm pulled from my family without him moving a muscle. Yet again, I play my role. I resist flinching when both of his hands cup my cheeks. I swallow the nausea that rears up every time he touches me.

I kneel before him, because I know it's what I'm supposed to do. Because that is what's demanded of me—what's been taught to me. And because I'm not a fool. Vinguard already sees me as their great slayer reborn. And now they see me kneeling before *him*.

"May the Etherlight bless our hunter!" he says in an overly loud voice that makes me flinch. "Make her strong. May Valor's blessings guide and invigorate her as she enters her Tribunal. May her performance carry her to the ranks of the Mercy Knights. For when she emerges from this crucible and their training, it will be as Valor, prepared to reclaim her birthright. Blessings. Blessings. *Blessings.*"

"Blessings of Valor," the majority of those gathered intone.

The vicar helps me to my feet, guiding me to the front of the line. Exactly like I didn't want. It's like he can read my mind and does the thing I hate the most.

I find Saipha as we walk, and she gives me a look that speaks volumes. She might cheer me on as Valor Reborn, but she disapproves of the vicar's showmanship, since she knows how uncomfortable it makes me. And she's seen the bruises he's left behind from training. I can't say anything to her now, as I'm dropped at the very front of the parade of supplicants.

Lucan is right behind me, and I fight with all my might to ignore his presence. But I can *feel* his eyes on the back of my head as his father ascends a stone pulpit that's built to the right of the massive doors of the monastery. I never thought I'd look forward to listening to the vicar, but when the alternative is listening to this guy breathe...

"Welcome, supplicants, to this year's Tribunal." He gestures across the crowd, and those not wearing the basic uniform step aside from the pack of eighteen-year-olds gathered. "As you embark on the next three weeks, you will commit yourselves to study, training, and prayer. Here, in the blessed monastery that usually houses the Creed's curates, you will deepen your faith and connection with the beating heart of Vinguard—the Font. You will emerge as full citizens. You will be gilded, and with that connection to the Font, you will be able to use sigils.

"The Tribunal is Vinguard's crucible. Here, there is no hiding; the cursed are found and shown mercy. While precautions will be taken, no life is guaranteed in Vinguard, not even here. And forcing the curse out can lead to unfortunate repercussions. But this is a risk we must take to ensure our home remains safe for centuries to come."

There is a beat of somber silence at the idea of this. Life is precious and rare in Vinguard. Losing a citizen for any reason is a tragedy, even if it is inevitable in the case of a dragon cursed.

I try to wipe my sweaty palms on my pants as subtly as possible. *This is it.* There is no going back... Dragon or dragon hunter—I'm about to find out which I'm destined to be.

"Now, submit yourselves to be tested, to reveal if you are among the hunters...or the hunted." The vicar raises his hands, and the massive doors open with a groan and a sizzle of Etherlight that's drawn across hidden sigils.

I take the signal and begin to march, breath thin. My pounding heart threatens to rip through every layer of scar tissue that holds it in place. *This is it.* This is when I find out if I am their savior or their greatest shame—when I discover at last if the dragon halted when it could've killed me not out of terror because I am Valor...but because I am one of *them*.

No sooner have I stepped into the monastery than I find myself face-to-face with a dragon.

9

The maw of the beast is parted slightly. I inhale sharply as my head spins. But its gaze is not burning, and hot breath doesn't batter me. Its eyes are two glassy pieces of obsidian.

It's just a statue. I'm freezing up over well-crafted metal. How in the dragon-burned hells am I going to survive the Tribunal to the wall and beyond if I stall in terror at the mere sight of a *replica* of one of the creatures? Even if this is one of the most terrifying renditions of a dragon I've ever seen. Given its pale hue, I assume it's the Elder Dragon.

A warm hand slips into mine, and my eyes meet Saipha's. I was already grateful that she'd be going through this with me. Now more than ever. The other supplicants have entered around me, and she caught up. My eyes dart to Lucan's back, now ahead of me. I'm honestly surprised he isn't looming over my shoulder still.

"Your hair looks good." She flicks a strand over my shoulder.

"Thanks," I whisper. She knows what it means when I wear it down. "I'm really glad to see you."

"Where else would I be?" She releases my hand with a grin. "Can't exactly say no to this. Plus, I wouldn't miss Valor Reborn's grand entrance for anything."

I roll my eyes. "I'm *certain* you had your own entrance."

"Father couldn't come." She shakes her head and shrugs. "He's doing a patrol on the wall. The safety of Vinguard comes first. You know how it is."

"I do." It reminds me of my mother's absence. My heart is already trying to beat out of my chest. There's no way I'm making it through this without her tincture.

"I'd bet you've seen him more recently than I have." She looks at me sideways. "Valor Reborn running to battle a dragon, huh? Pretty sure it was dead before I let you go."

The vicar speaks, saving me from having to think of a good excuse, cued by the heavy doors shutting behind us. "You are now, formally, supplicants of the Tribunal."

I take in the large hall we've entered. There are six tapestries hanging along the walls around the one dragon statue in the center, each one depicting a life-size dragon in embroidered detail so fine my fingers ache at the thought of the effort they took. Vicar Darius is perched upon a narrow metal balcony close to the roof that's accessed by a spiral stair.

"Over the course of three weeks, you will be watched, examined, and tested as the inquisitors see fit, to ensure that you are not cursed to transform into one of the beasts that ravage our lands and attack our city." Vicar Darius motions to the people who line the edges of the room.

All of them look young, no more than three or four years older than us. They wear stiff leathers in a rusty-brown shade, clearly a simplified variant of the plate the Mercy Knights wear up on the walls, and short capes with hoods that hide half of their faces. Their capes are dyed black, rather than the dragon-blood red that the Mercy Knights and curates wear.

The silver daggers at their hips, each pommeled by a dragon, tell the truth of what they are. Those daggers are laced with a venom so deadly it could kill a dragon—not that it would ever be able to penetrate one's scales. But they're not meant for dragons. They're meant for humans.

These people surrounding us might be in different clothes, they might be young, but these are trained killers; these are Mercy Knights, and every one looks ready to administer that mercy should someone's eyes go to slits. Because the mercy of death is better than becoming one of the beasts.

"In addition to the challenges the inquisitors present you

here, there will be three greater tests that will bring you closer to understanding the truth of Vinguard—to *earning* our secrets to emerge as full citizens and join our society as contributing members," he explains. I suspect this is where the "tri" in Tribunal comes from. "Those who make it to the end without showing signs of the curse will stand before the Font and receive their gilding."

Restless excitement has supplicants shifting from foot to foot.

"There will be times during your Tribunal where others might come to observe—guild leaders, curates, and, of course, Mercy Knights. They might come to give you lectures. Or you might not even be aware of their presence. Even if you do not see them, know they could well be watching you."

Every other supplicant continues to stare up at the vicar, but there is a new glint to their eyes. A spark ignited by what we all know—those observers will be guilds and masters searching for talent—but even more, they are thrilled by the mention of Mercy Knights watching, scouting. One cannot apply to be a Mercy Knight. They are only invited.

"All is to ensure that those who live within our walls are free of the curse, contribute meaningfully to our society, and are loyal to the cause of Vinguard alone." The vicar stands slightly taller, looming. His words take on a harsher, more ominous tone. "Remember: The deadliest dragon is the one within."

My skin feels too tight, stretched across sinew and bone that is suddenly dragon-sized. I rub my palms along my pants and glance at the other supplicants near me. Their faces are wide with smiles. What it must feel like to be one of them…

"Be prepared to be pushed to your limits to ensure that you are not cursed." The vicar finally reaches his conclusion, voice booming. "And should you have indication of another being cursed, you are required to bring them forward or it shall be considered treason and both your lives will be forfeit. No child of Vinguard harbors a dragon or dragon sympathizer. May Valor bless your lives and mercy be swift at your death."

I swallow the lump in my throat as the vicar descends the spiral stairs, the click of his heels echoing ominously throughout the cavernous room. No one moves, clearly unsure of what to do next. His departure invites my gaze to wander the atrium, settling on each of the six dragon tapestries.

A master weaver has captured each in an eerie likeness, poised for an attack in its own, unique manner.

There's the green dragon that clouds the air with a noxious haze, its maw dripping with acid. That imagery is a little too fresh for my liking.

The purple dragon, a shade short of midnight, with its black eyes and roar that is said to spark madness.

Nimble, rare, a silver dragon whose scales might as well be hammered plate reinforced with artificer sigils, its claws sharpened steel.

A blue dragon with woven ice around its mighty talons. I can almost imagine the storm clouds that plume from every flap of its wings.

The largest of the group is the yellow dragon, a monstrosity whose size alone renders it formidable, but its shielding and healing auras also make it nearly impossible to kill. What it lacks in offensive magic, it compensates for in brute strength and defensive capabilities.

And the smallest but most fearsome. The nastiest dragon: the copper. The copper beast is nothing but rage and fire. That last one hooks my gaze longer than any other. My heart flutters, scar itching, skin suddenly too hot all over. I'm trying to force the memory away when my friend starts speaking.

"Wild to think that one of us could become one of *them*," Saipha murmurs.

"It's unlikely. There hasn't been a cursed in the Tribunal in ages." The words are scripted. I've said them to myself a thousand times to try and sleep at night.

I force my gaze away from the copper dragon before I'm

consumed once more by the memory of the creature that attacked me that day...

Smoke so thick it blotted out the sun. Running through darkness and flame, smoldering ash filling my nose and clotting my mouth. Bodies littering the ground. Every way forward blocked by rubble and fire, only one way—the worst way: up.

Unbearable heat on an upswell of wind... Then those two unnatural eyes, staring back at me. A parted maw, crackling with a blaze that threatened to consume me.

Until it didn't...

"It still hurting you?" Saipha asks.

I quickly lower my hand from my chest. "Just itches today." Damn that habit of mine. I can't show weakness here. They're all watching me, expecting me to be Valor. And every inquisitor is looking for a reason to suspect the curse.

"It's not going to—"

"No, it won't interfere." I finish her question before her, sounding more confident than I feel.

"Good! Shall we go see our rooms?"

"Sure." Most of the supplicants are headed that way anyway.

There's a staircase with a carved stone sign over its archway that reads RESIDENCE HALL.

I'm the last up the stairs, since the rest passed me while I was transfixed on the center statue when I first walked in. That little slip-up does have the benefit now of giving me a view of all the other supplicants—which is also a way to spin my pause as intentional, should anyone bring it up.

I recognize a good few, I think, but it's hard to be sure. But I can't tear my eyes off one. I still can't believe Lucan went on ahead of me. I don't trust him for a second.

As if he senses my stare, Lucan's attention is pulled in my direction. His hazel gaze locks with mine. I hold it just long enough to be clear I'm not going to back down but not so long it feels weird. He turns to look ahead, and I let out a relieved breath.

I grab Saipha's elbow. The stairs are too narrow for us to walk side by side, so we're awkwardly half sharing steps so I can whisper in her ear.

"You finally get to see him. The vicar's son." Lucan rarely leaves the Grand Chapel of Mercy, so despite knowing him pretty well through all my stories, Saipha hasn't yet had the displeasure of meeting him. "The guy with the blond-brownish hair, darker underneath."

Saipha follows my gaze, finding Lucan. "The one whose broad shoulders are presently winning a fight against the seams on his shirt?"

I roll my eyes, pretending like I didn't notice. "Yeah, that's the one."

She makes a noise of disgust. "You neglected to tell me how good-looking he is."

"I mentioned it." Once. Before his loyalty to the vicar got in the way of me ever seeing him as attractive again.

"You might have conceded it in passing. But you did not sufficiently emphasize the strength of that jawline."

"Saipha. *Gross.*"

She sighs dramatically. "You know I'm weak for messy hair and sad eyes."

"I have faith you'll persevere," I say flatly.

Supplicants break away at different levels. Long halls of doors await. Saipha and I continue heading up and around. The stairs seem to go on forever—most buildings in Vinguard are capped at two floors. The Grand Chapel, Mercy Spire, and the monastery are the only three that stretch higher.

The monastery is usually home to many of the curates of the Creed, particularly those who are young and without family dwellings of their own, though it's fully evacuated for the three weeks of the Tribunal. There are many more rooms than there are supplicants, so we can take our pick...and I want to be as far as possible from everyone else—especially Lucan. So, when I see him go down the second-floor hall, I hastily make my way to the third, then fourth.

We're the only two who decided to go this high up. It's instinct for most in Vinguard to stay close to the ground, me included. I'm warring against that frightened part of me and doing what a Mercy Knight, a dragon hunter—what Valor would do. We check out the six doors on this hall—one of them is a bathroom at the end—to ensure we're alone. Then I pull us into the hall and wait, watching the curve of the spiral stair.

"What is it?" Saipha has the sense to keep her voice down.

I don't answer. I hold up a hand, listening. Footsteps are approaching. I hate it when I'm right in the worst possible way.

Lucan crests the stairs, and our eyes meet again. This time, he stops, holding my gaze. A chill sweeps over me. He just... stands there, *staring*. As if he's waiting for me to do something. Say something.

I step forward and open my mouth to speak, but another supplicant's panicked words fill the void.

"Are all the doors locked?" someone exclaims downstairs.

A commotion is rising. More confusion. Similar exclamations from supplicants.

I look back to Saipha, whose eyes are as wide as mine must be. We all know what the vicar said, what we've been told our whole lives: the Tribunal has one purpose—to *force* the curse out. By any means necessary.

And like it or not, all my worst fears are about to come to a head.

A copper box on the wall rattles with the crack of Etherlight and the voice of an unseen speaker. Their words boom through the halls.

"Keys to the rooms have been hidden across the monastery. Acquaint yourselves with your new home. But do it before the day bleeds out. Like the rest of Vinguard, in the Tribunal, safety at night is not a promise."

I look over at Lucan. Then Saipha. Then back. He turns and bolts down the stairs.

"Chances of there being enough keys for all of us?" I ask Saipha, emotion draining from my voice.

"Slim." She says what I also suspect.

"And whatever they're going to do to us at night?"

"Horrible," she agrees with my thoughts yet again.

"You ready?" I roll my shoulders back and take a breath.

Saipha cracks her knuckles, tosses her short hair. "Yeah, you?"

Even though I feel like I could vomit. Even though this is the nightmare I can't run from. Even though I've spent years training for this and yet feel like I'm somehow unprepared... My voice doesn't crack when I say, "More. Than. Ever."

We only need one key. Saipha and I can share a room, I tell myself as we race down the spiral stair. What matters is that we're not left out at night. Whatever the inquisitors have in store for those unlucky souls isn't going to be good, I feel it in my marrow, and I'm not going to let it be me.

Once afflicted human bodies have matured enough to physically hold the imbalance of Ethershade that causes the transformation, it can happen any moment. But times of intense physical or emotional distress—pain, fear, danger—are well-established triggers. Knowing this, I can only imagine what kind of situations they've crafted to draw out a change.

The other supplicants seem to have the same take on our circumstances. They're racing down the stairs, shouts and grunts echoing back at us. Saipha and I are all the way on the fourth floor, so beating anyone out to the main areas is hopeless…unless we resort to more ruthless physicality.

Is that what we're supposed to do? Harm each other for an edge? Would the inquisitors stop us? I've no idea. For the first time, it dawns on me what that really means… *Anything* could happen in here. The notion sticks in my brain as though pinned there by a Mercy dagger, poisoning my blood with fear.

Suddenly, not telling us about the inner workings of the Tribunal feels less like an effort to prevent the cursed from avoiding discovery…and more like another way to mess with our minds. And cover their asses. Mum's words echo in my ears. *But they will do things to you in there…horrible things that should never be forgiven, and they'll tell you it's normal.*

"Down here." I make a quick decision and pull Saipha into the third-floor hall.

"Here? Why?"

"We're already the last of the group. We're not going to catch up. Let them dissipate, maybe find a few keys, and we can see if there's some sort of trend in where they're hidden. Plus, there's nothing to say a key can't be hidden in plain sight here in one of the hallways," I explain, skimming the long stretch of doors for a key already in its lock.

"Sometimes the right solution is the most obvious," Saipha immediately agrees. "I'll go back up to the fourth floor and check there."

"After this, I'll check the first." Concocting a plan already feels better than racing headlong into the chaos.

"And I'll take the second."

"Then we can split up to search the rest of the building."

She pauses at the entrance to the stairwell. "We only need one, right?" I love how we arrived at the same conclusion without the need for discussion.

"Yeah, but let's get as many as we can find. They could be good for bartering later." It's probably far too optimistic to think we'll find more than two, but if we do... I'm taking any advantage I can get here.

"Great minds." She grins, no doubt having already thought much the same again. Saipha is going to make an exceptional Mercy Knight, I already know. "The vicar or your father wouldn't have happened to teach you any find-the-thing-I-need sigils, would they?"

I snort at the notion. "You know Father would *never* go against the rules of the Creed." And those rules state that only full citizens can see a sigil—even then, most in use are obscured. Their full designs are kept guarded in Mercy's records.

"You spent a lot of time in his workshop. I didn't know if you peeked." She leans against the stone archway with a smirk that tells me she absolutely would've if she'd been in my shoes.

"You can't imagine how tempting it was."

She picks up on the note of bitter longing in my words. "So why didn't you?"

"The vicar said that I would draw Etherlight without a sigil or not at all."

She drops her voice, taking a step forward so no one else hears when she says, "You hate the vicar. And you lit my father's lantern."

I sigh. "I know, it's probably silly, but it's because my father asked me not to."

"I don't think loving and respecting your family is silly at all." She smiles. "Meet back on floor four by dusk?"

"Done." No sooner do I say the word than she's off.

I continue my search in earnest. I skim every keyhole and run my hands along the top of every door trim. Much to my dismay, there are no hidden keys here... Nor any on the first floor.

Damn. I'd been thinking that I was clever for that, too.

Reemerging into the central atrium, I see a supplicant who's climbed up onto the back of the Elder Dragon. He's fishing underneath scales, trying to see if any of the spines that trail down its back are loose. Another has her arm in the dragon's mouth all the way to her shoulder. I suppress a shudder and head for one of the many doors that line the circular central hall. If there are keys hidden inside the dragon statue, the others can have them. I'd rather not pass out in my first few hours of the Tribunal.

I find myself in the heart of a two-story library packed with shelves of scrolls and—even rarer—books. I don't have time to appreciate it as I step into the middle of a fight.

Blood splatters, nearly blending with the dark-gray carpet. A supplicant tumbles to the ground. A boot slams down onto their wrist, and their fingers unfurl.

Someone else reaches down to pluck a key from their now-open palm with a familiar grace in her movements. Despite the scuffle, not a hair of the braids her delicate, light-brown waves have been tamed into is out of place. My lip nearly curls in disgust.

It would be her *getting into a fistfight on the first day.*

"You should learn to mind your betters." Cindel sneers.

Before I can do anything, the supplicant on the floor rolls, grabbing Cindel's ankle and biting down. She lets out a yelp that's more surprise than pain.

The one on the floor then grabs Cindel's other boot and yanks, hard. She topples, and the black-haired supplicant is on top of her.

"Give. It. Back!"

Cindel comes from a wealthy, well-connected family. Money and power buy one thing in Vinguard: training. Which means an easier time in the Tribunal and a higher likelihood of becoming a Mercy Knight, or attracting the eye of a first-rate guild or craftsman, at least. She's almost as skilled as I am. Cindel shifts her weight, bringing up a knee and rolling. Her opponent is pinned.

"I saw it first," Cindel declares.

"I *got it* first!" The other supplicant attempts to pummel Cindel's thighs.

I scan the room. There's an inquisitor nearby, at the end of one of the shelves. Another leans against the railing that rounds the second-story mezzanine.

Neither move.

They're Mercy Knights in a different uniform, I remind myself. They might be young, but each is a trained killer. They don't care about violence; it's second nature to them. All they're here for is to ensure none of us are cursed and bestow mercy if we are. They'd probably let us do *anything* to each other, if that's what it takes to be sure none of us spontaneously transform into mindless killing machines in the middle of a market someday. *Which seems fair enough, when I put it like that…* Still, my mother's words are gaining new clarity by the second.

"Stop." I step forward. The duo ignores me. *"Stop!"*

I grab Cindel's fist before it can be thrown. Another blow flies in my direction. I dodge it effortlessly and keep my balance. Begrudgingly, I admit there may have been something to all the training the vicar put me through.

Cindel's eyes meet mine. There's a flash of recognition, then hatred. *"You."*

Feeling's mutual, I want to say. But instead: "That's enough."

A cold mask shutters the flash of genuine emotion on her face. Cindel never lets more than a second of weakness show. Her wrist quivers in my grip, key locked in her fist. "What do *you* want?"

The other supplicant looks between Cindel and me through their thick lashes set against light-brown skin. After a quick assessment, the black-haired individual seizes the moment to regain their footing and rub their nose with the back of their hand, smearing a trickle of blood.

"It's not worth it," I say.

"I never thought Valor Reborn would shy away from a fight." Cindel looks me up and down.

"Save the violence for our real enemies: the dragons. We have a lot more to gain by helping each other. Like knights on the wall."

Her lips twitch downward at my mention of them. She must hate that I'm making her look bad. But then, she shouldn't make it so easy.

I grab her closed fist with my other hand, feel her body shake in anger. "Give it up." I could tell from the beginning that Cindel has no right to the key. She's always fighting a scowl whenever she's in the wrong.

"I'm not going to give this to you just because you're Valor Reborn." She lowers her voice, as if afraid someone else might hear her being anything less than deferential to me. This is her eternal torture—trapped between her resentment of me and her fealty to the Creed, which tells her to revere me as her savior returned.

I don't relish in this dynamic, but I'll use it to my advantage. "I'm not keeping it. I'm going to give it back to the person who found it."

For a second, I think she's going to swing for me. Instead, she uncurls her fingers, and I take the key. I toss it to Cindel's victim, who snatches their lifeline out of the air and promptly scampers off, throwing a quick thanks over their shoulder. I don't blame them. Got what they needed and got out before anyone else could add bruises.

"*So noble.*" The way Cindel says it, I know it's not intended as a compliment. "Such a luxury to be idealistic."

"Luxury?" Feels more like a suffocating responsibility.

"Not all of us are guaranteed a position in the Mercy Knights."

I scoff. "I wish." It's my turn to drop my voice to a hush and lean into her personal space. "You really think the vicar is going to let me just don a dragon-blood cape and stroll onto the wall? To let anyone doubt the strength of the *savior*? I'm going to have to fight for a spot just like you. If I want a life after this Tribunal, I'm going to prove I am as good—no, I'm *better* than everyone else here." I say that last bit louder, for everyone's benefit.

"Good. I look forward to seeing how I measure up against the great *Valor Reborn*." Cindel steps away.

"You know, I meant it—we've a lot more to gain by working together than fighting each other." It's futile to say to her of all people. She's always seemed to harbor a dislike for me. Even before I was Valor Reborn and we were just two young girls living a couple of blocks apart. Her father's another high curate and seems to dislike mine just as much as she does me.

Cindel slowly shakes her head and checks that the pinnings of her hair haven't come undone. I've never missed how she wears it in a similar style to what the vicar requires of me: pinned up in braids around a bun. "Might is earned through conflict and sacrifice. I'll be praying you have the will to be who Vinguard needs, Isola."

"I appreciate your prayers." While I'm of average height and Cindel slightly taller than me, I try to give off the energy of staring down at her. "But I have the blessings of Valor himself. Save your breath for someone who needs it."

"So confident. Let's hope it's not misplaced after all our dear vicar has invested in you." Her gaze shifts over my shoulder and slightly up.

At first, I think it's some kind of ploy to distract me, and I don't move. But, when her focus remains stuck on whatever it is, I finally turn slightly and glance over my shoulder. There, with forearms resting on the railing of the mezzanine, is Lucan.

I fight a groan. *Of course he's shadowing me.* It was too much to hope he wouldn't just because he didn't stop next to me when I did at the dragon statue.

But then I realize that it's not *me* he's looking at. Lucan is staring down Cindel like a Mercy Knight would stare down a wounded dragon in the Nightgale Mountains. It's absolutely murderous. And, judging from Cindel's uncomfortable shift, she sees it, too.

"It's so unfair," she mutters under her breath. "You get to be Valor *and* have him."

My head jerks in her direction, and my jaw falls from shock. Cindel isn't even looking at me. She's transfixed on Lucan. No… it's like she's looking straight through him. At what he represents: power, status, a connection with the Creed. I can practically *see* the fantasy she's constructing where Lucan is the vicar and she's his doting wife, the spiritual mother of Vinguard.

With a noise of disgust, Cindel shakes her head and strides away before I can object. "Benj," she calls out, and a man that looks like he could be Lucan's cousin comes running from between the shelves. Benj has slightly darker hair, but still with lighter highlights. His eyes are a light brown, however, not hazel. It's so obvious what she sees in him I nearly gag. "Find me another key," Cindel commands, and away he runs.

Shaking my head at her as she walks out, I look back up at the balcony. Lucan is gone. *What in Valor's name was that about?* Usually I'm the one Lucan is glowering at. So why did he look like he was ready to shoot down Cindel where she stood?

I can't leave the library fast enough, sweeping my gaze at every turn for any other sign of him.

The back of the room connects to a tower of dusty artificer workshops that I wander through until I find myself at a greenhouse, hot and humid upon entry. It's strange to see a room with this much glass in Vinguard—the ceiling and one wall are made of thick, clear panels to allow light in for the plants that grow throughout. Lucan enters just as I'm leaving, and I make it a point to say nothing to him. I've nothing to say.

Lunch is called by way of another booming announcement over the copper boxes that project inquisitors' voices. I make a quick pass through the refectory to grab a flat roll, but I don't linger. I use that time when others might be taking their breaks to search inside every toolkit in the workshops, then backtrack to paw through the potting shed and garden bed in the greenhouse.

I hunt for a key like my life depends on it. Because it just might.

In the process, I learn the overall layout of the monastery. The building is four stories high, though that much I knew from the outside. It's ancient, not as old as the wall, but shows its age with patches of fresh brick and mortar. Much like the wall, it seems to have been made from a handful of combined towers. There are walkways that lead to nowhere, closed off as it's been built on over time, or barred by locked doors, winding inner corridors, and new structures wedged where they fit. There are stairs that dead-end in dusty storerooms filled with nonsensical things like massive casks that could fit a person, rows of empty weapon racks, or crates that have all been nailed shut and bolted together—probably filled with ritual supplies we don't need to be getting into. There are more prayer rooms than I can count, each bearing tiny tokens on the walls of the five tenets of the Creed. I quickly search them all but find nothing.

The chapter house and library are in one of the connected towers, physical training and combat arenas in another, then residence hall, gardens, workshops for artifice and renewing, and myriad other rooms whose original purposes seem lost to time. I find myself turned around more than once, but I eventually begin to navigate by memory.

Yet, for all my exploring, I don't find a single key. But I do spot

Lucan several more times and immediately strike out in the opposite direction. He's following me, no doubt at the vicar's direction, but I refuse to give him the satisfaction of even acknowledging his existence. I ignore him repeatedly, until he eventually gives up, wandering back toward the central atrium as I search high and low. Backtrack. Double-check every nook and cranny.

I remain empty-handed as dusk turns the sky orange. I glance over my shoulder, half expecting to find the vicar's watchdog lurking in the shadows again, but I'm alone, which is…irritating? And that irritates me even more.

It's not like I wanted him to complete this challenge for me… But I'd be lying if I said at this point I wouldn't appreciate it.

Defeated, I take a deep breath and head for the residence hall stairs. Every step of the climb to the fourth floor feels like a funeral procession. If Saipha didn't manage to find a key…we'll both be at the whim of the inquisitors tonight. And, based on how tight my skin feels, I'm not sure if I'll survive it.

11

Saipha is waiting for me on the fourth floor, a key in her hand held triumphantly aloft. "Got one!"

I hug her so fiercely it's practically a tackle. "You're a lifesaver."

"They let me pick the room, too. Exchanged the key I found for one to a room of my choosing—I picked the one up here."

I lean away, beaming. "You are brilliant."

"I take it you didn't get one?" She pats my back.

"No." I release her with a sigh. "Where was it?"

"I noticed all the keys people found were in or around something related to dragons," she says.

And here I am, too scared to even look at the statue, much less stick my hand in its mouth and rummage around. I've never admitted to my friend how dragons make me freeze up. Part of me has always been afraid of what she'd think.

So instead of mentioning it now, I just say, "I'm glad you noticed. I only ever saw one person with a key."

No sooner have my words left my mouth than the copper box on the wall pops to life with a sizzle of Etherlight. "All supplicants with a key are to report to the residence hall. Only one supplicant is permitted per room. Those without a key may continue searching into the night to find their refuge."

Our gazes meet, and her eyes widen with guilt. "Isola, I—"

"Don't worry about it. You got your key on your own. You earned a good night's rest. I'll be fine." The words leave a foul taste on my tongue, soured with how wrong they are.

"Yes, you will." Saipha nods and takes a few steps back, then opens the second door from the top of the stairs. We share a last look before she closes it behind her.

As the lock on her door engages, the confident smile I was giving her falls. I'm reminded of just how exposed I am. I look to the window at the far end of the hall. The city is vanishing in the quickly fading light. My heart shudders. I lose a breath and a beat at the same time.

I could wait out the night holed up in a defensible location, or I could keep searching for a key. I know what a Mercy Knight would do.

I walk down the stairs again and out to the central atrium, then stop mid-step. All the exits to different stairwells and hallways are closed. I check the nearest door, jiggling the handle. It doesn't budge. I try the next. Locked. Every single one refuses to open.

The idea of being locked in *this* room has me dragging my eyes to the statue and tapestries. Every dragon seems more realistic as night falls, their eyes shining as if they could come to life at any moment. The individual stitches glisten in the fading light like they're about to leap off the fabric.

Daring to approach the blue one, I scan the threads that perfectly depict large shards of ice coming off the monster's claws. Maybe they locked this room to force me to check here. I try to warm myself up to the idea of getting closer to dragons than my body wants to allow. Yet, as I draw closer, my skin prickles and my throat feels hot. I massage my neck. *Is it bulging more than normal? Hotter than normal?*

Another set of footsteps draws my attention back to the residence hall. My eyes meet Lucan's, and my heart beats harder as I remember what Cindel said earlier: *You get to be Valor* and *have him.*

Gross, I think in reply.

No, my heart is beating like this because I am relieved not to be alone in a room of dragon imagery—even if not being alone means being near him. Definitely not beating hard because I'm alone with a boy, and this might be the first time ever in my life when that's happened.

Determined to not let him see my nerves, I fold my arms, mirroring how he was last night with Mum and me in that cell. I wonder if he catches it.

"You didn't get a key, either?" he asks. His voice is low and soft, meant for cloistered halls and prayer studies. But there's a hard edge under its almost gentle hum. *That's* what I don't trust. That rougher part of him that his put-together, holier-than-thou facade hides. But I know it's there—he wouldn't be the vicar's son without it.

"No, I just thought it would be fun to give myself an extra challenge by staying out the first night." I walk to the next tapestry as he approaches, making a point to keep distance between us without ever putting my back to him.

"You really don't trust me, do you?" Lucan has never said anything so blunt to me, so it startles me, even if the observation is right.

"I don't know you." Cautious. Truthful. Better than the way-too-honest answer of, *I'd trust a copper dragon not to eat me before I trusted you.*

"You've spent years with me." He steps closer, and my whole chest is tighter as he draws near. I'm focused on the slightest sway of his shoulders. The small bounce in his hair. Maybe my training is really paying off. He's not going to get a surprise attack on me when I'm this aware of every move he's making.

"Years *around* you," I clarify. "There's a difference."

"You might have spent years *around* me, looking through me like nothing more than another one of the vicar's sycophants. But I've always seen you." The way he says it causes my heart to race again. His hazel eyes are big enough to see the entirety of my soul.

"What do you mean?" I work to keep my head and voice level, wandering to the center statue to get some distance. He follows after one last glance at the tapestry. He looks almost…wary? I don't dare think that maybe he's also unnerved by the sight of dragons.

"I've seen how you never pray, yet you ask the curates for prayers upon you so you can retreat into your own mind. The way you stare out at the wall like you're searching for something—no, *yearning* for it. How you scratch yourself whenever an artificer sigil is being drawn," he says, and I'm grateful for the waning light. It hides the heat in my cheeks at realizing I've been so thoroughly observed.

He continues, "How you pull the collars of your shirts up when he isn't looking, probably for the same reason that you wear your hair down even though it's more likely to get you hurt in a fight: because it upsets Vicar Darius." His gaze drops to my chest. It's only then that I realize I'm pressing my palm into my scar. It's throbbing, as if the scarred seams of my flesh are about to rip back open and *something* is going to escape. If he could see all of this, then what else might Lucan know about me? What else that I try so desperately to hide... And what right does he have to know it? "And, of course, how you rub your scar in the presence of Etherlight."

"So studious. I'm flattered." I can't even feign sincerity as I turn away. This is...creepy.

"And I bet that, even now, you're so scared around these tapestries that your heart is almost beating out of your chest. So scared that I'm shocked it doesn't finally stop entirely."

I halt, looking back to him warily. He knows *too* much. This is why he knew just what to say to make me trust him that day. Fooled me into thinking he was someone else.

Lucan approaches with slow, deliberate steps. He almost infringes on my personal space but stops short. The air in the room is suddenly too thin, the laces of my jerkin too tight, and I wish he was closer and across the room at the same time. There's something completely foreign to his stare. Something that I couldn't name even if I tried...and a part of me does want to try.

"Why have you never shared these observations before?" The question is as sharp as the point of a crossbow bolt, and the next shoots from my tongue just as fast. "Saving them for your evening discussions with the vicar?"

He scoffs at that.

"No?" I lean forward, trying to regain the edge in this conversation. But closing the gap myself only makes me more aware of just how *hot* he is—he's warmer than the stones of a hearth that's been blazing all day. Warm enough that my cheeks are definitely flush, and I hate that he'll probably read into it. "You're always so eager to run to him."

"Is your hatred of me all because of that day?"

That day. It absolutely is, you two-faced liar. "It's because you do nothing but *his* bidding," I retort a little too hastily. Then I add, "But what you did that day didn't help."

"Isola—"

"One day off. *One.* That's all I wanted, Lucan! You made me think I could trust you." *Made me think you liked me.* I've had very few friends since becoming Valor Reborn. Not many want to genuinely spend time with the "savior of Vinguard"—most are insufferable suck-ups trying to get close to me to improve their position somehow. I thought he'd know what it's like being stuck under the vicar's shadow. But I'm not about to tell him any of that. Instead, I take a deep breath and lower my voice so that no inquisitors lurking in the shadows will hear. "One day on my mother's birthday to be with her."

I shake my head and turn, walking away. I'll do laps around this room all night if that's what it takes to keep my distance from him.

His footsteps follow, because of course they do. "I told you I didn't advise it."

"But you *let me leave*. Which obviously seemed a lot like agreement." I don't look at him. "If you were just going to run to the vicar, why let me go at all?"

"I couldn't say no to you without going against the teachings." He laughs. That gets my attention. It's a bewildered sound, steeped in disbelief. "You really thought I could? And that I, an eighteen-year-old apprentice of the Creed, could cover for *Valor Reborn* when she was suddenly missing—the most watched person in all of

Vinguard—and everyone would just accept my word for it? You're even more delusional than I thought."

The words hit me like a slap across the face. When he puts it like that... Anger has my chest to the tips of my ears burning, but I can't tell if it's directed more toward him or toward myself. "Excuse me?"

"I'm just a cog in the vicar's automaton, Isola." He sounds... tired. "Grinding away at his command. Heeding his whims and executing his wishes."

A cog? "But you're the vicar's son."

"And you've seen me live such a privileged life because of it," he says sarcastically.

When I think about it, he's always in one of the same few outfits, unlike the vicar, who regularly changes his regalia. But I've attributed that to the rank and file of the Creed wanting to model the behavior it expects from the citizens of Vinguard. Though I've never seen him eating anything special, either. And even around the vicar, the two seemed... Lucan seemed more like a dog heeding its master's call than a son.

"What did he do to you, Isola, for leaving that day?" Lucan comes to a stop before me once more, staring down at me. Why does he have to be so damn tall? I can't even posture my way into looking down on him, and I am not short by any measure.

"I got a measly half hour with my mum, and in exchange he made my training hell for six weeks."

"How do you think he punished me?"

That silences me. I've gone from too hot to cold all over. I hadn't thought about it at all. Hadn't seen him as anything more than...*a cog.*

I'm about to reply when the lights in the hall extinguish at once, like they do in all of Vinguard an hour after the sun sets. Lucan disappears before my eyes as we're plunged into near-total darkness, though I can feel the heat rolling off him in small waves that crash against the chill realizations I've just been having.

"Are you all right?" he breathes.

Did he move closer in the dark? Sounds like he's only a few inches from me now. "I'm fine," I lie. I am not fine with that massive silhouette looming in the dark. The dragon sculpture seems even more real now that my imagination is filling in the details… "Why?"

"Your breathing changed." His fingertips land on my cheek, and I gasp. It's a clumsy movement. I know he was likely searching for the statue or my shoulder. He withdraws his fingers as quickly as they landed. "Isola?"

His warmth. The sound of his breath. Knowing he is *right there* and I can't see him. It's all so distracting…enough that I nearly miss the movement to our right: the brief flicker of light before we both dive in opposite directions and a ball of flame tears through the air, exploding half a scale's width from where I was just standing.

12

I dodge the attack, throwing my body weight into a few extra tumbles in case the flames caught on my clothing. A glowing trail streaks across the floor where Lucan and I were standing. Tiny flames dance over the tile, giving off barely enough light to see the ominous shadows of the dragon statue looming over us. I inhale deeply, an unnatural, metallic, ozone-like scent filling my nose. It's followed by a soft, rhythmic clicking sound overhead.

"Move!" I scramble to my feet, jumping over the line of flames. There's nothing more I can do to help Lucan without endangering myself even more. He'll have to manage on his own.

Another ball of flame lights up the darkness as I skid to a halt in front of the blue dragon tapestry, chest heaving. Movement to my right and a series of curses tells me Lucan heeded my warning, but barely.

"What the—" Lucan is cut off by his own shock.

There's not just one dragon statue in the room with us any longer. The flames might as well be a beacon in the near-perfect darkness. They glitter off the copper sheen of a second metal dragon. The tapestry that depicted the copper dragon has rolled up on the wall, and the dragon stands proudly in the room, as if emerging from its roost.

"It's an automaton. Not real." I pant softly. My heart is galloping inside my ribs, wild and erratic. Even if I know it's not real, my body sure thinks it is, including my scar, which is itching unbearably.

Another burst of flame from the copper dragon finally illuminates Lucan's face enough for me to see the exasperated look he's giving me. "*Obviously* it's not real."

"Well, I—" I don't get to finish. Cold has sunk through the leather of my jerkin, and I realize that it's not just the copper dragon that was waiting for us. My breath frosts in the air.

He seems to realize the chill haze slipping under the blue tapestry at our side at the same time I do.

But where Lucan dashes away, I freeze in place, eyes closed, panting.

"Isola?" he calls back.

I can't reply. *Move*, I command my muscles as the churning of gears and rattling of metal fill my ears. *Move! They're not real.*

"Isola!"

The tapestry rolls up like the curtain of the worst stage play I could ever imagine. A massive statue of a blue dragon rumbles out at my side, and all I can do is stare wide-eyed and utterly terrified. My whole body is locked up.

"I seriously thought you were better than this!"

Spite is apparently the motivator I needed.

I push away from the automaton before the frost creeps over my shoulders. Lucan has sprinted to the silver dragon that's materialized from behind its tapestry. I follow his lead. Not because I want to team up with him, but because he has the right idea. The silver dragon might be bloodthirsty, but it doesn't spit fire or acid or freeze the ground it's standing on. And for as long as we stay in its blind spot by its haunches, its scales should shield against the other three...at least until the green dragon emerges next to us.

"Thanks for finally following my lead," he says dryly.

"Shut up," I snap back, breathless from the run.

"Wish you showed the dragons that same ferocity. Some hero you are." He and Cindel will get along amazingly in here. Maybe she can have him after all. *Not that it's any of my business.*

"Weren't you the one to say I'm 'stronger than any of them could ever imagine'? Or was that just to make me think I could trust you?" I jerk my face in his direction with a glare, repeating his words from the one day we had one-on-one training together. The day he was in charge and I thought I could convince him to let me skip.

He returns the intensity of my stare with equal challenge. Both of our chests are heaving. My body is flush with shame, embarrassment, anger, and whatever this annoying feeling is that he twists in me.

"I want to believe it, but you're proving me wrong."

He just *knows* how to get under my skin.

I'm not who they think I am. I really believe I survived that dragon attack because I am some kind of weird dragon cursed—one that showed early and in a way people haven't seen before—rather than because I'm Valor Reborn.

Without warning, he grabs my biceps, and a jolt surges through me at the touch. It's like the rush of the first time Saipha and I raced up one of the towers in the wall. Like the first gust of wind from the outside world that battered my face. I inhale sharply and, for a second, can almost taste that crisp winter air that rolls off the Nightgale Mountains.

"So prove me right, Isola. How do we stop these?" he challenges.

I'm about to ask why in the dragon-burned hells he thinks I'd know, but I quickly shut my mouth. Maybe I do know... These are *automatons*, and my father is the best artificer in all of Vinguard. If anyone knows how to mix metal and magic, it's him. Which means it's something like one of the various projects he's shown me over the years in his workshop. This is a puzzle I can *solve*, not just survive. My thoughts scatter again the moment a burst of flame shoots over the blue and silver drag—no—*automatons*, exploding against the wall behind us.

"How is it still tracking us?" he grumbles.

"A sigil that senses Etherlight. If I had to guess, it's been designed to recognize the other dragons as friendly and anything else that uses Etherlight as a threat. Even if we're not actively drawing Etherlight, it still flows through us and around us. It's in everything." I explain the theory Mum taught me about Etherlight as I simultaneously try to think of how my father might go about building these. He might not have let me see any sigils, but that doesn't mean he didn't tell me theory.

For all I know, he did build these. Actually... *Is this what the vicar was asking about last night?*

"Oh, thank Valor's legacy." It's almost impossible to see Lucan in the few lingering flames from the last explosion, but I can hear the faintest hope in his voice when he asks, "So you *do* know how to stop them?"

I press my back into the wheeled podium that the silver dragon—still blessedly immobile—rests upon and close my eyes, forcing myself to imagine Father's workshop. He's explaining how fire ignites along a line of rare sludge collected by Mercy Knights from the swamps outside the wall. My eyes follow Father's movements as he shows me the gears, the oiled springs, and the threads that connect artificer sigils to allow Etherlight to be drawn through the machine to bring it to life. He asks me questions about how I think it works, inviting me to find solutions for myself—he loved to give me little puzzles as a girl.

"Even if it flows through them, objects can't actively draw on Etherlight, since they're not conscious. So there must be a primary sigil to draw it from the Font to power the other sigils that are making them move and attack. Think of it like a heart. If we can disrupt that core sigil, then the rest should—" At last, the moment I've been dreading arrives.

The silver beast comes to life with a swing. Its claws shear through the dim light. I fall and press my body against the floor, trying to make myself as small as possible when suddenly my bones feel three sizes too large.

All I see is death coming for me years ago. *The dragon on the rooftop and its smoldering maw. The talons that will rip me to ribbons. Its claw puncturing my chest.*

A scream tears from my lips as the talon becomes real. My back is pierced by the silver dragon, straight through my leather jerkin and shirt to the flesh, severing a line between my shoulders. My body shrieks with pain as blood warms my sides.

And still, I can't move. I'm frozen. My heart skips and sputters, and my joints ache as though every one has been dipped in acid.

The whir of the machine fills my ears. I brace myself. Another whiz of a strike through the air, this time low, followed by a violent thump that rattles and cracks the marble floor. That must've been its tail.

But it missed me.

I'm pulled up and away from the spot where I was cowering and find myself yanked halfway across the hall, past the center statue that—thank Valor—is still unmoving. For a dizzying moment, I think Saipha's come to my aid. But it's not her.

Lucan slams me against the far wall, his body shielding me. I cry out at what feels like an explosion in my back where I was injured. Then he pulls me by my collar to the right. We tumble as another burst of flame strikes where we just were. The smoldering remnants illuminate his fury.

"Pull yourself together, Isola! We're not getting out of this without you." He shakes me, and I fight stars of pain as my eviscerated back cries out in protest. This is worse than every one of the vicar's beatings during training, but somehow I'm not crying. "Where's this 'heart' sigil?"

"Somewhere at the center." My words are thin, caught between shallow and labored breaths. The gouge on my back sends shock waves of pain throughout my body.

"Great, so do we just politely ask them where their entry hatch is, or…?"

"Are you always this charming?" Scowling at him miraculously dulls the pain.

"You think this is charming? You should spend more time with me not during near-death experiences." He flashes a broad smile that I make a show of gagging at.

"I need light. If I'm going to get into the guts of these beasts, I'll have to see what I'm doing." I quickly uncinch the laces of my jerkin.

"Moving a bit fast for my liking." The words are playful, but he speaks in a very uncertain manner.

"You wish." I step away from him and shout, jerkin balled in my fist. "Hey, copper piece of dragon shit! Over here!"

Fire collects in a distant point, and the head of the copper dragon turns. The world seems to slow down as a fire ball shoots toward us once more. I wave the jerkin right through it. The flames collect on it, smoldering.

"How is it not burning the jerkin away—not burning *you*?" Lucan asks.

"Flammable swamp sludge. Flames ride on the sludge, and the sludge buffers the fabric, more or less." I oversimplify. The fire isn't going to burn forever…not even for a while, but it's better than nothing. I scan the dragon statues with new eyes. *Not real*, I remind myself and charge ahead, dodging more attacks like I dodged the curates' mallets as the vicar had them beat me while reciting verses of prayer.

I skim the perimeter of the silver dragon's podium. A claw sweeps overhead, and I duck. Everything in me wants to freeze up. To curl into a ball and hide. Instead, I fight the urge as I search for—

An entry point.

There's a seam around the base that's raised higher than the others. A side panel. Tossing my jerkin, I dig my fingers into the opening, seeking purchase, ignoring the pain as my nails crack and snap back.

Another swipe whizzes through the air. This time, I narrowly avoid it. The creature was going right for my head. They really don't care if we die in here, do they? A horrifying thought occurs to me: How many "cursed" deaths in the Tribunal's history have been anything but? The notion makes this whole place suddenly feel like a mausoleum more than a testing ground.

"Over here!" Lucan shouts to the dragon, waving his hands.

It spins on its stand, swiping its tail. Lucan dodges with surprising grace. Nimbler and more adept than I'd expect of a guy who's been trained to uphold the Creed, not deliver mercy.

Unless the vicar did train him for Mercy Knighthood so that he could get in and watch me there, too...

Something to worry about in the future. Right now, I'm getting this panel open if it's the last thing I ever do. I dig my fingers in and really put my back into it. With a shout, I pop the sheet of metal off and scramble inside.

Sure enough, there's a maze of metal gears and pulleys. The dragon's underbelly glints in the faint light of my still-smoldering jerkin, as though alive with silver and copper bugs. A buzzing so great it's almost like a roar hums in my chest. How am I going to find anything in this mess?

It can be sensed... I hear Mum's words. *Ether, the balance of both Etherlight and Ethershade, as nature intended, is a natural flow in us all. In the world itself. It is life and death, creation and destruction—true power is found in the middle. In the balance. To feel magic, you only need to reach out to it with your whole self.*

I draw in a slow breath and try to clear my senses. It's hard when I still hear the explosions of flame, the crackle of growing ice, and the endless whirring of machines. I block out the overwhelming scent of my own blood. My whole body begins to itch, muscles twitching, heart skipping beats. Through quivering breaths and furrowed brows, I keep my focus, even when I feel as if the only relief would be ripping my skin off starting with my scar. I persist further than I ever have before because I'm either turning as a dragon cursed or dying here.

And then, as though I've pushed past the point of exhaustion, everything fades, and I feel it—the spark of power she spoke of. A familiar sensation, deep within. Clearer than ever before.

A glint catches my eye. *There.*

My eyes lock onto a small point off to the side. A tiny panel upon which a simple design has been drawn—a square with a circle inside, a single vertical line. My eyes widen, and my breath catches.

An artificer sigil, complete, unhidden. Forbidden knowledge laid out before me. Time seems to slow, and my thoughts quicken. A hundred constellations are forming in my mind as a dozen seemingly unrelated points connect. It's like my father gave me all the pieces—I just needed to see the picture.

This sigil hasn't been carved or embossed onto the metal but rather drawn in what looks like chalk. I swear I recognize my father's style in it. As if he intended for this to happen—for me to find it.

The thought makes me bolder, braver. Makes me feel less alone because, in a way, he and Mum are here with me. Looking out for me. I track the movements of the gears and pulleys around it, any of which could snap off my fingers.

One...two—three.

One...two—three.

With a grunt, I lunge. My hand smears across the sigil. The second the design is smudged, everything halts. It must've been the sigil that was drawing Etherlight into the machine.

I collapse, rolling onto my back with a groan of pain and staring up at the still gears, catching my breath. That's when I see another tiny sigil. A square with a smaller square inside of it, an X connecting the center of the smaller square to the outermost points of the larger one.

Reaching up, I rest my fingertips on it. I was right...it's Dad's marking. If the first sigil was the primary draw, then this one was...

I follow the threads, eyes widening. Something in me is clicking into place with the same precision as the gears around me.

"Isola?" Lucan calls out, frantic. More bursts of flame return me to the present. A dragon roar—magnified by a copper box—rips a chill through me.

I scramble back out. Lucan's eyes find mine instantly.

"Do you trust me?" I ask.

"What kind of a question is that?"

"I'm not hearing a no." I reach around and smear my fingers across my lower back. Using my own blood, I replicate the second sigil I saw inside the automaton on the back of my left hand. Lucan's eyes widen. *Most* people can't feel Etherlight enough to activate sigils until the gilding. But I am not most people, thanks to whatever happened in me that killed that dragon when I was twelve, and I have the dual golden eyes to prove it. "Why don't we find out what this does together?"

I hold out my hand to the side in case my recreated artificer sigil will cause me to unleash a burst of flame or ice. This is exactly why the Creed doesn't want regular people trying out sigils. One wrong line and it can either not work at all, or Etherlight can explode with horrifying consequences.

But I'm surprisingly confident in my abilities for having never done this before, thanks to all the hours I spent with Dad. For the first time, it feels like something is going to simply *work* for me, and the sensation is intoxicating.

I suck in Etherlight with a breath—the way I did for years, trying with the vicar—and this time, it feels as though all this power has somewhere to *go*. The skin on my fist puckers, spreading down my arm and even tingling across my chest. A thin sheen across my arm is illuminated in the fading light of our fires.

The copper dragon turned my way while I was drawing forth Etherlight. I almost miss the surge of power. Lucan lets out a shout, but he's too far.

Using all the information I've learned about drawing Etherlight through sigils from my father and my training with the vicar, I raise my fist and position my body behind it. Etherlight is warm, like the sun rising after a long night. More flows through me than I've ever felt before—so much more than opening a lock or lighting Saipha's little lantern.

As a ball of flame is hurled toward me, I really hope this sigil does what I think it does. This is going to be either a really stupid end to my life…or the most brilliant thing I've ever done.

The ball of fire splits in two on my knuckles, shearing away into ribbons of flame. Tiny embers glow around my fist before fading to black. The thin sheen across my flesh vanishes as the Etherlight dissipates.

To think, *this* is what the vicar wants me to do, but without a sigil. What Valor could do. It's impossible to imagine just how powerful I'd be if I could.

A shocked laugh escapes me. *It worked. That worked.* I guessed they'd put an armor sigil with the silver dragon—the most armored of them all—and I was right.

The copper dragon clicks; it's readying another blast. I sprint forward and, with my free hand, grab Lucan, who lets out a yelp of surprise. We head in the direction of the door closest to the greenhouse.

This is going to hurt. Releasing Lucan, I call on Etherlight again but this time shift the flow of magic to my leg. I suck in a breath and take a step back as the copper dragon begins to gather its own Etherlight. Then I lift my leg and kick straight out with all my might, right at the doorknob. Even with a leg like steel, the rest of my body is not. My joints scream. My back continues to ooze blood to the point that I'm dizzy. The door budges but doesn't break.

"Isola—"

Ignoring whatever Lucan is about to say, I bounce back and kick again. Then a third time. On the fourth, the doorframe shatters and I'm left panting, sagging.

Lucan catches me before I fall over and drags me to the other side of the door as a burst of flame explodes where our heads just were. Again. And I don't know how many more near misses I can take.

He curses under his breath, a sentiment I share. My whole body is wrecked. Sweat and blood soak my clothes to dripping. Trembles are beginning to chase an unnatural cold sweeping through me as the Etherlight vanishes with my focus.

"Come on." Lucan keeps his hold on me, beginning to pull me up the stairs.

"Where are you taking me?"

"Greenhouse," he says with a grunt, as though having read my mind. I'm basically dead weight as I stumble down the hallway at his side. I'd probably fall over if it weren't for him.

"Why are you taking me there?" I glance in his direction. There's enough moonlight through the windows here for me to see him better.

"You can hardly walk."

"I'm fine."

Without warning, he lets me go, and I instantly sway. I'd drop to the floor if the opposite wall wasn't so close. I barely get a hand up to support myself in time.

Our eyes lock. Lucan folds his arms. "Absolutely fine. The literal picture of 'fine.'"

I scowl at his sarcasm. "You don't have to help me. We're even."

"Even? What're you talking about?"

"You helped me in there. I saved you in return. We can go our separate ways now."

"We're stuck here for the next three weeks. There are no 'separate ways.'" He sounds about as pleased as I am. "I was wondering why you helped me get out, though, when you could've left me. You can tell me on the way." Lucan wraps his arm around my waist, careful to avoid my wound, grabbing my arm with his opposite hand for additional support.

I knew the man was muscular. His shirts do little to hide it. But feeling him at my side... He's raw strength, and a part of me I've never known before wants to melt into him. To surrender to the safety he offers, even if I know it has ulterior motives.

"I don't like being indebted to anyone." My circumstances with the vicar have made that clear enough to me. He holds my life over my head, and I can't do anything about it. I hate that feeling of owing and never knowing when it'll come due. Of lacking that control. "So don't help me anymore."

"Your stubbornness is going to get you killed."

"My *tenacity* is how we survived."

He snorts. "After I snapped you out of your catatonic terror."

This guy is so rude. But I'm not about to say so out loud. *I'm far too strategic for that*—is what I tell myself. Even if he's the vicar's son, he's been useful so far…as much as I hate to admit it.

I scan for dangers as we emerge into the balmy greenhouse, grateful to find none.

"This way." He guides me to a shed that's been built off the back wall of the greenhouse. "In here." Thank goodness it's unlocked. We both do a quick search of the interior, but it's small enough that there can't be many surprises. He says what I'm thinking. "Defensible."

I nod.

"Now, you stay here. I'm going to collect what I need."

"Which is?" I let him ease me into a seated position on a bench. The world is starting to spin a bit from either blood loss or exhaustion…or both.

"Something to patch your back up."

"Are you some kind of healer now?" I narrow my eyes slightly.

"Would it be so bad if I was?" Lucan shrugs and heads into the rows of plants.

I should have paid closer attention the past six years I've been stuck around him. I shift to a more upright position and wince at the multiple stabs of pain. He returns with two types of leaves clutched in his fists. His knee bumps into mine as he sits, and I jerk away from the touch. He doesn't even seem to notice it happened.

"I'm feeling better," I say, not only because I'm dubious of what he plans to do with the sprigs and leaves in his fist, but because being this near him is uncomfortable.

"Sure, sure," he says in the most dismissive way possible as he begins to grind the plants together in an empty pot. I pay close attention to what he's adding when and how much water is needed to form a thick paste. If there are plants here that can heal, I need to learn how to use them. He stares at me for a moment, and I adjust my back, wincing at the pain. "But you don't look like you feel better," he says.

"Looks can be deceiving."

"You're a bad actress."

I scoff at that. If only he knew how decent an actress I can be. I've kept all of Vinguard thinking that I'm Valor Reborn—blessed by my position, loving of the Creed. High Curate Kassin Thaz's good little daughter, following the path he'd always dreamed of but could never achieve, straight into Mercy Spire.

Despite the fact that I'm fairly certain that, out of everyone, I'm the one who's cursed.

"Turn around." Lucan has a glob of the plant mush on two fingers. I never realized how big his hands were until I had a reason to focus on them.

"You expect me to put my back to you and let you smush that into my wound?"

A pause. A lift of his brows. "You want to do it yourself? Or would you prefer just sitting here with it bleeding and hurting?"

He's so annoying when he's right. With a grumble, I banish my desire to be childish and turn. Lucan's touch on my back is strange, his fingers callused and warm. When he pushes the torn edge of my top to the side, I shiver. I almost prefer to focus on the pain than think about him touching me. When he's this gentle, I can almost forget all the reasons I have to be skeptical of him. *Almost.*

I'm not going to let him win that easily, I vow to myself. *This is what he does. He shows kindness and then turns on you.* I'm in a vulnerable state. Of course it's natural to want to literally and emotionally lean on someone helping you. *Take what you need from him now and get what information you can, Isola, and sort through your thoughts about him later.*

There's a bit of initial pain at the pressure of him pushing the mixture into the wound, but the makeshift medicine immediately begins to take effect, and the ache numbs. My shoulders relax, and a soft sigh escapes my lips without a thought.

"I really don't need, or want, your help," I murmur.

"You might not want it, but I challenge you on needing it."

I glance over my shoulder and study his face. Square jaw, strong nose, hazel eyes—the brown-and-gold sort more than green. All the pieces fit together perfectly, and I really hate that I notice. Because he's right…I still don't know if I trust him. He's either the vicar's loyal heir—in which case he would help me—or he's a zealous, jealous sycophant like Cindel and would gladly poison me to expose I'm not really Valor.

"How'd you learn how to do this?" I ask.

"The one good thing about being in the Creed is access to the library. There's a lot of information there, and I've had a lot of time to read."

A lot they don't want us to know, I think, but I'm not sure if they're my words or Mum's.

"But you already know that, don't you?" he says.

"I'm sure I don't know what you're referring to," I say, thinking of all the maps of the wall I studied.

"They lock the door with a sigil. Somehow never occurred to them that the girl with the gilded eyes could open it."

He knows I sneaked into the library. Am I to think he told no one? No… Why wouldn't he? This is a trick. It has to be.

"You were…impressive back there," he says. No doubt changing the topic so I don't probe too deeply.

"You going to tell the vicar I used a sigil?" It goes against not just his ethos when training me—the vicar always insisted that if I were to draw Etherlight it'd be with a sigil or not at all—but also the rules of Vinguard. I'm not a full citizen yet. I haven't passed the Tribunal. I shouldn't even know the full design of a sigil.

"If they didn't want us to get them, they wouldn't have put them here."

I'm not sure if that's the case, but I like the theory too much to argue.

"I always suspected you had spark to you that you weren't letting show around the vicar." There's that low, thoughtful voice of his again. The one usually reserved for prayers. The same one that praised me and made me believe I could trust him... *Who are you, really, Lucan?*

"You're different, too," I reply cautiously. He's never said so many words to me in one sitting. Never been so forward or blunt. I see the outline of the kindness that he showed me before, but this time it's in full detail.

"Guess we both had parts of us we protected from him." His sentiment startles me. It feels almost like a peace offering. Or an invitation.

I try to glance at him from the corner of my eye. All I catch is a furrowed brow as he works dutifully on my back.

"It's strange to see someone being part of the curates before the gilding...before it's confirmed they're not cursed. Did they make an exception for the vicar's son?" The words feel like putting my fingertips into bathwater to test if it's too hot. Saipha theorizes that Lucan has been trained from a young age to be my keeper—perhaps it's time to find out if that's true.

He scoops more of the paste and then resumes treating my wound, which now is blissfully numb. "It's strange that you've known me for years and never once inquired about my background."

He's right. Since I began at twelve, he's been at almost every one of my training sessions and history lessons from the vicar. Silent and in the background, dutifully doing the vicar's bidding.

"You were around. I saw you. I don't *know* you." Because he was always lurking, mostly expressionless, sometimes scowling, but never interacting, so I refuse to accept the premise of his accusation. The first time Lucan and I ever properly spoke to each other was a few months ago when he alone was assigned to train me one day. I tried to convince him to let me leave to spend my mum's birthday with her, and he promptly ratted me out to the vicar. I shift out of his reach and lift my chin in challenge. "And when we did officially meet, you told me you believed in me, let me leave, and then turned around and screwed me over."

That same raw anger from months ago rises, hot and sharp-edged in my throat, as if his betrayal just happened. I turn my head away to stare at the empty plant pots stacked haphazardly in the corner.

He wipes the remaining salve off his fingers in harsh, jerky strokes on his pants leg. "Sorry, not all of us have the privilege of wearing Valor-named armor to be able to rebel against Vicar Darius when it suits us." His hands still, and he huffs softly. I think he's trying to stop himself from saying anything more, so I let the silence hang like an invitation. He takes it. "He calls me his son, but I'm really just another ward of the Creed. Orphaned after a dragon attack."

"What?" I can't stop a gasp. "You're adopted?"

"The vicar is *so charitable* for taking me in, don't you think?" If looks could draw Etherlight, several plants would be on fire now from his glare alone.

"But...you're still his son, aren't you?" I say softer, gentler. Something isn't adding up here.

Family is the blood you choose over the blood you're born with; all of Vinguard knows this. We're a city where people lose their loved ones with painful regularity. Just because he's adopted shouldn't mean he's loved less... But the way Lucan is acting makes me worry that it's true. Then again, the idea of the vicar loving anyone but himself is as strange to me as a Mercy Knight in the Undercrust.

"In name." He shrugs, then adds, quieter but just as angry, "As long as I'm useful to him." Lucan rakes his fingers through his hair, letting out a noise of disgust. "To be fair, I asked him for this."

"*You* asked *him*? To be his son?"

"Just to join the Creed. The whole 'adoption' business was his idea."

"How old were you when you asked to join the Creed?" It's a big decision. The Creed takes in orphans, but if it was all he knew...

"Twelve."

"That's so young." My gaze softens. Twelve was when I found out I was meant to be Valor Reborn. "Too young…"

"I've always been someone who knows what I want." His voice is quiet, but there's a weight to it of things I don't quite understand.

"No one ever came forward for you?" Obviously not, if he stayed with the Creed. *Nice one, Isola.* He gives me a look that suggests he's thinking the same, and I mumble, "Sorry."

"The only thing I remembered when I came to after the attack was my name…and just my first one at that. Everything else was hazy." He pauses, his movements and words becoming weighted. "So it's not like I could go off looking for my family."

And then he asked to join the Creed, because he had nothing else. And the vicar turned around and made him his son… I would bet my entire life that it was because, in Lucan, the vicar saw an opportunity. A desperate and impressionable young man who just happened to be the same age as his Valor Reborn. Someone the vicar could mold to follow me into the one place the vicar couldn't go: the Tribunal.

"I'm sorry." I mean it, too. So many in Vinguard secretly blame me for not fulfilling my role faster and killing the Elder Dragon already. As if every death that's happened since being named Valor Reborn is my fault. As though that's not a guilt that I, too, bear.

"Sorries won't fix anything." *So he is one of those types…* One of the people who shrugs off the weight of the world like it's nothing because you "can't do anything about it" even though you're quietly being crushed to dust.

"I know."

"But I'm sorry, too." His tone has completely shifted—the words feel a bit lighter and come easier.

"Oh?"

"If things had been different, I would have helped you spend the afternoon with your mother. I owe the vicar everything. I can't go against him, Isola. He controls my life as much as yours."

Maybe more, I think and stare into the middle distance, through the plants. I wasn't expecting his kindness and didn't really ask for it...or want it, for that matter. What can be said? We all wish things were different? Understatement of the century.

Before I can find a response, shadows emerge from the door we entered through. Three inquisitors stride with purpose to where we sit. I slowly shift, muscles tensing in case I need to run.

I can't see the eyes of the woman in the front because of the shadow her hood casts on her face, but I can feel them darting between us. "Who between you held the fire without being burned?"

I'm about to answer when Lucan says, "Her."

My stomach drops, and my eyes swing to him. Lucan doesn't even look my way. After helping me, patching me up, baring parts of our souls, he just outs me like that? I want to shout at him, but my anger would undoubtedly be used against me. Flying off the handle is something a dragon cursed would do.

I know, logically, he had to do it. But it's hard to be logical when at the first opportunity, he's eagerly offering me up. *Again*. It doesn't matter that I was about to take responsibility. He had to ensure it. *So much for budding comradery.*

"Isola Thaz, come with us," the woman in the front commands in a tone that tells me she's not about to take me to a healer to get patched up.

"Why?"

"Based on your display tonight, we've reason to believe that you might be cursed."

My whole body goes cold, jaw slack. I'm amazed I can still form words enough to say, "My hand was in my jerkin. The flames were from—"

"If you do not come willingly, it will only earn more marks against you." The woman is so matter-of-fact, it's painful.

"I..." Objection or further attempt at explanation will only make things worse. There's only one thing I can do now, and that's go with them. I stand and lie when I say, "I have nothing to hide. Let's go."

The inquisitor nods, turns, and starts back for the door. I follow, the two others with her close behind. There are no faces and no names to them. Just specters ushering me back into the darkness of the hall.

Lucan says nothing as they take me away. I don't even bother looking back at him as the cold shadows envelop me. I've no idea where they're taking me. Or what they'll do to me.

I rub the center of my chest as all my previous fears return. *Why didn't the dragon kill me that day?* It probably wasn't because I am some prophesied person. It was probably because the dragon recognized me as one of its own. And now I'm alone with the people who are experts at finding dragon cursed.

My worst nightmare is coming true.

14

My stomach is in my throat as the inquisitor leads me up the stairs. I press my lips shut to stay silent. They're not going to answer any questions I have, and I doubt they'll think better of me for asking.

Brave like a Mercy Knight, I tell myself. *Brave like Valor.* It offers little reassurance. I work to keep from trembling at all costs, clenching and relaxing my fists, controlling my breathing to calm the frantic beats of my heart.

At best, looking terrified will hurt my chances of being invited into Mercy. At worst, it's going to make me appear even more suspicious.

The only way I can salvage this is by exuding a strength that I'm honestly not sure I have anymore. Drawing that much Etherlight put my body in revolt. My back is still agonizing, even with Lucan's makeshift medicine.

Can't imagine how bad it'd be without it, though…

"Out." The inquisitor opens the door at the top of the staircase.

Wind batters my face before I even emerge. I swallow thickly, eyes immediately drawn to the skies. It's cloudy tonight…which makes being outside even more dangerous. There's some moonlight, but not enough to confidently tell what is shifting cloud cover and what could be a dragon. The jagged peaks of the Nightgale Mountains pierce the sky in the distance—the perfect launch point for a dragon to swoop down in attack.

The rooftop is barren, save for ten shackles.

I'm guided to one of the sets of irons, still clenching my fists as they lock in my feet. Little good the chains will do if my worst nightmare comes true and I turn out to be cursed. They're meant to stop me from running, not transforming.

My gaze drifts to Mercy Spire, its imposing silhouette standing out against the night. One of the inquisitors lights a lantern, and on the distant windowsill of a tower, another flickers to life in reply. Lamplight glints off the cannon barrel as it shifts toward me, and I swallow down the knot rising in my throat.

They know I'm here.

I wonder how many Mercy Knights are perched in their vantages. Do they realize that the cannon they're leveling is against "Valor Reborn"? Did my father ever imagine that his greatest weapon would be pointed at his daughter? And I can't stop the trembling in my hands now, so I clench my fists until the skin turns white.

The woman who led the way here comes to stand before me, drawing my eyes to her. It's then that I notice a thin scar that runs perpendicular across her jaw and down her neck. It's impossible to tell how far it stretches up her face with her hood drawn. I can't see her eyes, but I can feel them… Their disapproval. Their sharp displeasure. She seems older than the rest of the inquisitors here, in control.

"I am going to ask you a few questions. All that is expected of you is complete and total honesty." She speaks almost sweetly. The sound is like perfume over blood—impossible to fully mask the sinister note. "Do you understand?"

"I do." In my mind, I'm with Mum in her apartment laboratory, with Saipha on a clear night testing our bravery by sitting on her roof, with Father in the market. I'm anywhere else but here, now. Thinking of everywhere I've ever felt happy keeps my words from cracking.

"Are you cursed?"

Would anyone honestly say yes to that? "No."

She draws a leather-covered baton with movements that promise violence and places it under my chin, as though sizing up her distance. "Do you have reason to suspect you're cursed?"

"No." A bold-faced lie. I've suspected I'm cursed for years. Even as I say the word, I fight a shiver that has my skin puckering into gooseflesh.

"Have you ever had dreams about becoming a dragon?"

"No," I lie. I've had dreams about my nails elongating and my eyes turning to slits. Nightmares about a tiny dragon clawing its way up my throat and crawling out of my screaming mouth.

"Have you sympathized with dragons?"

"No." Half-truth. I've felt for them as one would any animal that's being slaughtered. And, if what Mum says is right, because killing them might be doing more harm than good.

She drags her baton along my cheek. I can almost see the tally running behind her eyes—does she believe me? Does she think she sees a lie in my words?

"Remember, up here, you are mine," she threatens with a whisper. Leather squeaks as she tightens her grip on the baton. For a second, I think she'll finally strike, but she refrains. "We shall collect you when the sun is risen." She leaves, and the others dutifully follow her.

The door closing is loud on the suddenly too-quiet rooftop. There's nothing but the wind and open sky, and I feel so terribly small. I stare up at the talon moon, and then my gaze falls back to the cannon. It's still pointed straight at me, and I give in and let the shivers overtake my entire body; they can't see it from that far away. Even my teeth chatter—from the cold or fear, I'm not sure anymore.

I'm fodder for any dragon that spies me. I glance at the cannon again and wonder if I'm actually bait. Because chaining someone to a rooftop to force them to surrender to their curse seems mild compared to having a room of deadly automatons attacking me.

I stare up at the pale moon and blink, sinking down to the gravelly roof. Waiting. Waiting for the dragons to come for me— either to investigate one of their own...or kill an enemy.

Thin clouds drift over the slender moon, making it writhe just like I can feel the shivers of magic underneath my skin. I ball my hands into fists. My knuckles feel stiff, fingertips aching. Is it because I ripped off that panel? Or because claws are pressing from the inside out?

Why didn't you kill me that day? I ask the dragon that lives in my memories the silent question that's haunted every beat of my scarred heart since. *Why spare me? And what was that light just before you flew away?*

My dark thoughts drift to Lucan. Was it as easy for him to turn me in as it looked? Or was it truly another time where, had circumstances been different, he would've done anything else? That haunted look in his hazel eyes as he asked if I knew what happened to *him* after he turned me in that day is seared in my mind.

An orphan taken in by a powerful man. A boy with no choices and no options. *What else could he really do that day I tried to skip training, or tonight?*

Are his kind words and gestures the real him? What is the mask and what is the man?

I shake my head. None of it matters right now, and I have been awake all night long. I close my eyes and let my shoulders sink, giving in to the exhaustion. If I'm still here when they come for me again, I will figure out what to do about Lucan. But right now, I just want to sleep.

I wrap my arms around my bent legs, rest my head on my knees, and do everything I can to ignore the sharp jabs from the gravel below, the ache in my back, and the overwhelming fear that looms over me.

As I drift off to sleep, my last thought is a hope that if I don't wake up, it's because I'm eaten by a dragon. Anything other than turning into one.

15

I crack my eyelids as the door leading back inside the tower scrapes open again. By some miracle, I'm not dead. Or, worse, a dragon.

Maybe I'm not cursed after all... The thought is as bracing as the cool breeze that drifts down from the already snow-capped peaks of the Nightgale Mountains. I'm not sure if it, or the wind, is what sends a chill down my spine. But, for the first time, it doesn't feel ominous. I was pushed farther than I ever have been before last night, and here I am.

The sky is brightening steadily with a hazy dawn. The woman who called the shots earlier has returned with her lackeys, striding out from the door. They stand around me like I'm some failed experiment.

"Let it be recorded that Isola Thaz has spent the night exposed, without dragon attack, and shows no sign of change." Disappointment is apparent in her voice. I grit my teeth. She *wanted* me to be cursed.

It's astounding how I can be so loved *and* hated at the same time in Vinguard. The inquisitors unlock my shackles and step back as I struggle to stand. The wound on my back feels swollen and crusted with the paste Lucan applied. Gravel is indented into my side from where I slept on it all night. No help is given. Even this is its own test.

None of them stop me as I head for the door and stumble down the stairs, using the wall for support. I wait for someone to bring up how I found and used a sigil, since they only focused on me handling the fiery sludge last night, but no one does. So I don't linger. One foot in front of the next... I'm not sure how I make it back to the residence hall, but I do.

Other doors are opening, supplicants stepping out for the day. Most don't notice me, but one does. The same dark-haired, androgynous teen from the night before—the one who had been fighting Cindel for a key. They open their mouth as if to call out but close it as another supplicant steps into the hall. Almost like they don't want to draw attention to my state. I give them a small nod of appreciation and finish dragging myself up to Saipha's room right as she's emerging.

"Isola!" she exclaims, rushing to me.

My knees give out at the sight of her, and she catches me. I wince, and she adjusts her grip on my back, seeing the wound. "What happened?"

"Would you believe me if I told you I fought a dragon?" The dragon automatons were concealed again behind their tapestries. The inquisitors must have realized my sabotage of the silver one.

"You have all the fun." Saipha half carries me into her small room.

It's a simple setup: a cot, a tiny table, and a stool. The table is empty. There's no dresser or armoire—not enough room for it. I suppose that makes sense. Curates living in the monastery don't need much space, and the Creed supplies all they need. Which makes the small lockbox at the foot of her bed stand out.

"What's in there?" My voice cracks from the exhaustion I can finally let show.

"Nothing yet, I checked—was hoping a kind curate took pity and left us something good." She helps me sit on the floor rather than the bed. I don't blame her. I wouldn't want me bleeding all over the sheets, either.

"Too bad they didn't break the law to help us." I wince as I sit.

"I'm guessing they left them because we're going to be encouraged to collect our own supplies at some point, or hoard whatever we find. What happened to you?"

I lean against the wall and explain the events of the night. She listens attentively to everything—Lucan, the mechanical dragons, using the sigils, the greenhouse, and the rooftop.

She makes a low noise, somewhere between contemplation and disgust, and then stands, pacing to the window and opening the shutters to get a breath of fresh air.

"What is it?" I ask.

"You're not going to like it."

"I figure. Tell me."

One more second of hesitation, a slightly apologetic look, then, "I think we should stay out tonight."

"What?"

"If what you said is true, there are more sigils on the dragons—good ones. We should find them all. It'll give us a big advantage because, unlike anyone else here, you can use them." *She has a point, but...*

"I'm in no position to take on more automatons. I barely made it out of that room with my spine inside my back." And, if I'm being honest, I never would have without Lucan's assistance. "You want to do it again?"

"I know, I know." Saipha sighs and runs a hand through her short red hair. "If we had time, Isola, you know all I would want to do is bring you soup and fresh bandages and tell you all the market gossip I could find until you were better. But we don't have those luxuries in here."

I look away. She's right, of course. But I just want a warm bed and a proper night's rest. *Not like I have a room to do it in.*

"Besides, if the silver dragon gave you a sigil that gave you armor—like a silver dragon—then maybe the other ones have similar sigils. You could get the yellow dragon's and—"

My head snaps back to her, and I finish her sentence. "Properly heal myself."

Saipha kneels and locks eyes with me. "Here's what we'll do. I'll go to the workshops; I'll find bandages or something that can be used as such; I'll get food, too; *and* I'll keep an eye out for a key for you while I do it, just in case. Rest, for now, then I'll patch you up.

Won't be as good as a proper renewer, but I'll do what I can. Come sunset, if you're still unsure and we found you a key, we can make a final decision if we want to try. But key or no, I think we should."

What would a Mercy Knight do?

Not back down.

"You're right. We should," I say with more confidence than I feel. If last night is any indication, this Tribunal is only going to get worse. We will need every advantage we can get. And, maybe since I've survived this long already, I'll actually make it through.

But despite my forced optimism, I can't help but feel like this plan is a terrible, terrible mistake.

16

Saipha and I stand on the last stair at the bottom of the residence hall's staircase. Night has fallen on the Tribunal.

I spent the entire day in her room but still feel like I've fallen down a set of stairs…twice. Bandages fashioned from torn strips of cheesecloth she found in the workshops are wound tightly around my torso underneath my shirt. I almost asked Saipha to find Lucan to ask him to refresh the salve he made, but I'd rather be in pain than go to him for help.

Expectedly, no one else is out. No one else is reckless enough to do something like this.

That's probably why Saipha likes it.

She would never say it, since I got hurt, but I know a part of her is genuinely a little jealous I had "all the fun" last night. That I've had a chance to prove myself as a candidate for Mercy already and she hasn't. This drive is what will make her an excellent Mercy Knight.

I kept an eye out for Lucan on our way down, but he's nowhere to be seen. I wonder if he used the rest of the night, or the day, to find a key. Something I should have been doing—would've been, if not for being shackled on the roof and then needing to recover as much strength as I could, as quickly as possible.

"Ready?" Saipha asks.

I'm not, but I'll need days to heal, and we don't have them. The best I have is a chance at a sigil that'll do it for me. "Ready."

With that, we both lunge forward. I go straight for the yellow tapestry and shove it aside to reveal the dragon automaton, hoping Saipha's right and this yellow dragon replica has a sigil that'll help fix me. Between that and the silver dragon's armor sigil, I'll be nearly invincible. Getting the rest would almost be easy.

Saipha runs in the opposite direction, straight for the copper dragon tapestry. She stops right before it, holding herself in place, waiting for the tapestry to roll up.

I'm searching for the yellow dragon's pedestal panel when it hits me.

Something's wrong.

None of them are moving. I'm squeezing into the narrow nook the dragon is tucked within. It should have wheeled out by now.

"Isola, how long does this take?" Saipha calls.

I don't answer, instead ripping off the panel door and crawling underneath. It's nearly pitch-black inside, and I struggle to find my way by touch alone. My movements are nearly frantic, fingers gliding over the completely still springs and gears as I inch my hand toward the center point, where the sigil should be.

There's just enough light to see that it's gone.

Did the inquisitors disarm them? No, there's no way they would make this place *less* deadly. Unless they didn't want us to find more? But if that were the case, I imagine I would already have faced their wrath for finding and using one.

I study the remnants of the chalk where the sigil was. There are only a few pieces of lines—nothing I could connect with confidence. It was smudged off with a handprint that I know. My back tingles.

Lucan did this. As I was distracted by just how large his hands were, he was scheming. I curse under my breath.

"They're gone," I announce as I emerge from underneath the mechanical dragon. "All the sigils are gone."

"What?" Saipha crosses over with urgency. "How are they all *gone*? Did the inquisitors disable them?" She's looking around the room. There's barely a sliver of moonlight to see by streaming through the slitted windows high above.

"You really think they'd make this place easier on us?" I ask flatly.

"Then how?"

"I bet Lucan saw what I did, and last night after I was taken away, he smudged them so I couldn't get any more advantages." My fists shake with barely contained rage.

"Given how hard you said it was to get one, I'm not sure he could've."

"He's perfectly capable, I assure you," I say, thinking of how easily he moved to dodge the dragon attacks.

"Spoken like someone who's been carefully watching the way he moves." Saipha calls me out.

"Only so I know the sort of person we're up against." My tone is way more defensive than I'd like.

Saipha scans the room to hide a smirk. "Well, whatever happened…it seems safe here, for now."

Clearly, nights are the inquisitors' hours. This is when they're going to push us in whatever ways intrigue them. And here we are, exposed. I've no delusion that they'll spare me if they come upon us, even having tested me last night. The Tribunal isn't about one test—it's about pushing us until we break. They say it's the only way to ensure the safety of our city, but I can still feel that inquisitor's baton under my chin. The way it was so, so obvious she wanted to hit me with it. I can't help the thought that she *enjoyed* watching me suffer…

"Why don't we check the other automatons, just to be sure?" Saipha says. "And then, if not—"

"If not, you go back to your room," I say firmly, not wanting my friend to endure what I suffered last night.

"I'm not leaving you out here alone again." Saipha folds her arms. "And the more you argue with me, the more time you're going to waste."

"Fine." I move to another dragon.

One by one, we check the remaining dragons. Saipha helps me maneuver the panels off. I know, though, even before I look, all the sigils are gone based on the automatons not trying to tear our heads off.

"At least we have each other," Saipha says in an attempt at optimism. I do appreciate her for it. "Let's go to the greenhouse. The shed where you hid last night sounded defensible."

I agree, and we make our way for the side door that I slipped through after learning the sigil last night. The stairway is quiet.

"Stay on your guard," I whisper.

"Don't have to tell me twice." She sounds confident, despite being frustratingly unarmed.

One floor up, we find a dead end. I pause, blinking like my eyes can't quite focus on what's in front of me. I don't remember this from last night, or when I was searching yesterday for a key. Eyes adjusting, I notice a door the same shade as the stone that surrounds it. I shake my head and push the door open, and I am met with a long, dark passage.

"Is this right?" Saipha steals my thoughts, sounding just as hesitant.

"I thought so…" I shake my head. "Let's go back. We must've made a wrong turn."

"Things can look different in the dark." She gives me an encouraging smile, but it doesn't spread across her face like normal. She's doubting herself, too.

We turn around to retrace our path but only make it a short way before my heart begins to stutter and my steps falter. The flat hallway now feels as if there is a slope to it…a slight angle that wasn't there before. I try to ignore the creeping sensation of dread and convince myself I must be mistaken. But I'm not. I know it.

Saipha sighs with relief when the door we entered through comes into view, but I'm still fighting to keep my breathing even and my fear in check, hopeful the changing slope was only my imagination. Back in the stairwell, we wind down and down. Hope is short-lived. My heartbeat picks up again.

"Was the central atrium this far down?" Saipha's voice is strained.

"No… Something's not right."

We move faster. The walls of the stairwell begin to blur, lines warping. They seem to oscillate as if the monastery is a living, breathing thing, and we are being pulled to its core.

A flicker of light catches in the corner of my eye. I turn, but there's nothing there. The air has gone cold, and it creeps down my spine, forcing me to fight shivers and chattering teeth.

"Where...are we?" Saipha presses even closer to me, and I immediately appreciate the warmth and security.

"I don't know."

The stairwell opens into a vast chamber. But it is certainly *not* the central atrium. The air is thick here, with the peaty smell of damp earth and...something else. Something sharp. Almost stomach-churning. It's a strangely familiar aroma, but try as I might, I can't seem to place it...

"We should go back." Saipha staggers backward and out of view. It's as if the shadows themselves have come to life, consuming her in one bite.

"Saipha?" I whisper. No response. "Saipha!" Louder. The darkness swallows her name, not even giving me an echo in reply. I shuffle through the inky blackness in the direction she disappeared, breath and body trembling. "Saipha!" I shout.

I'm met with nothing but silence, and the feeling of danger looms over me like a predator.

Something catches my eye. I spin in place. A blue flame hovers in the distance, casting the dirt floor in an otherworldly glow. If I can see it, maybe Saipha can, too. I run toward it.

The blue fire darts away just as I'm about to step into its glow. I pivot hard, trying to keep up. It teases me through a seemingly endless space that holds nothing but shadowed mists and dirt floors. All the while, I'm calling for Saipha.

Still, no response.

The ball of flame darts right, and I turn, then stop when a gust of warm air is accompanied by a low growl. Freezing in place, I notice a dagger-sharp talon the size of my leg curling by my foot. Mercy, I nearly tripped over—

My chest locks tight as my gaze drags upward to a thick, monstrous arm and across a broad, scaled chest. Up a neck that coils with terrible grace toward a face carved from every nightmare I've ever swallowed down.

Behind it, terror seizes my chest as wings unfurl, vast and silent, blotting out the dark with something darker still. I can't move.

Then I see its eyes. Obsidian pools split by lilac slits—cold, unblinking, and locked on me.

The sound that leaves my throat isn't a scream. It's a whimper. Small. Broken.

And far too human.

17

I scream as something slams into me from the right, knocking me to the ground with a thud and forcing the air from my lungs. The dragon's tail, maybe? With a groan, I roll and gain my feet, arms spread, ready to defend myself from talon and tooth and whatever else the beast has planned.

But I take a step back and trip on something.

"Isola," Saipha rasps, and I almost cry at the sound of her voice coming from the dirt floor at my feet. I reach down, and her fingers find mine, gripping me almost painfully. "S-sorry I ran into you," she whispers. It was my friend, not a dragon that knocked me down.

Saipha releases my hand, and I spin in a circle, expecting death for both of us at any moment. But there's nothing. No purple glowing eyes. No hissing. And no dragon. Nothing. We're alone.

"Did you see it?" I whisper.

"I saw a lot of things." Her voice is thin and trembling. She sounds as shaken as me. "I don't know what in the dragon-burned hells this place is, but I want out of it. Now."

How could she not have seen it? The monster was right here. I scan the void. There's not even enough light to see Saipha at my feet. It scares something primal in me, causing the fine hairs on the back of my neck to rise. Closing my eyes, I rely on my other senses, strain my ears and focus on feeling vibrations in the floor.

There are neither of those, but a certain sense still flares. When I was a little girl, Mum called me talented with Ether. Father even said he thought I had the senses of a future artificer. But everything changed after the attack. Their enthusiasm turned to worry. My body no longer felt safe, but like some dangerous object I happened to inhabit.

Maybe...I should stop being afraid of it. Maybe my worst fears are true, and it's not Etherlight but Ethershade I feel. Maybe my earlier hope was misplaced and these senses are further proof I'm cursed.

But, if being cursed is about to help my friend, then I'm going to use it.

I take a deep breath and focus as Mum taught me—just like I did last night under the dragon automaton, allowing my mind and body to relax and receive. Points of dense energy on each of the walls coalesce in my mind, and I can feel the invisible currents of Etherlight strung between them, forming a web. One we're currently stuck in.

I know what this is. I read about it in one of Father's journals years ago—it didn't have any sketches of sigils but was full of theories on them. He might have even created the web and sigils himself. And then there's the smell...

"It's not real," I whisper.

"What?"

"None of it is real." I help Saipha to her feet. "No matter what it shows you, just hold on to me and keep walking."

Slowly, I lead her to where I still envision one of the points of energy on the wall. But before I can reach it, she shrieks and jerks from my hold, her footfalls pounding over the stone in the darkness like she's running for her life.

Instinct tells me to chase after my friend. But undoing this is what'll really help her.

"Not real, Saipha!" I shout after her but continue heading to the point I'd been guiding us toward. I pull off my boot and use it to get enough height to smudge it across the stone where I sense the energy coming from, hoping that this sigil, like the others, is drawn in chalk and not anything more permanent.

My gamble pays off. The magic flickers, then crackles, then

dims, breaking the web connecting it to the other sigils and the horrible visions it induced. I lean back against the wall, catching my breath as the sense of the sigil on the opposite side goes dark as well, then another, and another. I can't help but grin. Sigil circuits are like a house of cards—they all rely on one another to work. Pull out one, and the rest fail.

"It's over, Saipha," I shout into the darkness. The lack of light wasn't a fabrication. "It wasn't real." I can hear her on the opposite side, drawing in ragged breaths. My senses are my own once more. "It's safe now, I promise."

"How can you be so sure none of it was real?" Her voice quivers slightly, breathing reluctant to settle. I wonder what form the illusions took for her.

"The stink." I should have put it together right away. I smelled this aroma recently. "Take a second. Take a breath," I counsel, since I don't think we're in any real danger now that the artificer sigils have been disabled. Saipha follows my instructions. "You know that smell." It's faint now that the sigils are not spreading it throughout the room, but it still lingers.

She inhales again, sharper, faster. "Green dragon." She probably smelled it on her father's uniform when he returned home the other night while my mum and I were being questioned.

Their acid can eat through anything, even steel—most people focus on that. But inhaling their gases can cause horrible hallucinations.

"This room is just magic and mechanics," I say to keep us both calm. "I bet they used some of the venom from the green dragon that attacked the other day to make the sigils." I stand and shove my boot on, really glad I didn't touch the stuff with my bare hand. Then I shuffle toward where I heard her voice.

"Does that mean the sigils were drawing from Ethershade?" she whispers, scandalized.

The question makes sense, given that the Creed says dragons are the embodiment of Ethershade. But... "I think the sigils merely vaporized the acid. I don't think they actually drew from Ethershade."

"But we breathed it in," she whispers from only a short distance in front of me. "We breathed in green dragon vapor—that *must* have Ethershade in it, right?"

"I don't know," I admit.

"How could it not? It's a part of those monsters." It's her words now that are all venom.

"Maybe that was the point." Reaching her, I grab her hand and hold it for a moment, stabilizing both of us. My next words are as solemn as a funeral horn. "The curse is brought on by a buildup of Ethershade."

"So they're willingly exposing us to it?" The words are small, barely more than a breath. The one thing in the world that terrifies Saipha.

"I don't know," I repeat. I want to reassure her by telling her Mum's theories—that dragons are not actually beasts of Ethershade—but I know my friend, and all she will hear is treason against the Creed that guides us. "I don't know what the inquisitors' logic is here or what they might do next. All I know is that I don't think it'll be good."

"I don't like any of this." I can hear the scowl in her voice.

"I don't, either. So let's get out of here while we can." I guide us along the outer wall. One palm glides against smooth stone, and the other still clings to Saipha's hand. I walk us around the room, knowing that, eventually, we'll have to find some way out. At least both of us are breathing normally, and my heart doesn't feel like it's going to explode.

A vertical gap in the stone, no wider than my little finger, has me stopping. I release Saipha's hand, and I push against the stone next to the seam. With some effort, it gives way. The moonlight is almost blinding after the total darkness of the chamber. We emerge with tandem sighs of relief, and I can't shut the door fast enough behind us. It blends nearly seamlessly with the brick and mortar of the wall. A hidden exit.

My hands ball into fists at my sides. The inquisitors were ready to let us wander that room all night, caught in a web of focused dragon venom, scared out of our minds. *The Tribunals are designed to push us to our limits*, they say. But now I'm even more certain it's to break us.

I can't help the shudder that runs down my body at the thought of what awaits us next.

18

"I never thought I'd be so happy to"—Saipha glances around and scowls—"be in another dark corridor."

"At least this one has a candle." I point down the narrow passage at a sconce.

"The epitome of luxury." Saipha fakes a swoon, and I fight a laugh that feels so out of place but so welcome right now.

I lean against the wall and gulp in air, exhale fully, and do it again. It's a fair bet this narrow passageway is without booby traps, since I don't think they intended for us to find it, but that's not where my mind really is.

"You were brilliant in there." She leans against the wall next to me, catching her breath as well. When I just stare at the floor in response, she shifts, leaning, tilting her head to try to catch my eyes. "What's wrong?"

"I froze up." I can't help the surge of frustration and helplessness that accompanies those words. It's enough to make me want to scream. "Twice."

"Isola..."

"It happened last night, too."

My friend pushes away from the wall to stand in front of me, grabs both of my shoulders, and gives me a gentle shake. "You did great in there. *You* were the one who got us out. Just like you did last night for Lucan. Right?"

Inadequacy hovers like an axe over the back of my neck. "I froze up then, too. He had to help me. And if it wasn't for you, this time, who knows how long I would've been stuck staring at the illusion of a dragon, knees jelly."

"Hey, *hey*. You disabled those sigils. I couldn't even see them. Stop this foolishness. You're the Isola who breaks into the Creed's library to find ancient towers in the wall to climb to test her bravery. Who stands up to the vicar whenever she can. Who's *Valor Reborn*."

She's not understanding—because I've never told anyone my secret, not even my best friend. But if we're both going to be locked in trials like the last, where she's going to need to count on me…she deserves the shameful truth.

"Who can't even look at a dragon without her whole body locking up, let alone fight one." I finally meet her gaze. Saipha's lips part. And I'm already being crushed by her disappointment.

"I had to hold you back from running to attack a dragon the night before last," she whispers. The truth she was going to ask me about on our first day returns to the front of her mind.

"No, you didn't." Disgust and self-loathing taste more bitter than the faint aroma of dragon acid that still clings to my clothes. The Celests are the one family who's been good to me, and I've lied to them. "You weren't holding me back. I was frozen in terror. You know I left after the dragon was dead; I wasn't running because I felt the pull of Etherlight and a need to slay. I ran because of Mum and was utterly terrified the whole time even though it was dead. I'm no hero reborn… I'm sorry I never told you."

My shoulders cave in on themselves.

When my friend just stares at me, I rush to explain. "Every time I freeze…I think I'll get over it, that next time I'll be fine. But every time I see one of them, I'm that scared little girl on the rooftop again. Every time I see one of those monsters, I can feel the claw of the one that tried to kill me, puncturing through skin and breastbone, reaching for my heart like it wanted to toy with me before its kill." As I speak, that same scar aches. It's been bothering me since we entered the monastery, but now the discomfort and itchiness have grown into a throbbing pain so unbearable I can't stop myself from rubbing at it.

Saipha's expression softens. Her hands slide down my arms,

fingers lacing with mine. "And then you *killed it*. That day, even when you were small and most afraid, you killed a dragon. That little girl with no training, no fancy sigils, no crossbows."

"But I don't even know how I did it," I whisper. *I don't even know what power I used.*

"It doesn't matter. You did it. *You*. And you have the eyes to prove it." She leans away. I'm shocked she's not running or yelling at me. "Why didn't you tell me all this before?"

"I… I didn't want to disappoint you," I admit.

She blanches. "That might be the most offensive thing you've ever said to me."

"What?" I repeat the words in my head, trying to figure out why.

"You think our friendship is that weak?" She smirks. The mischievous spark is returning to her eyes. Not even a room full of green dragon vapor can shake it. "I'm not abandoning you, Isola. You're brilliant. And you're my best friend."

"Even if I'm a coward?"

"You're one of the bravest people I know." There's not a trace of hesitation in her voice. "Bravery isn't about conquering easy challenges. It's about facing what scares you and doing it anyway."

My eyes sting, and I look down. She's far too kind to me. "I could be a liability to you in here."

"For once, I can say with confidence that you're not *that* special, Isola. Pretty much everyone in Vinguard is afraid of dragons."

"But—"

"And besides, I know how we're going to get you past it."

"Oh?" I doubt she can think of anything I haven't tried, but I'd welcome any suggestion at this point.

"By becoming Mercy Knights."

Laughter bubbles up in me, small and brief but genuine. If the wall was mortared with Saipha's will, it'd never need repairs. "All right."

"Good, now that we've settled that—" She stops herself, looking at me from the corners of her eyes. "You don't have anything else you've been meaning to tell me, do you?"

I open my mouth and nearly tell her about my deepest fear. *I might be cursed.* But I don't say it. The last thing I ever do might be betraying her...but at least I'll get to live these final days as her friend. It's selfish, but I consider it a dying wish, should all that come to pass.

But I haven't changed yet. Not even after tonight. Maybe I'm really not cursed.

"Not at all." Despite my attempt at optimism, the words are ash in my mouth. All I can see is my mother's expression when I asked her if I was cursed, panicked and afraid.

"Good. Now, let's see if we can find our way back."

I don't object, and we begin walking in the general direction of up.

"Where do you think we are?" Saipha asks.

"I don't know, maybe—"

We hear the voices at the same time. Both of us rush to press against the wall, but the muffled sounds don't change. We dare to continue slowly, crouched on instinct. There's only one way to get up, and we're risking whatever's around the bend because we're certainly not going back down there.

Around the next corner, the streak of orange underneath the crack of a door ahead is almost blinding. It's where this narrow passageway ends. And behind that door is where the voices are coming from.

I glance at Saipha. She nods encouragingly. We creep forward until we're close enough to listen through the thick wood.

"...too soon. We'll need to do more things that involve all of them. Push them as a group to weed out prospects—look for any signs of weakness that might be attributed to the curse. The major tests will be a good opportunity for that." *It's the woman who left me on the roof last night*, I realize. Given how she's speaking, she really is in charge. "I expect plans for the first test with the dawn."

"Could it be a false alarm, prelate?" one of the other inquisitors asks.

"No, the dragon curse alarm was made by High Curate Kassin Thaz himself."

Father? A chill sweeps through me from the top of my head to my feet.

"Could we run it again?"

"Unfortunately, the prototype was unstable and broke under the strain. Kassin says that he won't have the proper supplies to make repairs for several months."

Broke? My father's inventions don't break. Unless he was forced to make it in a rush? Even then... The notion is like a shoe on the wrong foot. It can't be right.

"Even if we could fix it, it uses too much Etherlight," the prelate continues. "The Creed doesn't want us drawing on the Font like that. Besides, we don't need any sort of alarm. We have the same tried-and-true methods that have been used in the Tribunal for centuries. You all saw it when the supplicants first convened. Its signal was clear—" She pauses before confirming the truth churning in my belly. "At least one of the supplicants this year is cursed."

19

Saipha and I ease away from the door and share a look that has a thousand words wrapped up in it, though both of us keep our mouths pressed shut to prevent them from slipping out. Still, our worried expressions speak volumes.

At least one of the supplicants this year is cursed.

That sentence is going to haunt me the rest of my time here. It's already consuming my thoughts as we slink away. It's whittling at my hollow optimism and false hope. We pick up the pace as we gain some distance, forced to backtrack and hope that there was some way we missed.

Just around the bend from where we started—but in the opposite direction from where we went, of course—is a door with a lever embedded into the wall at its side. I glance to Saipha. She shrugs. *Not like we have any other options*, is what I'm sure we're both thinking. As she pulls the lever, we brace ourselves.

The door slides open sideways, into the wall, and we emerge into a familiar staircase. As soon as Saipha releases the lever, the gears start to turn, and the door begins shuddering back into place. She slips through with a side-step just before it seals shut.

"A hidden passage…" she murmurs, keeping her voice low.

The doorway is now nothing more than a tall painting on the side of a staircase landing.

"There must be more of them. Remember how the vicar said people could be watching us even if we didn't see them?" I run my fingers along the picture frame, looking for what mechanism might trigger the opening on this side. Whatever it is, it isn't immediately obvious, and Saipha cuts my search short. I reluctantly agree that we should go before any inquisitors notice where we ended up.

We might have managed to give them the slip. For all they know, we're still stumbling around in that dark room, screaming until our voices give out. Which means we might have a shot at getting to the greenhouse before they can manage to trap us in that horrible basement again. Or worse.

Ice coats my spine as we emerge into the familiar greenhouse. Its lush greenery and soft, filtered moonlight feel at odds with the fear coursing in my veins. *One of us is cursed.* It's the only thought I can think. Over and over and over...

"Do you think we'll be safe here?" Saipha asks, eyeing the walls.

"I don't think we're 'safe' anywhere. But I think sometimes you have to pretend the monsters aren't real to be able to sleep." I sound braver than I feel, and I guide us to the back, holding my breath as I pull open the door to the shed. It looks the same as yesterday, with all the pots and shelves appearing untouched.

"I doubt either of us is getting any sleep tonight." Saipha steps inside, stumbling to the very back and collapsing with a huff.

My gaze flickers from the small table to the bags of fertilizer to a few tools for digging. I was hoping the little bowl Lucan mixed that poultice in might still be here. But it's not. Did he take it with him to smudge the other sigils? Did he clean it up so no one else could use it? Did an inquisitor remove it?

I realize that I don't actually know what happened to Lucan after I was gone, and that has something shifting uncomfortably within me. I spent the day in Saipha's room only to come out as night fell. Did he get a key? What if the inquisitors got him? Or worse?

No, I am not going to worry about him. I imagine him casually walking away after handing me over to the inquisitors without so much as a blink to then make it a point to screw over any advantage I could have. Whatever compassion I was feeling for him evaporates like water off hot stones.

I settle down next to Saipha, and she leans her shoulder into mine.

"That passageway... You think we were supposed to find it?"

Her voice is barely a whisper, and the way she asks tells me she already knows the answer.

"No, not at all." Even though the air in the greenhouse is humid and rich with the aroma of damp earth, I'm still cold. The stink of green dragon acid is burned into my nose.

"There're probably a lot more like it," she muses.

"Probably. This whole place suddenly feels like a gameboard, and we're the pieces."

"Sure, except the board changes whenever it suits them."

It makes me think of the various levers and pulls my father would design. The little boxes with hidden compartments he'd surprise me with on my birthday. The tiny puzzles he'd give me "just to see" if I could figure them out.

Were you training me, even then? I wish I could ask him. Another question for when I make it out of here. I imagine there'll be a lot to talk about when all is said and done. *If I make it out of here...*

The silence is heavy. I know what both of our thoughts are drifting back to. The one thing that's going to keep us up all night, flirting with our worst nightmares and fears.

"Who do you think it is?" she whispers. "My father told me being cursed is incredibly rare."

"I don't know." The back of my head rests against the cool stone as I look out onto the raised gardens. "Hopefully Lucan."

"You *really* don't like him, do you?"

"Can you blame me?" I shrug even though a part of me already regrets what I said. *It's not his fault he's like this,* one part of me says. *Oh, Valor bless, stop making excuses for him!* another rallies against him.

"He seems like he's been nice enough to you."

I don't respond, too busy mentally arguing with myself over a boy. An utter waste of my mental energy.

"I bet you could win him over," Saipha continues. "Flirt with him until he's putty in your hands?"

"Saipha. *Gross.*" I repeat my earlier statement, and she laughs. The sound is thin and somewhat hollow. But genuine.

"I'm just saying, we could use all the help we can get in here." Saipha sounds noncommittal.

"Yeah…" I trail off. I can't get any more words out anyway. Only one thought is circling my mind right now.

It's me. I'm the cursed one.

I don't know how, but eventually I must have fallen asleep, because Saipha shakes me awake. Sunlight streams in through the windows, and I let out a long sigh. We've survived another night.

I stare out into the dim light of the greenhouse, forcing my attention to stay sharp. We're still the only ones here, so it must be very early. The other supplicants aren't roaming the halls yet, keeping themselves busy with whatever they find.

"I'm eating everything they serve in the refectory this morning and then having seconds." Saipha stretches and then extends a hand to me, helping me up. "Then we're finding you a key."

I can't help but agree. But, as we're leaving, a tiny cluster of red, poofy buds catches my attention. The little plant is growing happily in a pot on a high shelf.

"What is it?" Saipha stops as well.

"Surely not..." I mutter.

"What?" She blinks.

I cross to the pot. It's just slightly out of line from the rest. As if someone moved it more recently than the others. I lift it, and sure enough, underneath is a shining key.

"Oh, Valor bless." Saipha curses under her breath. "How did we miss that?"

The flower—more like a weed—is called dragon's breath. It grows in the cracks of stone near the wall. We pull it up and burn it because it's poisonous. Pretty much anything with the name "dragon" in Vinguard is going to try to kill you.

"I swear I checked this greenhouse top to bottom on the first day," I grumble.

"I wouldn't be shocked if the inquisitors added it later." Saipha's tone is just as sour as mine.

"This place is the worst."

"Well, at least that's one thing done for the day." Saipha tries to shrug it off.

I want to smash the pot against the wall, but instead I put it down delicately and grab the key.

"Let's get food...and try not to look so murderous on the way?" she suggests with a wink.

I force a smile. "Better?"

"Somehow worse." She laughs, and it's a bit forced but still genuine. I can't help but join her. If I don't laugh, this place is going to make me weep.

The refectory is connected to the central atrium by way of a short staircase down—as we pass the dragon tapestries, I give Lucan another angry thought. On the way, we stop to exchange my key with an inquisitor for a key to the room across from Saipha's on the fourth floor.

By the time we reach the refectory, the other supplicants have already settled in for the most part. There are seven round tables set for eight, which is three tables more than necessary—my original count for the number of supplicants was only two off. I wonder if this is how many tables there always are in the monastery, or if they intentionally set it up so not every table would have to be full. So people could pick and choose who they wanted to sit with—ally with.

Already, it looks like factions are forming. Cindel holds court with a group of four. She straightens as I enter.

"You look awful. Rough night?" She tries to paint it as concern.

I see right through it. "This is what someone who spent the night hunting for knowledge and skills looks like, Cindel. But thank you for asking."

I turn away, scanning the room. But I don't see the boy coming straight for me until the last second. I try to dodge out of the way, but I swear he walks straight into me intentionally, bumping my shoulder, and I nearly end up with an entire bowl of hot stew down my front. Never thought the vicar's training would come in handy for dodging food.

"Watch where you're going!" A familiar set of light-brown eyes meets mine. Benj, Cindel's creepy Lucan look-alike.

"Sorry," I mumble and take a wide step around the spilled soup.

"Why are you apologizing to him?" Saipha steps in. "He walked into you on purpose."

"Why would I do that?" Benj can't even fight a smile to avoid looking guilty. "Now my soup is on the floor. I guess I have to take your portion."

"Fine," I sigh, not really wanting to deal with this after the past two nights I've had.

"No, it's not fine." Saipha takes another step, nearly going chest-to-chest with Benj. "You're not walking into her, then taking her food."

"I only think it's fair, since Benj lost his because of her," Cindel chimes in without getting up from the table, because of course she does.

"It's all right, Saipha, just let him take mine."

She grumbles the entire time he goes up for another portion but doesn't fight. That's how I know she's also exhausted. As Saipha gets her bowl, I scan the room, searching for a familiar tall frame. When I don't see Lucan anywhere, I pretend the tightening in my chest has nothing to do with wondering if he survived last night.

Saipha is stepping away from the communal trays when I feel a set of eyes on me. I pointedly ignore Lucan *and* the relief flooding my body. It will do me no good to soften an inch for this guy. Every time I'm the least bit vulnerable, he reminds me that he'll turn on me if he has to. Him having a choice or not in the matter doesn't change that it's dangerous for me to be vulnerable around him.

But also...I'm glad he's all right.

I pick a table at random and end up sitting with a boy that has one blue eye and one brown. It's weird to see someone with different-colored eyes when one of them isn't golden. Saipha sits down across from him and slides her tray between us. I don't fight the offer, taking a few bites of the mushroom soup.

"Horowin Kael," he introduces himself. "And I know who both of you are, obviously."

I take a bite of fried egg. "Where are you from?"

"Undercrust, second level."

I pause, spoon hanging in midair. "Undercrust?"

"You say it like *I'm* the special one here." He laughs. It's a warm, full-bellied sound.

"I don't meet many people from the Undercrust." Even though travel between the upper and lower halves of Vinguard is freely available, it's rare for citizens to traverse the two. Those who live below do so to avoid the skies. And those who live above see it as a quiet shame to retreat into the depths. We've given up so much of our land, few of us can bear the thought of ceding one plot more.

"Me neither," Saipha adds.

"We five are." He gestures to the other people who were sitting at his table when we arrived, introducing each of them. *So this is the little group he's forming...* Good of them to let us join, though. "You're looking at all the eighteen-year-olds this year rounded up from the city underneath the city."

"Only five?" That surprises me, considering many women go to the Undercrust for the duration of their pregnancies—the one time doing so isn't met with judgment from those living on the surface.

I can't imagine having a child. Partly because I've never been sure if I'm going to survive long enough, be it curse or dragon attack or something horrible befalling me for not actually being Valor Reborn. But also because it's hard to imagine bringing new life into this world.

"Most people in the Undercrust want their children to grow up with the sun," Horowin says.

"They think it'll make them braver," Yenni, a girl with a thick, dark braid, adds.

"Is this the first time you've seen the sun?" Saipha asks. I hope on her behalf the question isn't offensive…because I want to know as well.

Horowin nods. "My first time on the surface. I've studied it a lot, though."

Others nod as well.

A guy named Ulven says, "I've been up once. But just during the middle of the day to avoid the dragons. Too bright up here for my taste." Given the ghostly hue of his skin, I don't blame him. He's even paler than me, and my skin sometimes seems like it burns at the idea of the sun. "I'll be very happy tending a farm in Font light when all this is over."

The idea that someone could live their whole life and never hear the bells. Never experience the horror of a dragon attack… It's so foreign, these people might as well be from a different world.

I've a thousand questions I want to ask, but I don't have the chance. Everyone's attention is suddenly on the entrance of the refectory. I follow their wide-eyed stares.

Vicar Darius holds my gaze and smiles.

21

For a breath, I think the vicar's about to single me out. His gaze lingers on me for just a second too long.

But just as I brace for it—whatever *it* is—he shifts his stance. His eyes sweep across the room. Cindel nearly leaps from her chair the brief moment his focus is on her.

"Supplicants, future of Vinguard, join me in the chapter house." The vicar pivots on his heel and leaves, blood-red robes billowing in his wake.

Cindel is the first on her feet. Her freshly formed group of sycophants scrambles to keep pace with her as she strides for the door. The rest of us are much slower, shoving the last few bites of food in our mouths.

As we head out, I try to get a feel for how the other supplicants regard the vicar. A few appear pleased to follow—though without the same level of zeal as Cindel and her cronies. Some drag their feet, but most seem neutral.

The vicar mentioned that lectures would happen while we're here, but I haven't given it much thought. The inquisitors have kept me busy enough, so far. My stomach knots as I realize their tests and trials are only just beginning, especially because they already have proof one of us *is* cursed.

I force the thought away as we pass the dragon tapestries in the atrium, unable to ignore their lifeless eyes staring accusingly at me with every perfect stitch. Even if the automatons behind them are disabled, knowing they're there and all it takes is someone who knows the right sigils to arm them once more keeps me on edge.

Lucan comes up along my right side, completely silent, like it's normal for him to be there. I shoot him a wary look from the corners of my eyes. Saipha at my left does the same, leaning forward to meet his gaze.

"I'm sure the vicar will want to see that I'm properly looking after you," he says.

"Like you 'looked after' me when you quickly told the inquisitors that I was the one who handled the fire without being burned?"

"They have eyes, Isola." He's suppressing a roll of his.

"Or you wanted to make sure you had time to sabotage the other sigils so I couldn't get them," I say under my breath and leave it to fate if he hears or not.

"I'm sure I don't know what you're talking about." He has better hearing than I thought. Good to know.

"Don't you?" I fire back, my tone daring him to deny it again.

"All I remember is helping patch you up after you were injured. And maybe saving your life, at least once." He glances at me from the corners of his eyes. His lips press into a hard line of frustration, like he's fighting to keep himself from speaking. But his eyes are all warning—*We'll talk later*, I think I imagine seeing in them.

"I've no idea what you mean," I say and leave it at that, for now, hoping I'm right that this isn't the final word on the matter.

The chapter house is at the end of a cloistered passage. It isn't very large, but it's filled with an air of importance that subdues conversation as our small group files in. Stone walls rise three stories to a lofty ceiling supported by thick, wooden beams. Hanging from the center of the ceiling is an iron chandelier humming with Etherlight that casts the room in a warm glow. Five tapestries are strung up in a semicircle opposite the entrance, behind the lectern. Though I've never seen these exact works before, I recognize their contents—each tapestry carries symbolism representing the five tenets of the Creed.

The first is a dragon's face emerging from thick clouds meant to signify the scourge: *Dragons are the enemy of life.*

The second, a vertical sword with a dragon curled around the pommel, like the Mercy Knights carry, meant to represent Valor's legendary blade: *Mercy is given through the sword.*

The third has a swirl that is meant to represent Etherlight, stars dripping from it: *Etherlight is sacred.*

The fourth, a scroll in a clenched fist: *The Creed is the absolute truth.*

The fifth, an armored helmet with dragon's wings rising from the temples, void of its wearer, the style well out of use for what Mercy Knights currently wear: *There is Valor in sacrifice.*

Five tenets that begin with the enemy and end with the savior. Every time I see the symbols, unease overcomes me. It's as though both the dragon's and Valor's void eyes stare at me…and only me. As though both are trying to claim me.

Multiple rows of stone benches, worn to smooth divots from countless supplicants throughout the centuries, await us. It all reminds me vaguely of the Grand Chapel of Mercy. The vicar begins speaking before the last of us have even taken our seats in the middle of the room but the back row of all the supplicants. The room can easily fit double. Lucan stays to my right and Saipha on my left.

"Who can tell me why you are here?" The vicar radiates power.

"To find out if we're cursed," someone responds in a small voice.

"Precisely." The vicar grabs the lectern, leaning forward slightly. "The scourge might rot our lands, but the curse is a scourge upon our souls. Those who bear this hidden, sinister mark, who are weak to the draw of Ethershade, are among us—hidden in plain sight. They might be sitting beside you. Or perhaps that draw is *inside you.*"

Everyone glances around. I shift uncomfortably in my seat.

"It starts with a racing heart, then an unsteady mind. Doubts and fears rise as the humanity of the cursed begins to be consumed by the dragon within. Many will even show signs of compassion to our enemies—because those beasts are the cursed's true kin."

"Compassion? Toward a dragon?" Saipha says under her breath.

Her eyes settle on me. "Not likely."

I look away, reaching up to rub absently at my chest.

"The Creed, Mercy Knights, and each one of you holds a sacred duty to rid the world of these beasts. They destroy our Etherlight, weakening Vinguard's Font every time one manages to breach the walls. For they carry within them Ethershade—the fuel of the scourge—and that is why they must be slain and their corpses must be properly handled to avoid the blight entering our city and our Font further weakened."

Saipha straightens a bit at my side as the vicar goes on, waxing poetic about the role of Mercy Knights. He reiterates how they are an extension of the Creed. That their mercy is a holiness almost akin to Valor himself.

At that, the vicar's eyes dart to me, drawing everyone else's attention as well. I sit a little straighter, trying to appear as enraptured as the rest. It's no small effort.

"And that brings us to the most sacred tenet of the Creed—of living as a citizen of Vinguard: there is valor in sacrifice." The vicar moves from around the lectern. "Survival demands more than bravery; it demands the sacrifice of those who hold life itself sacred. To give up yourself for the many. Valor did not hesitate. He struck out fearlessly to slay the Elder Dragon."

And what did it get him? The stories paint Valor to be this great warrior, but no one seems to linger on the fact that Valor left to kill the Elder Dragon and never returned. Here we are, centuries later, still with an Elder Dragon, a horde of lesser dragons beneath it, but without a legendary hero.

"That is why the Tribunal exists—to ensure that you are not a risk to this city that has raised you, that will keep you for the rest of your days. And when you leave these halls, you will serve. But take the lessons of this place with you forever."

He pauses with dramatic flair before continuing, "We are the last barrier against the scourge. We are all that stands against the dragons. We are the last guardians of the Etherlight. Any souls beyond these walls are scattered and doomed in a desolate land."

When I was a girl, I would imagine what those beyond the walls might look like. Mum spoke of them in a way that was in direct contrast to the Creed—she said should any other humans still survive, they would be just like us. Resourceful and determined.

Once, in my first year after my eyes turned gold, I asked Vicar Darius about them, and he showed me a drawing of them in a book. Every pen stroke outlined unfortunate souls twisted by the scourge and Ethershade. Claws extended from their hands. Parts of their flesh were scaled. Broken wings protruded from their backs at odd angles like some unholy abomination of a human-and-dragon union.

Whatever is actually out there is long dead. The scourge has become too widespread and Etherlight too thin for any pockets of life to survive beyond Vinguard. We're all that's left, and that's why, more than ever, we have to fight to preserve our home.

As though stealing my thoughts, the vicar finishes, "We are a beacon of what could be. We are the last hope for all of humanity."

Cindel jumps up, clapping wildly. The others around her do the same. Many of the supplicants bow their heads in reverence, asking for blessings of strength and duty. Even those that looked mildly skeptical upon entry now seem…bolder. More confident. As though with a few compelling words, they're ready to lay down their lives for the vicar.

"You gotta give it to him… He knows how to motivate a crowd," Saipha says softly.

"It's all normal chapel fodder." I don't risk saying anything more against the vicar in such a public setting—especially next to Lucan, whose eyes I can feel on me.

Saipha shrugs and stands, stretching. "This has made me want to train."

I'd like nothing less than to make use of the training rooms right now. My whole body still aches, my back is a mess. But instead, I say, "Sure."

"Isola, can I have a moment?" Lucan asks. When Saipha lingers, he adds, "Alone."

"I'll meet you there?" I say to her.

Saipha tosses me a wide grin. "See you there. Or not. If you get hung up, you know."

I groan at her obvious attempt to get me to manipulate Lucan into our soldier and repeat, "I'll meet you there *soon*."

But she's already turned and gone before I finish speaking. I sigh. She might be my best friend, but sometimes I want to murder her.

I stare at Lucan, but he doesn't move to stand. I roll my eyes at him and straddle the bench to face him. Now, it's just the two of us and the heavy silence. Very alone in this massive room that somehow suddenly feels too small.

I try to ignore the pit of dread growing in my stomach as he holds my gaze. He has something he wants to say, and somehow, I'm more terrified of whatever it is than I am of a dragon.

22

Lucan shifts on the bench to face me and reaches out, palm up. "Give me your hand."

I lean back slightly, instinctively putting more distance between us the moment he asks me to get closer. "Why?"

"You'll see."

Yeah, that's not convincing me at all. "Tell me what you want first."

He holds my gaze, hand still extended toward me, and I'm suddenly very aware of how close we are right now. I've never noticed the subtle, darker greenish tint around his pupils or how inky his eyelashes are. I stiffen. *Why am I noticing his eyelashes?*

"What do you really think I'm going to do to you?" He keeps his voice low, so it doesn't echo in the cavernous space, but it also emphasizes the teasing note to it.

The truth is, I've no idea what I think he'll do—or why I'm hesitating. Perhaps it's because he asked. All the other times we've touched, there's been an unavoidable circumstance—training at the Grand Chapel, or the other night when I was injured. But doing it here, now, feels different. Dangerous, even. And I can't place why. His presence puts me on edge, every nerve vibrating with energy, despite my exhaustion.

"Well?"

"This isn't some trick you're going to turn against me?" The question sounds far more vulnerable than I'd like.

"No, I swear it."

I stare at his open palm for a moment longer, then I place my hand in his. Lucan's fingers slowly curl around mine, warm and firm, as if he's savoring the movement. With his other hand, he presses his fingers to his chest. At first, I think he's mocking the motion I make when I rub my scar, and I nearly rip my hand away. But then, a flood of Etherlight rises from around his hand.

The air between us hums.

He *glows*.

Not from the light of the chandelier above but from raw energy that collects around him. I gasp as the faint haze unspools like a ribbon. It surrounds him, sparks shimmering. I've never seen anything like it. I've beheld nothing more beautiful, and for a heartbeat, I forget to breathe.

I've been able to sense Etherlight, to see what it creates when drawn, but the only truly visible *Etherlight* known to humanity is the Font itself—it's so much power condensed that it illuminates the Undercrust. But it's never visible beyond how it manifests when drawn through an artificer sigil, like fire, lightning, ice, or noxious gas. This is something else entirely. It's as if I am catching a glimpse of the currents of life and magic swirling around him. Like I'm witnessing strands of the Font itself.

The orange-gold Etherlight flows like the hot spring water that's piped up from deep in the Undercrust. It seeps into my skin, easing tension from my muscles, healing bruises that I didn't even realize were there. I can't see my back, but I can feel the wounds smooth over. Then the aches vanish entirely as I'm healed.

The entire time, I can't tear my eyes from his. He's...stunning. The Etherlight highlights the strong edge of his jaw and casts shifting shadows over his cheeks. Lucan is intensely focused on me, but the expression is more tender than I've ever seen from him. The gold in his hazel eyes seems to glow. As the magic relaxes, his focus shifts from my face to our joined hands.

For a breath, neither of us speaks. The Etherlight dissipates into the air like stardust, fading entirely from view like embers on a breeze. I can even faintly smell sulfur.

Did you see the Etherlight, too? The question burns my tongue, but I can't bring myself to ask. Drawing attention to it would expose that something about me is different, which could be explained away as me being Valor Reborn. But, in here, it could also be something that's used against me as an indication of the curse.

It's not a risk I can take, especially not with him. Lucan continues staring at me. I hold his gaze, breathless, determined not to be the first to speak. The gold flecks are still there in his eyes, and they've never looked more beautiful.

"You can let go of me now." His voice is barely above a whisper, but it doesn't lose its playful edge.

I hadn't realized how tightly I was gripping his fingers. I quickly retract my hand, and all my thoughts slam back into my skull at the same time.

"You used a sigil," I say as understanding dawns.

"I think the words you were looking for are, 'Thank you.'" He smirks slightly. *Smirks!* Lucan, of all people, Mister Stoic-beyond-reason-and-impossible-to-read-or-scowling-at-best, is *smirking* at me.

I ignore the remark. "You're not gilded. People who have enough of a connection to Etherlight that they can use sigils without the gilding are…"

"*Very* rare," he finishes when awe silences me.

I'm not alone. It's the first thought that crosses my mind. It's not at the level of "Valor Reborn," but he also has something that makes him very special. Something that the vicar no doubt has wanted to keep for himself ever since he found out Lucan has this skill. Maybe he knew when he declared Lucan his son. Like he's some kind of disgusting collector of particularly gifted individuals.

Just like Saipha said, he's useful. I force the thought to the front of my brain, replacing the other. But all my heart wants is to pull him closer and talk about…everything. How does Etherlight feel for him? When did he find out and how? What other sigils does he know, if any?

"You were right. I did go back to the atrium two nights ago, but only to get this sigil." He tugs at the lacings of his jerkin and then pulls it and the loose collar of his shirt aside, exposing the top of his chest. I fight a flush that instantly rises to my cheeks at the sight of his collarbone and instead focus on the thick, black line that's been stained onto his skin like a tea ring from a mug—it's the start of an artificer frame. "I thought it'd be helpful for us."

"*Us?*"

"Consider this my application." He releases his shirt, and I hate how much I resent the fabric falling back into place.

"For what?"

"To be your ally in the Tribunal." Perhaps it's the lingering Etherlight, but his eyes still shine with flecks of gold, like an unintentional gilding.

"You want to be my ally when you're keeping secrets from me left and right?" I narrow my eyes, and he has the audacity to seem amused by my annoyance.

"We all have things to hide, don't we?" He gives me a pointed look, expectant. There's no way he could be referencing my fears about being cursed, yet it feels like he is. I look away.

"And, to think, four days ago I thought you hated me." I tease a hand through my curls, not sure if I'm more annoyed *at* him or at my reaction *to* him.

"Never hate, Isola." His gaze softens, though I can't say why. Something stirs in his expression, like admiration.

I place both hands on the bench, lean forward, and look him dead in the eyes. Trying to see through to all the things he's not saying. "You've never made an effort to endear yourself to me."

"Are you *still* on about your mum's birthday?" He sighs.

"More than that."

"It's not like the vicar would just let me casually spend time with his Valor Reborn when you were in the chapel."

"You could've found me outside the chapel."

"Would you have let me?" he asks as if he's thought it through countless times. "Be honest. Could I have walked up to you and asked you to spend an evening with me and you'd say yes?"

I fold my arms as I think about just how intently I'd been avoiding him specifically when I ditched my training. "Well, you weren't exactly *nice* to me that first night here."

"We were literally being attacked, and you were doing your best statue impression." Lucan shakes his head and returns his attention to me. "If I didn't like you, why would I go out of my way to patch you up then or help you now?"

"You did it to get something out of it," I point out.

He laughs, and the sound nearly makes me jump as it echoes off the floor and ceiling. "You are an astoundingly stubborn person." It reminds me of what he said the first night, and I realize what almost stuck out to me then—he says it as if it's a compliment.

"Teach me the rest of the sigils that were in the dragons, and I'll consider this whole 'allies' thing."

"You think so highly of me." He rolls his eyes but turns serious once more. "I could only manage to get one by myself—and I went for the yellow dragon because I was hoping it was healing. I got pretty beat up in the process, so thankfully it was. I hid under the yellow dragon until morning. The inquisitors must've disabled the others while I was asleep."

"Did they ask you about seeing a sigil?" I ask. Lucan shakes his head. "Me neither. So, they must be all right with us using them…"

"Right. You have one that protects. I have one that heals. That's a good team right there. Why not work together?"

"And what about Saipha?"

"Two allies are better than one. We're all stronger together." His proposal hangs in the air as I consider it. *Can I trust him?* Other factions have begun to form. Saipha and I are less outnumbered if we have a third.

She would be screeching at me to say yes, or dying of laughter, if she knew that I have him begging to help us without even having to do one little bit of batting my eyelashes.

Luckily, I'm not Saipha, and my caution is going to keep us safe. "How do I know that you haven't asked others this same thing? That

I'm not being played?"

"I wouldn't expose my advantage like that to just anyone." Not a particularly convincing argument... As I'm weighing the risk against potential reward, he continues, "Take some time and think about it. I don't need to pressure you now because I know you'll come to the right decision."

Arrogant. "Fine." I stand and start for the door.

"You're welcome, by the way." He draws my attention back to him. The very corner of his mouth curls slightly. "For healing you."

I'm actually incredibly thankful—and ashamed I haven't thanked him yet—so of course I bite out my, "Thank you."

Lucan smiles, and the whole room brightens. Once more, he seems to glow. But this time there's no magic involved...it's all on his own.

I quickly leave before I'm caught staring. The last thing I need is for him to think I *like* looking at him. But as I step out of the chapter house and back into the cloisters, I hear two voices coming from a hallway ahead.

Voices I know all too well.

I spot Saipha talking with Cindel and immediately wonder, *Am I about to have to break up a fight?*

Before I can walk over and find out for myself, Cindel spots me, and she lifts her chin and walks away. Saipha turns and heads over.

"So…" she begins, dragging out the word. "What did you and Lucan talk about?" One eyebrow is raised to match the teasing lift to the corner of her mouth.

"You first," I say, waving a hand in the direction in which Cindel slunk off. "What were *you* two talking about?"

Saipha's smile thins. "Oh, I pulled her aside to tell her that if she tries to come at you again—or send her cronies to do it—she's going to be dealing with a lot more than words from me—and I can hit back harder than her and her little lackeys could ever imagine."

"Benj wasn't that big of a deal."

"He wasn't, but you know Cindel. She'll make it a big deal." Saipha's serious expression lightens, a slight smile quirking her lips. "And you know me. I get angry when I'm hungry, so the last thing we want is me continually having to split my portions with you."

My chest tightens, and I grab her hand, squeezing it. "You're the best, you know."

"I know," she says without missing a beat, and we both share a little grin. "But you're not going to use my greatness as a distraction from telling me about Lucan."

"Right, speaking of having each other's backs… Lucan had an interesting proposition for me—for us."

"Oh! So you did use your looks for good." She doesn't let go of my hand and pulls me closer. "I knew you had it in you."

"I did not, and I'm not sure if that would be 'for good,' Saipha," I say with mocking scolding.

"We need to use every advantage in here." She shrugs. "Stop stalling and tell me what he said."

I repeat what Lucan said and detail how he healed me. When I'm finished, we lay out the risks and the upsides of agreeing to take him on as a formal ally. If the vicar is looking out for him...maybe there are benefits to be gained from having him in our fold. Maybe he has important knowledge. Being able to also use sigils is a pretty significant item on the "upsides" list.

But he also clearly feels the need to comply with anyone above him, like the vicar or inquisitors. And worrying if we can trust him with our secrets when times get tough is a pretty major risk. I tell Saipha in no uncertain terms that I will feel profoundly stupid if I trust him only to have him run off, *again*, and rat me out about something at the first opportunity.

We debate on and off for the rest of the day—during our time at the training rooms, where we keep to ourselves, at lunch and dinner, and until night falls and we're forced to retreat into our respective rooms.

For the first night since we arrived, I have a pillow under my head. An evening when I can just relax.

Or...so I thought.

Right after sunset, the inquisitors come through and take our keys. That test is done, apparently. All I can think of now is that my door is unlocked and *anyone* could come right in. My mind likes to torture me with messed-up imaginings of inquisitors from the first night coming in and dragging me back up to the rooftop. I'm sure that's what they want—that this is just another form of psychological torture designed for the Tribunal to draw out the curse. I wonder if it's the first taste the other supplicants are really getting of what's in store for them.

As a result, sleep is restless the first night in my room. Even though it's just Saipha and me up on the fourth floor, I *swear* I hear footsteps pacing the hall. Whispered voices just beyond my recognition—so clear that they jolt me fully awake, but faint enough that when I open my eyes wide…I'm not sure if they're a dream after all. I'm constantly sniffing for the faintest scent of rotting earth that heralds green dragon acid, ears straining for the pop and click of whatever machinations they might be saving to torture us with next.

Eventually, deeper sleep takes me by force, and I make it through the night. But I'm under no delusions that the inquisitors are done with us.

The next morning, I wake up as tired as when I went to bed. But there's no luxury of late mornings in the Tribunal. The copper box in the hall springs to life, loud even in my room as an inquisitor declares: "All supplicants are to report to the central atrium immediately."

We all hustle into our uniforms and line up downstairs as instructed. One at a time, the inquisitors pull us aside. Alone.

By the time I'm called, my heart is racing. The supplicants who were already taken have returned a little shaken but not harmed.

Two inquisitors flank me on either side and lead me down a long, narrow hallway at the end of the main hall and into a poorly lit room with a single chair in the center. A tall inquisitor stands to one side with a parchment in hand, and everything else is cast in shadows so dark that they could hide a whole other person.

The questions are few but straightforward.

"Have you experienced any signs of the curse?"

"Have you seen anyone exhibit signs of the curse?"

"Do you swear upon life and Creed to immediately report any who might be cursed?"

No. No. Yes.

I swallow the lump in my throat as the inquisitor holds my gaze, eyes narrowed. But then he turns and motions toward the door. "You may leave."

As I stand up, I can feel eyes on me from a far corner of the room. The hairs on the back of my neck stand on end. I don't dare look over my shoulder, but I'm certain it's the prelate. I just know it.

The heavy metal door echoes as it shuts behind me, and I'm released.

My hands shake as I walk back down the hall. The questioning was too brief, too clean. This wasn't the test we thought it was. How could it be? I can see the same fear gnawing at the others in the main hall, still waiting their turns. Unease thickens the air, eyes sliding sideways, measuring, mistrusting.

No one is showing any signs of being cursed. I can't decide if that's a good thing or a bad thing.

Usually, I'd think it's good. But knowing *someone* is cursed and still suspecting that someone is me is agonizing. If it *is* me, I almost wish the curse would get on with it already. Something I'd never admit aloud.

I pass by Lucan, still waiting to be called, as I head to breakfast. He doesn't say anything, but his presence is heavy with expectation. His stare questions loudly: *Allies?*

Heart pounding, I continue walking. I already know what I'm going to say when he finally asks outright again. No matter how many ways Saipha and I sliced it, there's only one real option that makes sense.

The thought follows me as I step into the refectory, the air thick with the scent of root vegetables and mushrooms. Trays clatter, voices rise and fall, people drift in and out. I meet Saipha's eyes—she's already grabbed a table—nod, and grab a tray with a baked potato and skewer of fat mushrooms before settling down next to her.

"How'd it go?" Saipha asks.

"Fine. Honestly, I was expecting more." The way I say it makes me sound like I'd been hoping for a challenge. When, really, I couldn't be more grateful that it wasn't.

"Same." Saipha probably *was* really hoping for more of a challenge. I study her as I chew on a mushroom. She's twirling a strand of her short red hair around her index finger and fighting a grin.

I know exactly what that look means. "What is it?"

She glances around, and her voice drops. "As I was leaving the questioning, I overheard one of the inquisitors ask another if everything was ready for the first test tomorrow. I think it's the first of the big ones the vicar told us about."

"*Tomorrow?* Tomorrow's only day five. It's too early." I try to hide my words with eating, keeping very aware of everyone who walks close.

"That was my thought. But, on the first day, the vicar just said there'd be three significant tests across the three weeks. He never said *when* they'd happen. Why would they make them orderly, like one per week? For all we know, they'll be back-to-back." Saipha's words are heavy. They'll do whatever it takes to mess with our minds and weed out the weak—the cursed. "To think, even after all we've been through, the real tests haven't even started…"

And, whatever the test is, it won't be good, neither of us says, but I'm sure we're both thinking it. It's bound to be something worse than anything we've already endured in here. And it's coming whether we like it or not.

24

After lunch, Saipha and I split up. She's happy to let me go to the library on my own while she heads for another workout. I swear Saipha would spend every hour of every day in the training rooms if she could, but there are only so many heavy things I can pick up and put down and pick up again before I need a reprieve. Studying was never really her thing, so she's happy to wave me goodbye, and I waste no time getting to the library.

There are so many scrolls here—more than I've ever seen in my life. There must be *something* that'd give us an advantage. And with the first test looming, I'm more determined than ever.

The other supplicants apparently don't agree with me, as the library is completely empty. I head upstairs to the second floor, which has small study rooms and even more bookshelves crammed together in a chaotic, almost claustrophobic manner. Ladders cling to their sides, and each is stuffed with scrolls bound in ribbons of every faded color. The air tastes more thickly of dust and old ink the farther back I go.

I round the corner—only to stop short.

Lucan.

He leans against the shelf I was headed for. Muscles strain against the long sleeves of his linen shirt, making him look less like a boy and more like the carved figure of some warrior scholar. In his hands is an ancient-looking scroll, the ink half faded, that he studies as though it was written just for him.

He doesn't glance up, but his voice carries across the stillness, low and deliberate. "You certainly know how to keep a guy waiting." He turns the scroll a little, though I suspect he's not actually reading anymore.

"I don't remember saying I'd meet you here." I make my way to his side and pretend to focus on the shelves, not wanting him to see that being this close to him has me slightly...off. Like I can't find my footing when he's near. I feel the phantom swell of Etherlight resonating between our bodies like it did the last time we were close.

His eyes flick in my direction. "Have you and Saipha reached a decision regarding my proposal?"

"Still considering."

"How much time do you really need?"

I hum and can't resist a playful glance in his direction as I run my fingertips along the ends of the scrolls. Their vellum is soft to the touch. "As much as it takes to feel like I can trust you."

Being stubborn only makes him smile. Not a reaction I'm accustomed to, given how it enrages the vicar, frustrates my friend, and exasperates my father on the best of days. In fact, the only person who's ever really appreciated my tenacity quite like him is Mum.

"You'd better decide quickly."

"Or what? Are you going to make the offer to someone else?" I probe to see if he's found out about the test tomorrow.

"I might start doubting you." He says it matter-of-factly, not a threat in the slightest. But I can't stop the pang of hurt that zings between my ribs at the thought of it. I tell myself it is because I don't like letting people down and has nothing to do with letting *him* down, specifically.

I shift the topic away from the notion and ask, "What are you reading?"

"Will telling you help my chances of becoming your ally?" he asks.

"It certainly won't hurt them."

He wraps up the scroll. The title on the wooden stave that protects the end of the vellum reads: PHYSIOLOGY OF ETHERSHADE AND THE CURSE.

"Seems dense." But fascinating...if I wasn't too afraid to find out those details and how they might relate to me. The idea of the test being tomorrow is getting under my skin. I haven't transformed *yet*. But they've only just begun doing their worst. I'm far from confident I'm safe.

"What are *you* looking for in this section?"

"Something on the scourge," I lie, instantly regretting my choice. *Why would I pick that?* Fascination about the scourge is dangerous in Vinguard. I blame Mum. The only research I've ever enjoyed has been for her.

"Ah, light reading as well." He shifts and reaches for a scroll on the shelves to his left. "You might find this one interesting, then."

I unroll it and skim the first bit—it's a standard summary of everything the Creed teaches about the scourge: That Ethershade blighted the land and twisted its animals. The pinnacle of this deformation was the dragons, tainted humans permanently disfigured into horrific beasts of Ethershade bent on destroying Etherlight. The first and greatest among them being the Elder Dragon, who now guides his hordes against the remnants of humanity—to destroy humans as beings of Etherlight so Ethershade can reign supreme.

As I try to focus on the words, Lucan shifts against the shelf next to me. His broad frame cuts the light streaming from a lantern at the end of the row.

I'm painfully aware of just how close he is, my body buzzing and restless. I look up to find him studying me, like I'm a puzzle he's close to solving. Too close. "Nothing new here. I think I might check the next row for something more stimulating." I pass the scroll back to him and turn to leave.

He catches my biceps. *Speaking of close.* Our noses nearly touch, and any words catch in my throat. Those bright, hazel eyes of his threaten to bore a hole into my soul. "Isola, I'm serious. I want to help you. Not for the vicar and not for your title."

A tiny, dangerous part of me wants to believe him. Aches to

believe him. I allow myself to be held in place, heart pounding.

"How can I trust you're not going to run to tell the vicar or inquisitors my secrets the second things get tough?" I breathe, wishing I sounded stronger and less afraid, less hurt.

"I only told them what they knew or would find out," he counters. "The vicar would've found out you'd left with ease, even if I'd lied. The inquisitors saw you handle the fire."

"But—"

"But I didn't tell them about you sneaking into the library," he interrupts me, and I pause. *I was right.* "Nor about you using the sigil. And I won't—even though the inquisitors probably saw that, too. I swear, never again will I run to the vicar, or the inquisitors, or anyone with any secret of yours."

"You expect me to take you at your word?" It's not that simple, yet...a small place in my heart wants it to be. My heart wants to believe in the good and ignore the bad.

"Yes." He speaks right to that tiny corner of me.

"How?"

"Is it crazy to think I like you?" He beams at me with a glint in his eyes that does indeed make him look a bit crazy. "That I like you more by the day? Especially now that the vicar isn't around, making us both act unnaturally?"

"Yes." *We don't really even know each other.* Anything he likes about me is the *idea* of me. Just like the rest of them...

Lucan releases me, his eyes still locked on mine, with a smile that could brighten midnight. "Then I'm positively insane."

The remark catches me off guard. He holds me with a look alone. Transfixed. Stuck. Wanting to lean in and run at the same time.

I take a step backward, and then another. This time, he lets me leave.

25

I barely sleep a wink. I know I need to, but I'm too restless, my body practically vibrating between anxiety and outright terror all night.

At breakfast the next morning, Saipha and I are so quiet that when her knife scrapes across her plate, it hits us both like a scream. We lock eyes. Swallow down dry biscuit. And return our focus to our plates. What can we say? I think we both feel far from ready. Especially after getting a taste of what the inquisitors might throw at us on our second night.

Immediately following breakfast, we're herded into the central atrium.

The inquisitors gather in the front of the hall, underneath the wrought iron balcony where Vicar Darius is currently perched. He grips the railing, eyes gleaming.

"Greetings yet again, my dear supplicants. You have made it through five days of your three weeks here." He projects his voice so everyone can hear with ease. "It is a delight to learn that none of you have shown signs of the curse, so far."

So far. Saipha and I share a glance. My focus shifts to where Lucan has positioned himself over her shoulder. Our eyes meet. He arches a brow and asks with a look, *Allies?*

I shrug noncommittally.

He rolls his eyes.

"But we must be thorough. We must ensure the curse is wrung from the bones of the already dead yet still living. There can be no doubt that when you are gilded, you are free of the pull of Ethershade. To do this, we shall challenge you. Test your mettle and your love and loyalty for Vinguard. You will act in service to the Creed and its Mercy Knights during these tests. Not only will you learn more about our city, its history, and our glorious purpose, but each of you will have the opportunity to prove whether you have what it takes to stand among the illustrious ranks of the Mercy Knights, defenders of Vinguard."

Whispers of excitement. Supplicants stand a little taller, Saipha especially. I'm sure they're already imagining catching the eye of a knight who will want them to be their page the second they step out of here.

"Now, follow the inquisitors and heed the commands of the knights who keep us safe," the vicar finishes.

The inquisitors encircle us like a tightening noose as we fall into place behind the prelate. She opens one of the previously barred doors in the atrium and guides us to a stairway. We spiral farther and farther down, and for a moment, I think we'll hit the basement where Saipha and I were tortured with green dragon poison. We descend even deeper, until the walls of the staircase give way, and a hazy underground metropolis shines up at us like stars through a labyrinth of bridges and catwalks suspended from the hollowed-out ceiling of this massive cave.

We're at the top of the Undercrust.

"I always forget how big it is," Saipha murmurs.

"Me, too." Mum took me down here once, long ago. She was doing some research on the Font when she was still an Earthwarden. It's impossible to see the Font from way up here. The whole city of the Undercrust is built into stalactites that hang beneath upper Vinguard and on ledges that cling to the walls as they stretch out over a vast abyss. Far, far below, somewhere in that golden haze of Etherlight, is the legendary Font. The last wellspring of Etherlight in the world. It's the only thing that gives us a fighting chance.

Saipha pauses at the railing of the bridge we're on, but only for a second. "It's hard to think people prefer this." Her eyes dart to Horowin and his group.

"You can't hear the bells this far below," I say. "There's a peace to that."

"True, but it feels like giving up. That's the last of our land up there."

Spoken like a true Mercy Knight.

We arrive at an intersection, then another, before heading up a ramp. I try to keep track of where we might be in relation to the city above, but it's impossible to tell from down here. The prelate opens a metal gate at the far end with a heavy *clank*.

The next set of stairs is so dimly lit that we're relying on the walls to keep us upright as we pass back into the bedrock that's the foundation of the Upper City. I hear supplicants behind me trip. Cursing. But no one stops.

As we ascend, the stone wall feels somehow softer under my fingernails. I imagine them sinking into it for purchase. There is a ripple in the darkness, like a breeze that shouldn't exist. No, not in the darkness—underneath my skin.

I shiver, and my head hums. Then my vision sharpens unnaturally for just a second before a door ahead opens and everything blinks back to normal.

I can feel Lucan's eyes on me, but I don't dare glance behind for fear I'll draw an inquisitor's attention. Nor do I rub my sternum, where my scar feels like it's been lit on fire.

We end in a massive, dungeon-like room. There are multiple pathways that extend farther into darkness—almost all of them barred. To the right is a heavy door, the old wood fortified with iron bars. The ceiling is so low that the taller supplicants, like Lucan, must crouch. And the air...

The air is thick with decay.

Supplicants around me gag. One boy with wavy brown hair I saw a few times in the library sways, leans against a wall, and turns up his breakfast. The inquisitors grab his elbow unceremoniously and wrench him away, dragging him across the room.

"I'm not— I was just—" Whatever else the supplicant was going to say is lost with the closing of a heavy door.

Don't show weakness. The inquisitors know that a cursed is among us and are no doubt on edge. They will do whatever it takes to find who it is.

"I think I know where we are," Saipha whispers. I glance in her direction. "Sundering pits."

My jaw slackens slightly. It'd explain the stink, the strange in-between feeling of these rooms—not quite Upper City and not Undercrust—and the unnerving sensation I felt on the way here.

Slain dragons are taken to the sundering pits. According to the Creed, they can't be left to rot aboveground because they might attract scavengers in the form of other dragons. Moreover, as they rot, the Creed says they release Ethershade, which could cause the scourge to break out within Vinguard.

The sundering pits break down the corpses of the dragons slain. The belief is that when the carcass is disassembled, the Ethershade is less potent. Less focused, less of a possibility to create harm to Vinguard or the Font with the thick crust of the earth protecting both above and below. The dragons are broken down until the Ethershade is so minimal they can be left to rot in these passages that look right out of a nightmare.

Though Mum disagrees with all of this, of course.

"You will be assigned two to a room and given instructions by our knights," the prelate says, her voice as sharp as a Mercy dagger.

All of us start looking around, sizing up who we might be paired with. I grip Saipha's hand.

"Your performance will be scrutinized and judged. Remember that everything you are about to do is in service of Vinguard, the Creed, and those who lay down their lives upon the ramparts to keep us safe."

No one dares say a word, every set of shoulders tight.

The prelate points to the heavy door the boy just went through. "Perform well. Do not give us a reason to take you through this door and administer a harsher test to ensure your heart has not been softened toward a dragon due to the curse."

With no further warnings needed, the prelate begins to call out names, pairing people off with each other. Horowin is paired with Rovin, another boy from the Undercrust. Cindel with Benj. Nelly, the supplicant I saw fighting Cindel on the first night, with Daisy, whom I've only met in passing but I know is another Upper City supplicant.

The list goes on and more supplicants step forward, exchanging wide-eyed glances but with set, determined jaws. As the prelate reads, Mercy Knights arrive, emerging from the halls in full regalia. Saipha's eyes widen, and her fingers tense around mine as she beholds them, like she hasn't grown up seeing those dragon-blood capes and armor of leather dotted with silver plate that crackles with flames, sparks with lightning, or shimmers a nearly iridescent silver, depending on what sigils have been etched on the underside.

The knights guide the pairs down seemingly random hallways. The idea of no longer being in the care of inquisitors somehow feels more comforting.

"Isola Thaz," the prelate calls.

I stand a little straighter and exhale a steadying breath, share one last look with Saipha, who dips her chin slightly, and move to the front of the pack. Even though I can't see the prelate's eyes from underneath the shadow of her hood, I can feel her piercing stare. The sensation of it prickles across my skin like the first frost of winter.

"Lucan Darius," she calls next.

Lucan moves to my side with easy, confident strides. His expression is calm, gaze detached, as though he's a world away. I never noticed how different his demeanor and expressions have become when we've been alone in the Tribunal. *This* is the Lucan I'm most familiar with—the vicar's adopted son, the unaffected, dutiful servant of the Creed.

Our eyes meet, and I quickly look away. Out of everyone, of course I would be paired with him. The vicar's hand is all over this match. But...maybe it's not the worst thing? Lucan's proposal of an alliance with Saipha and me still dangles between us. This could be a prime opportunity to test the mettle of his offer and formalize the obvious choice.

A knight steps forward and guides us away. Our walk down the corridor is far too long and incredibly claustrophobic, and I force myself to keep my breathing even. I imagine we've walked two or three city blocks when we finally arrive at a door.

The room we enter next feels even worse than the passage.

Before us is the head of a green dragon—one I *recognize*. It's the beast that attacked Vinguard the day Saipha and I snuck into the wall. It's festering with rot, scales barely clinging to the sludge that was once flesh and muscle. Its neck has been unceremoniously hacked away. Sinew and bone jut out at odd angles. I can't prevent the shudder racing down my spine when I realize its eyes are now only empty, oozing red holes.

A trail of crusted blood connects the dragon to a colossal chute jutting out from high up on the wall. Judging by the permanent stain at its opening, I assume it connects to the city—an easy way for Mercy Knights above to send pieces of dragon into the thick rock of the crust, away from both sky and Font.

"Your tools." The Mercy Knight gestures unceremoniously to the wall at our left.

I stare at the wall and the tools that line it, stomach churning, knowing exactly what I'm about to be asked to do.

26

Hanging on the wall before me are all manner of saws, thick metal needles, chisels, hammers, and pliers. The dragon carcasses are quickly processed on the surface—just enough that the pieces can fit down the chutes. This must be where they are broken down completely to finish the job of dispersing the Ethershade.

"Reduce the skull to small enough pieces that it can completely fit in that barrel." The Mercy Knight points at a vessel to the right of the door that's surely far too small. We'd have to reduce the skull to little more than pulp to get it to fit... "I'll return in an hour to assess your progress and ensure neither of you are particularly susceptible to Ethershade." *Cursed, he means.* That's why we're really here. Put us all in front of a whole bunch of Ethershade and see if anyone transforms.

"Put on those," he says, pointing to two pairs of gloves that look long enough to stretch past our elbows. They're resting atop an equally tall pair of thick leather boots in front of heavy leather aprons hanging on the wall. They're all red like the Mercy Knight robes, but uneven—and I want to vomit as I realize just how much dragon blood has stained them, year over year, without a proper wash.

At least if we are dragon cursed, we won't die covered in dragon innards. I'm learning it's all about the small victories during the Tribunal.

With that, the knight leaves, and the door closes behind him with an ominous thud. Shivers dance down my spine at the distinct sound of a lock on the outside of the door engaging.

Lucan doesn't say anything. Instead, he stares at the head of the dragon, mouth pressed into a hard line.

I cross to the wall and shove on a pair of boots and gloves, then sling the apron over my neck and tie it on. It's all slightly too big for me, but I'd rather the extra space over pinched toes. Then I turn to the tools hanging along the wall. Beside them is a basic anatomical chart of a dragon. It bears the seal of Mercy in its lower right corner—an impaling blade, a dragon wrapped around it.

"Which would you like first?" I select a bone saw. When Lucan doesn't immediately answer, I glance back at him. He's still staring at the dragon's head, shoulders curled in slightly. *Relatable.* I cross and hand him a hammer. "We should get to it."

His eyes drift toward the hammer, then to my face. Lucan's skin is ashen, and a fine sheen of sweat beads his brow, like he might pass out at any moment. I bite back a sigh. I didn't want to find something in common with him, but if he hates this as much as I do...

"They're going to be back before we know it," I say, softer. What I don't say is what I know he well understands: they're going to want to see results, and not having them is a grave risk.

"Right." He takes the hammer from me, his jaw tightening.

"There's a chart over there. The softer spots and good break points are marked." I gesture, then go right to the head.

It's a truly disgusting sight. Bile creeps up the back of my throat as I lean in. Being this close to a dragon's head—even a very, very dead one—has my throat tight. Innate fear wars with disgust as my saw sinks into the squelching, rotted flesh. The scales part with ease, the meat below no longer holding on to them.

"You...are very good at that." Lucan still has yet to move.

"Almost half my conscious life has been spent under the tutelage of the Creed."

"As has mine. That's how I know they didn't teach you this."

I should've expected that offhand excuse not to work on him. Straightening, I debate if I can tell him the truth. If he wants to be allies, this is a good test. "My mum."

Comprehension dawns on his face.

"She studies the dragons as much as she does the scourge. She believes *dragons are not the cause of the scourge.*" I echo her at the end.

"Study of anything related to Ethershade is prohibited if not in service to the Creed or Mercy." His voice lacks conviction, as if he's simply reciting it out of habit.

I give him a dull look that I hope conveys he can stop echoing the vicar around me. "You going to turn her in?"

"No," he responds easily, glancing away, as if ashamed he even brought it up. The tension in my shoulders eases some. I'd intended to be sarcastic, but there was a nugget of something genuine in that question. He's passing the test, so long as he keeps his word on that.

"She's already been disgraced—cast from her guild, research support taken. I think she's suffered enough." *Lost her happy family, as it were...* "Anyway, let's focus on what we have to do."

He walks over and shoves on his own boots and gloves, then comes up beside me, adjusting his grip on the hammer before delivering a blow to the chunk of neck vertebrae still attached to the head. I narrowly avoid projectile goop. "I'm sorry for what they did to her."

I pause mid-saw, staring at the chunk of bone I'm hacking in two rather than him. Lucan glances my way, I see it in my periphery, but I don't turn to face him. I don't want him to see my expression; he might read too much into it.

It was easier to not like you when I thought you were a Creed sycophant, I want to say.

My saw vibrates in my hand as I hit a particular hard piece of bone and is now wedged stuck. I yank on the handle, trying to wrestle it free.

"Do you want me to help?" Lucan straightens from his last swing.

"I got it."

He gestures at the bone above my saw. "Here, that's the thickest part. Let me—"

"I said I got it." I give him a firm look.

"What's your problem?" Lucan rounds the massive head anyway. "Why are you *still* fighting me when all I'm trying to do is help you?"

"Why are you helping me at all, though? You haven't given me a good answer." I grunt without making eye contact and try to force my saw through the thick knob of bone it's stuck on.

"I told you: I like you."

I willfully ignore that. "Is it for your father?"

"That man is *not* my father," he says with enough venom that it startles me, even knowing more of his history since coming to the Tribunal. "How many times do I have to tell you: I will do what I have to, never because I want to screw with you."

"I..." All of my warring thoughts silence me. The tidy tally Saipha and I made of pros and cons is a mess. "No matter what I tell myself, I can't seem to move past the idea that I just can't trust you!" I thrust forward, and the saw pops free. My grip slackens in the moment of surprise, and the handle slips from my fingers. The saw scuttles across the floor, skidding all the way to the back corner of the room. But instead of going after it, I lift my gaze to his. Neither of us move. "I can't stop thinking you're one of *them*."

"Them?" His voice is low and quiet, and his brow furrows.

I realize I could have been referring to those cursed as easily as the Creed.

"One of the vicar's mindless sycophants." I look away. "I shouldn't have said that."

Lucan takes a step closer. I go to move around him, making for the saw. He catches my elbow, holding me. Not hard enough to *make* me stay, just enough to ask me to. Face-to-face, I'm struck by just how much taller he is than me. I can almost feel the bulk of his muscles, which I've been unable to ignore since Saipha so aptly pointed them out, straining against pulling me closer. For the first time, he feels like someone who could protect me, if I were to ever need it. Not because he's of the Creed or can use sigils. Not even because he possesses power within Vinguard as the vicar's son...but because he might also have the will.

It's a dangerous fantasy that I try to kill as fast as it sparks to life in my mind.

"Why would me being one of 'them' matter? Don't you trust the curates as Valor Reborn?" Lucan's gaze roves over my face—my brow, my lips—as if he's searching for a hint of a lie.

I swallow thickly and manage to say, "Of course I do."

He narrows his eyes slightly, and the corners of his lips twitch, but I can't tell if it's with amusement or disapproval. "Say it like you mean it this time."

"Excuse me?" My words are barely more than a whisper.

"That might work on the rest of them, but not on me. I see you, Isola, even the parts you wish I didn't." His gaze doesn't waver. It's as though he's reading me like a scroll and he just got to the best part.

"Is that a threat?" My body is on edge. Breaths short. Never have I been studied like this before.

"If it was, you'd already be in trouble." Lucan frowns as a flash of pain crosses his eyes. "You can trust me. *Please*, trust me."

"I want to," I whisper. "You've no idea how hard it is, being Valor Reborn. I don't have people lining up to be my friend for the right reasons often. I thought you'd understand that as the vicar's son. Maybe even understand me."

"I do."

"So then you know why it hurt so much when I put trust in you and you betrayed me to the man I hate the most. I know it was small and unimportant. I know I'm being immature about this. But it's like there's a part of my mind that knows better and a part that's scared." My words are as fragile as I feel, and Lucan accepts them as delicately as his hand rests on me. "Look, I—" The words are stuck in my throat, and I force them out. "I want to trust you again. I'm getting there."

He nods and releases me.

I walk to where the saw landed, kicking up motes of dust with my oversized leather boots, all the while wondering when the last time anyone set foot on this particular chunk of stone was. Anything to run from my mess of thoughts and feelings surrounding Lucan. From my fear of giving someone my trust when it's so possible that they might disappoint me. Or worse, that I might care enough about disappointing them.

I'm so focused on everything else that I don't realize what's happening until it's right upon us.

I don't notice the sudden drop in temperature until the chill passes through me. The cloying smell of rot accosts my senses—but not of dragon flesh. Instead, it's of flowers and soil. Of stone crumbling to time. A rot that's as sweet as it is acrid. A slight burning on the end of every inhale. It's distinctly different from the green dragon's acid. This is brighter. It burns my nose and sizzles across my skin. It's a scent I last detected on the wind as I stood on the wall with Saipha.

I look overhead, and terror grabs me by the throat. A thin curl of rusty haze ripples across the ceiling. I stagger back.

"Isola?" Lucan asks, his voice sharp with concern.

Spinning, I lock eyes with him. "Scourge."

27

I'm running back toward Lucan as he's trying to formulate his next question. Grabbing his wrist, I charge toward the door. I'm about to scream for help when he flings a glove off and his bare hand clamps over my open mouth.

Releasing him, I turn and glare. "What do you think you're doing?"

"What if it's part of the challenge?"

"Have you lost your mind? They wouldn't expose us to the *scourge* just to see if we're cursed."

A shadow passes over his eyes as his chin tips downward, severity overtaking his gaze. I shake my head.

"No," I whisper. "There's no… There's no way."

"You know what the vicar is capable of. Dismantling a dragon to get it into the chute should've prevented the scourge." Lucan speaks with such authority that all I can think is that he knows something I don't. "And if we call for help, I've no doubt they'd use it against us, claiming we're overly sensitive to Ethershade."

"Everyone is 'overly sensitive' to literal death! What in the dragon-burned hells are we supposed to do?" Even if I'm not screaming for help, I can't stop my voice from pitching up. "Die?"

"Even if it's not a test, you know they won't open that door. They won't risk the scourge getting out."

Disappointment and despair unlock every joint in my body, and I nearly collapse. They will let us die in here if they think opening the door would let the scourge spread farther. I stare up at him and wonder if his is going to be the last face I ever see. Is this it? My final moments are to be spent in a room filled with rot and blight, staring at a guy I'm not even sure I *like*?

He flings his other glove off and grabs my shoulders, holding them tightly. "You figured out the automatons; you can figure this out. Death isn't ready for us yet. You're going to get us out of here, Isola, and I'm going to help by doing whatever you tell me to."

"I'm not—"

"Isola Thaz. *You* are going to get us out of here." There's something familiar in the way he says my name that makes me realize it's how he's always called me. Isola. Not Valor Reborn. To him, I've always been Isola.

He's telling me to save us. Not me as the vicar's well-trained favorite. Not as Valor Reborn and whatever legendary powers I may or may not possess. As Isola. The girl who has been trained, not just by the Creed, but by her mother. Her father. As someone who *can*.

Damn it. Why does that work on me? Why does him saying he's putting his trust in me suddenly have my mind searching for a way out of a hopeless situation?

I drop low, speaking hastily. "We have ten minutes, *maybe*, before the scourge haze replaces the air in this room. Before that, our lungs will start burning. Our skin will itch and peel. We will go mad as we begin to rot from the inside out until we're nothing but mindless, moving husks before we're completely consumed." *And that's all assuming neither of us is cursed*, I don't say, deeming it unnecessary and unhelpful.

"A great summary of a horrible death. Now, how do we stop it?"

"Well, if I knew how to do that, our world would be saved."

"No time like the present to figure out how to save the world," he quips far too easily when facing down near-certain death.

I glare at him. He just smiles in a way that says, *Go on*. And…I do. I look at the room, not with the eyes of the Creed but with the understanding of the scourge as my mum always taught.

To the masses, the scourge is a festering blight, a plague upon the earth itself. And that's not *wrong*…but it's also not completely accurate, either.

Think of the scourge as the by-product of a void, my mum would say. Places where Etherlight has been sucked dry can create an imbalance toward Ethershade. That's how the scourge forms. It is, in that way, like a rot. It manifests where death is—where life has left. Once the scales of our world were no longer balanced, it was impossible to put them back. And that's why the scourge runs rampant. It continues feeding on life until there is nothing left. Which, right now, is Lucan and me.

So I have to do three things:

Put the room magically back in balance.

Protect Lucan and me while doing so.

Not. Die.

Frantically, my mind searches all I know—all I've learned from Mum and Father and, as much as I hate to admit it, the vicar. And as I stare into Lucan's hopeful eyes, it hits me like the sun piercing the clouds.

"I think I know how we're going to survive this. But you need to do *exactly* as I say."

28

"Tell me." There's no hesitation.

"You need to get in the chute."

He eyes the opening. "For Mercy's sake, why are we going in there?" His eyebrows are almost in his hairline now.

"What happened to doing whatever I tell you to?" I plant my hands on my hips. "Either you think I can get us out of here or you don't."

"Okay, fair." He flashes a tiny grin at my zeal.

I move, grabbing a glob of dragon gore, the soft squelch of sludge making me nauseous. The rotting flesh is already singeing away in the presence of the scourge. There's no time to linger on what this means.

Lucan is at my side.

"Are you sure about this?" He gags, barely getting the words out.

"Not in the slightest." I'm still crouched, drawing a symbol with dragon guts on the apron over my upper breastbone—a circle with a square and a vertical line. Lucan regards me warily, and I wonder if he knows what this sigil does. It had to have been in the yellow dragon automaton, too. "I'm going to need you to heal me." *I imagine this is going to hurt...a lot.*

"All right." He tugs his collar aside, and I see the familiar edge of the sigil stained on his skin. *I need some of whatever he used to do that.* "I'm ready."

Adjusting my shirt to cover the lower half of my face, I reach down to fill my gloved hand with more dragon guts, then stand. My lungs burn instantly, and my eyes water as the scourge thickens the air above us. But I stay focused.

With blood and guts, I draw a square around the chute's opening, barely able to reach the top.

"Your artistic pursuits leave something to be desired." A cough follows his remarks. The scourge is getting to him, too.

I ignore him and draw a square on my torso, then a crimson line from one of my wrists to the opposite foot, cutting the square into two triangles. I swallow the bile that claws at my throat. Then I make another from the other hand to foot. I certainly hope they're going to finally give me new clothes after this...

"All right." I wheeze and cough. "Get in."

"Isola—" My name is desperate on his lips. I wonder if he's figured out what I'm about to do.

"Don't get sentimental on me now. There's no time."

He scrambles in and extends a hand to me, and I use it to help raise myself into the opening. He grunts and shifts back, making room, until both our bodies are fully inside the chute. The scourge is so thick up here, my eyes are watering, and I blink several times, desperate to find the lines I painted on the rim.

I'm so relieved I almost cry when I see them. My fingertips touch them as I steady my grip around the top two corners. I extend one leg out from under me, pressing my right foot into the bottom right corner, and the pressure keeps me wedged.

I take a deep breath, trying to slow my racing heart. I look up at Lucan. "Ready?"

"I'm almost scared to say it, but yes." His eyes are filled with worry.

There's no time to waste. No time to doubt or further mentally prepare myself for what's to come. I shift my left foot out to the left corner. The lines drawn across my body connect with the symbol I drew around the outside, making a complete armor sigil.

There's a breathless surge of Etherlight the moment the lines merge. My body glows a hazy gold that flickers weakly against the thick, crimson scourge.

"Isola! You can't turn yourself into a human sigil, that's—"

"The best chance we've got," I grunt between breaths, pinning him with a glare. We're so close in this tiny chute. Close enough that I can feel his panicked breathing. "The armor sigil will keep us safe in here—it'll block more scourge from coming in. The other one draws Etherlight from the Font. I'm going to use it to balance the Ether of the room, to put Etherlight and Ethershade in balance and, hopefully, clear the scourge."

"You should've let me do this." He reaches up. His fingertips graze my cheek, warm and callused.

"Too late for that." I give him a wild grin. I think it's an expression Saipha would wear—far braver than I feel.

"The scourge eats Etherlight, no? Won't this just draw it to you faster?"

"The scourge is a product of imbalance. That's the secret, Lucan. Too much Ethershade is bad, and so is too much Etherlight—but the Creed doesn't want to admit that part," I say softly, as if someone is listening through the door. "But if you put them back in balance, you have harmony. You have Ether, just *Ether*, as it was meant to be. I'm betting that I can draw enough Etherlight to neutralize what's in the room."

His fingertips have yet to leave my jaw. "Will it be enough without killing you, though?"

"I'm betting *I'm* strong enough." The words are little more than a whisper.

When I was a small child, I never dreamed of going on the walls. I never wanted to play hero. I wanted to be a researcher, like Mum. I wanted to save the world, but not with valiant acts. With pen and a vellum-packed journal and a workshop.

It doesn't matter if I'm Valor Reborn or not. As long as I draw breath, I'm going to do whatever it takes to defend my home.

"Then I'll bet on you, too." His hand leaves my face, and before I can ask what he means, a hazy yellow glow combines with the light radiating off my body. It outlines him, filling in the gaps and gilding his face.

Lucan's eyes are locked with mine. We share a single inhale and exhale, perfectly in sync. His hands drop to my waist, and the glow envelops both of us. I still can't tell if he sees it or not. But something in his gaze assures me he does. Like this is *our* secret. Precious, dangerous, and forbidden.

I steady myself and draw through the first sigil I drew on my body—the one to pull Etherlight up from the Font.

The rush is so overwhelming that it goes straight to my head, making everything spin. Making me feel like I'm weightless. Like we're the only two people in the world.

Even as my breathing thins, and it feels like a thousand hands are clawing at me, scraping under my skin, searching for purchase. Even as the freshly healed scars on my back throb, there's only us.

I stay focused on the Etherlight that flows around us, between us, *within us*. The barrier I've created with Etherlight and my body with the armor sigil is enough to keep more scourge from attacking us. Thanks to the flood of Etherlight drawn from the Font, the clawing at my back lessens and the scourge in the room begins to ease.

But, as the seconds drag on, my skin begins to feel too tight. My scar is on fire. My heart flutters, shuddering.

Skip.

Skip. Skip.

I draw a shaky breath and sag, fingers pressing hard into the stone opening to keep myself upright. *Not yet.* I'm not done yet. He's not safe.

"Are you all right?" Lucan's grip tightens on me.

"I'm fine. It stings, a little. But not very much."

"You're such a bad liar."

"Fine, the pain is excruciating." My vision blurs, and my thoughts jumble.

"Stay with me, Isola," Lucan whispers, pulling me back to consciousness. "You're safe with me." Those hazel eyes, illuminated by gold flecks, are all-consuming. If not for the laughably dangerous position we're in right now, I might believe him.

"Lucan...are you really on my side?" I whisper.

"Always." No hesitation. No change in his tone.

I don't want to believe him...but I do. "Because the vicar told you to be?"

"Because I *want to* be."

The last of my resistance shatters. I want to collapse into him and surrender completely. I try to form words, but none come.

The agonizing tear of the scourge at my back finally abates. My fingers tremble before giving out the second I think it's safe enough—hoping I'm right. Hoping he will catch me if I finally let go.

My foot slips on the opening, and I tumble backward, consciousness wavering. Lucan jolts forward. His hands tighten on my waist, holding my weight. He comes crashing down with me. We twist in the air, tumbling.

I try to wrap my arms around his neck and brace.

Then everything goes black.

29

Somehow, Lucan must have taken most of the fall. I feel his body thud beneath mine, his arms tightening around my waist and pulling me close. I try to lift my lashes, let him know I'm fine, but my eyelids feel as heavy as a dragon landing on a rooftop. My whole body groans from the strain of trying to exist.

Lucan clutches me tighter. His breath is hot against my cheek as he pleads into the now-clear air, "Stay with me, Isola. I have you." He sits us up, settling me across his legs. My head lolls against his chest. *"I have you."*

Waves of exhaustion and dizziness course through me. I shudder, cold all over. I wouldn't be shocked if frost coated my flesh.

I can't believe that worked. The vicar swore I was never to touch sigils, claiming they would only slow any progress I made, that I had to learn to draw from the Font directly—like Valor, like I did on the day of the dragon attack when I was twelve. But as my chest lightens with victory over the scourge, a darker thought claws in. What if he never meant to guide me? What if he only meant to keep me weak and afraid, pliable to his whims?

I don't know how long we sit there, each lost in our own thoughts. Finally, when I've leeched enough of his warmth to open my eyes, I pull away and struggle to my feet. Every muscle aches. Red dust coats the room, the harmless remnants of the scourge. We both turn our gazes to the dragon head. It's nothing but a blackened skull now.

"You must've released a lot of Etherlight."

He didn't intend for it to happen, but the remark sets off a gnawing guilt within me. I did just use a lot of Etherlight. The Font, for as massive as it is, refills with Etherlight very slowly due to the imbalance of the world. Every draw on it—from the Mercy Knights' weapons to tiny repairs—removes a little more and weakens it. Vinguard is slowly dying by a thousand small cuts.

I shake my head and ignore the guilt. *We didn't have a choice.* "This wasn't me. It was already blackening earlier in the presence of the scourge."

"I thought dragons are immune to the scourge because they're also made of Ethershade? Shouldn't it still be intact, then?" He sounds genuinely confused.

"You assume what the Creed has told you is true." I also stare at the skull, thinking of everything my mother told me. With one blackened and brittle skull, her wildest theory has evidence: dragons are also creatures of Etherlight.

Lucan stares, expression impossibly unreadable. He's too smart not to piece it together with what I've heavily implied. Everything he's ever been told is proving untrue. Yet…he doesn't seem surprised or horrified? There's a grim acceptance of it. But not the shock I'd expect.

I don't have time to read into it now, and he doesn't have time to stand there lost in thought. "Help me break down the skull. It should be easy to get in the barrel now."

As soon as I grab the hammer, my knees wobble. I'm about to collapse to the floor when Lucan's arm slides around me, pulling me against his body tightly.

"I'm here." He says it like he plans for it to be true far longer than this singular moment. But that's absurd. I shake the thought from my mind. "Let's put you over here where there's less dust, then I'll take care of the skull and clean up this room."

He must have the same thought as me about how bad it would be if they find evidence of the scourge. Anything out of the ordinary is going to be used against us.

Lucan helps me over to where the tools are, by the door. I'm still catching my breath, but, oddly, I don't feel out of sorts. In fact, despite drawing directly from the Font more than I ever have before, my whole body feels at peace. My heart isn't erratic, my skin doesn't itch, my eyes and nails seem…normal.

Without warning, the door opens to reveal a Mercy Knight, hood pushed back, draping his shoulders. His eyes widen to where I can see the whites all the way around his irises, and he staggers back.

Lucan raises his hands. "We can explain."

"Scourge dust?" he murmurs. Then, louder, *"Cursed!"* The man draws his silver blade in a blur and charges.

Lucan dodges with a speed I didn't think him capable of. He doesn't retaliate, even though I swear I can see the twitch of his fingers as though he quenches the urge to disarm the man. I definitely wasn't the only one the vicar gave special training to.

"We're not— Please, I—" Lucan dodges another near miss.

The dagger the knight is brandishing has enough poison in it to fell a dragon with a single nick, provided one makes it through their scaly armor. Lucan is going to get himself killed.

"Cruelty!" Lucan jumps back as the clamor of more Mercy Knights' armor echoes in from the hall. "We demand cruelty."

Killing a dragon cursed is to show mercy. Mercy might be swift and painless, but cruelty at least demands an audience with Vicar Darius.

"There are no second chances for cursed. You brought the scourge upon our walls!" The man snarls and lunges as the others pour through the door. Two go right for Lucan, and two more advance toward me. I hold up my hands.

"We demand cruelty," I repeat, shaking my head. "Show no mercy!"

But they don't hear me. Flashes of silver. What was the point of fending off the scourge if I'm just going to die by their blades?

No. I refuse. "*Please*, let us explain."

"We will not poison our ears with the words of a dragon cursed," one shouts.

They each take a step apart and draw back their blades, readying attacks. My heart hammers. My hands tremble. Is this it? Is this all I'll amount to? Just when I've finally managed to do something monumental with Etherlight, they're going to kill me?

No. All my life, I've rolled over and given in. I'm not giving up now. I'm going to prove Lucan right—death isn't ready for us.

"I am Valor Reborn," I say with as much conviction as I can summon. "Stay back."

"You are like any other cursed, and you will die before you bring further harm to our city."

They lunge.

And something breaks inside me—not a crack, but a collapse, like a tower finally falling under its own weight. My life was never mine after the attack at twelve. Every meal chosen. Every hour dictated. Every order obeyed, even when my body shook and begged to stop. Stand longer. Train harder. Or suffer.

Day after day, I've buried my own voice, pressed it into a hollow inside my chest, an ember smothered and starved.

No. More.

My hands tremble as that ember ignites, stealing the breath from my lungs as it sweeps through me. The Creed has stolen six years of my life. They will not take my death.

My heart is a drum, beating so fast I can't breathe. But I don't care. Fury rises unbidden—a flood of heat and light. If I don't release it now, it will consume me.

I lift my hands. All the years of silence, of bending under someone else's will, tear free like invisible shackles snapping. Useless to ever hold me again.

Fire arcs.

Screams pierce the air as flames shoot from my palms toward the knights, sending them scattering.

I stagger, slamming into the wall, but I manage to keep myself upright with nothing more than a hand for support. My fingers find purchase in the stone, and I remain on my feet.

"I don't think you heard me." Despite gasping for air, my voice is steady. Not a single word cracks. "I am Isola Thaz, Valor Reborn, savior of Vinguard, and I *command* you: show no mercy."

30

To my amazement, the knights step back. Even as a rush of nerves has me fighting shivers, my stance is strong, my skin doesn't crawl, my pulse is even and steady.

The knights all stare at me, open-mouthed. None of them are seriously injured. A few scorched capes. Burned cheeks that are paid no mind. These folks are accustomed to worse.

My gaze finds Lucan. The tightness in my chest loosens at the sight of him unhurt—and loosens more when I catch the pride burning in his eyes. Heat rushes to my cheeks, and I look away before a flush can settle there.

I straighten away from the wall, even though my knees threaten to give out, attempting to project strength. My head spins. It's like something—or someone—else took over and spoke for me. As if here, in this scourge-encrusted room, I truly became Valor.

"The prophecy—" One of the men who was just lunging for me sinks to his knees.

"She must be... She truly is..."

A woman speaks for them all. "Valor Reborn has truly returned."

The man who was first into the room looks between Lucan and me. His eyes narrow. I can almost feel him wanting to believe. Knowing that no dragon cursed has ever commanded flame—at least not in any stories *I've* ever heard. But judging from the sheen of Etherlight that covers his armor, he's of higher rank than the rest of them.

So I'm not surprised when he says, "There are ways this must be handled. Take them for interrogation."

The woman looks aghast. She continues to speak for those on their knees. Those looking at me as if I'm a goddess come to life. "Sir, this is Valor Reborn. We cannot—"

"And she stands in a room coated with scourge dust. There are processes for what has occurred. Take them to the interrogation room, *now*. Doing only that is already a deviation from protocol." He barks his orders.

"Take us for interrogation," I say before the woman can object again. Arguing is only going to prolong the inevitable. The woman looks between me and her leader uncertainly. I give a slight smile. "I am not afraid. As Valor Reborn, I gladly uphold the laws of Vinguard."

"Do it," the leader commands again.

Their training takes over. They do exactly as ordered and encircle me. One man pulls my hands to the small of my back, grabbing my wrists and holding them in place. Another keeps his hand on the hilt of his dagger, though he doesn't draw it.

Lucan is behind me. I can't see him, but I can hear his footsteps. Like me, he doesn't resist. We're escorted through the dark, dank halls that slope upward. The smell abates as we leave the sundering pits and continue down the long hallway. Sunlight streams in through little holes punched through the ceiling to what must be the Upper City.

One such porthole illuminates the room where Lucan and I are taken. There's nothing else inside the small stone space, leaving me to wonder about this room's original purpose. I don't think interrogations are all that common in Vinguard—not outside the Tribunal, at least. Probably why we had to walk for a while. This must be part of a sentinel tower similar to the one Mum and I were taken to after the dragon attack, before the Convening.

"Wait here." The commander leaves, and the rest of the knights follow. Once more, a door is closed on us, and a heavy lock engaged.

My knees give out.

Lucan is at my side in an instant. He grabs me, but his grip is awkward. Rather than keeping me upright, he manages to ease us both to the floor. I hunch and hang my head. My arms tremble as my palms press against the cold, hard stone beneath me. Lucan gently loops his arm around my shoulders, one hand hovering above my arm, as though ready to catch me should my elbows unlock.

"What were those flames?" he whispers.

"I don't know." I shake my head and try to gather my scattered thoughts. "I... If I had to guess, it's something lingering from the artificer sigils."

"You didn't draw any for fire." He states the obvious.

"I know. But maybe one of the symbols on me smudged into something new. That's exactly why the Creed doesn't want untrained people messing with them. It could happen. And I... I don't know enough sigil symbols to recognize what might be there."

"You know as well as I do that sigils need to be precise. It's unlikely you 'smudged' one sigil perfectly into another." A pause. "Isola...did you just draw Etherlight without a sigil?" Lucan has never revered me like the others. Even though I've only just come to realize as much, hearing him regard me now with awe feels like a wound.

"I..." I shake my head. "I don't know what happened." I manage to lift my gaze, meeting his eyes. Worry gives me a convenient excuse to move the topic of conversation off me. "Do you think other supplicants were affected by the scourge?"

"You know what I think." *That the vicar sabotaged us... probably hoping for just this outcome.* His arm tightens around my shoulders. I've never had someone hold me like this before. Saipha always is there for me. She always has my back. But this is something more. This feels like...

Like if I were to lean on him, he wouldn't pull away. As though he's a break against a storm I didn't even notice on the horizon.

"It's all right," he says softly, tenderly. "No matter what it was, I'm here with you."

I want to lean into his aura of safety. Into his sturdy yet warm hands. To collapse and sleep for a thousand years only to wake and have him be the first thing I see.

And what feels more dangerous than actually doing any of it is how badly I want it. I've never desired the comfort of another as desperately as I want his in this moment, and the idea of it…of risking myself in that way—of creating that sort of a vulnerability… is almost too much. Especially when it comes to this boy whom I've always seen as the vicar's son. Even if my heart knows so much more about him now, so much that changes everything, my head has to catch up.

The door opens again, and the prelate stands in its frame. "Lucan. Come with me."

"What?" He frowns. I've *never* seen him openly defiant to authority before. The knit in his brow and firm set of his jaw suit him. It ignites a spark in his eyes that lends a maturity beyond his eighteen years.

"You will be interrogated separately. Now, with me." She dips her chin. Lucan doesn't move. "I said, *now*."

He begrudgingly stands. The moment he's gone from my side, I'm cold again. I tense back up, push myself into a seated position. Lucan gives me one more wary glance before following her, the door closing and locking behind them.

I'm not alone for long, nor am I surprised to see who comes in next.

"So, you finally did it," Vicar Darius says quietly the moment the door closes. The glint in his eyes immediately puts me on edge. He stalks across the room, coming to a stop a step away, looming over me. The light halos him, as radiant as it is horrible. "My Valor…"

"I don't know what I did." Terror has smothered my voice to a whisper.

"You focused raw Etherlight without an artificer sigil."

"I actually drew one," I say hastily.

His eyes narrow a fraction for only a second. "Ah, yes… The ones you saw in the automaton." I can only assume the inquisitors told him. The vicar's smile widens. "Do not be so modest. You know as well as I that one sigil was to draw Etherlight but not apply it, and the other was for armor."

"My father always said I was a great artificer in the making—just like Valor was said to be. I must've made something new, by accident." Continuing to object to him isn't a good idea for my well-being, but allowing him to think what he's clearly thinking feels equally dangerous.

"Don't be so modest, Isola. You bent the essence of life itself to your will." The vicar looks right through me, as if pulling back the curtains to peer into my soul. "You are so very close to claiming our destiny."

Our destiny. I say nothing. I can't imagine what he wants to hear, so I keep my mouth shut. I've never seen this side of the vicar, and I thought I'd seen everything.

He leans forward, light shadowing the deep wrinkles of his face. "Now, show me."

"I... I can't."

Vicar Darius leans away. "You would dare defy me?"

"No," I say. His stare sparks something in me, a survival instinct. My palms are clammy with sweat. "Of course not. I don't know what I did, not really. And even if I did, I'm too exhausted. I—"

Vicar Darius grabs my cheeks so hard my lips pucker. He towers over me, eyes shadowed yet gleaming with something I can't place. It's not malice, but it is the opposite of kindness. It's desire but not lust. It's something that puts the taste of bile in the back of my throat. An expression sweeter than the scent of roses and twice as putrid as decay.

Run, that primal instinct within me whispers.

But there's nowhere for me to go. I'm trapped in a room, alone with this man. Part of me searches for a way out, envisioning a sprint to the door. The other part of me wants to reach for the magic I might have just found and *fight*.

I'm trapped, suspended between the two and exhaustion. The

only thing I know for sure is that I want it to be over. I want this moment to be done and gone—to be free of him and everything he represents.

"Show. Me," the vicar snarls through clenched teeth.

My heart quickens. "I can't." The words are as harsh as steel across stone. Scraping the corners of my mouth where his fingers press on my cheeks. "I'm too tired. I'm sorry. Please."

"So, you'd like it to be the hard way, then." He releases me and slowly steps back, composed and calm.

"Vicar Darius, if I could, I would. I swear it." I don't even know if it's the truth, but the drive to protect myself has me bartering and begging him.

"You responded to pressure well." *Does he mean the scourge? Was Lucan right and he really did sabotage our room?* I've always known the vicar to be a man who would do anything to achieve his goals. But I never thought he'd actually do something that could harm Vinguard. That could kill me. "Let's test it again."

He knocks on the door, and it opens. Two Mercy Knights step in. Their hoods are drawn like the inquisitors. I resist the urge to plead for any kindness.

Mercy is death.

Cruelty means you are still breathing.

So I take a deep breath and brace.

The two Mercy Knights pin me to the floor with ease. My arms and back slam into the cold stone. Inside, I'm all molten panic. I'm torn between trained submission and the need to fight back.

My exhaustion makes the choice for me.

"I swear," I plead to whatever humanity is locked behind the vicar's hungry eyes. "I swear I cannot summon Etherlight right now. Give me time. *Please*." My voice cracks.

The knights look to the vicar, who merely nods. Vicar Darius rounds me slowly, staring as if I am another piece of a dragon carcass for carving up. As he does, he speaks, and one of the knights begins dragging chalk along the stone surrounding me. The other stands, placing his armored boot upon my wrist. He doesn't press down hard enough to wound me, but I know he would if needed.

"I saw the remnants of what you did in there." The vicar's voice is low and ominous. "I see the markings on you. You turned *yourself* into an artificer sigil." He crouches down and drags one of his bony fingers along the crusted, crimson line of dragon blood on my shoulder. "It would've killed anyone else. But not you, my Valor. Not you…"

I'm inside another sigil, I realize as I lower my eyes to the lines the knight continues to draw on the stone around me. The vicar is going to try to force me to draw Etherlight through my body again. Even if it didn't kill me before, it surely will now.

I stare up at Vicar Darius in horror. But there are no words. Any further pleading will only make things worse.

"Begin." The vicar stands and takes a full step back.

The knight who was doing the drawing finishes with a flourish. Instantly, the lines are cold enough that they burn. The knight steps back and draws a second symbol off to the side. The searing panic turns to actual lava in my veins as the other knight places a token in the center of my chest that feels just like Lucan's healing—a sigil that will, hopefully, ensure I survive this.

The reaction to all three sigils at once is instant.

I scream.

The knights leap away as my body is trapped by an invisible weight, and I'm pinned to the floor, unable even to writhe as endless and unbearable pain pulses through me. It feels as though monsters have crawled underneath my skin and are sucking the marrow from my bones. Just like before, my vision blurs and my head buzzes, only this time, I don't have Lucan touching me, sharing the pain, holding me steady, and encouraging me to hang on.

"Show me. *Show me.* I know it's in there. Show me the product of my work. Break free, Isola. Use your power without a sigil of your own to break free," the vicar snarls, but his voice is distant.

My eyes roll up in my head, and my veins burn with liquid fire. Through earthquakes of Etherlight, I am reshaped from the inside out. Something pulsing, writhing, seeks escape but cannot find it. I will explode into dust if this continues. My back arches and falls, time and again. I almost feel my ribs popping out of their places on my spine, arcing in reverse.

My vocal cords give out.

"Your holiness?" one of the knights says uncertainly.

There is no response.

My mind splinters, and suddenly I'm elsewhere—Mother's apartment. On the floor, just like this. But her hands are gentle, and her magic seeps into me like tea leaves to water. She gives me a tincture, a formula she said will help, one that Vinguard's healers would not touch. One that I can go to her for and must keep secret from everyone else.

My one hope.

Am I cursed, Mum? The question rings across my mind. Still unanswered.

Nearly...I so very nearly...beg for mercy. As my skin splits and peels from my muscle. As my mouth is dry, throat burning from the inside out. As I am destroyed by the outer sigils and remade again from the one on my chest...a thousand times.

But I do not.

There is something within me. Something that burns hotter than the vicar's endless thirst for power. Something that lights my way.

Rage.

He wants me to become his Valor. His killer.

I might *be* a killer, but I will never be his.

My power is my own.

My eyes find focus again. They find the vicar in the blur of the room and the endless waterfall of rage and pain that crashes through me. And there must be something in my stare that even he can't bear witness to, because he sucks in a slow breath.

"Enough," he says at last.

I'm doused with cold water. It washes away the chalk sigils and sends the token on my chest skittering across the floor. I cough and sputter.

"Enough for now," the vicar clarifies, taking a step closer to me. I can barely see him through swollen eyelids and tangled lashes. "Do not let me down, Isola. Remember, I control everything you love." He crouches next to me, tucking a piece of hair behind my ear almost like a father would. "I have invested much in you. Vinguard needs you. I need you." He says it gently, voice contrasting with the violence of what he just did. "You are not yet ready, but you are so close. Soon...*soon*... This power within you must be freed. Destiny awaits us both."

They leave.

A wheeze escapes my lips. Trembles rack my body, and I twist to the side. I want to scream, but the only sound is my dry heaving. No bile. Barely spit. Nothing within me. I collapse back onto the floor and try to get myself under control. Fighting the tears only makes them fall faster. Trembling lips and quivering hands.

I don't know how long I lie there before the door opens again. This time, it's an inquisitor, and I can't decide if I'm relieved to see them instead of a knight.

The inquisitor throws me a bundle. "Freshen up." They place a bowl of water on the ground next to a bar of soap and a rag. And leave.

Every muscle screams. I close my eyes—and the darkness turns traitor. The pain floods back, every moment of pain and helplessness replaying. My breath jerks. My eyes fly open.

I don't dare close them again. Sleep feels like surrender, like shackles waiting to slam shut. If I drift, I'll never claw my way out of the nightmares waiting for me. I manage to make my way to the bowl and freshen up. Valor bless, the bundle is fresh clothes.

The door groans open, and the inquisitor steps in again as I finish. I force myself to stand, body shaking, and follow her back into the black halls.

I pray they'll let us rest. The healing sigil sputtered out long before it could knit me whole. One wrong touch and I'll splinter.

And yet, when I think of the vicar's eyes glinting with hunger, I know rest will never come. Not while he still has pieces of me left to break.

32

When the inquisitor guides me to the entrance of the main cavern again, I see fewer supplicants than before by two or three. I suspect I wasn't the only one being interrogated and they'll be escorted back later. Hopefully their experience is better than mine, though.

Everyone looks as though they got fresh clothes, too. What a luxury. Saipha is here, and her worried eyes find mine. She moves to my side, and I instantly feel more confident on my feet. Yet my gaze searches for another...

Lucan stands on the outer edge of our group. He doesn't look any worse than when I last saw him, as if his interrogation was hardly more than a chat. Our eyes meet, and I open my mouth to say something, but he looks away sharply. He turns his gaze to the prelate instead.

My chest tightens at the unexpected pang of his rejection.

Eventually, we're taken back to the monastery. And the entire walk, I can't help but feel like something has changed within me forever. The moment we step into the Undercrust, I'm nearly overwhelmed by the flow of Etherlight from the Font. Never have I felt it so clearly—as if I could reach out and touch it. Threads of warmth tangle with my fingers, like the handshake of an already familiar friend.

I keep my eyes forward, hoping no one else notices. But Lucan is behind me, and somehow I know he's seeing it. He never misses anything. I stiffen my shoulders, chin high until Saipha and I are finally alone again on the fourth floor of the residence hall.

"What happened in there?" The question practically explodes

from Saipha. "I can tell just by looking at you that *something* happened." *That's certainly a way to phrase it.*

"You first," I respond as the door to her room closes. I don't risk saying anything where inquisitors might hear. "Did you... Were you attacked by scourge, too?"

"What?" She gasps. "Scourge? Why would I— Were *you*?"

I nod and stagger to her bed, sitting heavily.

Saipha sits next to me. "You were... There was scourge in your room?"

"A flood of it." It's so strange to say. Again, it's like my consciousness has left my body.

"How did you survive?"

I tell her, sparing no details. The entire time, Saipha's expression shifts between shock and horror. She interrupts me toward the end.

"Hold on just a second." Saipha holds up her hand. "You fend off a scourge flood by turning yourself into a human sigil-in-a-chute, then command Etherlight without drawing it through a sigil and shoot a fireball out of your hands... And the vicar— I don't even know what to call that! *Experiments on you?*"

"Keep your voice down." I place my hands on her knees, leaning in with a severe look.

"You don't think someone's listening in, do you?"

"I've no idea what might be happening. Things seem different now. Vicar Darius has never done anything like that before." I fight a shudder. Somehow, it's even more terrifying after the fact. As if what he did to me is only just now settling into the corners of my mind. I can barely comprehend it. In retrospect, it feels as though I stood before a dragon once more and lived to tell the tale. "I don't want to risk him finding out anything or having reason to think I'm less than loyal."

Saipha shakes her head and lets out a noise of disgust. "What do you think—"

A knock on the door interrupts her question, and we share an uneasy look. My heart races, my breath shaky, but I grit my jaw and force myself to get up and open the door. To not give in to the fear.

"Lucan?"

Every muscle in his face seems to relax at the sound of his name from my lips. The furrow between his brows smooths, but the concern that pains his eyes doesn't abate. His lips part for a second, ever so slightly, then close, and then he speaks. And I know that what he says, while true, isn't what he originally wanted to say.

"I wanted to see how you are." He seems sincere, but it's all a complete turnaround from him making a point to not even look at me earlier.

"I'm fine. You?"

He nods, and we stare at each other. Almost awkward. Do a thousand words burn his tongue, too? Does he know that everything has changed in an irrevocable way?

Saipha stands, hands on her hips. "And what were *you* doing while she was being tortured?"

"Saipha, volume." I shush her. I spare a single glance down the empty hall, pull him inside, and close the door.

Lucan's eyes narrow. "What does she mean? You were tortured?"

"Just the vicar seeing if he could get me to use Etherlight without drawing it through a sigil by ripping me open and healing me over and over." I can't look at either of them as the moment replays in my mind. My hands ball into fists.

"Isola…" My name is heavy on his lips, but delicate. No one has ever said it like that—filled with so much pain. So much quiet fury. As if he has to whisper or else he'll scream.

It's enough to form a lump in my throat, and I shake my head to signal that I don't want his pity. His well-intended sympathies make me feel far too weak for what the Tribunal demands.

A long stretch of silence. I bring my eyes back to his and find the muscles in his face bulging with how tightly he's clenching his jaw. Regret contorts his features.

"What about you?" I ask, mostly to move the focus from myself.

He looks down as if guilty. I already have my answer, but I respect that he doesn't try to lie. Lucan rubs the back of his neck. "I was questioned. But it wasn't physical."

"The prelate must like you," I mutter. I don't want to blame him for his good luck—for the choices of others that led to the brutality I faced and the relatively painless interrogation he got by comparison. But it's difficult to be mature about things when you can still feel your skin ripping from your muscle, flayed by a magic knife beneath your flesh.

Lucan rests his hand on my shoulder, his touch gentle and his voice sincere. "Are you all right?"

I shrug. "I'll live," I say and avoid his gaze once more. I really don't want any more attention for now.

"I'm sorry." Lucan frowns.

"Are you?" Saipha narrows her eyes.

He turns his displeasure in her direction. "What's that look for?"

"Strange, I think, that you are assigned to work with Isola as partners when there's a scourge flood, then you leave her side, and *then* come back looking fresh as sunshine on a spring day. She's tortured while you just get a stern talking-to."

Lucan removes his hand from my shoulder, and I'm surprised to find I miss the weight of it. "And that's probably because they didn't care what I did or didn't do, since I'm neither Valor Reborn nor the person who drew Etherlight without a sigil."

"Convenient excuse," Saipha mutters.

Lucan shoots her a glare. "Why are you acting like I'm your enemy when we should be allies? I'm not keeping secrets from you—no need for any of us to keep things from one another."

I catch Saipha's eyes, and she arches a brow that asks, *So you finally agreed?*

"He's on our side," I say to her with a shrug, then give him a sidelong glance. "At least, I'm pretty sure he is after what happened today." So much is wrapped into those words. Even as I say them, I can still feel the sensation of his arms around me. Him supporting me when I could barely keep myself upright. *I have you.* Those words are etched on my brain, embossed on my heart.

"You know I am," he says, as if reading exactly where my mind is.

"No more secrets? Fine. Are you reporting to the vicar?" Saipha is still skeptical.

"I'd need to speak with him to report to him." Lucan tears his attention from me to give my friend a dull look. "I'm as trapped here as you are. When could I be 'reporting'?"

"Mercy Knights ultimately report to the vicar, and inquisitors are part of Mercy's ranks. You could get information to them to be funneled back."

"I'm not reporting to the vicar." Lucan rolls his eyes. "But even if I were, it's not as though I have anything to tell him that he doesn't know. You think the inquisitors aren't already telling him *everything*?"

Saipha opens then shuts her mouth, stilling her retort. She clearly considers this. "But he did ask you to watch her."

"Yes, so?"

"He did?" I ask softly.

Lucan looks back to me. "Obviously, he did."

I nod, wishing the admission didn't sting. I assumed as much... so why does it hurt to hear him say it out loud?

As if he can read my thoughts, Lucan adds, "But he asked everyone loyal to the Creed to do so. I wanted to ally with you for my own reasons."

Saipha speaks before I can spiral too deeply around what those "reasons" are. "So the vicar—"

"Enough of him. I don't even *like him*." Seething hate is evident in his trembling fists. "Yes, he asked me to 'help you' as much as I could. Yes, he asked me to keep an eye on you. But I've already sworn to you I won't tell him your secrets." Lucan shakes his head and looks directly at me. I can feel the question, even if he's not asking it. *What must I do to prove myself?*

This moment feels like it's a million years long. What more could I expect of him? He's proven himself time and again, hasn't he? Yet I don't trust him… Or is it that I don't *want* to? The longer our eyes are locked, the less sure I am. What do I feel underneath it all? Underneath the traumas the vicar has inflicted upon me. Is there a genuine distrust of Lucan as a person?

This shouldn't feel as major as it does. And yet, I sense that whatever I say next will change my life forever. I'm on the knife's edge, and I'm not sure what in me ultimately pushes me to one side over another, but when it happens, I don't look back.

"I trust him," I say to Saipha, even though I keep my eyes on Lucan. "I think he's going to be a good ally."

She nods, as if she already knew that was coming. "Lucan, answer me one more thing: Why does being our ally mean so much to you if you're not reporting back to the vicar?"

"Because I'm tired of being alone," Lucan says plainly.

I…can relate. I look back to Saipha, more confident than ever in what my gut has told me. "He's strong and capable, and he can use sigils even though he's not gilded."

"You think I'm strong? You're too kind," Lucan playfully mocks me. I shoot him a sideways glance that he just smirks at. *Is his face a little red, though?*

"You're absolutely sure?" Saipha puts the final call in my hands, knowing how many knots I've twisted in over this.

I nod.

"All right. The three of us, then." Saipha stands, stretches, crosses, and claps him on the shoulder. "Now, can we eat? I'm starving."

"That's it?" Lucan clearly has whiplash from her personality. I fight a laugh. After everything I put him through, I get why he'd expect more from her.

"We can't go in circles all day. Isola trusts you, and that's good enough for me…until you give me a reason not to. Then I'll just have to destroy you." Saipha squeezes by him to leave through the door.

Lucan blinks, turning his confusion to me.

"You'll get used to her." I offer a smile and follow Saipha down to dinner.

Lucan's hand brushes mine as I pass him. He doesn't pull away, and I glance up at him. But he doesn't even react. It's like it didn't happen at all.

I'm tired of being alone, he said. Is that one of those "reasons" he mentioned earlier? Or is there something more? Something related to this tension that— I halt the thoughts. I don't have to examine where my mind was just going to know it's dangerous. Yet, I still hear the echo of what he said, twice: *I like you.* I could read a whole library's worth into those three words.

I suck in a slow breath, chest tight, hoping that by trusting him—by letting him in—I didn't just make the worst decision of my life.

33

The sundering pits clearly took it out of all of us supplicants. Everyone is ravenous and eats all they can. The buffet is picked clean on the first go-round tonight—none left over for seconds.

Very few words are shared, though I strain my ears for any mention of the scourge. There are none. It must have been isolated to just Lucan's and my room, lending more credence to his sabotage theory. *Do the others even know?*

A few wary glances are cast our way, perhaps taking note of Saipha and me now sitting with Lucan. Especially since we didn't pick the table with those from the Undercrust as Saipha and I have been doing most days. But no one says anything to us, for now.

"I didn't really ask how you were," I say somewhat guiltily to Saipha. "How was the rest of your time in your room? Did it go all right? Were you interrogated at all?" I asked about the scourge in Saipha's room, and then the conversation became all me...and Lucan.

Why is it suddenly so unnaturally difficult to not *think about him for more than a few minutes?*

"No, I wasn't." She shakes her head. "It was... I can't really say 'fine' because I spent my whole day looking at a third of mostly rotted dragon thigh."

"You are a little pale." I take my own bite of food, though it's a bit harder than the last with the images of dragon carcass fresh in my mind.

"Well, it was *gross*."

"Understatement," Lucan mutters.

"At least it didn't seem to ruin your appetite," I say as Saipha shovels in another large bite of potato.

"I'm so hungry I could eat an entire barrel of potatoes." She goes for another bite, moving so quickly her fork nearly slips from her fingers. "It was so much worse because I got stuck doing it all with Mikel."

My eyes tug in the direction of Cindel's table, but only for a second. Mikel is one of her bunch. A mousy-looking boy with short brown hair and dark-brown eyes set against fair skin a similar shade to Saipha's. I've only seen him in passing and never have heard him speak. I only know his name because I've heard Cindel bark orders at him.

Luckily, they don't catch me looking.

"Let me guess, he spent the entire time telling you how amazing Cindel is?" I whisper.

"If only that were it. He wouldn't stop asking about you." She gives me a genuinely worried look.

"Me? Why?" I try to exude calm I don't quite feel.

"Spying for Cindel would be my bet." She leans in as she talks, voice barely above a whisper. "No matter what I tried to talk about, it'd come back to you—how you were handling the Tribunal, what it was like being friends with Valor Reborn, what you could really accomplish."

The food is now ash in my mouth. But stopping eating would let Cindel win. And if the vicar can't break me, I'm not letting *her*. "Whatever it is, we'll handle it."

"Cindel isn't also some kind of mole for the vicar, is she?" Saipha glances in Lucan's direction. As she lowers her fork to her plate for the next bite, she nearly drops it. The utensil is shaking in her white-knuckled grip.

I speak before Lucan can reply. "Saipha, are you *sure* you're all right?"

"Wha— Oh." Saipha looks at her hand, then violently stabs a hunk of potato. When she lifts it next, it's stable. "Other than mentally scarred with images that'll probably haunt me for life, I'm fine. Hands are tired, is all, from using bone saws and mallets. Now, focus. Cindel and the vicar?"

"It's doubtful," Lucan replies. "The vicar is indebted to her father. As the master renewer of Vinguard, he's done a lot of repairs on the chapel after attacks, as that's what he specializes in. But I don't think there's any love there."

"Does the vicar love anything but himself?" I murmur under my breath. I don't think Saipha hears, but Lucan's eyes flick toward me, and there are a thousand things unsaid in that stare. Hate wars with worry that competes with a defensive edge I want to pretend doesn't exist because it'd be so much simpler if it didn't.

The moment evaporates as that same man enters, as if materialized at the mere mention of him like a nightmare I can't escape.

My whole body goes cold as he walks down the stairs with the prelate at his side. Behind them are three faces I haven't seen before—one boy and two girls, all wearing supplicant uniforms. Behind the three are two more inquisitors, like a wall to prevent them from running.

As odd as it is to see three unfamiliar supplicants, I can't take my eyes off the vicar. I still see him looming over me. Still feel the magic ripping me apart as if I was little more than paper.

Lucan's knee presses into mine under the table so firmly that our thighs touch. The warm, steady contact jolts me back to the present, and I glance his way. But he's looking straight ahead, eyes on the prelate.

"Supplicants, there are three late additions to be counted among your ranks." The prelate steps to the side and gestures to the inquisitors in the back. They shove the three new additions forward aggressively. "We found these three *hiding* in the Undercrust, avoiding reporting for Tribunal."

All eyes dart between Horowin's table and these new additions. Horowin and his crew look as bewildered as the rest of us. Hiding from the Tribunal? It seems impossible. And even if it were... Is there any greater shame in Vinguard?

I'm shocked they're still alive. That they weren't slain outright from suspicion. But Vinguard needs all the citizens it can get. And if they haven't been tested yet, they've no reason to receive mercy.

"Some Mercy Knight is getting reprimanded for *this*," Saipha murmurs. I glance her way, lifting my brows. She leans in, whispering hastily. "Two years ago, there was a pair of siblings in the Undercrust who didn't report in. Mercy Knights were sent, Father one of them. According to him, they were made such an example of in the Tribunal, no one would ever try again. Didn't stop Mercy Knights from doing sweeps since, though."

I shudder to think of what making an example of someone here would consist of, given what we've been through.

"We weren't hiding," the boy snaps at the prelate. "We didn't even know about the Tribunal. It's not like we had a home or parents to teach us."

"Excuses." The prelate scoffs, disbelieving.

The vicar holds up a hand.

"Street urchins, hiding in the caves of the Undercrust. Fighting for scraps. The Creed has failed you," the vicar says solemnly. Like he cares. "Which is why we shall show you forgiveness and allow you to join late. But do keep in mind that you have already missed the first test—something we must remedy tonight."

I suck in a slow breath. My heart is starting to race as though I'm the one about to go into another test. I've no idea what the inquisitors might do to them. But I am sure the vicar will punish them in his own way for this.

The wicked gleam in the vicar's eyes turns my way, as if he knows how aware I am of his worst tendencies. "You also missed the blessing on the Convening. Perhaps Valor Reborn would like to assist me in placing it upon you."

I'm going to be sick.

If it weren't for the sturdy bench under me, I would've collapsed here and now. I'm honestly surprised I don't melt under the table.

Anything to get his eyes off me.

"My Valor Reborn, come. Your vicar commands it."

My body betrays me. It moves on instinct and without thought. It moves because he commanded it and I have been trained for six years to jump the moment he tells me.

Everything seems to occur at half speed, happening in a faraway place. I'm at the vicar's side. He places a hand on my shoulder, and keeping myself from falling over is all I can manage.

"Blessings of Valor upon you," he intones.

"Blessings of Valor upon you," I repeat like a puppet.

But inside... Inside, that fiery ball of rage is burning hot. So hot that it's looking for any escape. If the vicar were to cut me now, nothing but molten lava would slide out.

The vicar continues to speak, and I echo his words. It gives me an opportunity to get my first real look at the new supplicants—anything to take my mind off another Creed prayer.

The tallest is a broad-shouldered guy. He has brown skin and short, dark-brown hair that is shaved on both sides, longer on the top, and pulled into a bun. He studies me with dark eyes as one might a scroll.

The two girls have fair skin and light-brown hair with streaks of gold. One's is cropped short and messy, not even past her ears. The other has hair down to her waist, a shining, unbroken curtain of it. Their features are identical, down to their button noses and green-blue eyes. Twins, undoubtedly. A rarity beyond compare.

The prayer reaches its end, and the vicar declares, "So sayeth the Creed, guide and guardian of Vinguard."

"So sayeth the Creed—" My voice cracks. *Guide and guardian?* The people who tortured me? Who dictated the life of a young girl?

"Isola?" the vicar almost growls under his breath, even though his face stays passive.

I look up at him and feel a sliver of that heat escape me. It unspools as a golden thread that lashes harmlessly against the vicar's cheeks. It looks identical to the Etherlight I've seen before.

No one else must see it, because they don't react. But the vicar must feel it. He leans back, eyes widening.

"Guide and guardian of Vinguard," I finish hastily, and, without a second thought, I move, leaving the vicar and pushing past the inquisitors. The second I'm out of sight, I dash up the stairs, heart pounding in my throat. Burning with every beat.

I almost unleashed Etherlight again—more than just a little curl. I know it in my marrow.

What's happening to me?

34

When I reach the atrium, I suck in a breath, trying to cool the burning inside of me. Everything is so overwhelming. My chest is too tight. The scar-knotted flesh is so tender it hurts with every shift of my jerkin over my shirt.

I want to scream.

But instead, I force myself to keep calm and head toward the residence hall, pausing at the central dragon statue to catch my breath. As I do, I try to ignore the lifeless eyes glaring down at me, the way fear prickles under my skin. It knows what I am.

This power... Maybe it's because I'm Valor Reborn. Or maybe because I am dragon cursed. If the dragons are beings of Etherlight, then of course I could draw magic. And both times it emerged as heat. This burning inside of me, threatening to consume me.

My gaze is drawn to the copper dragon tapestry.

Am I one of you?

A pair of footsteps comes up quickly behind me, and I straighten. The hairs on the back of my neck stand on end, and my stomach twists. The vicar must've followed.

He's going to take me away again. I know he sensed it, the moment I drew from the Font without a sigil again in the refectory, however slight it was.

A shoulder brushes mine as someone comes to a stop beside me, and I nearly break down in tears when I find myself face-to-face with Lucan and not the vicar.

He stares down at me through his mess of dark-blond hair. In the fading sunlight, there's something almost radiant about him, despite his exhaustion. I still see the strands of gold threaded around him, in his eyes, in his hair, in the air that surrounds where he walks.

"Lucan," I say softly, keeping this conversation just for us and not possible nearby inquisitors. Somehow, his name eases the tension from my shoulders, as if my body still remembers earlier—how comforting his presence was as he held me steady. The way the Etherlight of our sigils danced together alongside our breaths.

He props an arm on the dragon statue, looking completely at ease, but his eyes dart to the corners of the room. "Don't let him get to you."

I force the corners of my mouth up. "I'll be fine."

"You will...but you also won't." Lucan's expression doesn't change in the slightest at my hollow smile. He sees right through it. "You'll tell everyone you're fine. You always do. But when you think no one's looking, you stare like you want to save us all but know you can't." His voice drops, low enough to cut. "And that resentment is going to make you want to burn it all down."

My jaw slackens. Mercy, he's so close to the truth.

"I'd never burn it all down," I whisper, though my throat tightens. "I want to save Vinguard. I want to see children playing in the sunlight, to walk beyond the gates, to know the world isn't just stone and shadows and the red of the scourge." The vicar and his Creed, however, could be nothing more than cinder if it were up to me. "But I can't seem to find the strength. No matter how much they train me, I always come up short."

"You are stronger than you think, Isola." His voice is soft but firm.

I sigh. The pretending to always know what I am, what I'm supposed to be, and what I might really be is suddenly too much. "I want to be enough, Lucan. But I'm not who all of them think I am. I'm afraid I might never be."

He shifts and leans even closer. Close enough I can feel the heat rolling off him. Close enough to touch if I just leaned in ever so slightly.

"You *are* enough." His warm, hazel gaze holds mine.

I shake my head, shoulders sagging, thinking of how the vicar could reduce me to such a pathetic state with such little effort. "No, I'm not. Not by any measure."

"You are," he insists. "I know you."

"You know the *idea* of me, Lucan." Guilt compels my words, making them hasty and messy. "I want to be enough to save Vinguard, save everyone—but I'm *terrified* of dragons." The moment the confession leaves my lips, I want to pull it back, but I can't. "You saw me on the first night—I freeze up. I run. I can barely handle them when they're lying dead in the street."

"You did fine in the pits." He tries to get an edge in on the conversation.

I don't let him. "It took a lot of effort just to be 'fine.' And that's not even the half of it."

He doesn't say anything. Just holds my gaze, giving me the space to figure out my own words.

"I finally drew from the Font without a sigil—but not intentionally and not with purpose."

Still nothing from him. So I keep going, the fear dragging the confession out of me. "It finally happened, I finally did it, and nothing has made me feel less like Valor Reborn. I didn't feel like a crusader of hope. I felt..." My voice cracks, dropping. "I felt like I might be the monster. Something dark and twisted. Like fire was in my bones and I could turn this whole place to ash faster than I could save it."

He continues to hold my gaze, patient. I don't want to share any of this with him. But it's like he knows I want to—*need* to. And, damn it, he's right.

I speak even faster, little more than a hasty whisper. "I don't know what's wrong with me. Why sometimes I have this power and sometimes I don't. And it feels as though not knowing might tear me apart...if whatever this thing inside of me is doesn't do it first. My skin itches, sometimes doesn't even feel like my own. My scar burns, my heart skips, I'm hot and cold all at once. Without my mum's tinctures—"

"Tinctures?" His tone hardens.

I flinch. "Her research, generally, led to her finding a tincture that helps with...with whatever it is I have. Something changed in me the day that dragon attacked me—and not for the better. Maybe I'm just broken." I don't dare say *cursed*.

I watch the muscles in his jaw tense. He's too smart not to hear what I'm avoiding saying. "You're many things, Isola, but broken isn't one of them."

"Maybe I'm not *broken*," I admit. I try to shake the pathetic mood the vicar has put me in. It's just so hard when an entire city expects more of you than is fair. "But I'm also not Valor Reborn."

"Maybe you're not Valor." He says it so easily, like it's not borderline treason, like every fear and worry I've ever had was unnecessary.

In a breath, it's almost as if he's lifted the veil of an identity that never fit. It might still be attached to me, but there's a whisper of freedom that I've barely dared to imagine. Saipha is the only one who's come close, but even she always carried the weight of a said, or unsaid, *But what if you are?* No one in my life, other than Mum, has ever accepted that I probably am not Valor Reborn.

"But that doesn't mean you can't save this world," he continues. "If anyone can find a way, it'd be you. And if not, Isola... You didn't break it in the first place. It's not even your responsibility to fix."

"That's...liberating." The skipping in my chest finally calms. "But I want to fix it. I want to help humanity and heal the world, if I can."

Lucan shifts, his hand sliding against the base of the dragon statue. His fingertips touch mine, and I can't decide where to look: the contact or his face. We were closer than this in the sundering pit, and yet something feels different now.

It's because this is a choice. Him leaning closer. The way he seems to hold his breath. I ache, but it has nothing to do with what I fear is the curse. Every part of me feels so brittle. And, for the first time, I want to break. I want to be weak, just so his strong hands can be what puts me back together.

"Isola!" Saipha calls. The moment—whatever it was turning into—evaporates the instant she comes running.

Lucan straightens away, barely perceptible to anyone else, but it's all I see. Especially as he curls his fingertips into a fist away from mine. Why is it that he always withdraws? Every time he does stings more than the last.

"Oh, good. I wanted to make sure there wasn't anything bad happening up here. You missed Cindel absolutely losing it, furious that there are new kids joining the group from the Undercrust. Says it's 'against the Creed's teachings' like the vicar doesn't get to dictate what those are."

"That's all we need. An even more pissed-off version of that girl," I say. But it is odd to hear anything but utter deference to the vicar from Cindel.

"Yeah, probably best to give her space," Saipha murmurs, starting toward the room.

"Already my plan," I agree.

"Want to plan our strategy between now and the next test? Assuming it's not tomorrow?" Saipha asks.

"I'm exhausted. Can we do it in the morning?" I say, starting for the stairs that lead up to my room.

"That works for me." Saipha yawns, as if I've given her permission to be exhausted as well.

"I'll meet you both on the fourth floor at first light," Lucan says, splitting off at the second-floor landing. He pauses for a second, eyes meeting mine, steady and unguarded. For the first time ever, my heart skips a beat for a reason unrelated to dragons or Etherlight. My chest squeezes, and I'm breathless as I wait to see what he has to say next.

Dragon-burned hells, what's happening to me?

"Good night, Isola," he says after a tiny eternity.

A million unsaid words dance across my tongue. None escape.

"Good night, Lucan," is all I manage.

"And good night, Saipha," he adds hastily.

She glances between us. "You too."

I can't get up the stairs fast enough. As if I could outrun Saipha and the question that I know is burning her tongue. But, of course, I can't. Not when her room is right across the hall from mine.

With every other step, I scold myself: one day, one firm set of hands and soft eyes, and I'm twisting in knots for him. I'm better than being distracted by this. But, then, on the opposite steps, I suppress a smile. I fight a tiny giggle. He's not what I thought he was, and maybe...maybe I like that? I've never given much thought to what I "like" in the ways of romance before. I always thought it'd find me if I was lucky. And maybe it has? But in Lucan of all people... And then it's back to scolding myself...

"What was that?" The question explodes from her as we reach the top and are more than confidently out of Lucan's earshot.

"What was what?" I try to play dumb.

"Oh, I don't know, maybe him coming to check in on you earlier—because it certainly wasn't for me. Or him chasing after you, after the vicar made you his living doll. Or *that look* you two gave each other." Saipha leans in, excitement shining in her eyes. "I thought you said you didn't flirt with him to get him to ally with us?"

"I didn't." I look away, fighting a blush.

"Does he know that?"

"Saipha, it's nothing."

She repeats, "Does he know that?" I glare at her, and she just laughs. "Look, would I have expected you to pick the vicar's son? No. But there are worse choices out there. Especially when he's showing us by the day that he's not as bad as we thought."

She makes a fair point. But... "I can't focus on that right now," I murmur, trying to douse my own feelings. "I'm just trying to survive in here."

"Yeah, yeah, we're all trying to survive, Isola. Not just in here. But in general. To be alive is to survive. That's why you've got to look for the things that make it worth living."

I give my friend a smile. Small but sincere. "You know, for being obsessed with seeing what's the biggest crossbow you can lift or how fast you can climb a wall, you're pretty insightful."

"Oh, I know." Saipha turns to her room, a triumphant sway to her steps. "That's why I'll leave it be, *for now*."

"Why do I get the feeling you're threatening me?"

"Because I am." She winks and retreats for the night.

I smile after her. At how she can make even one of the worst days of my life bearable. Fun, even. At least for a second or two.

Because the moment I open the door to my room, my jaw drops, I freeze, and all other thoughts vanish as I meet a pair of all-too-familiar eyes.

"Come in and close the door," Mum says.

35

I blink. Then blink again. And *again*.

Mum is sitting on my bed as though this is all perfectly normal. She stands with a slight smile.

"I'm not an illusion or a dream or an imposter," Mum says softly, clearly understanding why I'm blinking over and over. "I wouldn't linger with the door open, though. You never know who might be listening or watching. The walls have eyes here, Isola."

Even though she says this isn't a dream, it feels like one. My body is disconnected from my mind. My spirit has flown away. Even as I ease the door shut and the latch engages with a soft *click*, the movements barely register. All I hear is blood rushing through my ears as my heart pounds.

This is bad. This is bad. This is so very, very *bad*, every beat says.

Mum should not be here. And I shudder to think of what they'll do to her if she is found.

"What…are you doing here?" My voice is so tight that the words are barely audible.

"What else? I'm here for you."

She looks older than I remember, worn down. Her cheeks are a bit hollow and eyes a bit listless. There's a grayness to her skin that has never been there before. It's only been about a week since I last saw her, though, so it must be a trick of the lighting.

"You can't be here." I say the obvious, struggling to find words.

"I know. Why do you think I sneaked in?"

My eyes dart to the door, as if the inquisitors will come rushing in at any second, and then back to her. "Are you trying to get yourself killed? No, really. Are you?"

"Isola—"

"You are risking not only your fate but mine." I press a hand to my chest. "If they find you here with me, what do you think they'll do to me?"

Hurt flashes through her eyes, but Mum keeps her composure. It's not the first time she's held herself together as I've lashed out. Hopefully, it won't be the last. "And what do you think they'll do to you if you finally collapse? If it comes to light that their great 'Valor Reborn' is not as legendary as they all think? They're already asking dangerous questions, Isola. Do you want to give them room to ask more?"

Her question stings like scourge in my throat.

She takes a step closer. "I'm here because I care for you. Because—as much as I wish it wasn't the case—you have been declared their foretold savior. I know how long it's been since you last had a dose, what happened today, and how much Etherlight you drew. You need this." Mum reaches into the pocket of the threadbare robes she wears and produces a small vial. It's a shade of crimson that was always unnerving but palatable when I considered its benefits.

I reach for the vial. "You...brought me a tincture?"

"I told you I would."

"Is it the new formula?" I dare ask, hope flickering back to life in me from embers I long thought dead.

"It is." Two words, but she might as well have said, *You can survive this.*

"Thank you," I whisper, clutching it tightly.

Weariness softens her face at the appreciation in my tone, but her eyes sharpen. "But listen to me, Isola. It is no longer safe for me." She swallows hard, but it's the only sign of uncertainty. "The vicar is making moves."

"What kind of moves?" A thousand ideas dance across my mind like a thousand magic blades danced under my skin at his command hours earlier.

"I fear he wants me gone. For good."

My stomach drops. "Gone?" *Oh, so she is actually trying to get herself killed.*

She cups my face and kisses my brow. I lean into it like a child, though terror grips me.

"The vicar is fighting for absolute control," she whispers. "He's been playing the long game. Now that you're in here and on your way to the Mercy Knights, he doesn't need me to hold over you any longer for your compliance. Your path is set."

"You knew," I breathe. "You knew the threats he made about you the whole time."

"Of course I did." She huffs, slightly exasperated.

The truth I've dreaded all along has never been clearer. What was merely monsters in the night are now walking these halls. The vicar will do anything to tighten his grip on me—on this city. Even if it means killing my mother.

"Everything I do, dear, is to keep you safe, even when you can't see it." Her hands tighten on my shoulders, refusing to let go. "It was my job to know exactly how I was being used against you."

"The Mercy Knights, even as a page, isn't like the Tribunal. Once I'm through, I'll have more freedom. I can—"

"He won't wait that long," she says, calm in the face of my rising panic.

"Why? Why is he so urgent now?" I ask, dreading the truth. This is more than me being in the Tribunal and out of the way. I finally drew from the Font without a sigil. He's so close to getting everything he ever wanted. Of course he'd start tidying loose ends.

She holds my gaze, glances away for half a breath—long enough that I think she'll tell me. But she doesn't, leaving me to assume I'm right. "It doesn't matter. All that matters is that you're safe, so focus on staying safe."

"I deserve to not be kept in the dark anymore, Mum," I say in a rush, fury helping my words gain speed. "You never tell me anything I need to know!"

Her gaze darts to the door. "Keep your voice down, Isola. *Please*."

"Then tell me what's going on. What's *really* going on. There's more to this, I know there has to be. What am I missing?"

We lock eyes, but I refuse to give in. I've been giving in my whole life. It's about time I started standing my ground. Especially now. The vicar will stop at nothing to force me to draw from the Font directly again—and something in my mum's expression has my heart racing faster.

"There is a mighty force drawing on the Font."

"What?"

Her eyes dart to the door again, then back to me, her fingers nervously raking through her hair, snagging on curls. "A weapon, or what will become a weapon unlike any other. Something your father helped create. The vicar plans to use it to go on the offensive."

My thoughts immediately go to Valor's sword. In the Grand Chapel of Mercy, his legendary blade is held by a statue of his likeness. But that sword would be ancient, not something Father helped make. Unless he modified it? No, the vicar would never allow it.

"*What?*" For a second, that's the only word I know, laced with fear and panic. "Offensive?" The knights venture forth on their hunts from time to time as resources allow. But at most it's searching for what small game they can find, or killing wounded dragons on nearby mountain ledges. Not a full-on offensive.

"Against the Elder Dragon…and soon," she finishes, as though it wasn't bad enough already.

"I'm not— Vinguard isn't ready."

"Don't fret. Stay the course, Isola."

My skin feels tight, the room smaller, as I stare into her eyes creased with worry. Even the air smells different—colder, sharper, as though it has blown down from the high peaks that loom over Vinguard, emanating from the Elder Dragon himself.

"Easy for you to say," I snap before I think better of it. "Easy to say *don't fret* when you're not the one expected to take Valor's sword and go up against the *Elder Dragon*." My voice cracks on *Elder*. The Creed says the beast is the oldest of them, the leader, and the heart of their power.

"You'll be fine." Her voice is steady—too steady—like she's reading a script.

"You don't know how I feel." I swat her hands and back away, wrapping my arms around myself and hanging my head.

Mum just stands there, a pillar of calm in the flickering lamplight. "I can only imagine the pressure."

"No, Mum, more than that. You don't know what it feels like underneath my skin. The nightmares of something trying to claw its way out of me." I look at her through a curtain of hair. "Tell me, please…am I cursed? Is that why you made me the tinctures? Why you risked everything to get me one?"

A beat of silence.

"Do not let this be like that night. Do not leave without telling me," I whisper, pleading.

"You are not cursed." Her words are gentle but leave a hollow echo in the small room. "But you are not like the rest of us, either, Isola. You're special."

If it were anyone else, I'd groan at *special*, but with her it's different. Mum doesn't use that word like the rest do—she doesn't mean Valor Reborn.

"The tinctures help regulate your Ether."

"Like how I drew from the Font without a sigil?" I ask. She nods. "But it's not because I'm cursed?"

"There is nothing about you that I would call cursed." All the admiration in the world lights up her eyes as she tucks a rogue strand of hair behind my ear. "Now, I should go."

"Where?" My voice sounds small even to me.

"It's better if I don't say…" She glances at the window. "But know I'm still a step ahead of the vicar, and I'm not without friends.

I'll find a way out of his clutches. Until next we meet, stay safe and hold on. Their cruelty is only just beginning."

I nod, but my throat closes. Love, anger, confusion—they knot under my ribs, sharp as claws. I throw my arms around her shoulders, desperate for her warmth, and clutch her until my fingers ache.

She doesn't move, only holds me until I'm ready to pull away.

"I love you more than Ether," I whisper.

"I love you more than *all* the Ether in the world." She smiles at me softly. "My methods might be unconventional, Isola, but my intentions have always been to protect our family. But now, the best thing I can do for you is leave…which means I won't be able to get you more tinctures."

Leave? I shake my head, unsure of what to say, and tighten my grip on her robes. There's no "leaving" Vinguard. "Where would you—"

A knock. Both of us freeze.

"Isola, are you asleep?" Saipha calls softly from the other side. I thought she went to bed. Did she hear anything? No, she couldn't have. If she had, she'd be breaking down the door.

I open my mouth to answer, letting go of Mum and making it halfway to the door on instinct, but then stop. Should I just let her think I'm asleep? I can't explain this.

Saipha makes the choice for me as her soft footsteps fade away, and I feel a twinge of guilt. Should I have let her in? Emotions warring, I turn and look back to Mum—

But she's gone.

Only a soft breeze drifts through an open window. I stand in the middle of the room, vial clutched in my hand. The room seems emptier than it's ever been, like the air itself has been scooped out.

More questions echo in my head. Where is she going? Who are her friends? But one swells louder than the rest: Why does she seem more afraid at the idea of me being "special" than if I were cursed to become a dragon?

36

I hardly sleep that night. Every sound jolts me awake, alert and straining to hear if the shutter of my window is creaking open, or if the inquisitors are coming to interrogate me—if Mum was caught—but nothing of the sort happens.

Even though I barely managed a wink of sleep, I feel better than I have in weeks when I wake in the morning, thanks to the tincture.

Cindel wants nothing to do with me today at breakfast. Instead, she shoots daggers at the new kids. She's clearly standing on the principle that they should've been put to death for suspicion of the curse. Selfishly, I'm a little happy to have her attention not on me for a while.

I eat with Lucan and Saipha, and we spend our day split between the library and training area. The three of us work quite well together. Better than I would've expected.

Two days crawl past.

Everyone grows a bit more on edge as the hours slip by. Probably because it seems...almost peaceful in a way that's like the quiet before a storm. Like something bad is happening—gnawing at us—but we don't realize what it is yet.

"What's wrong with you?" Saipha asks on the fourth quiet afternoon. We're in one of the training rooms with just Lucan.

"Nothing's wrong with me." It's not the first time she's asked. Ever since my meeting with Mum, I feel like a "guilty by association" sign is plastered across my forehead. I stride to the weapon rack to put space between us. We came here to get away from everyone else more than to train, so I just stare at the array of blunt practice weapons.

"You've been broody and all-around...off," she insists, following me.

"You've been more testy than normal, too," I counter, not wanting to be prodded or examined.

"Maybe if you weren't acting so weird." Saipha folds her arms.

I look to Lucan for assistance.

He surprises me by coming to my aid. "You *have* been more testy, Saipha."

"Rude." Saipha narrows her eyes at him and selects a javelin from the rack. I think for a second she considers flinging it at him.

"And you have *also* been 'off,' Isola," Lucan says, raising one brow at me.

"And you haven't?" I fire back.

Lucan considers this much more thoughtfully than I expected. "I suppose I have..." He stares at the corner of the room for a long minute. "We're all on edge. Let's just keep doing what we can while we wait for the next challenge. There's only two to go, and then we're done with the worst parts of the Tribunal."

Later that afternoon, there's a small reprieve when we have a lecture from the head librarian of Vinguard. He runs a small association that's dedicated to maintaining and recording the histories of the city on behalf of the Creed—the histories they let citizens read.

Better than the vicar.

He's a short, balding man with ill-fitting robes that look like they're an attempt at some sort of draped fashion but miss the mark. He prefers to pace the stage in front of the lectern, rather than stand behind it as he speaks.

"Every historical record we possess speaks of Valor's skill with Etherlight. Not only could he identify the locations of the Fonts—which he did when he settled Vinguard upon the deepest and most robust one remaining in the world—but he was also one of the last humans to possess the ability to wield Etherlight without sigils to focus the power."

"When, exactly, did humans lose the ability to use Etherlight directly?" Daisy asks.

"It's difficult to pinpoint an exact time, as we have lost many recorded histories in tandem with the loss of our lands and the lives of our forefathers to the blights that assault us. We know there were originally four Fonts with cities built upon them—one among the clouds, one in a vast sea, one deep within the earth, and Vinguard. But the histories of the other three were lost with them." He totters and paces in the opposite direction. "Based on this limited documentation, we have concluded that humans' connection to Etherlight was disrupted as the scourge spread Ethershade and extinguished the other Fonts."

His attention lands on me, and I move uncomfortably in my seat. Lucan shifts next to me, his hand sliding closer to mine. He knows my discomfort when it comes to Valor. He knew it well before the Tribunal. I once considered how well he knew me—how closely he paid attention—unnerving. But now, it's a surprising balm. I almost wish he'd reach for my hand because I know what the lecturer is going to say next before he says it, and I know it's going to be targeted right at me.

"Before Valor left to battle the Elder Dragon, he swore that, should he fail, he would return to usher Vinguard into a bright new age. That there would come a day when the scourge would be banished and the Etherlight would flow to empower every citizen within our walls. But Valor didn't return...not until six years ago, when a human drew upon Etherlight without a sigil for the first time in centuries to slay a dragon. A human who now possesses two golden eyes, as it is said Valor did."

Every set of eyes that turns to me is like a stone. Up and up they stack. When the lecture is over, I can barely walk from the weight. My shoulders are heavy, and my gut feels hollow. Like I've been worn out from the inside, crumbling in on myself.

· · ·

THE NEXT MORNING is not like the rest.

Lucan pulls Saipha and me aside following breakfast. He shuts the door to the small study room on the second floor of the library and waits, clearly listening. Saipha and I remain silent, though we share a wary look. His caution has us both on edge.

"How do you two feel?" he asks as he eases away from the door. I assume he was listening for anyone walking nearby and heard no one.

"Fine." I glance between him and Saipha.

"I'm all right." She nods but somehow sounds like she wants to fight about it.

"Seems like a lot of nerves about someone overhearing just to ask us how we are." I regard him skeptically.

He obliges my skepticism. "They're starving us."

"What are you talking about? They've been giving us the three normal meals a day." Saipha's tone is already annoyed. She wanted to go to the training grounds, again, to "hit something." It's the only thing that seems to keep her from snapping at us both these days.

"The frequency is the same, but the quantity is not. They've been gradually reducing portions every day since the first day, so it wasn't obvious."

Saipha places her fists on her hips with a huff. "If you don't want to train today, you could've said so."

"We should hear him out," I counter.

"Maybe you can waste time, Isola, because you're Valor Reborn, but some of us actually must work for what we have," Saipha snaps. I open my mouth and then slowly shut it. Not about to let the conversation rise to a fever pitch.

The harshness of her words settles on her, and Saipha presses her palms down on the table in the study room, murmuring a soft, "Sorry."

"He's right." I realize it for the both of us. The agitation. The empty feeling in the pit of my stomach that seems to never abate. I thought it was just guilt and nervousness.

"I know what hunger feels like." Lucan leans against the wall. His gaze grows distant, as if he's seeing straight through the present, back to a past that turns his usually brilliant eyes lackluster.

"What did the vicar do to you?" I whisper. What the vicar did to me in an attempt to achieve his ends is too fresh for me not to ask. I've only just begun to understand Lucan's hatred for the man I thought was a father to him. Now I suspect the vicar was more of a captor.

"It doesn't matter." Lucan moves from the wall, pushing past us to stare out the window, as if physically changing his position can help him avoid the question. "All that matters is I'm very aware of how much I'm fed. Consider me an authority on it."

"All right," I say quickly. I'm inclined to believe him, and I don't want to go in circles about it. Saipha seems content to agree as well. "So, what do we do? Start stockpiling and rationing?"

"I think it's a solid plan," Lucan says.

"We'll take what we can at lunch." I pick at my nails in thought. "Since that's the time people can wander in and out of the refectory, we'll be able to do it without drawing suspicion."

"Fine with me," Saipha says.

Lucan nods in agreement, then adds, "If they're starving us, I'll hunt for edible plants in the greenhouse. They'll undoubtedly restrict access soon."

"Good thinking." The quick rise and fall of Saipha's eyebrows indicates she's impressed by the suggestion. An odd feeling of pride overcomes me, as though I've somehow done well by bringing him into our group.

We implement the plan immediately. Now that Lucan has pointed it out, I'm acutely aware that my plate at dinner is much lighter than it was the day we arrived.

The next morning, we linger after breakfast, going around and scraping up the last few bites left behind by others.

The inquisitors see us do this but say nothing, just like they see us skip eating our lunches in favor of saving them for later. We stuff the flat loaf of bread, bag of dried mushrooms, and wedge of hard cheese we're given under our shirts and make our way back to our rooms to seal them in the lockboxes at the feet of our beds. Then we go straight to the greenhouse, where Lucan continues to impress as he guides us in what plants to pick. "A few can be dried," he says. "These are best fresh." And those we eat first so we can have less breakfast or dinner on days when it's a meal that will keep well if we save some.

By the time the rest of the supplicants begin to notice the diminishing food, we already have a decent stash put aside.

Their recognition starts as some passing mentions—said loudly enough that it's clear the possible negative ramifications of speaking such aloud hasn't occurred to them. More people begin to talk. And, just as the three of us have come to expect, it gets much worse from there.

Lunch is the first meal to completely stop being offered. We aren't the only ones who had the idea of taking the shelf-stable foods and using them as rations. As soon as enough supplicants begin to do that, the inquisitors remove it entirely.

The whole point is to hurt us. No one has shown signs of the curse yet, and part of me thinks it's beginning to worry them, given we overheard them say that one of us *is* cursed. The question of *Who?* must be looming larger than a yellow dragon for them.

Breakfast is the next to vanish. People begin to sleep later into the day. Unconsciousness makes the hunger more manageable. When people are awake, irritability is the default.

We're well past when we thought the next challenge might reasonably be, and no one has any idea when this might end. And that makes it somehow even worse.

One night, we show up to the refectory at dinnertime and find it still locked. Everyone hovers uncertainly in the central atrium like ghosts. No one seems surprised in the slightest. We all stare with hollow gazes.

With a roar, Benj lunges for the door. It's the first time I've ever seen him do something that Cindel didn't directly command. He grabs the handle with both hands, rattling it. His frustrated shouts echo off the ceiling between the ominous clanks of metal.

"You bastards, let us in! You can't starve us. That isn't the point of this place." He roars and bites the chain on the door like an animal.

"Enough, Benj," Cindel says, but she doesn't move from where she's standing with the two guys and two girls that surround her. Her nose is scrunched slightly with disgust, rather than concern, even as Benj is snarling. Snapping. Almost frothing at the mouth.

He keeps rattling the door. "I'll break it down. I'll do it!"

"Benj, I am going to leave you if you do not come." Even half starved, she exudes an air of "better than."

"We should leave, too," Saipha murmurs. "This could get bad."

I don't disagree, but I'm rooted to the spot, grimly fascinated as Benj begins to beat his fists against the door until they leave smears of blood.

"Isola." Lucan steps into my field of view. "Let's go."

"Benj, please." Horowin steps forward to try his luck. But if Benj isn't listening to Cindel, he's certainly not listening to Horowin.

I nod at my friends, and we begin our retreat toward the residence hall, but a shout stops us in our tracks. "You three."

Benj has turned his attention from the door. The others who have lingered with him have placed their focus on us as well. All the attention feels deadly.

"You have food."

"What?" I furrow my brow.

"You have food. I can smell it on you," he snarls.

"That's enough." Horowin tries to step in again, ever the good-natured peacekeeper. "You need to go to your room and rest. Wasting this energy is pointless."

"*They have food.*" Benj points a bloody finger at us. "I know they do. They're hoarding it. They're the ones who took it all."

"Maybe we should let him speak," Cindel says in an almost singsong way. Her eyes find mine with a predatory glint. "If they have food, shouldn't the rest of us know? It's not very Mercy Knight—like to be hoarding resources as your comrades struggle."

"Let's go," Lucan says again, giving Benj a withering look like his words are little more than the ravings of a madman and wildly inaccurate.

Saipha looks positively murderous toward Cindel. Obviously, her warning after the vicar's lecture has done little.

"I'm going to find it. I'm going to take it. I'll eat it—eat it all—*eat you* if I must!" Benj's ravings echo off the ceiling.

"Benj." Horowin doesn't get another attempt at calming the man. The inquisitors approach, and Horowin readily backs away, making room as they encircle Benj. Horowin knows as well as the rest of us that nothing more can be done.

"Wait, no." Cindel steps forward, but it's far too late. "He was simply jesting. This isn't that serious."

The inquisitors ignore her.

Realization strikes Benj—of his circumstances, of what he said. He staggers back, but there's nowhere to go. And the rest of us are powerless to help as the inquisitors close in.

"I didn't... I wasn't..."

The inquisitors grab him.

"Let me go!" he yells. "I wasn't— I'm not cursed. I'm not!"

"Stop this!" Cindel shouts shrilly. "He's just hungry. He doesn't know what he's saying." Even though panic is rising in her voice, she doesn't move. She knows if she did she'd be tying her fate to his—and Benj is now a lost cause.

They begin to drag him away. The rest of us are rooted in our horror. There's nothing we can do. For the first time in my life, something other than a dragon has made me feel truly helpless—truly terrified.

Benj's eyes dart around the room and find Cindel's. They share a long look and, for a heartbeat, I think that they might have had something real between them. At least as real as any of Cindel's emotions can be.

"Please don't," she whispers as a deathly silence overtakes him.

Benj is limp in their ironclad grips. Then a sound almost as horrifying as the bells begins to echo in the cavernous atrium:

Laughter.

Low and crazed. Then higher pitched. Faster. He roars bitter delirium with ferocity.

"Fine. *Fine!* You think I'm one of those beasts? You think I'm in league with the enemy?" His eyes swing to me again, but this time it's me alone. "Or are you protecting your precious Valor Reborn? Is she afraid of me? You think I'm cursed? *Are you afraid, Valor?*"

"I don't— I'm not—" I stumble over my words. Should I be stepping in? Should I try to stop this? *I'm as helpless as the rest of you*, I want to say when all their eyes turn to me. But I can't say that as Valor Reborn, even if it's true. Yet again, I'm trapped in a prison of the vicar's making.

The inquisitors attempt to maneuver Benj through one of the many doors of the atrium, but he continues to resist. Without warning, Benj bites one of their arms.

"Kill me, then! Be done with it! Show mercy!"

They do.

A flash of silver. A dragon-curled dagger, laced with poison. And he falls, dead.

37

There's no ceremony. Benj's body is dragged off with the same regard as a sack of dirty laundry. Death is so common in Vinguard—more so among the Mercy Knights—that none of them spare it a second thought.

But, for the supplicants... Even if we've all seen death in one way or another, this *feels* different. I know all of us are now imagining how effortlessly their blades would strike our flesh. How quickly we would fall.

For a second, smoke hits my nose and I see the bodies on the rooftop. I press my eyes closed and suck in a breath through my mouth. When I open them again, I'm still in the monastery, and the memories abate.

"He wasn't cursed," Saipha whispers. "Merely hungry."

"He asked for Mercy," Lucan says solemnly.

"And it was given gladly." She shakes her head and looks away.

There is nothing in Vinguard more unforgivable than being dragon cursed. But disobeying Mercy Knights, and the will of the Creed, are close seconds. He signed his fate multiple times over.

"We should go." Lucan starts for the stairs once more.

The three of us make our way to my room as the sunset glows orange through the window at the far end of the hall. Lucan shuts the door with purpose, putting his weight against it. His expression is calm and collected, probably the result of years of practice under the vicar's roof, but I can tell he's as stressed as Saipha and me.

"They know. They all know we have food." Saipha begins to pace. This is the most on-edge I've ever seen her. "They're going to come for us."

"Saipha, they don't know if it's true or not. Benj sounded absolutely crazed—he asked for Mercy, for Valor's sake. I doubt most of them will put any stock into anything that came out of his mouth," Lucan says calmly.

If Saipha hears him, she doesn't react. She's half a world away. "They will come in the night, and they will kill us for our food. We should get rid of it."

"We are not getting rid of our food, Saipha," I say firmly. "That's the only reason we have any strength at all, and we'll need that strength to fight them off if they *do* come."

"We only have a little left anyway." Lucan opens the lockbox at the foot of my bed with a grimace. Two stale rounds of flatbread. Three bags of dried mushrooms. And who knows how long we have to hold on before the next test... Assuming they stop starving us after that.

"Why are they doing this? Why would they do this?" Saipha continues pacing.

"To try to force the curse to manifest," Lucan says.

She stops and shivers, wrapping her arms around herself.

After a moment, I suggest, "Let's all sleep together."

Saipha halts.

Lucan tilts his head and quirks a brow, and I quickly realize what I said and clarify with a soft cough to clear my throat. "We'll pull my mattress to Saipha's room, since hers is farthest from the stairs, at least by a small margin, but it's something that might give us a better chance to hear someone coming down the hallway. The doors open in, so maybe we can use her lockbox as a barricade. Two can sleep while one stays on guard duty."

"Sounds good to me." Lucan nods.

"I'd probably feel better not being alone," Saipha agrees. It's a relief to see her calming.

We do exactly as I suggested. My mattress takes up nearly all the floor space in the small room, but it does fit flush between Saipha's cot and the opposite wall. Then I take the first watch. Saipha is on her bed, and Lucan on my mattress on the floor, each falling into a restless sleep. Nothing happens. No inquisitors and no supplicants come for us. Not on my watch. Or Lucan's. Or Saipha's.

"Did we really make it through the night?" Saipha's disbelief is palpable.

"Looks like." I yawn.

"The day can pose just as much of a threat," Lucan says grimly. He's sitting on the lockbox in front of the door. "We should stay here. They're not feeding us anyway."

"Wouldn't it be suspicious if we don't leave?" I rub my brow, trying to alleviate the pain pulsing between my temples. I've never been this hungry before in my life.

"That's a good point. Maybe we go out in shifts? One here while two go out?" Saipha suggests.

"Then they could know that there's only one person here guarding." Lucan frowns. "I don't think we should leave."

"I suppose if we don't, it conserves our energy," I muse. "Everyone's been sleeping later and napping more…maybe it won't actually look that suspicious?"

Saipha sighs in agreement and stretches back out, staring up at the ceiling. There's not much conversation the rest of the day.

We're down to just one wheel of cheese for the three of us the next day. None of us are convinced that they're going to feed us even after the test. The fear of the other supplicants has lessened some the longer the days drag on. Everyone is too weak to launch any kind of meaningful attack on us, even when we venture to the bathroom at the end of the hall for water or other needs. And while we're in a much better position than most thanks to our rationing, a toll has been taken on our bodies.

"I feel like someone has scooped me from the inside out." Saipha groans. She's perched on the lockbox in front of the door. "I won't be able to stand by the time the test comes."

"You still have strength you don't realize." Lucan doesn't really sound optimistic. More like grimly determined based on experience he has yet to share with us.

"We can't do poorly on the tests. They look at those most of all for entry into Mercy." Saipha presses her eyes closed and shakes her head before opening them once more.

She has a point.

I sit on the edge of the bed. "I have an idea." I've been trying to avoid it, but I don't think I can.

"I know that look of yours…" Saipha leans forward. "What kind of an idea?"

"Neither of you have to be involved. I can do it alone." The risk of this only needs to be on me. If the inquisitors have any reason to suspect I've been given outside information about the Tribunal, they might think I have even more. Maybe even enough to hide the curse. I think of Benj and fight a shudder. The inquisitors are ready to jump at any opportunity.

"We're *not* leaving you alone." Lucan's conviction startles me.

"I think I might know where we can get food. *Maybe*," I say. *Down the red staircase, behind the black dragon shield for food.* I repeat in my mind what Callon told me on Convening Day before I entered the monastery.

"How?" Saipha's voice has dropped to a whisper. She knows the implications of what I'm saying. If there's a way to get food when they're intentionally starving us, it means breaking rules.

"A hunch. An instinct." I meet her gaze and hold it, bidding her to understand that I'm not going to say anything more. Saipha bites her lip. She's too smart not to suspect that I have some kind of information I shouldn't if I'm being this confident but this cagey. But she knows better than to ask. It's safer for her not to know; if she doesn't, I can take the fall alone. "It might not be anything." His information is out of date, and I know better than to assume the monastery's Tribunal layout is consistent from one year to the next. It's clear that they open and close different sections to us as supplicants that I imagine are all open for the curates usually here.

"But if there's a chance, it's worth it to get our strength back before whatever they throw at us during the next challenge," Lucan says my exact thoughts.

"You're both thinking with your stomachs." Saipha folds her arms and raises her knees, curling into a ball. "It isn't worth the risk." She definitely knows I was given illegal information about the Tribunal. "They know we're all starving...they won't throw something too intense at us for the next challenge."

"Do you honestly believe that?" I ask her. She has no response, so I add, "They are determined to root out the curse by whatever means. No one has shown signs—yet—so they're still hunting."

"They won't ease until the very end," Lucan adds grimly. "Two more tests left."

"They had Benj," Saipha says weakly.

"He wasn't dragon cursed, and we all know it." We all sit in tense silence until I add, "I'll be careful, but I don't see any other way. They could use our weakness against any of us, claiming it's a sign of the curse manifesting. Let's not give the inquisitors any more reasons to suspect us."

Saipha sighs. Lucan says nothing. Finally, as if reaching the same conclusion at the same time, they both nod.

We make the decision to go the next night. Better sooner than later, while we still have some strength. Saipha is still resistant to the plan. Being even proximally related to anything that has to do with someone revealing secret knowledge about the Tribunal has her on edge.

The problem is, I don't know where to "go" other than a red staircase. Which I haven't seen. And I've been up and down this whole place multiple times. While I haven't been explicitly looking for one, I think I would've noticed.

"Are you sure you want to go alone?" The slow dragging of the lockbox across the floor almost hides Lucan's soft words. Saipha is still sleeping.

"I'll be all right," I tell him, a little surprised at how worried he looks. It almost makes me want to touch his arm to reassure him.

But the idea of reaching out and closing the gap between us has my stomach fluttering in a way it never has before, so I don't.

"If you're not back by the time the sun is fully up, I'm coming looking for you." He nods toward the window. The first beams of a gray dawn are threading through the slats.

"Don't worry. You won't have to." I flash him a bright smile, more confident than I feel. And I think I imagine him leaning forward slightly. But I leave before I can be sure.

The monastery is quiet. Everyone is still asleep, but I still am alert as I strike out on my scouting mission. Benj's death still hangs over the monastery like a shroud, and some part of me knows that Cindel is going to blame me for it. Then there are the late additions, who are wild cards—I've no idea what orphans who grew up "fighting for scraps" will do when pushed like this. Not to mention all the other supplicants...

I take a breath and steady myself before my worries spiral. I mentally prepared my route last night, so I can keep my head on a swivel as my feet carry me where I need to go. Callon said "down" the red staircase, not up. Assuming he spoke from ground level, that substantially narrows my options. He also said explicitly regarding food, which draws me in the direction of the refectory.

I check the short stair that leads to it first for any signs of red. I scan the walls for the ghosts of old signposts and see none. There's no artwork hung. I do find holes left behind from a long-gone runner bolted over the stone and hope that wasn't it. I scan for any kind of string or lint left behind but find nothing.

I do the same on the next staircase. And then on the third. That's when I see it, in the corner of one of the stairs that dead-ends in a storeroom I wrote off on the first day: a fleck of red paint that's been almost completely scratched away. Easily overlooked if you aren't searching for it.

Glancing down the stairs, I debate going now, but instead return to Saipha and Lucan. It's getting later in the morning, and I don't want them to worry. Or for Lucan to come searching for me.

"How'd it go?" he asks when I enter.

"I think I know what I need to do."

"What *we* need to do." Lucan shuts the door behind me.

"Lucan—"

"I don't want you to go alone, Isola. Scouting is one thing, but whatever it is you're about to do... I know the look you get in your eyes when you're about to do something risky."

I stare up at him, realizing how close we are. My throat is tight. Body hot. But the way he looks at me, it's like he wants to devour and savor me all at the same time.

"It's not worth you taking the risk, too."

"You are always worth the risk." He doesn't flinch, doesn't waver. Lucan speaks so matter-of-fact that the fluttering in my stomach I felt earlier is now full-on soaring.

Saipha murmurs in her sleep, rolling over.

We both jolt slightly away from each other, like two children caught sneaking. Finally, Lucan says, "You should get some sleep while you can. I'll take the first part of your watch."

"But you need rest, too." *Especially if you're coming with me tonight.*

"I'll be fine." He smiles reassuringly and takes his place on the lockbox.

I feel his attention on me as I stretch out on my mattress, pulling the covers up to my chin. I have to fight for sleep. I'm anxious about what tonight will hold. But also...excited? I'm excited at the idea of going alone...with him.

We wait for night to fall and everyone to—hopefully—be in their rooms.

Saipha hovers at the door, sucking in a deep breath.

"You'll be fine," I reassure her.

"Oh, I know I will be." She flashes me a confident smile that doesn't reach her eyes. I don't point it out, though, instead giving her shoulder a squeeze. "I'll let you both know when everyone is definitely tucked in for the night."

With that, she leaves, and I drift to Saipha's bed, sitting heavy on its edge.

"Don't worry," Lucan says as he settles on the lockbox. "She'll be fine. Most people are likely asleep already."

As soon as she returns, we'll leave.

I stare out the window. Suddenly, this tiny room feels both too large and even smaller than normal. This is the first time I've been alone with Lucan in days. The first time since we stood together at the statue of the Elder Dragon after the late admissions from the Undercrust arrived. And, even then, there were inquisitors not far.

Right now, it is very much just the two of us, and the silence is unbearable.

"Do you want to be a Mercy Knight?" I blurt, and Lucan jolts.

"Well, that came out of nowhere."

"I'm just making conversation, and we've never spoken about it." I shrug.

"Of course I want to be a Mercy Knight. Everyone does," he says, absolutely emotionless.

"*Of course.*" I roll my eyes at him.

"What is *that* tone?" He laughs softly. "What's wrong with wanting to join the ranks on the wall?"

"As you said, *everyone* wants to go to Mercy. It's such a boring answer." *And you also didn't really sound like you want to*, I refrain from saying, not sure if I know him as well as I feel like I do.

He shrugs his broad shoulders. "I'm a boring man."

"You are anything but boring, Lucan." As I say the words, it hits me how true they are. He's been my shadow for so many years, since we were just kids; I've never really let my thoughts dwell on him. He was the enemy. The vicar's watchdog. But now I realize I'd never really given Lucan a chance to be anything more. Now that I have, I'm finding curiosity is getting the better of me.

"I assure you, I am. Orphaned and raised by the Creed, wanting to get into Mercy to avenge the misfortune that must have befallen my family... It's such a standard story that you could throw a stone in any direction on the wall and hit a knight with similar motivations," he laments somewhat mockingly. *It is, but that doesn't make it less traumatic.* Then he adds so softly that I almost don't hear him, "Plus, *you're* going to be there."

Something in the rough timbre of his voice sets butterflies loose in my stomach. "Because the vicar asked you to keep watch over me?" I ask.

"I told you once, and I'll tell you a hundred times: Screw the vicar." That elicits a smirk from me, but it's abandoned quickly when he adds, "Not to keep watch over you. Though I will always protect you, if you'll let me. And not because of the vicar, or the Creed, or Valor Reborn, or any superstition or titles."

My heart catches. Those are all the reasons anyone in Vinguard has ever cared about me, outside of my family and Saipha. "Then why?"

"Because it's *you*." His gaze is steady.

I swallow and force myself to ask, "But *why*?"

He's looking at me as if he hasn't looked at me nearly every day of his life for years. "So many reasons, but the first is because of that day six years ago... You saved me that day."

Wait. That makes no sense. My hunger must be affecting my

mind. I scoot a bit closer to him. "What are you talking about?"

"I was there that day. On the rooftop with you."

His words hit my chest with the same force as the cannon shot to the green dragon.

I'm suddenly back on that rooftop. The rubble. All those bodies scattered around, dead.

Was Lucan one of the people I'd thought dead?

"You were there," I repeat. "Which means you survived, too?"

He nods.

"I—" The words stick in my throat. It all begins to click into place. Why Lucan, even though he hates the vicar, remained in the Creed. Why he was drawn to me—would want to look after me. Why he endured the vicar's horrors just to stay on a path parallel to mine. Not because I was supposed to be a legendary hero, but because I'd been *his* hero.

And that's why he was appalled when he first saw my terror at a dragon. He'd seen me as someone who saved his life, and there I was, running scared from the very first moment I was tested.

But right now, he looks at me with sheer admiration. I've seen it from him before, but I always thought him a zealot of the Creed. Now that I know where that admiration comes from, the truth inspires panic. It's somehow worse than all the rest of Vinguard seeing me as their savior.

I actually saved him. And I don't even remember him. I couldn't even do it again if I tried. Guilt slips between my ribs, squeezing my scarred heart until it aches.

"I'm sorry, I didn't know..."

"You passed out from your injuries and the surge of Ether. I was unconscious when you would've seen me anyway. I understood perfectly why you wouldn't have known." His tone makes it clear there's no animosity.

And just like that, a weight shifts in my chest. That day, that moment that had othered me—that placed me on an unreachable podium to most—is now shared with someone else. *I wasn't alone.*

"Why didn't anyone tell me?"

"The vicar said not to." He shrugs.

"Why didn't *you* tell me? Screw the vicar, after all, right?"

Lucan's lips quirk in a wry smile, one I mirror. "You're right. Outside of here, we never really spoke. And it didn't feel like something I could just come out with right away when the Tribunal started." Lucan pushes off the lockbox, standing. "So, I tried to look out for you as best I could, what little I could manage over the years."

I look away, rubbing my scar, replaying that day in my mind. If I'm not careful, it's so easy to get lost in the memories. Which is why I usually avoid them at all costs—I don't want to remember that day, don't want to let it have a hold on me.

But, for the first time in maybe ever, I let myself remember. To see it with a slightly new and different lens.

Mum has a meeting with some of her other guildmembers. The guildhall is small and always smells of soil. I love going because the saplings they cultivate are tiny wonders. To think, from dirt, things could be grown—that, long ago, the world was filled with green and not the pale stone of streets and buildings, or the rust of the scourge, or the scars of dragon attacks.

I can't hear what they're speaking about—it's always behind closed doors. But it sounds...tense. Even at twelve, I can tell that much.

She comes out of the back door in a whirlwind. We leave without saying goodbye and emerge onto the cramped streets of Vinguard.

The sky is clear.

So...strikingly blue.

It makes the dragon's roar echoing over the rooftops all the louder. As if the clouds manage to muffle them somehow. They don't normally attack in clear, daytime skies.

But the beast streaks overhead, trailing cinder and smoke like a cursed falling star. It rounds and hovers, as if looking for me.

Mum pulls me aside and into an alcove of a doorway.

"Stay here, Isola. You'll be safe here," she says.

Is anywhere safe? I want to ask, but she's gone before I can, running off into the street.

The dragon roars again, closer, louder. Fire lights up the sky and stings my cheeks. Flames catch on the shutters of the buildings down the street. I turn and bang on the closed door. "Let me in. Let me in," I beg. But the door doesn't budge. I hear people inside, but they don't dare open it.

Looking back onto the street, I see people running, their clothes ablaze. They're... No, it's not screaming. It's a guttural, horrible sound like a dragon's roar. A dying breath as their skin blackens.

Tears well in my eyes. I bounce from foot to foot, clutching my shirt. The dragon roars again, and I flinch.

I don't want to be alone. I go to find my mom. If I'm with her, she'll keep me safe. She'll know what to do. Mum always knows what to do. She's brilliant like that.

Dragon fire explodes before me, hot enough to melt stone. Most of those fleeing are killed instantly. But I hear the screams of those who aren't. I smell them. There's so much fire and black smoke. Claws scrape against roof tile, and I see a flick of a dragon's tail.

I run. The chaos pushes me down a narrow alley—I think I saw Mum go that way.

"Mum! Mum!" I scream, coughing up smoke to the point that I'm nearly sick.

So many screams. I get turned around, and soon there's only one way forward. Fire behind me. Burning rubble in front of me. A single iron stairwell that goes up.

Up is death. But so is fire. Maybe there's a rooftop door or hatch?

I crest the flat rooftop, between more rubble and bodies—remnants of some family enjoying their afternoon—and as I search for a way back down, the monster lands. Right behind me. Metal wrenches as the stairs I ran up break away from the stone that cracks under its weight, and I'm trapped.

My stomach is in my throat. My legs tremble. I stagger and fall, trying to scramble back. The bodies around me, singed, barely recognizable as human, now look like a promise. The building groans under the weight of the beast.

How would you like to die? its molten gaze seems to ask me.

Be it by crumbling building, dragon fire, or being eaten alive, I will not survive.

The dragon leans forward and huffs, clearing the dust and smoke enough that I can see the details of its face. Copper scales, dotted with gold, turn rusty and black around its glowing eyes. Curls of thick smoke trail from its nostrils. Teeth as large as my arm cut from its gums.

It reaches a clawed hand forward. I press my eyes closed and brace for what comes next. I expect it to grab me. To lean forward and devour me with a massive bite and sickening crunch. But it doesn't. Instead, that claw scores my chest. It burns so sharply, I'm certain it has punctured my breastbone. I scream.

Then…light.

"Does it hurt?" Lucan jolts me from my thoughts. He's standing before me at the bedside. I was so distracted, I hadn't even seen him approach.

Lowering my hand from my sternum, I bring my attention back to him, banishing the memories to the recesses of my mind. "No, it doesn't hurt. Sometimes, it feels as though there's wire corded around my heart—like it cannot fully beat as it should. The scar itches, and that can send tiny, invisible bugs across my skin. Or every part of me feels too stiff. It's all uncomfortable, but not painful. And fortunately inconsistent."

I can feel the warmth from his body and shift backward on the bed. He must take this as an invitation, because he settles into the space I've left on the edge of the bed, the mattress dipping under his weight. I resist leaning into him.

"May I see it?"

Even though I usually hate showing people, something about Lucan feels…different. I don't instantly grate at the question. More than that, I find I don't mind if he sees. This scar is mine, yet part of it is shared with him—he was a part of that day, even if I've never known it. My hands move to the laces on my vest, loosening them. I pull down my neckline, but it's still comfortably above my smallclothes. Even so, I'm less fastened up than I've been in ages in front of someone else, and I'm unable to resist taking a deep breath.

Lucan's eyes drop to my chest, causing heat to rise up my neck. He's not looking at me romantically. I know he's not. Despite this, his attention feels different than any other who has ever beheld the mark that made me Valor Reborn.

The scar is a splintered web of shattered skin fused together by white, gnarled scars. Its thickest point is between my breasts, at the center of my chest. But it extends to just under my collar bones.

He raises his hand. I don't stop him. Lucan brushes his fingertips lightly over the lines at my clavicle. I inhale sharply as a jolt passes through me.

He flinches, withdrawing his hand. "Did I hurt you?" I almost grab his fingers to put them back on me.

"No. I… All the scarring feels a bit strange." It's true. It's also a lie.

The skin around the scar is riddled with dead spots—places I don't feel anything at all or feel less sharply. Other areas, the tissue mended right. It causes an uncomfortable sensation of disappearing and reappearing touch.

But it's also *his* touch. It does something to me. Sends a flush underneath my skin. I want him to touch…and keep touching. To run his hand across the scar and underneath my shirt. It's an urge that I've never experienced before, and it's as thrilling as it is terrifying.

"You can continue," I manage, wishing I could say the rest. Maybe it's the hunger making me delusional. Maybe it's how this whole place feels more desperate by the day.

Lucan's fingertips glide over my chest, right above my breasts, expanding to make room for his palm. His touch is so searingly hot my lungs ache with every thin, strained breath.

"Did you ever figure out what the light was?" he asks, eyes focused on his hand.

It's hard to formulate an answer when he's touching me like this. "No, I didn't."

"The light was one of the first things I saw when I came to. I remember it well," Lucan says softly, lifting his gaze to mine. A shiver races along my spine. He has yet to pull away.

"Me too," I say softly.

"You honestly don't know where it came from? It wasn't a lie you told the vicar?"

"I…" My brows knit, the day fresher in my mind than it has been in years. "The dragon reached for me, its claw scraping against my chest, and then…light." I was told later that the light consumed the creature, and it vanished. A feat of Etherlight unlike anything anyone had ever seen—a feat that was described as similar to the legendary Valor. "When I woke up next, I was in the Grand Chapel of Mercy being stitched back together by the renewers under Vicar Darius's control."

He nods and shifts his gaze back to my scar. "My consciousness faded in and out, but I was taken alongside you. They noticed me after retrieving you." Lucan's fingers press a little more firmly, almost as if he's trying to touch something within me. "They told me I was alive because of you."

"I doubt it."

"I don't."

This time, I know it's not my imagination that we lean in slightly. I want to ask him everything he remembers of that day, everything that happened when I was unconscious, but I doubt he was in the room when the renewers worked to stitch my chest back together.

"Like it or not, Isola, you're something special," Lucan whispers.

Mum said I was special, too. Not cursed, but special. The dragon attack, unleashing fire at the sundering pits, my eyes... It's too much to ignore. *Maybe I'm not Valor Reborn*, but perhaps I do have a power that can help save this world.

I've just opened my mouth to speak when there's a knock on the door. "It's me," Saipha says from the other side.

We both stand, and I hastily tighten the laces on my vest as Lucan opens the door.

Saipha slips inside, stepping around me to stretch out on her bed with a groan as she grabs her stomach. I don't think she's even aware of the motion. We're all so exhausted from hunger. "It's quiet. I haven't seen anyone—not even inquisitors—for a good fifteen minutes. If you're going to go, I'd go now."

I look to Lucan. He nods.

"Let's do this," I say, and we slip out together.

My chest tightens as we walk down the silent hallway, and I'm not sure which terrifies me more right now. The way I can't stop thinking about the warmth of Lucan's hand against my chest, or what will happen if we can't find more food before the next test.

"This way." I guide us down the residence hall steps, into the central atrium, and straight for the stairs where I saw the fleck of red.

Black dragon shield. As we descend farther, I scan for anything that might even suggest a black dragon shield, trusting Lucan to keep an eye out for others who might have followed us—or inquisitors. I suspect we're hunting for a place we're not supposed to be.

The stairway ends in a room lined with enormous wooden casks on either side that are twice my height in diameter. I ignored this room after a brief search on the first day because it seemed like a remnant of a bygone era. Alcohol is an extreme luxury. It's not necessary for survival, so very little resources are allocated to it. Most production is private and funded by the super wealthy. There would never be enough produced in a single year to fill even one of these casks. Maybe long ago, when Vinguard had more fertile land around the Upper City, but not now.

So why are they still here? It must mean something.

"What are we looking for?" Lucan asks, keeping his voice low.

"A black dragon, and a shield." I walk down the rows of massive casks, studying the markings on the ends. There's nothing remotely resembling a dragon or a shield. They're all stamped with the marks of vineyards and vintners long gone.

He follows my lead, also scanning the casks. "I don't see either."

"Could we be in the wrong spot?"

"I—" I'm silenced as I spot a small label I overlooked. The name has almost completely flaked off: SHIELD VINTAGES. The name is painted in a delicate, flowing script on a field of black-and-white flowers.

I cross to get a closer look.

"Shield Vintages," Lucan reads aloud as he joins me. "But I don't see a black dragon."

"It's not obvious," I agree, a smile curling my lips. Callon knew I'd find it. He knew because he knows just how much I learned from Mum about the earth. "There is no 'black' dragon. Copper, green, purple, yellow, silver—no black."

"There's no dragon at all here." Lucan squints, as if trying to figure out what's making me so confident.

"No. But there is this." I press my finger into one of the painted flowers: dragon's breath done in black ink. "Black Dragon... Shield."

"It seems like a stretch."

"Unless you have a better idea?" I give it a knock, and it's hollow, just as I suspected. I start searching for an opening or seam somewhere on the sides of the cask, thinking of the hidden door in the basement.

Lucan shifts to cover me as I search, his gaze trained on the stairs. "Maybe—"

"Ah-ha." I find what I'm looking for—a vertical cut through the curved planks, not visible from the front. There's another to the left of it. It's a tight squeeze between the two casks, so I assume the door pushes in, and I'm proved right. It's the same rush as whenever I managed to find a new door on the wall. A heady burst of hope.

Lucan's eyes widen. He squeezes in beside me. "Do we go inside?"

"I didn't come this far to back down now."

"And here you want to call yourself a coward." His breath is warm on my neck, sending shivers down my spine. For a second, I very nearly lean into him. To surrender, selfishly, to the safety he unknowingly offers. No starvation, no Tribunal, no dragons—only his warm hands and kind eyes and reassuring words.

"Isola?" Lucan's tone shifts to concern.

"Sorry," I murmur, duck my head, and step through the secret door, still far too aware of him as he follows me inside.

The interior of the cask is large enough to fit three people comfortably. There's no back to it. Instead, it's flush against the wall, with an opening carved through the stone. The inquisitors' ability to create secret passages for themselves continues to impress me.

Light streams in through the gap. We share a look and slowly make our way toward the end, leaning against the strip of stone wall on either side of the opening, backs pressed into the curve of the cask, making ourselves as small as possible as we peer into the bright room beyond.

It's a well-appointed kitchen. Pots and pans hang from hooks over darkened stoves. It's spotless and completely vacant. Unsurprising, since it hasn't seen much use for days now. My stomach grumbles and burns at the thought.

I get Lucan's attention and point to a far corner, mouthing, *Over there.*

He leans a bit more to follow where I'm pointing—a door that looks very much like it'd be a larder. He returns to the safety of cover, locking eyes with me. We both share a wordless exchange I've only ever experienced with Saipha before. Without a sound, we know exactly what we're going to do.

With a nod in unison, we move, keeping ourselves low while darting through the empty kitchen. Lucan is faster and opens the door. Luckily, it's not locked. Like two little rats, we scurry inside.

The aroma of food hits me harder than the blow of one of the curates' mallets during the vicar's training in the months before the Tribunal. I stare in awe at the stocked larder. My stomach rumbles again, and a bit of saliva escapes from the corner of my mouth.

There's dense barley bread in flat loaves, salted pork, dehydrated fruits and mushrooms, wheels of hardened cheese, even fresh kale and root vegetables... It's all here and more. Food that we never saw, even from the start, as supplicants.

So much, and we can't even bring back any to share with the rest of the supplicants whose stomachs are twisting in knots just as painful as mine. There's no way we could carry enough. And even if we could, it'd risk the other supplicants thinking we've "held out" like Benj accused us of and actually turning on us. Or, worse, the inquisitors knowing we found their secret passage to the kitchen. And who knows what they'd do to us then.

Still, I can't stop a scowl that's directed at the inquisitors who aren't even here. *How dare they do this to us.* Rage, as hot as the vicar made me feel when I was helpless on the floor, flares in me. I'm so sick of feeling helpless, crushed beneath the authority of people I don't even respect.

Lucan grabs my hand and leans in to whisper, "We can only take a little of each thing, so they won't notice missing food, but eat what you can while you do." He continues to read my mind.

I grab an empty burlap grain bag from a hook near the shelves and alternate between shoving fistfuls of dried mushrooms into the bag and into my mouth. Tying up the strings on the bag, I attach it to my hip. The snap of a carrot between my teeth is immeasurably satisfying.

"You cannot bring that," Lucan whispers when he catches me staring at a massive chunk of honeycomb.

"I know." Even as I say it, I'm contemplating if there's some way I can. "I've only ever tasted honey once before. It was Saipha's birthday present, and I feel like it'd really mean a lot to her if she could have it now—give her some strength."

He catches my hand midair as I'm reaching for it. "It'll mean a lot more to her to survive, or even excel in, the next challenge with more substantive food."

"Absolutely." I lower my hand, and he turns back to stuffing dried peas in his bag. When he's not looking, I slice off a small piece of the comb and wrap it in a nearby waxed cloth. Sometimes it's about feeding your soul as much as it is feeding your belly.

I run my index finger where honey has pooled on the edge of the tray under the comb and bring my finger to my lips. The explosion of sweetness is almost enough to make my teeth ache. I wonder if it's here for the prelate. Imagining her lounging and eating honey on toast has me violently shoving slabs of salted pork in my bag—far more pragmatic. Though I don't miss the opportunity to filch a handful of berries, too.

I've never stolen anything in my life, and after years upon years of being the "good girl" and staying in line, there's something immensely freeing about it. Especially here and now. *And you thought you'd beat me*, I want to tell the inquisitors.

The screeching of hinges as a door opens, followed swiftly by it snapping shut, has Lucan and me freezing mid-grab. It's followed by footsteps, then voices.

"...downside of the kitchens being closed is we don't get a hot meal, either," a man says.

"No one is stopping you from cooking," a woman responds. *It's not the prelate.*

Lucan and I lock eyes. It's impossible to tell what direction the voices are coming from, but they're getting closer. Lucan grabs my arm and tugs. We wedge ourselves between the wall and some barrels of potatoes. He grabs a large, empty grain bag from the hook, and we kneel down as he throws it over us like a blanket. And not a second too soon.

The door creaks as it opens. Crouched low, I can see this section of the larder through the gap between the two barrels we're hidden behind, but they're still around the corner. My heart is racing in my chest.

"I'm a shit cook," the man says, his footsteps growing closer. I hold my breath as Lucan keeps the sack in place. "Maybe you could?"

She snorts. "I'm no better a cook than you, and you know it."

My breath catches as they turn the corner. The inquisitors have their hoods lowered, and it's surreal to see them as...people. They're not faceless, brutal shadows. They're as much flesh and blood as either of us. I knew this, of course. But it's so easy to forget when they're the ones enforcing the rules in here with iron fists...

"The kitchens will open after their test tomorrow," the woman says. "Eat then."

"I certainly will. But I'm hungry *now*." The man heads our way.

Lucan shifts, trying to press his large body farther back. The man halts, eyes locked on the honeycomb. Lucan looks my way, and I know I should feel guilty for what I did—especially if I get us caught… But the rage I felt is still too fresh in my veins. I'm hungry, and tired, and fed up with feeling scared, and I'm about to throw fists over my friend having a taste of honeycomb if I must.

"Didn't we just get this, like, an hour ago?" the man says, leaning close to see my obvious cut corner of the honeycomb. "Who was here?"

"No one. Everyone else is getting ready for tomorrow." The woman walks over to check it out.

My whole body tenses. My better sense screams to be quiet and wait. They'll leave to investigate. But that other part of me is still ready to fight. If they—

Bells.

Frantic. High- and low-pitched. It's the sound of fear in Vinguard.

They both sprint from the room, leaving their food behind.

Lucan and I wait, but only a second. The inquisitors are not coming back. Not with the bells ringing…

A dragon is attacking.

40

"Let's go." Lucan grabs my hand, wrenching me toward the barrel-disguised entry we came from, and we don't even bother to hide ourselves as we bolt through the kitchen.

He drops my hand as we burst from the cask, closing the secret door heavily behind us. I don't think anyone will hear it. Even down here, the bells are deafening.

Lucan moves for the stairs, and while I force myself to follow, I stall on the first step. Go up? *Up, when there's a dragon?* I'm nothing more than a girl again, about to take a step onto that rooftop. But this time, the dragon is waiting for me, calling…

Lucan pauses a few steps ahead, and our eyes meet. The image of the dragon in my mind is replaced by him, reassuring and steady. He extends a hand, and I fully return to the present. "You can do this, Isola."

Our fingers wrap together, firm and unyielding. For a second, I believe him, and that's all it takes for me to begin ascending. Almost running. I don't let the fear win. My heart is hammering to the point of bursting by the time we make it back into the central atrium.

We stop a moment and catch our breath. I expected utter chaos, but there's nothing. The central atrium is alarmingly empty. The bells still toll, singing their frantic, ominous hymn across Vinguard, and we warily ascend the stairs to the residence hall.

The moment our feet hit the fourth-floor landing, a flash of light fills the window at the end of the hall, followed almost instantly by a deafening *boom*. Etherlight strikes me, and I wince. But it's not quite as uncomfortable as I remember the last cannon shot. It feels like too-hot bathwater. Prickling my skin. Painful, slightly, but in an almost refreshing kind of way.

"Cannons?" Lucan runs to the thin window at the end of the hall, peering out. His lack of self-preservation is both astounding and alarming.

"There must be more than one, if they're using cannons already." Which means I'm not wasting time. I burst into the room to find Saipha already on her feet. Without a word, I throw a small roll to her, and she tears into it like her life depends on it. I'll give her the honeycomb later. She needs more solid food first. And I want her to be able to savor it.

"Your success is delicious," she barely manages to say between bites. Lucan walks in the room and closes the door behind him, then shoves the lockbox back against it. He flips the lid open. I quickly unpack and store our score.

Saipha has barely finished when the copper boxes throughout the monastery sizzle to life.

"All supplicants are to report to the central atrium." Direct, to the point, and leaving no room for questioning.

"I wonder if they'll move us into the basement." Saipha still sways a little, but there's a satisfied smile on her face that I haven't seen in ages.

"I hope so," I say as I start out the door. Lucan catches my eyes. We share a look that suggests neither of us are particularly convinced that will be the case.

The three of us join the flow of the other supplicants down the stairs. It only takes a few minutes for everyone to gather, staring at one another uncertainly.

Inquisitors emerge from the staircase that I vaguely remember taking with Saipha on our night out together; it's the one that leads to the basement. A sigh of relief escapes me. We'll be safe down there…so long as they don't use this opportunity to put all of us under the effects of the green dragon vapor. I'd like to think the inquisitors have other things to worry about, but given how they've acted so far, I'm not optimistic.

"Please follow us." It's the prelate. My stomach knots, acid eating through tissue, burning muscle. I don't trust her...not for a second.

My fears are proved well-founded when she leads us up, rather than down.

"What's going on?" someone asks, voice pitched high.

"Is there a fortified room this way?" another supplicant asks an inquisitor standing off to the side, clearly thinking along the same lines that I am: *"Up" during a dragon attack is never a good decision.*

"No questions," the prelate snaps, her voice echoing around all of us, the words tightening like nooses on our necks.

They funnel us like livestock. Every step up feels like a funeral march. More cannon fire rattles the upper windows. Flashes of light mingle with the darkness.

We're nearly on the fourth floor when the roar of a dragon seems to shake the very foundations of Vinguard itself. Some of the supplicants let out screams. I falter, grabbing the wall for support. My other hand goes to my chest, and I take a shuddering breath.

My thoughts waver, turned to liquid; I can't hold on to them. *Trees aren't real. The scourge is actually my blood. Punch Saipha in the nose.* Laughter threatens to bubble up, as though that's the funniest idea I've had in ages. *Talk like a dragon: Roar, roar roar. Hiss.* I snort.

"Isola." His hand is firm on my shoulder, jostling me.

I shake my head and catch a hiss in my throat. What was that? *Purple dragon madness.* Exposure to one's roar can cause delirium. It's the only explanation. But purple dragons are extremely rare.

Given how everyone else seems to be emerging from a daze, it must have been.

The inquisitors don't even give us a second to catch our breath. The prelate begins marching again. Up and up...

The supplicants at the front of the line begin to shout objections at the prelate. They curse at her, beg and barter, because they see now where she's leading us. She ignores them all and throws open the door to the rooftop where I was interrogated far too recently.

Icy wind billows down into the stairwell. Someone screams as though it's a dagger stabbing them. Another weeps. "You can't do this to us!" Mikel shouts.

"Out!" the prelate barks, ignoring all the protests.

"You're going to kill us!" Daisy yells over the wind.

"You can't force us to stand out there with dragons in the air." Cindel forces all her misplaced authority into her words to try and seem calm.

I can't see the prelate's face, but I can hear what almost sounds like delight in her words when she says, "It will be assumed that those who refuse are hiding the curse."

"How is not wanting to go out on a rooftop during a dragon attack any sign of the curse?" one of the latecomers, Dazni, asks. His sunken eyes are blazing in the shadows of their sockets. Bruises dot his skin. The other two latecomers—the twins—slide in closer to him as others cast wary looks their way, maintaining a full step of separation even in the cramped hall.

"Being in the presence of a dragon can force the dragon curse to activate. Therefore, any who avoid being near one will be presumed cursed and will be shown Mercy." The prelate continues to exude utter calm. I think she gets some kind of sadistic amusement from this, and I *hope* I'm wrong.

Given no choice, the supplicants at the front begin to march out onto the exposed rooftop.

One woman stops at the threshold. Yenni, one of Horowin's group. Of course a girl who spent her life in the Undercrust would be terrified by this prospect. Even those of us who have grown up under the skies are terrified.

"I can't." Her words quiver.

"Go," the prelate commands coldly.

"I can't go out there. A dragon will kill me. You can't honestly expect us to go out there." She pleads to the prelate's compassion—her better sense. A futile endeavor, from all I've seen.

"Go, or you will be assumed cursed." There is no emotion behind the words, a simple statement of fact.

I try to push forward, but there's no way. We're too compacted in the narrow passage. No one is moving; we're all blocked by Yenni and the prelate.

"Please, I'm not cursed... I don't want to die." Yenni worries the end of her braid.

"This is your last warning," the prelate snaps.

Yenni tries to take a step forward but falters. She shakes her head and lets out a whimper, turning. We all watch her eyes go wide as the prelate's dagger sinks between her ribs.

She's so weak and malnourished, she barely has enough life to let out a shocked, choking noise before she collapses into the prelate. The head of the inquisitors tosses her body aside, out the door to the rooftop. Another inquisitor moves to collect the corpse.

"Leave it," the prelate commands. "Fresh blood will draw them."

My hands ball into fists. From the first night on the rooftop, I didn't trust her. I *knew* she was waiting for an excuse to strike me with that baton.

No one moves. Everyone stares in stunned silence. Someone behind me begins to hyperventilate.

"Move!" she snaps.

We march once more. My hands are shaking, knees weak. I'm going to throw up. The only thing that keeps me moving is when I reach behind me with both hands and Saipha's fingers lock against mine in my right hand. And Lucan in my left. Saipha trembles, too. She's just as terrified as I am. Somehow, that makes me feel better. And then the guilt of taking solace in her fear makes me feel worse.

But all emotions leave me the moment we cross the threshold. I suck in a gulp of cool nighttime air, and my eyes are drawn to the sky.

It's another overcast evening. This time, the moon is full enough that the drifting clouds are mostly illuminated. Dark shadows dart between them. Wide wings. I immediately see four of them.

Four dragons.

A once-in-a-decade attack.

Still forcing myself to move, we shuffle toward the group of supplicants that is condensing at the center of the rooftop. Ulven kneels by Yenni's body, and Horowin and the others from the Undercrust stand nearby in shock. Wind whistles softly in my ears like an ominous undercurrent to the rising cacophony of a city in panic.

"You should go mourn your friend." Cindel pushes Dazni, and I swear I see one of the twins hold the other back from punching her. A part of me wishes they wouldn't—Cindel should get what's coming to her eventually. But they don't look strong enough to stand up in a fight, and now is not the time. "You're all Undercrust cowards." Cindel casts a withering gaze their way and leaves.

Lucan pulls us off to the side farthest from the body. "We don't want to be an easy target," he whispers. "Seeing so many together, vulnerable, might draw a dragon."

I look up at him, searching his face for some kind of fear.

But his brow is furrowed with intensity. In fact, he doesn't seem afraid at all. If anything, he's furious. He's ready to roar louder than the cry of the dragon that screeches across the sky and sends half of the supplicants to their knees, covering their heads, muttering as our thoughts scatter once more.

He looks like a Mercy Knight, already vetted and ready to do battle.

A dragon swoops down, charging the wall in the distance. The pale moonlight might just be playing tricks on my eyes, but I think it's a Silver Dragon. Mercy Knights fire ballistae and weighted nets, covering its wings. The ropes, even woven from metal, won't hold its steely wings for long—every scale is sharper than a knife. Knights rush the beast, overwhelming it. Silver Dragons are hard to shoot down from the sky, given most projectiles do nothing to them and they're too nimble for cannon fire. So getting in close is the best chance to get under their scales.

The kill demands a high cost from the knights. The dragon swings its tail and arm, sending Mercy Knights falling from the wall like little more than scattered dolls. I'm too far to see them hit the ground, but I can feel it in my bones, and it knocks the wind from me.

Finally, the beast is felled.

As if in retaliation for its fallen friend, another dragon roars—louder than any before—and explodes over the sky of Vinguard. I collapse this time, my knees meeting the stone. *Steal the inquisitors' daggers. Eat a rock. Kiss Lucan. Jump off the roof.* The thoughts are scattered, racing. *Maddening.*

The purple dragon is still alive.

"Isola!" Lucan shakes my shoulder. As I come to, I nearly heed the suggestion of the madness and kiss him. But I refrain, grateful for the night to hide the flush that covers my face. He points at the shadow in the sky. "Purple dragon. Snap out of it."

"I know; I'm fine, I'm fine."

We get Saipha back to the present, barely. She doesn't want to stop rocking and shivering. The rest of the supplicants are struggling worse as fear and purple dragon madness overtakes them. Some have scattered to the edges of the rooftop. Others tug on their jerkins and hair. Some are laughing.

A deafening boom resounds from behind us. *That* pulls everyone back to reality.

A beam of pale light streaks across the darkness in response. Whatever knight took the shot will be awarded with a handsome feast for sure, because it's a direct hit—rare to shoot them down from the sky. The purple dragon cries out in agony. The sound rips between my ears, and I grip the sides of my head with my hands. It feels as though it's tearing my mind apart as its final act.

But its dying cry is short-lived. The dragon falls to cheers from the other supplicants. I force myself to clap as well...to look happy. But I feel no joy. Relief, maybe. All joy within me has been rotted away by blood and chaos. By one near-death experience after the next. By having sense beaten from me at the vicar's hands—by being his toy, his experiment. By starving at the hands of people who'd call themselves my fellow citizens.

This can't be the only way to live... *There must be a better way.*

It's treasonous to even think, but I can't accept that all this death and destruction is good for our world. I can almost feel the flow of Ether shift as the dragon draws its last breath. A void where there was once vibrancy.

My eyes drift to Lucan's profile. He's as still as a statue. Expression unchanging. Somehow...I know he's thinking the same as me. That he feels the same. As if sensing my attention, he turns all that intensity on me. There are a thousand words unsaid. Words I can't even fathom but ache to know.

Do you think like me? Feel like me? Do you want to see the dragon scourge ended without blood? Or, Lucan, are you really the Mercy Knight I caught a glimpse of shining in your eyes?

"Lu—" I'm interrupted by a screech so close I can feel the heat of the dragon's breath.

We all turn in unison, facing the monstrosity that glides toward the rooftop with outstretched wings and a body larger than most houses. It's a yellow dragon. Gold glimmers off its slick scales in the moonlight. Etherlight fills the air with an effervescent quality. My head spins from the sensation washing over me.

The dragon lands on the edge of the rooftop, talons sinking in. Spiderweb fractures splinter the stone, and supplicants frantically attempt to keep their balance. Saipha lets out a scream unlike any sound I've ever heard from her.

I don't say anything. I can't even breathe. It's just like that day six years ago. It's as if I summoned the beast by allowing myself to remember. My heart feels like it's stopped completely and abandoned me.

But the only people who have abandoned anyone are the inquisitors. As I search for someone to help us—to intervene—I realize they're absent from the rooftop. They just...left us here.

The dragon sweeps its unfeeling gaze across the rooftop, as if assessing which tasty morsel it wants to consume first. No one moves. Everyone is too terrified to even make a sound. For once, I'm not alone in my fear.

Maybe now, they'll see it's not so unreasonable... Now that they've all been face-to-face with one of the monsters. It's so easy to imagine yourself as brave when you've never known true fear.

The dragon shifts, leaning back. Its long neck stretches. Jaw relaxes. It's going to bite and take out all the supplicants clustered together at once.

Someone has to do something.

I look for the inquisitors, but they're not here. I look to Mercy Spire, but I don't see the glint of a cannon. It must need to collect more Ether.

Someone has to do something.

Someone...

You saved me that day. Lucan's words from earlier resonate within me, repeating with every quickening beat of my heart. Being Valor Reborn was always a hollow title placed upon me by a man I've come to hate more than anyone in the world. It felt unearned and undeserved, especially when I've never been able to do anything else befitting of Valor. But Lucan...he really believes I saved him that day. Maybe I did.

And then there was what happened in the sundering pit when I drew Ether without a sigil.

Something wild and untamed pulses through me. I lunge forward, sprinting across the rooftop.

"Isola!" Saipha shouts after me, Lucan's voice joining hers in shock.

The silver of the inquisitor's dagger protruding from Yenni's body glints in the moonlight. Clumsy of the prelate not to sheathe it again. Mercy Knights are supposed to guard their daggers at all costs.

I grab it as I run, using the blood that's collected on the guard to draw a sigil on the back of the hand clutching the knife.

I take my stance, holding out the blade. The dragon looks at me, and I can almost imagine its scaly forehead rising as if to say, *What do you intend to do with that?*

Ether moves within me and around me—deep below, churning in the Font. Rising through stone and mortar. It moves through me, to the dragon, and back. The sensation is so sharp and present, it's almost as if the magic replaces my own breath.

The dragon's eyes shimmer like molten gold, as though it can feel it, too. As if we're having a conversation with magic alone. As though I can almost understand the beast.

Something about standing here, now... I can't imagine killing it. Maybe that's why even though Ether begins to collect around me with tiny sparks and hazy swirls, I can't bring myself to unleash it. I was prepared to have the dragon lunge for me and use the armor sigil to protect myself while I cut out its throat from the inside.

The dragon leans forward. Its massive neck is able to span halfway across the rooftop to me. In so doing, its forearms come forward, sending the other supplicants scattering. One doesn't get out of the way in time, and in my periphery, a splatter of crimson accompanies a sickening crunch. Others scream, but I don't react. I can't. I can hardly breathe.

The dragon's eyes bore holes into me, consuming me.

The air between us begins to spark like stardust. The dragon's face is so close that I can feel its breathing. Its face is monstrous, wider than I am tall. But I don't sense any animosity from it. It doesn't lunge for me. It doesn't bite. Just like the dragon that day, it studies me with curiosity.

With a huff through its nostrils that blows my hair from my face, the shimmering magical aura that surrounds the beast lowers. The act almost feels like...it's saying *hello*.

The moment it drops its barrier, I can sense even more about the creature. Etherlight runs along its scales—that must be how it makes the protective aura. *It's not using Ethershade… It's using Etherlight, just like us…*

My elbow unlocks. Muscles relax. "Tell me," I breathe, audible only to the beast and me. *Everything beyond the walls, the truth about the world and magic, about your kind. Tell me…*

It lowers its chin, as if to say in reply, *You already know.* Its eyes drag down to my chest—right to my heart, where the other dragon's claw carved into my skin. There's something akin to recognition within them.

I open my mouth again to demand to know what secrets it holds. As if it could speak. As though it's a breath from returning to whatever unfortunate soul it once was before the person transformed into a monstrous dragon.

Without warning, a deafening *boom* explodes from an upper level of Mercy Spire. The beam of light blinds me. The meditative flow of Ether that had surrounded the dragon and me is disrupted by what amounts to the sensation of a cleaver striking stone. The cannon fire strikes true, straight through the beast's center. For its final second, its eyes widen, staring straight through me, as if to say, *How could you?*

An apology burns my tongue unbidden.

Then, the yellow dragon rears back and lets out a dying scream. It staggers, shudders, and tips away, falling off the edge of the monastery and into the dark night.

41

No one says anything. No one breathes.

Ears ringing from the cannon fire, none of us hears the buffet of massive wings as the remaining dragon retreats to fight another day. The bells fall silent, in stark contrast to the cacophony that rattled the city. The other supplicants slowly regain their footing. Some are injured. All are shaken. None can bring themselves to look at the bodies of those claimed by the attack.

All eyes turn to me instead.

Their expressions are unreadable. Did they see my action as bold and brave? I stare at the dagger still in my grip. Was it enough to make them think I had the capability to take down that dragon, and the Mercy Knights merely beat me to it? Or do they all know now, beyond any doubt, that I am nothing more than a fraud? I felt the Ether gather...but I didn't unleash it. Could they somehow know that part of me held back?

My hand falls limply, and the dagger clatters to the ground. The motion triggers Saipha, and she sprints over. Past her, I see Lucan shifting, a few steps forward, halting, then back. Our eyes meet.

What do you think of me? I want to ask of the man who looked so ready to slay a dragon. So filled with righteous fight. My throat has gone dry.

"Are you all right?" Saipha asks as she comes to a stop right before me. I can't tell if she's actually whispering or if my hearing is still muted from the cannon fire and the rush of blood from the surge of Etherlight.

"I'm fine." I nod.

"What were you thinking?" she hisses.

"I wasn't. I was acting on instinct," I admit. "Maybe it was the call of Valor in me." The words are hollow even to my ears. But something *did* possess me to step forward. If not Valor, then what? Do I even know who I am anymore? My mind feels like mashed potatoes, and I don't think I can blame it entirely on the purple dragon.

"Armed with a dagger? Valor was brave, not stupid." She shivers and grips herself, quickly getting it under control. "I feel like I'm going to be sick. Your recklessness made me sick. How dare you, Isola."

"I'm sorry." I give an apologetic smile at the touch of teasing she managed to add in at the last moment.

"That light…"

"You saw it, too, then?" So it wasn't just my imagination? I stare at my palm.

"I saw it," she says, and a million questions flood my mind.

But before we can say anything else, the inquisitors emerge from the door to the rooftop. It hangs a bit ajar now. The prelate is surrounded by the others.

"Let it be written that none of you have shown signs of the dragon curse," she declares. "Now, inside with you all."

There's no talking amongst the supplicants as we're shuffled back to the residence hall. Saipha, Lucan, and I don't even say a word to one another, readily falling into our normal rotation. As I sit on the lockbox by the door during my shift, I decide then and there that I'm telling the other supplicants about the way into the kitchen in the morning. This has gone too far for too long. Risks be damned. They won't say we're all dragon cursed and kill us.

Would they?

The thought haunts me, and later in the night, sleep only comes for me out of overwhelming exhaustion. Even then, it's restless and broken by memories of eyes like cold fire—eyes that felt like they looked into my very soul with something akin to recognition.

In the morning, we eat in our shared room in silence. I notice that Saipha's hand still quivers from time to time, but I avoid pointing it out. None of us are fully recovered from the rooftop experience, and we're processing the lingering terror in our own ways.

"I have something else for you, Saipha." I finally have a chance to give her the honeycomb.

She unwraps it, and her whole face lights up. Her hands are steady, and the deep furrows in her brow relax. I didn't realize how much older the stress was making her look until it's gone.

"They had honeycomb?" she whispers in awe.

"Yeah, thought it was much more deserved in your belly than theirs." And I'm further vindicated after what the prelate did.

"Do you want some?" She goes to break off a piece.

"I had some in the larder."

I sense Lucan's gaze on me, but when I glance at him, I don't find the censure I expect. Instead, he looks almost...approving. "Enjoy it," he tells Saipha with a small grin.

She takes a bite and lets out a soft sigh. "It feels like my birthday."

"Happy birthday." I nudge her with my shoulder.

Saipha snorts. "It's not for, what, four more months?"

"Early birthday."

We share a grin, and she finishes the honeycomb, chewing on it thoughtfully. For a quiet, peaceful second, it almost feels like we're not in the Tribunal. Like we can breathe and just be three eighteen-year-olds sharing a little treat.

But it's just an illusion, and the truth sneaks back in faster than any of us would like.

"Do you think one of the people who died was cursed?" Even though Saipha speaks softly, the question breaks the silence like shattering glass. Lucan and I both turn to her. She licks off the last of the honey from her fingers, and with it, any sense of levity vanishes. "No one transformed last night. And if someone was going to...surely that would've been it. Right? What could push us more than that?"

"Maybe..." I murmur.

"We were never able to find any leads on their sensor, even poking around here for weeks," Saipha says.

"Sensor?" Lucan interjects.

We share a look, realizing we never told him. I take the opportunity to fill Lucan in on what we overheard back on our second night.

He frowns. "They know someone among us is cursed? No wonder they're being so extreme."

"But maybe the sensor wasn't working properly from the start?" Saipha suggests optimistically.

"They seem convinced it was accurate." *And my father made it*, I don't say. But there is a slight, almost defensive edge to the thought.

"I'd like to think that the cursed supplicant died last night." Her tone becomes wistful, almost dreamy. "And the rest of our time here can actually be enjoyed."

A snap of Etherlight tickles the back of my neck. I sit straighter and fight a shiver.

"All supplicants are to report to the central atrium for the next test," an inquisitor announces through the copper box.

For a breath, none of us move. We all stare at one another and then at nothing. They aren't even going to wait a full day between the rooftop horror and the next test. Not even going to give any of us a proper meal first. Which must mean they think the cursed is still among us.

"Thanks again for getting us food." Saipha stands, breaking my momentary panic.

"Isola did the hard work. I merely helped," Lucan says, mentioning nothing of how I almost got us caught.

"We all played our part," I say firmly. "We're all surviving together."

"Or not at all," Saipha murmurs under her breath as she steps out the door.

Lucan and I share a look, but neither of us respond. Her being so defeatist is even jarring to him. Not even the honeycomb could get her back to her usual self. Hopefully after this test she'll feel a bit more at ease.

We make our way down the stairs, trudging alongside the other supplicants. Their gaunt cheeks and dragging of feet fill me with a pang of regret for not telling them about the larder last night or running to do it first thing this morning. But there's been such little time. An unnatural chill fills the air, fueled by their listless expressions. Lucan slides into step beside me, his warmth helping ward away the uneasy cold. He doesn't even look my way as he does it, though, like he just knew.

It's only about a minute after the last of us gather in the central atrium that the vicar appears. He moves through the inquisitors and supplicants, ascending to his balcony.

I wonder if he sees us as the husks we are now. If he does, nothing in his expression suggests as much. A slight smile quirks his lips, nearly impossible to see from where we stand. The glint in his eyes is almost sinister. He looks so satisfied to the casual observer. As though delighted by our pain.

I'm no casual observer.

A shiver rakes down my spine. *He's upset.* I know it as well as I would if he were my father.

"Supplicants, you have done well to make it this far in your Tribunal. It bodes well for each of you to have reached this point, as we are now more than halfway through, and you are that much closer to being full citizens of Vinguard." He grips the railing, leaning forward. "Every moment of this Tribunal is a test—a test to ensure that a dragon cursed does not draw breath within the walls of Vinguard. To know you may live without the fear of one day transforming and mindlessly killing all those you love. In fact, you will become the last bastion against the scourge and the dragons. Even those of you who will not enter Mercy will be part of the brigade—the family, the fortification, the people in arms that is Vinguard.

"And I know the journey to get there is hard. But remember,

there is Valor in sacrifice. What you are enduring here is a noble pain."

The manner in which the vicar speaks is almost like food for hungry stomachs. The supplicants stand a little taller, their eyes a little brighter, even though they still lack sustenance.

I have a different reaction. I feel the Ether surging violently through me at the vicar's words. But I remain completely still.

They will do things to you in there...horrible things that should never be forgiven, and they'll tell you it's normal. Don't let them win. Mum's words come back to me yet again.

They starved us, then offered honeyed words in place of food. They have made us fearful, while presenting themselves as the only form of protection. They have shown us horror but have wrapped it in noble ideals so we don't dare question why we were forced to endure it to begin with.

My hands are relaxed at my sides and heartbeat steady as I stare up at the vicar. I am just like one of the Tribunal's dichotomies: looking the part of a dutiful supplicant, but filled with a quiet, brutal rage.

"Even though you might not often see me, I assure you, I am here with you, for all of you. I fight your fight, and I feel your pain." The vicar sweeps his hand across the crowd.

"He has never known the pain of hunger," Lucan mutters under his breath with an absolute gut-wrenching amount of loathing.

"We are one, in Vinguard," the vicar continues. "We are united by our fight and by our connection with the Font. And today, as your second test of the Tribunal, that is precisely where you will go."

"What?" I breathe.

"We're going to the Font?" Someone else steals the question from my lips.

"That's... We can't..." Lucan barely manages to say the words through his slack jaw.

"Aren't only those who are gilded permitted access?" Saipha looks at both of us, even though she's just as familiar with Vinguard's laws as we are.

"That's just to the springs before it. To the Font itself is usually restricted to just the vicar, high curates, and a few others the vicar handpicks." Lucan squints his eyes, as if trying to see what the vicar is planning.

But I've never seen anything more clearly. I keep my voice down as I speak. "I suspect they're trying to see if being in the presence of Etherlight causes anyone to transform. I'd bet their theory is that the Ethershade within them might reject the presence of Etherlight enough that it revolts."

Of course, the Creed is wrong in all of it—I'm certain now. Dragons are creatures of Etherlight, not Ethershade. But, in that case, being in the presence of so much Etherlight would bring out the curse. They'll get the results they want but for the wrong reasons.

The vicar descends the stairs, eyes grazing over us like honed blades. "This way."

Supplicants and inquisitors fall into line, passing through the same door that we went through the last time we left the monastery and descended to the Undercrust. Previously, we kept to the bridges that skimmed the ceiling of the massive cave beneath Vinguard.

This time, we descend farther.

The Undercrust is shaped like a cone. Its widest span is at the top—closest to the Upper City above. The cone is split into three broad levels.

The first and highest is the city portion—this level boasts multiple-story homes that, instead of being built from the ground up, are constructed from the top down in the massive stalactites that curtain the rocky top of the Undercrust. Almost like a mirror of the city above. Bridges connect the spears of hanging rock. Pathways loop around and through them, mostly shadowed. The only light is from the streetlamps and the ambient, golden glow of the Font below. Horowin and his brigade seem more at home here as we crisscross through the people of the Undercrust, who readily part for us.

Surprisingly, the latecomers seem wary to be back here. Their sunken eyes dart around, and they murmur to themselves, hands covering the bruises on their arms. I wonder if they're remembering when they were caught...or maybe it had something to do with whatever replacement test the vicar gave them.

I shake my head and banish it from my thoughts. It won't do for me to dwell on all the horrible things the vicar can come up with.

Those whose skin isn't naturally a shade of brown are ghostly pale, much like Ulven. I doubt they've ever seen the sun. And they look at us with as much fascination as I imagine they'd look at the sky.

I can't stop myself from wondering if somewhere among them are Yenni's parents. I hope they were already told of their daughter's demise and this isn't how they find out. But everything involving the Tribunal seems so unnecessarily cruel, I doubt it. My hands ball into fists, and I set my jaw.

The cave begins to narrow in the middle section and brighten as it nears the Font, walls closing in and trapping the naturally warm, thick air that radiates with a golden glow from deep below. This is the farming section.

Terraces are cut into the walls, connected by fewer bridges throughout. Crops and livestock are fed and nurtured by Etherlight. The buildings here aren't privately owned. They are under the control of the Creed.

Beneath the farms are springs that pool on similar stone terraces in place of crops. The water is piped up to the Undercrust and Upper City above. But the springs themselves are a holy place of meditation—of connection with life itself, raw and eternal, bubbling up from deep within the world.

Then we reach an iron gate at the lowest of the ledges that hold the springs. It's set into a fence that spans the edge of the terrace we're on—a stone balcony that stretches over the abyss of the Font. Etherlight swirls so thickly, it manifests as a mist that I note with fascination is not unlike the scourge. This is the only place I've ever heard of Etherlight being potent enough that anyone can see it. Its golden glow illuminates the entire Undercrust, although the source of the Font itself is still impossible to see. An arched stairway carved from stone stretches away from the ledge and into the misty abyss.

I'm not the only supplicant that eyes the edge on the other side of the iron fence and the vast nothingness beyond. Even though we are deeper into the earth than I've ever imagined possible, it still keeps going. It's as though we will touch the very heart of the world itself.

The vicar opens the gate before us, and I suck in a breath as he passes through. *This is really happening.* We're going to head down to the point of the cone—the deepest part of the Undercrust: the Font itself.

Beyond the iron gate is another stairway that curves along the wall of the Undercrust. It's carved right into the stone, just like the ones above. Except, unlike the ones above, it's barely wide enough for one person at a time and has no railing. One slip would be our last.

I can almost hear every supplicant's heart pounding—from proximity to the Font, and the peril of the sheer drop to our right. The stone wall is warm underneath my palm as I brace myself against it. Almost too warm. Tiny jolts pass through me, as if a lightning storm is happening in each of my joints. I can't imagine how bad it'd be if Mum hadn't been able to give me a tincture.

Please be okay, my heart whispers at the thought of her.

As we plunge deeper into the swirling mist of Ether, it becomes impossible to see beyond the person in front of us. Saipha's shoulders are nearly invisible, awash in the golden glow. Somehow, all this light isn't blinding. Ahead, a shape comes into view—another landing.

It reminds me of the wide, flat cap of a mushroom. The haze makes it impossible to see if there's any structure beneath supporting it or if it's a horizontal shelf protruding from the wall.

As our feet meet the stone, we all let out a sigh of relief, grateful to be off the narrow stairway. It's hard to tell how big the landing is, but it's large enough that every supplicant and the inquisitors can stand upon it and there is still more beyond, obscured.

With the haze of Etherlight blocking the city above completely, it feels as though we've stepped into another world.

"Welcome to the precipice of the Font." The vicar's voice is muffled, weighted by the ambient Ether. "Here is where, once you have successfully completed your Tribunal, you will receive your gilding. Just as the Mercy Knights guard Vinguard's walls, I guard the soul of Vinguard. The Creed is the manifestation of the guiding light of the Font in all of us." He lifts a hand and places it on his cheek underneath his shining, golden eye. "It is from this power we come, and it is to this power we return. The gilding is a reminder of this—a reminder that we are all connected. Today, you will not receive your gilding, but you will meditate before the Font to seek Valor's guidance within you. You will spend time here, basking in the Ether, just as he did to empower himself before leaving to attack the Elder Dragon."

The mention of the Elder Dragon so soon after thinking of Mum reminds me of something else she said—something I'd all but forgotten in the fog of hunger and push of survival: the vicar is planning an offensive. Did he bring *me* here to make sure I'll be ready? Mum mentioned a weapon, too, something big drawing on the Font. I look around warily for anything that could be it, but of course there's nothing.

Questions on questions compound, filling the empty space in my stomach to the point that I'm nauseous. *What am I not seeing?* I'm missing something important, something that I know, through all my terror, has to do with me.

"Please follow the inquisitors to the spring of cleansing," he finishes.

We're taken to the right. Another narrow bridge comes into view, also without railings, suspended over a glowing abyss. The bridge takes us from the platform we arrived on to another.

On this vast arc of stone protruding from the cave wall is a wide but shallow body of water. It's impossible to tell exactly how large it is, as it extends into the haze that surrounds us. Stone benches line the closest edge.

"Strip down to your smallclothes," the prelate commands.

"Excuse me?" Cindel blurts, utterly aghast.

"The Font demands you as you were when you came into the world. Be grateful we're not demanding more." At the prelate's final word, the inquisitors step back to the outer edge of the ledge the spring is upon.

Supplicants regard each other warily, but Cindel is the first to move. She crosses to a bench and begins undoing the laces on her vest. Her expression is one of placid calm, despite her objection seconds ago. An ever-dutiful daughter of the Creed.

Others follow her lead.

I step off with Saipha and Lucan, moving with them instinctually. We cluster around one bench, starting with our shoes, placing them underneath. Then we remove our vests. Saipha has a moment of hesitation before she pulls her shirt over her head. I follow suit, trying to look calmer than I feel as my knuckles graze over the leather-and-silk brassiere covering my breasts as I pull off my shirt.

I can't stop my eyes from darting to Lucan as I untie my trousers.

My cheeks flush as his gaze briefly meets mine before he tugs his shirt up. He doesn't look the slightest bit uncomfortable. *I mean, I wouldn't if I were a guy with a body like his...* The fabric glides over his flat, muscular stomach, and the flush from my face flares through my entire body. He turns and drops the shirt on the bench.

My heated skin goes ice-cold as I openly stare.

In my periphery, I see Saipha open her mouth to say something to me. Make fun of my gawking, likely. But then her eyes dart to Lucan and also stick.

His body is a constellation of scars. Long, deep gouges. Pale and thin slashes. Raised and gnarled. Some look fresh.

"Who did this to you?" I breathe.

Lucan freezes, but he doesn't look at either of us. His eyes are downcast, shoulders rigid. "I am to say they are from the dragon attack I survived as a boy."

Yet it's everything he doesn't say that has me balling my hands into fists so tight my nails dig crescents into my palms. Suddenly, the pain the vicar has caused me is trivial. I can endure for my own sake. But when he hurts the people I care about? The heat returns, but it's completely different. I suck in a slow, angry breath through my nose, trying to remain calm.

Lucan has removed his trousers and steps to my side. His fingertips touch my white knuckles lightly. "Don't." His eyes are full of pain, but there's a faint smile curling the edges of his lips. He moves away, wading into the waters of the pool alongside others. The haze of Etherlight quickly consumes him, and he fades from sight.

"Bastard." Saipha strips off her pants and follows Lucan. We both know she wasn't referring to Lucan.

"Yeah," I murmur, pulling off my own trousers to nothing but a small, silken pair of shorts. The Font warms the air temperature to a perfectly comfortable level, even just in my smallclothes.

"I'm surprised you're here." Cindel's voice nearly startles me out of my skin. I didn't even hear her approach.

"Where else would I be?" I only glance her way, keeping my

attention on Lucan and Saipha. Mostly Lucan. All I can think of are the scars he's worked so hard to hide.

"I would think the great Valor Reborn would be going to the Font itself. Not merely basking in its glow like the rest of us." Cindel speaks loud enough that others glance our way. "I would hate to think that you have an opportunity to strengthen your power and you wouldn't take it. For the good of Vinguard."

"Indeed." The vicar's voice slithers across the open space. An unwelcome third party to this conversation.

I freeze, head turning his way, bracing myself. Or, maybe, holding myself back from launching forward in anger. There the vicar stands, barely visible in the haze. His hands are folded at the small of his back. Here, his golden eye shines as bright as the sun.

"Come, Isola," he commands.

An objection rises from my gut and burns my tongue as I remember vividly what happened the last time I was alone with him. I press my lips into a line to prevent myself from saying all the things I want. From cursing him for all he's done, to demanding to know what he did to Lucan so I know *exactly* what I'm going to someday make him pay for.

"Oh, it looks like you *will* have a chance to make yourself stronger. How good for you and for us all." Cindel's words have soured. Like she can't decide if she's glad to be proved right or perpetually annoyed that I receive special treatment.

"It is good for me." I try to stand taller as I stride past her to follow the vicar.

"You think you're so strong, don't you?" she mutters under her breath. "You're nothing without him, Isola Thaz."

I freeze for a heartbeat, nearly turning on her. I want so badly to put her in her place. To tell her that I drew Etherlight without a sigil. But I bite my tongue. *She's not worth it.* And something about sharing that fact widely feels...dangerous.

"Isola, *now.*" The vicar snaps, and I follow. I don't know what he intends, but instinct tells me it won't be good.

43

The vicar guides me back across the bridge to the first platform. We head toward the wall where the shelf originates, but instead of taking the stairway up again, we turn right.

"I didn't have an opportunity to meditate and cleanse my body." The moment the word "body" leaves my mouth, I'm reminded of how exposed I am. Part of me wants to curl in on myself and hide. The other part wants to stand taller. I will not give him the satisfaction of shame because there is nothing for me to be ashamed of. I am me. Wholly and unapologetically.

"That is not something to be concerned about, for you are Valor Reborn."

I roll my eyes at his back.

A new stairway leading down appears through the haze, and I swallow the lump in my throat. There is only one thing deeper than this: the Font itself. Not the general area we're in now. Not the mist of Ether. But the wellspring of magic and life.

I pause at the top of the stair, hesitant to follow. I don't want to go down there alone with him. But there's nowhere I can run. And I can't fight him.

Can I? The thought has sweat beading along my brow. *Could I fight the vicar?*

The notion is pure treason, and everything that he has trained into me rebels against it. But something was awakened at this man's hand in the sundering pits. Something that's intrigued by the notion of such a fight.

He glances over his shoulder. "Isola?" Impatience makes my name short and taut.

If I'm so powerful, why do I obey you? I want to ask. Instead, I plaster on a forced smile. "Forgive me, I was briefly overwhelmed by the Etherlight." And then I take my first step down.

Carved into the cave wall are depictions of dragon skulls, hundreds of all shapes and sizes. Human skulls are wedged between them, wrought from stone. I have no choice but to rest my palm on one for balance, and a jolt runs through me. The rock glitters under my touch, then darkens.

I stare at my palm but don't dare fall behind again.

The pathway plunges into the stone and becomes a tunnel that has so many carvings of human and dragon bones it's almost as though its constructed entirely from them. They stare at me with vacant, hollow eye sockets. Each one more lifelike than the last.

Upon someone's death, their body is returned to the Font, so that their Etherlight can be restored to the earth. What if these bones aren't mere carving from rock? Grim fascination stops me from looking away, even as a horrified shiver runs down my spine.

At long last, we end at an iron gate. On the other side is a narrow strip of rock that is the beach to a vast lake of molten gold.

I know what it is, and yet I can't believe it. My throat has gone dry. "Is that…"

"The Font." The vicar unlocks the gate and opens it, gesturing for me to step inside.

"I…" I'm rooted to the spot. This goes against everything I've ever been taught. "I shouldn't be here."

"This, Isola, is your destiny." He speaks almost gently, but his eyes shine with something that makes my skin prickle. His golden eye is the same color as the liquid of the pool and, suddenly, the gilding makes sense. I would bet anything he drops a tiny bit of the Font's liquid Etherlight into one eye of every citizen of Vinguard. That is how he connects them to the Font, and why they have a better sense of the flow of Etherlight after—enough that those who couldn't use magic even with an artificer sigil before can manage simple feats following.

"Do not stall." The vicar grabs my arm, yanking me toward the gate, shoving me in front of him and onto the threshold. He steps back into the tunnel, positioning himself behind me, blocking any hope of escape, and the harsher edges of his voice smooth as he adds, "Go and commune with the Font. Find your true power to slay dragons with Etherlight, Isola."

I look uncertainly between him and the final path to the Font.

The vicar leans forward and whispers, "Lest I try to wrench it from your body again using my own methods." He keeps his stare locked on me as he steps back. There's the making of a snarl curling his lip.

I try to think of a retort. Some way to get around this… But there's so much Etherlight flooding the area, I can't concentrate. My head spins. Something about it calls to me, louder by the second.

Unable to resist its pull—or the vicar's orders—I take timid steps along the narrow strip of rocky beach at the edge of this vast, underground spring of raw magic, awestruck and terrified. This is the last thing keeping the world alive. The power rolling from the golden mist is irresistible but overwhelming. I'm frozen in place, as though I've run into an invisible wall.

"Go, Isola," he urges from behind me, not crossing the gate, as though he wouldn't dare get as close as I am. His toes haven't even passed the threshold. "Show me your true power."

I press on when it feels like a thousand invisible hands are trying to force me back, pushing through to reach the edge of the molten gold. What will happen if I continue? If I touch it? I already feel as if I'm about to be torn apart—like the magic is grating against my ribs and tugging flesh from bone to pull me closer. It hurts, yet I yearn for it. Like the sweet pressure right before a joint pops.

"*Go,*" he commands.

Shuffling forward, I barely submerge my feet into the Ether. It's warm but not wet. The second it touches my skin, the whole world tilts, shakes, and trembles. I can see the patterns of Etherlight in the air. They carve shapes...no, lines. Like artificer sigils—like a secret language.

From the back of my mind come unrelenting screams. A thousand voices crying out in pain so loud, it's a roar. I nearly collapse.

"Continue, Isola." The vicar sounds far away.

Come, Isola, a voice whispers from the Font itself, cutting through the screams.

Then the vicar's rises above the roar of power and the screams in my head. "Bring Vinguard power and victory at last!"

I take another step, and another. My foot slips on rock underneath the Ether, and I tumble off an unseen ledge. Not liquid, not mist, the Font is something else, something indescribable. It sucks me under, and I fight against it on instinct. My feet find purchase on the rocky bottom, and I push up, frantically gasping for breath as my head clears the surface.

Waves of gold obscure the vicar before he comes back into focus. There's an inquisitor—no, a Mercy Knight with him now.

I'm pulled under again.

The Font cradles me. Every joint in my body aches with a distant and unyielding pain from the sharp, persistent surge of power. It's too much, but something in me wants more—needs more.

For a moment, I think I see someone, deep within the endless field of gold. There's a man, standing in front of countless others on a precipice. The vicar? No...*someone else*.

Another crash of power slams into me, and with it, I hear the screams of thousands in chorus. The weeping of a thousand more. It's as though I'm somewhere else entirely yet still trapped within my body. Like I'm on the edge of realizing something—knowing something—just beyond my grasp.

My heart is beating so fast, I can hardly breathe. This raw magic is going to destroy me.

I'm pulled farther down, or maybe I'm not moving at all. *This is the only way to save humanity*, I hear someone whisper between my ears—more like a thought.

I finally resurface, gasping. My eyes swing back to the entrance, but the vicar's gone.

I can leave.

Fighting with gritted teeth, clawing at rock, pumping my legs and arms, I struggle toward the rocky strip in front of the still open and empty gate. For something that looks light as air, the Font is as sticky as tar, sucking me down, as if trying to consume me. The world continues to blur and oscillate.

Tell no one. Distant screams persist. *What's happening?* I don't know what thoughts are my own anymore. *It must be done.* What is reality and what is the fiction of magic. *We will survive.*

I struggle to find my footing on the rock. *If I don't get out, I might die here.*

Gasping, I manage to climb out onto the narrow strip of stone at the edge of the Font. I catch my breath and look down, expecting to find my body bruised, torn, and bleeding under a coat of golden Etherlight. But even though the unbearable pain persists, I find my skin uninjured and clear, with only scattered patches of Etherlight remaining. I groan as it hisses off, evaporating in a blood-red haze. I think I'm going to be sick. I want to tear off my skin. It feels as though it doesn't fit. Like it's not *mine*.

What's happening to me?

The Font behind me is bubbling. *Groaning.* I force myself to find the strength to stand. I try to run for the gate, but my feet slip, and I land hard, the stone cutting my skin. My blood steams off the rock, making me wonder just how hot the stone is from the Font. How I'm not cooking alive.

Maybe I am?

I manage to right myself somewhat. I'll crawl to that gate, if I must. Hand over hand, knees and feet dragging, I make my way. The body isn't made for this much exposure to raw magic. No wonder humanity lost our ability to draw Ether on our own—it was a survival mechanism of our species. Those who could do it must've died off. Because this…this agony…

I grit my teeth so hard my jaw pops. I will *not* die here. The gate is close, and something tells me if I can make it to the other side of the threshold, it'll be better. There must be something about the threshold that buffers the overwhelming nature of the Font. Otherwise, how did I not feel such agony until I had crossed from the tunnel to the rocky beach? There is a reason the vicar didn't enter. If he thought he was safe there, then it must be safe. I'll work out by whatever magic later.

Just as I reach the entry, boots appear. The gate slams shut with a heavy *clang*. The same terror the bells inspire sinks into me, making my blood run cold even as my skin burns.

The prelate stands on the other side. I know her by the scuffs on her boots. "I don't think you're done in there."

"Let me out." The words are gravelly and low from pain.

"Make me."

I snarl at her like a beast. She lets out a low hum of amusement in response.

"The vicar had some urgent business to attend to but left me in charge—told me to ensure you don't come out until you can properly wield Ether." She crouches. "And if you can't make me open this gate, then it looks to me like you're not done."

From this angle, for the first time, I can see more of her face. It's still shadowed by the hood she keeps drawn to its fullest, but the haze and glow of the Font illuminate strange angles on her cheeks and jaw. I can't make out finer details, but I can see one notable absence.

"Your eyes," I wheeze. They're both a dark shade of brown. Not a particularly noteworthy color on its own. But the prelate is easily in her mid-twenties. She's a Mercy Knight. All that combined means she's a full citizen of Vinguard and thus should have received the gilding. The fact that it's notably absent has only one explanation: she didn't go through the Tribunal. Which is impossible.

"I don't know what you're talking about." She stands and, one blink to the next, the gold is there.

I try to make sense of what I just saw. "What…"

With a final look, so disapproving that it could wither fruit on the vine, she says, "Show us what you're really made of. If you're meant to save this world, then do it," and leaves, the gate locked shut behind her.

"Don't— Don't leave me here." I reach through the bars of the gate, but she's already gone. I run my fingers over the empty keyhole and let out a cry.

The bubbling and churning continue behind me, calling me back. I grab the bars, trying to pull myself up, but the effort almost overwhelms me. It's as though the Ether has had a taste of me, and now it demands more. Tendrils of magic wrap around my body like vines, pulling me back to the source.

I grip the bars tighter.

With a deep breath, I groan and pull myself to my feet.

And just as I do, the Font explodes.

44

I'm slammed against the gate by the force of the explosion. Etherlight pummels into me. For a moment, the world is awash in gold. I can't see or feel anything else.

In the distance, there are screams again. Did the Font's explosion impact the others? No. It's all in my head. I put my hands over my ears, and the screams transform into dragons' roars. They cry out by the hundreds. The very foundation of Vinguard trembles as my bones rattle.

My heart stops entirely.

I try to suck in a sharp breath, but my lungs don't fill with air. It's just endless magic. I'm drowning in the raw essence of life itself.

The air has been replaced entirely with Etherlight, and my body can't handle it. My knees give out, and I slump, sliding down against the bars at my back.

Gold turns to flames. I am ablaze, inside and out. The orange-and-white fire dances across my flesh. I feel the blaze tangling my hair as though fingers are raking through it, teasing through the dark curls. Endless agony rushing through me in wave after wave of pure magic.

And then, as if sensing I couldn't take one second more, the fire extinguishes.

I roll to the side and upturn the meager contents of my stomach. Red splatters across the hot stone, steaming instantly. *Blood?* Panicked, I wipe my mouth with the back of my hand. The crimson streak vanishes off my skin, singed away by the Etherlight.

Is this it? Did I survive this long to die like this?

It's getting so hard to keep myself upright. At any second, my body will give up. I fought and survived this long for what?

Footsteps rush down the walkway. I fight to turn my head and peer through the closed iron gate.

"Lucan?" I blink, certain my mind is playing tricks on me.

Worried eyes meet mine. Lucan rushes over and slams into the gate, shaking it. The Etherlight doesn't seem to impact him, confirming my theory that safety lies just on the other side.

"What are you doing?" I gasp. "How…"

"Hold on." With a flash of an artificer sigil sketched messily on his hand with dirt, the lock shatters. Never has anything sounded more beautiful than that fracturing metal.

"Lucan, don't—" I see what he's about to do before he moves, but he does it anyway. He opens the gate and is nearly knocked back by the force of the Ether.

With gritted teeth and every muscle straining, with pain so apparent in his eyes it nearly finishes the job the Font started and tears me in two, he reaches for me, pulling me up. Arm around my shoulders, he heaves me through and slams the gate shut behind us as we tumble against the wall.

It's instant relief.

Air—not Etherlight—fills my lungs. Skin and muscle settle back onto my bones. My head slowly stops spinning, but now it's filled by the most splitting headache I've ever experienced. I still see motes of gold drifting through my vision, even as I press my eyes closed.

My bones rattle. Though I'm not cold. I finally, slowly, crack my eyes open only to be met with Lucan's.

The hazel of his eyes seems to glow brighter, the flecks of gold in them shining in the light of the Font. Or perhaps it's just the sparks in my vision.

His back is against the wall, which must be uncomfortable, given that he's still in nothing but his smallclothes—which is now the only thing I can focus on.

There is so much skin.

Face-to-face, my body is flush against his. His legs are on either side of me. Lucan's fingers dig into my back and hip, holding me up. Our eyes are locked, and nothing else exists. The pain evaporates, as though I'm melding into him.

"How are you here?" My voice is little more than a pathetic croak.

"I was worried."

"Worried, but—" I try to push away, my fingers splayed out on the large, unbroken expanse of his hard chest. *Dragon hells*, the man is carved like one of the stone sculptures of Mercy Knights that loom over the Grand Chapel. I step back, breaking contact, and the shaking instantly returns, worse than before.

"Don't move." Lucan's arms tighten around me, pulling me against him again. One of his hands spreads between my shoulder blades. The other, at the small of my back. I'm held so tightly, I barely have room to breathe. The world spins. "Give yourself a moment," he says.

"But—"

"I'm helping you." He tucks a lock of hair behind my ear, hand hovering a second too long, knuckles brushing my cheek.

It's then I realize that the motes of light aren't just the haze of the Font or remnants of what I just endured. They're real and happening right now. Etherlight flows between us like it did in the chapter house.

"That's it," he murmurs. His hand still hovers, near enough to feel his warmth. "Let me lead, Isola."

Fingertips lightly brush my cheek, though I don't think he's moving any hair this time. There wasn't any reason for him to touch me at all. But he is. Lucan's eyes drop to my mouth, and his fingertips are quick to follow. His thumb drags slowly across my lower lip, and my breath hitches. He tightens his hold at the small of my back, like he needs to be even closer.

There is no space between us. I feel *everything*. Every flat expanse of muscle, every divot and curve. I feel him through the thin fabric of my smallclothes, and my skin aches.

What would it feel like if he brushed his thumb lower? Down my neck? Lower still?

The heat that started as familiar and comfortable is now a blaze, flushing up my chest and over my face.

"Lucan," I rasp. All I seem to know is his name. All other thoughts have vanished. It's just him. Endlessly glorious him.

"How are you feeling?" he murmurs. He's so close that I feel his breath on my face. Close enough that I could kiss him if I wanted to.

And I want to.

The realization is somehow more terrifying than facing down a dragon.

"I feel horrible." Yet also amazing at the same time. How is this so confusing? My body has just been torn apart and put back together. But as long as his hands are on me, I feel like I could do anything.

He nods. "There's only so much I can do with a healing sigil."

"You should go before they catch you."

"I'm not leaving you." His hands tighten further, if that's possible, as if to prove the point.

"If they find you, you'll be in trouble."

"Then I'll be in trouble."

"Lucan..." I search his face for a hint of doubt. He's ready to stay here with me until I'm ready, come what may.

"I'm not leaving you, Isola." He brushes my cheek with his knuckles again, and my whole body is ablaze. The light around us seems even brighter.

"Because I saved your life," I say on a broken whisper.

"Because you're *you*," he corrects me but doesn't elaborate further.

My breath catches and my body goes rigid as hasty, uneven footsteps echo down to us. I push away from him, and the moment I do—the moment I am out of his Etherlight aura—I instantly feel worse. Everything comes crashing down on me at once. My joints ache. My skin hurts. My eyes burn as though acid has been poured into them.

"Isola—"

"I'm going to need you to do me a favor, Lucan." With a groan, I manage to take another step back. And I'm nearly sick again. My symptoms are worse than ever before, and there's only one thing that I know that will alleviate this agony: Mum's tinctures.

"What?" He straightens away from the wall, concern blazing in his eyes. I probably look as awful as I feel.

"Lie for me."

Lucan doesn't have a chance to ask what I mean. The vicar looms at the base of the stairs, eyes wide with surprise, and then his brow furrows with anger. It's not outright, not yet, but I have to play this carefully.

"Vicar Darius." I stagger toward him. The hand I place on the wall for support isn't just for show. "I need my father."

"Excuse me?" His eyes dart between Lucan and me, then narrow. "What has occurred?"

"I was worried for her and—"

"When Lucan arrived, I already had broken out," I interrupt and gesture toward the gate. I must give the vicar what he wants. Give a little to keep him pliable and working with me to get what I need—a way to get a tincture before this power tears me in two. "I drew on Etherlight."

"Without a sigil?" the vicar breathes in what sounds like ominous anticipation. I don't nod. Don't affirm. Merely level my eyes and wait for him to draw his own conclusions.

"While the toll on my body was great, I now have a greater understanding of Etherlight. I think... I think I can help my father create a new weapon. Greater than ever before." *Perhaps even better than Valor's legendary sword*, I don't say but let him assume as I hold the vicar's gaze, easing farther away from Lucan with each word. "My father can help me craft a sigil that will help me stabilize this power and then..." I take one step too far.

The world tilts and goes dark.

45

I wake up in a room that I'm sure is part of the monastery. I know it by the rough, uneven mortar between the stone. This place is painfully familiar now. A simple tunic covers my smallclothes as I shift underneath a heavy blanket.

It's not one of the normal supplicant rooms. The finishes are a little too nice. Bed slightly wider. There's a dresser and a proper desk with a chair. Perhaps this is one of the inquisitors' rooms?

I turn my head and meet a familiar pair of gold and brown eyes. Father is seated next to me, shoulders hunched, as though he's been perched there for hours.

"Isola." He heaves a sigh of relief and leans down to plant a kiss on my forehead.

"The vicar actually summoned you." I exhale my shock. "I wasn't sure if he'd listen."

"When I heard what had happened, I wanted to come, regardless. There are benefits to being a high curate." He smiles weakly. "He said you wanted to tell me of a weapon?"

I see the vicar omitted my possibility of needing a sigil to stabilize the power within me. Strangely, I already feel better. Perhaps some rest—and not being in the Font—was enough. I glance toward the window. The sun is hanging low in the sky. I must've been out for a few hours.

"That was just an excuse." I sit up, locking eyes with him. "You know about the tinctures Mum made me, don't you?" His brows lift a fraction. A small amount I wouldn't have noticed if I wasn't staring right at him. It's not a no, and for my father that's a yes. "I need you to get me one."

He runs a hand through his hair, looking away and shaking his head. "I can't."

"I know the rules of the Tribunal. But the Font... I have never felt worse, Father. And I don't think I'm going to make it if we don't find a way to—"

"Even if I wanted to, *I can't*." That stills me. He continues, "Your mother is gone, Isola."

"Gone?" A sickening feeling churns in my belly. "Did the vicar..."

"No. She's gone missing."

I study him, letting those words settle on me. "Mum wouldn't disappear." I grip the sheets, my knuckles turning white. She wouldn't leave me. "The vicar killed her."

"He did not."

"Stop being obsessed with him for just a second and listen," I snap.

"Stop allowing your hatred for him to blind you to what's right in front of you." He grabs my shoulders, shaking me gently and locking eyes with me once more. There's a truth in them he's trying to get me to see. "She. Is. *Missing*."

See what's right in front of me... He's so unshakably sure. Father wouldn't be, unless... "You know something."

"Listen to me." His voice is low and urgent now. He speaks without letting me go. So quietly that even if there were someone else in the room with us, they wouldn't hear. "When you take your place back in the Tribunal, you must be what they expect of you as Valor Reborn. No matter what. If the vicar demands that you draw Ether without a sigil, you *must*."

"Even if it kills me?" The last thing I want right now is more Etherlight in me.

"It won't kill you."

"How do you know that?" I probe.

"You don't think you were the only person your mother shared the details of her research with, do you?" he says softly, almost sadly.

I'm frozen in place. Silenced by my surprise. "She knows something. What did she tell you?"

"More than you give her or me credit for." He chuckles softly. "I was married to her. You don't really think I could be oblivious to the woman I spent my hours and days with? You don't think that I—as a student of Etherlight—wouldn't be fascinated by her theories?" His face has a genuine but sad smile. "And we both knew, the moment you were attacked and became Valor Reborn, you'd need two champions—one within the system, and one on the outside."

I swallow hard. My throat has gone dry. "You and Mum…"

"We might have had our differences and troubles, but you, Isola, are the one thing we have always been able to agree upon."

"All these years…you were both looking out for me?"

"All these years," he repeats in a way that leaves no room for doubt.

"Why would you keep me in the dark?" I whisper.

"You were just a child, Isola. We told you what we could as we could, guiding you in our own ways." Father saying to follow the vicar but never pressuring me to really take the Creed's teachings seriously, despite him rising through their ranks. Mother educating me about her research in secret to ensure I knew the truths of our world… Suddenly, all the random points in my life align, drawing a straight line to this moment.

So many things are pulling into clarity. But there's one thing still missing.

"I know we probably don't have much longer, but there's one thing I need to know, Father. Even if you can't get me one, what *are* the tinctures?" Somehow, I feel like if I know that, then everything else will fall into place. And the way he seems to tense at the mere question tells me I'm right. "It's my life at risk, too, and I'm not a child anymore. I need to know what's going on if I'm going to keep myself or anyone else safe."

"No…you're not a child anymore." There's a wistfulness to his sigh, as though he's imagining me still as the girl sitting on his lap, fiddling with the gears of the crossbows he's working on. "The vicar intends to take your power for himself once it has fully matured."

Like I'm some kind of incubator. I grimace. "Is that even possible?"

"He's determined to find out. He believes he was the one destined to be Valor Reborn, and you were a…mistake." There's a flash of an anger in his eyes that I've never associated with my usually soft-spoken and level-headed father.

"What makes him think he could, though?" I keep rounding back to that question. "Even if I am a 'mistake,' how could he take whatever power made my eyes gold and allows me to draw on the Font without a sigil?"

"Your scar," he says solemnly.

"What about it?" I press my hand against my chest.

"I'm not sure how it healed… But have you ever really looked at it?"

Looked at it? I can't escape it a second of my life. "Sure. Gnarled. Twisted. Spiderwebbed. Like I'm some kind of clay doll that cracked. Ugly—"

"Don't look at it with the eyes of society and their narrow ideas of beauty. Look at it objectively, Isola."

I frown, and my brows knit. What's he trying to get me to see? "Father, I know your instinct has always been to teach me through questions and probing, but now isn't the time for it."

"It's a sigil."

I inhale sharply and straighten. "A sigil… That's impossible." Now that I think carefully, it could look like one…

"It's one we've never seen before. Not even I know what it does. My only theory is that the Etherlight you summoned was so powerful that it scorched the sigil into your flesh."

"And the vicar knows this." It was his curates who patched me up, after all. They would've seen the jagged outlines of what transformed into my scar. A sigil wrought in blood—my blood.

"I've dedicated my life to trying to figure out what, exactly, it does. I've tried to stall Vicar Darius and throw him off course, but he has so many resources. There is only so much I can do, Isola. I might be the master artificer, but there are others who are good. Maybe not as good as me, but good enough to tell the vicar if they realized I was being intentionally obtuse." He sighs heavily.

Is that... Is that why he worked so hard to become the best artificer in Vinguard and place himself right next to the vicar as a high curate?

I throw my arms around him again, hugging him tightly. Father lets out a soft, surprised *oomph* but doesn't say anything more. He merely embraces me just as tight.

"The tinctures are designed to manage the flow of Etherlight within you. Even if your mother and I couldn't figure out what the sigil does, it does seem to increase your ability to draw on the Font. You were always inclined toward Etherlight, but after the attack, everything was different."

"And if you minimize the flow of Etherlight in me with a tincture, you postpone me drawing upon the Font without a sigil." Or, seemingly without a sigil, since we don't know what the one etched into my chest does. "So the vicar couldn't get what he wants," I finish, pulling away.

The tinctures weren't suppressing a dragon from within. They were suppressing my abilities. Maybe, all along, I had Valor's power—it just wasn't safe for me to manifest it. Because the second I did, the vicar would at last have what he wanted, and he'd no longer have any use for me. He'd steal this power and wash his hands of me.

"If all this is true, Father, why would you say I should give in to his demands now? Why would I draw Etherlight without a sigil, even if I can?"

"Time is running out. The vicar made you Valor Reborn, Isola. He can unmake you just as easily," he says. An objection buds within me, but I don't dare to speak it. The Mercy Knights listened to me in the sundering pits because they viewed me as Valor, didn't they? And if I can control the Mercy Knights...who has the real power here? "You must buy the rest of us time. We're close, Isola, to solving this. But your mother and I need a little bit longer."

"I thought you hated Mum?" I whisper.

"We might not have been the best partners romantically. But that doesn't mean we can't work together in other ways. I respect her more than you know."

"And you never believed I was actually Valor Reborn?" I go to relax my grip, but he doesn't, so we stay, every word whispered and hasty.

"No. I never believed you were Valor Reborn. But I believed that you needed to oblige the vicar to keep yourself and the rest of us safe while we figured out the best path. And you must oblige him for just a little longer, Isola. The Tribunal is almost over, and when it is finished—when you get into Mercy, everything will change."

What he's saying... It's like I've waited a lifetime to hear these words. Dreamed of this moment, never realizing he understands me so completely. Proof that he was on my side, not the vicar's. And now that I know, I feel foolish for believing anything else.

My father is mine, not the vicar's. And it's our whole family against that horrible man.

Without warning, the door opens, revealing the vicar, and the air in the room is suddenly colder and thinner.

"Good, you're awake." His eyes dart between me and my father. "A touching reunion."

"It is. But I also shared with my father what I uncovered in the Font."

"Good," he praises. "And how are you feeling? Are you still able to draw on Etherlight without a sigil?"

I glance at my father, and he holds my gaze steadily. I borrow his bravery and the conviction in his words. This is all part of the plan. Even if I don't know the full scope of what the plan is, I have faith in the love of my family.

I hold out my hand and find the connection with the Font easier than ever before. Etherlight flows through me, souring my stomach and making my head spin. I'm still exhausted, but I push through, ignoring the slimy sensation that coats the underside of my skin. I focus on the Etherlight flowing through me. The magic he demanded I bring forth during years of training. I never could before, but this time, a tiny flame appears in my empty palm. It dances in the vicar's eyes like a fire that could threaten to burn down all of Vinguard.

He inhales slowly, as though he could breathe in the raw power that I've collected. As though I'm offering him the greatest gift he could imagine.

He takes a few steps forward, staring only at the flame. I close my fist, extinguishing the fire, and his eyes flick to mine. The spark I saw earlier still gleams within them. His chest rises and falls slowly, as though he's forcing himself to breathe evenly to conceal the wild excitement that I see behind his facade.

I hope whatever it is my parents have schemed, whatever has given my mother a reason to disappear, will bring an end to this soon. There's less than one week now in the Tribunal.

Because whatever the vicar has planned for my power—I now know he's not going to stop at anything to take it.

46

After a few more hours of rest and a hot dinner, the inquisitors give me fresh clothes and blindfold me. They take me through back passages, not pulling the strip of fabric from my eyes until I'm in a familiar prayer room. Alone, I make my way back to Saipha's room.

"Isola!" Saipha throws her arms around me the moment I enter. I squeeze her tightly, but my gaze is over her shoulder, locked with Lucan's.

Are you all right? I mouth, not knowing how much he has shared with Saipha about the Font.

He nods with a slight smile and eyes as full of relief as the Font is filled with Etherlight.

"I was so worried about you," Saipha says as she pulls away.

"Me too." Lucan's voice is soft and deep. I barely avoid shifting uncomfortably.

"What happened? You were taken away by the vicar, and then Lucan was summoned. He said you went to pray before the Font?" Saipha looks between us.

"Something like that." I fill in broad strokes for Saipha, leaving out the way Lucan held me, even though I feel it over my whole body. I also leave out drawing Etherlight without a sigil and the details of my father's discussion. Even though I trust them, that feels like too dangerous a secret to share for now.

By the time I'm finished, I collapse onto the bed, exhaustion heavy in my bones. Saipha catches me up on the other supplicants' tests—no one was exposed as dragon cursed, but Cindel seemed to get in a competition with three others for who could pray the longest, holding up the rest—as I fall into a deep sleep.

The next morning, we head down together to the central atrium, hoping to find the refectory open. To our relief, we find more than enough food for all of us. The supplicants fill the room, eating in silence like it's the most serious task in the world, and after what we've been through, it probably is.

The odd silence, broken only by the sound of cutlery scraping against plates and occasional whispers, is interrupted as one curate and two Mercy Knights enter the hall. The knights have their hoods drawn like inquisitors. It sends a shiver of dread down my spine. What is it they plan to do that would warrant covering the majority of their faces?

Wearing a pitying smile, the curate crosses to Cindel. He ushers her off to the side, much to her apparent confusion. The rest of us don't even bother to hide our curiosity.

Without warning, a shrill shriek reverberates through the hall, echoing off its rough-hewn walls. Cindel covers her mouth with trembling fingers, standing up, wide-eyed. The curate gives a solemn nod.

"You're lying!" Tears begin to stream down her face.

Whatever the curate says is lost to our ears, but her tremors become almost violent. The curate continues to speak in hushed tones, but Cindel says nothing more. Horror has overtaken her, an expression all of us know too well.

I think part of me understands what's happening even before the curate leaves, the knights in tow. I don't say anything, because the right words are just beyond the realm of my conscious thought. Yet, somewhere in the back of my mind, I already know.

It isn't until Cindel turns her eyes toward me that it really begins to crystalize in the forefront. She stalks over, tears staining her flushed cheeks. Hands balled into fists.

"What is your problem?" Saipha says. I wish I could tell her not to speak, but it's too late.

"Nothing with you," Cindel says, her eyes sweeping over Saipha to me. I swear the room drops in temperature as her focus rests squarely on my face. If looks could kill, I wouldn't be breathing. She's always resented me for being Valor Reborn, but this is something different. Jealousy is one thing, annoyance another. This expression is pure hostility. "Why are you here, *Isola*?" She spits my name like venom.

"Excuse me?" I don't know what I was expecting, but it wasn't this.

"What's the point of you?" She's suddenly screaming, lunging for me. Lucan is on his feet, practically jumping over the table. Even Saipha is scrambling. But Cindel's faster, my vest balled in her fists. "What good are you if you can't keep this city safe? You're supposed to save us, right? That's your job as Valor Reborn? Then do it. *Do it!*" Spittle flies from her mouth, landing on my cheek. I nearly gag but control myself for fear of her reaction. Her eyes are wide and bloodshot, hands worryingly close to my throat.

"Cindel, that's enough." Saipha wedges herself between us, attempting to pry Cindel's hands off me.

Cindel grabs a knife from the table and thrusts. Saipha barely has a chance to dodge. But she manages, mostly. The knife still gouges her arm, but Saipha barely flinches.

I stare at the blood seeping through my best friend's sleeve, and rage, hot and sharp, fills me from head to toe.

Cindel brandishes the bloody blade at Saipha. "Stay out of this." My friend remains perfectly still, even as blood drips down her arm. "This has *nothing* to do with you. I only have business with her."

And then she turns the knife on me.

"What do you want, Cindel?" I try to sound as calm as possible, when inside, I'm anything but. She cut Saipha, and hate beats at my chest like dragon wings.

In my periphery, I see Lucan inching closer. He's no doubt calculating a move as well, and Cindel's crew sees it. They've formed up and are moving closer. The air itself feels like a bowstring pulled taut, chaos ready to be unleashed.

"I want you to do what you're supposed to do or stop giving us false hope. If you're the savior of this city, then save us." The knife clatters as Cindel drops it and lunges for me. Saipha and Lucan move at nearly the same time. I hold up a hand and stop them, not wanting this situation to escalate further. Cindel grips my shoulders. She's not trying to kill me. If she was, she wouldn't have dropped the knife and this whole situation would be unfolding very differently. "What good are you if you can't help us? Why are you even here?"

"Cindel, you're being ridiculous." Saipha, even wounded and clutching her arm, doesn't know when to quit. It's what's going to make her an exceptional knight...or get her killed.

But Cindel doesn't move. Neither do I. She stares down at me with such resentment, such pure and utter and all-consuming hatred. *They're questions I've asked myself*, I wish I could say. Followed up with, *I'm just as scared as you.*

"First Benj and then... And then... You should've saved her." Cindel's whispered words are sharper than a blade.

"What are you talking about?" Saipha looks between us, clearly confused.

"The other night on the roof. The dragons. She died. She's dead. *My mother is dead!*" My heart shatters when I hear it. I can only imagine the pain if I lost Mum. "If you had done what you were supposed to do as Valor Reborn—if you had finished these monsters off already—she would still be alive." She shakes me, her fingers digging in painfully.

"I'm sorry," is all I manage, and I know it's not enough.

"That's it? That's all you have to say to me? To all of us to answer for your crime of inaction?"

"The dragon attack wasn't Isola's fault," Lucan says.

"If she'd killed the Elder Dragon, as is her supposed destiny, it wouldn't have happened." Cindel's eyes narrow on me. "So, are you going to do it?"

"I'm going to try." It feels like a lie, even though it's not. I would end all of this in an instant, if I could.

"Try? That's it? *Pathetic*." She releases me, staring down with tired and desperate eyes. I don't move. "You're no Valor."

With that, Cindel leaves.

Immediately, murmurs rise. I move to Saipha. "Are you all right?"

"I'm fine. It's not as bad as it looks." Saipha's attention drifts to where Cindel left—where her lackeys are trailing behind. I'll give her one thing, the girl knows how to engender loyalty. "She... Her mother died?" I can tell from the tone of Saipha's voice that she's imagining her own parents. Every supplicant in this room knows the pain of loss in some form. There's no one in Vinguard who does not.

Saipha, Lucan, and I exchange startled glances as the copper box on the wall sparks to life.

"All supplicants are to report to the chapter house."

47

When we enter the chapter house, a Mercy Knight is leaning against the lectern, arms folded. His commanding presence draws every supplicant's attention as they file in. My throat tightens with apprehension as I lower myself onto the bench between Saipha and Lucan. Saipha leans close and whispers somewhat giddily, "That's Commander Anton Salvis. He's one of the ballista sharpshooters. His accuracy rate is seven for ten—from the air."

I let out a low whistle.

"Is that what you want to do, when you get into Mercy?" Lucan asks across me.

Saipha shakes her head. "I want to be on patrol. On top of the wall itself. In the thick of it, with nothing but my wits, a crossbow loaded with sigils, and my silver dagger."

"I am Commander Salvis," the knight announces, drawing our attention. A few excited whispers suggest Saipha isn't the only one aware of his reputation. "I have been a Mercy Knight for two decades, serving this city and upholding the Creed."

As he speaks, the scars on his face tug and pull. I suspect in those twenty years of service, he spent time on the wall, like Saipha dreams of. You don't get scars like that perched behind a ballista in a tower or Mercy Spire. The other supplicants are hanging on his every word. I glance from the corner of my eye to find Lucan staring expressionless at the knight, as if he's attending a Creed sermon.

"Who can tell me why we are called Mercy Knights?"

"To kill a dragon is to show Mercy to the man or woman who succumbed to the curse," Nelly answers. I notice they're sitting with Horowin and his group. Daisy is still at their side. *Good, I'm glad they found someone to stick with.*

Unlike the others from the Undercrust. My gaze shifts to them for a second. They've never managed to find their footing here, and they look it, huddled together, gaunt. Horowin didn't invite them into his group. I don't blame him. Welcoming in confirmed cowards who skirt the Creed's rules is a risk for all of us who are trying to prove we're playing by those same rules. But it's still hard to see. I'd invite them to be with Saipha and Lucan, if I wasn't so worried about just keeping the three of us alive.

Anton gives a sharp nod. "Humanity is precariously perched upon a precipice. Outside our walls, the scourge spreads. In the mountains above us, the dragons soar, hunting for more Etherlight to absorb into their bodies, removing it from the world so they can better spread Ethershade."

Saipha is enraptured. Lucan remains stoically focused ahead, but the side of his hand brushes against mine, nearly startling me out of my skin.

Our eyes meet. For a breath, we're the only two not paying attention to the lecture. We're the only two in the room.

I know. I'm with you, his expression seems to say. My lips part slightly. I remember the last time we were in this room, so intensely focused on each other. I can almost see motes of Ether gathering in the air between us. And then our time alone at the Font. How his skin felt against mine. My hand twitches, and I imagine reaching over and entwining my fingers with his.

Instead, I place my palms safely in my lap.

The knight continues speaking, and the whole world moves on, oblivious to the seconds we stole.

"Within Vinguard, it is essential for everyone to do their part. All in this last bastion of humanity have a place, and all are connected to the Font." His words are hard as steel. Gaze unflinching. "Mercy commanders will be at the final challenge. What do you think they will be looking for?"

"Fearlessness," Saipha says.

"Boldness."

"Competency with a crossbow."

There are more guesses, all along the same lines.

The knight raises his hands, and the supplicants fall silent. "All of these things, yes. But a Mercy Knight is also someone with the resourcefulness and understanding of Etherlight akin to an artificer—someone who can find unconventional solutions to problems. A person who holds as deep a reverence for our faith and history as a curate of the Creed. One who cares for the people and places around them with the attentiveness of a renewer—for there are many breaks that happen on the wall. Who holds reverence for our world like an Earthwarden. And yes, above all else, someone who possesses the unending desire to ruthlessly hunt dragons."

Anton drops his arms to his sides and stands a little taller. "To this end, Mercy is offering an opportunity for all of you to hone these skills."

"Much like up on the wall, where there are outposts with supplies in the various towers and turrets, as I am here with you now, the inquisitors are hiding supply caches throughout the monastery," he continues. "These caches hold tools, weapons, and other resources that will help you survive between now and the final test."

Survive. My chest tightens at the word.

"Finding these caches and utilizing the tools within is certain to impress the Mercy Knights serving as your inquisitors. But, keep in mind, as a gift and a test from Mercy, this will not come easy. The wall demands a steep price, and so too will the caches." Anton steps down from the stage, strolling through the benches as he finishes. "And, even with the right tools at your disposal, survival is never guaranteed."

I grit my teeth at the implication.

The moment he leaves, the room is abuzz with excitement. Saipha leaps to her feet with a clap of her hands. "We are going to find as many as we can."

"Challenge accepted," Lucan says with far less enthusiasm.

"I agree," I say, pushing to my feet.

We step out of the chapter house and into the passage that connects with the central atrium. We're about to head off and begin our search when we hear a shout echo to us:

"What's the meaning of this?"

"Was that Cindel?" Saipha murmurs.

"Can't be good if it was," I say.

"Let's see what it is now," Lucan suggests.

"If we must see Cindel, we must... But she's better ignored." Saipha gives us a small, conspiratorial grin, one I return. It feels good to smile; it feels like forever since we last joked together. Even when things were serious, Saipha used to always find a way to lighten things up.

Ever since we entered the monastery...there's been an increasing weight to her. A desperate seriousness. Or perhaps it's me who's changed. Maybe we both have. This place isn't exactly kind. I never imagined Mercy would be where we'd have an opportunity to relax, but I never imagined the Tribunal would be this nightmare, either. After it's over, I can only hope things go back more to the way they were between us.

We emerge into the atrium to find a small group of supplicants clustered around the entrance to the residence hall—which has been walled off. The atmosphere in the room is a complete change from the enthusiasm following the lecture.

"What now?" Saipha murmurs under her breath, the words filled with dread.

48

"Where are we supposed to sleep?" Daisy asks the inquisitors, who line the edges of the room. I'm amazed she still thinks they care.

The copper box springs to life in answer.

"As outlined in the lecture from Commander Salvis, there are supplies now spread across the monastery." It's the prelate. "There are enough supplies for approximately five supplicants to live *very* comfortably until the next test. Or enough for fifteen supplicants to sustain without issue. Or…should you all share the supplies evenly and ration them well, for all supplicants to at least survive."

"All of us to *at least* survive," Lucan says skeptically. "They say that like it's not a given."

"After the last—" I pause, thinking. "What are we at? Eighteen days?"

"Seventeen, I think?" Saipha corrects, but she doesn't sound sure, either. Time became blurry during the depths of hunger.

"Either way, I doubt it is enough for the three or four days we have remaining. Especially not going into it as weak as we all are." It occurs to me that the remnants of the pantry we managed to build is still up in Saipha's room. Which is now blocked off. I wonder if they'll find it hidden in her lockbox. I assume they will…which means they'll figure out we have a way into the kitchens, so I doubt we'll be able to get in that way again.

The other supplicants are already beginning to cast wary, suspicious looks at one another. Outright animosity is beginning to fill the air like the sour aroma from green dragon acid. First, they took our safety by making us earn the keys to our rooms. Then they took our food away. Now it looks like they're taking both after just one good meal, and I can't help wondering why they're focusing so much on our resources.

The Creed teaches that dragon cursed are those more susceptible to Ethershade, and the dragon is brought forth when Ethershade builds up enough in someone's body to trigger the transformation. By their logic, the sundering pits made sense—expose us to Ethershade to see if anyone reaches saturation. I can make sense of the Font in their minds, to see if the Ethershade revolted and drew forth like a protective mechanism against the Etherlight.

Protective. If they think the transformation can happen to protect the host body, then it would also happen to save someone from starvation or exposure. It seems rational based on the Creed's teachings. But the word sticks on my mind like a crossbow bolt to a target.

I am my mother's daughter, and I don't believe the dragons are beings of Ethershade. I believe they're beings of Etherlight. And Etherlight is the force of life. Which means *it would make sense if it did protect.*

My heart thunders in my chest as my mind races. But, then, if Etherlight is what fuels the transformation, and it's a survival mechanism, why did the yellow dragon on the rooftop almost seem like it was wavering from mindless beast to sentient in the presence of more Etherlight as I drew it between us? Wouldn't the Etherlight just make it stronger?

Mum could help me figure this out. As soon as I'm out of here, I'm sharing this theory with her. It's not quite there. I'm missing something...something important. But I'm on the right track. I know it as clearly as I can now feel the flow of Etherlight in me.

I turn to Lucan on instinct to tell him, and the movement startles me. *I turned to Lucan, not Saipha.* All my life, I've been turning to my best friend, my only confidant—and it's not that I wouldn't want to tell her, I do. But, for the first time ever, I have someone else to turn to. The number of people I can trust has doubled.

Lucan's expression washes all the racing thoughts from my mind like a storm. He looks borderline murderous.

"I suspected something was coming, but not this. This could've been a challenging exercise to find supply caches, not a fight for our lives—pitted against each other." Lucan throws an inquisitor a not-so-subtle glare. If the inquisitor notices, he doesn't react.

"Breathing in Vinguard means fighting for your life." I paraphrase the familiar refrain from those who've survived the Tribunal. My stomach twists painfully. Is this what they all must think to justify what was done to them, what's being done to their children?

"We should find a place to claim as our own. Somewhere safe and warm." Saipha wraps her arms around herself, rubbing them. "Then we can find supplies and hunt for the caches. Maybe the little shed in the greenhouse?"

"Everyone will be going there." Lucan's tone suggests he's not interested in even trying that option.

"The study rooms, then?" Saipha suggests.

"We need somewhere that isn't so obvious." Lucan casts a wary gaze toward Cindel and her group. They all shoot us daggers with their eyes before trudging off. "We won't sleep at night if we feel like we'll be jumped any second."

"We can take rotations like before," she counters. "We just need something to barricade a door with."

I'm silent as they speak, thoughts whirring again but in a totally different way. *Safe.* Saipha's choice of words sticks with me. *A safe hiding place is behind the crossbow rack.* Callon's first tip was essential. Maybe this one will be, too.

"Let's go to the artificer tower," I say low so only Saipha and Lucan can hear. Others are shuffling toward the different areas of the monastery, casting wary looks at other supplicants.

There's a tautness in the air, like a bow being pulled back. We're all quivering, waiting to shoot in different directions.

And when the first person begins to run, we all do.

After slowly starving us, the inquisitors have successfully

conditioned us to expect the worst. Elbows are thrown, people are pushed down the stairs. I pull Saipha and Lucan into a side hall, wanting to get out of the main flow as quickly as possible. The fact that Cindel wandered off first and I now don't know where she is fills my veins with dread.

We take the back passages that loop along the outer walls of the various towers and wings that compose the monastery. It's a longer route to get there, but it's safer.

"Why the artificer tower?" Lucan asks. "You have something in mind. I can tell."

"A hunch," I say between heavy breaths as we start on the final length of stairs. From my search on the first day, I remember the various rooms in this tower—one had the supplies to make crossbows. It's the only place I can think of that might have a crossbow rack.

My stomach sinks when we enter the room. There are no bows at all, just shelves. I scan once and then scan again. The first clue Callon gave was precisely right—even if they changed something, like stair colors, the fundamental guidelines have been helpful. I refuse to give up so easily.

I press my lips together and focus, knowing our lives depend on figuring this out. Did they move the rack, or is there another meaning to what he said? Either is possible.

"What are we looking for?" Lucan steps in front of me, stopping me in my tracks. I hadn't even realized I'd been pacing between the shelves. "Tell us so we can help you."

"A crossbow rack," I say.

"A crossbow rack?" Saipha repeats. "The only place that has enough weapons to warrant a rack is the training area, but now that I think about it, the bows are all on hooks."

"I know...that's why I came here, hoping there might be a rack next to where you could make one."

"I know where one is," Lucan blurts.

"You do?" I turn at the same time as Saipha, my voice pitching up with excitement.

"I saw one when I was looking for a quiet place to practice with the sigil I discovered inside the dragon statue that first night. This way." Lucan leads us out of the room and back down the stairs. He takes another quiet, dimly lit hallway and comes to a stop before a rack for a single crossbow mounted on the wall. "Here. Is this what you're looking for?"

A replica of a crossbow has been cast completely in steel. A wide wooden panel surrounds it, embellished with carvings of flying dragons impaled with bolts. A steel placard is mounted at the top. It reads, *In honor of the first Mercy Kill.*

"It hardly qualifies as a rack." The disappointment is obvious in my voice.

"But technically it is," Lucan points out.

"How is this going to help us?" Saipha glances over her shoulder and down the hall. "At any second, someone could sneak up and trounce us. We need more than a decorative crossbow—we need the real deal, at the very least."

"I'm not looking to fight people," I say.

"I'll fight if that's what it takes..." Saipha murmurs, her voice trailing off.

I focus on the silvered crossbow. The weapon is firmly welded to the wooden panel. But the panel itself doesn't have obvious hooks, nails, or screws attaching it to the wall. *Curious...* Gripping it, I give it a firm tug. It doesn't budge.

"It's just a replica. What good will it do?" Saipha is being pushy today. Not that I blame her. More days of starving and fearing other supplicants is hardly appealing.

Lucan inspects the crossbow and its mount. "Try turning it."

I twist, and the crossbow swings easily on a hidden pivot. There's a click deep in the wall. I pull, and the whole placard swings open like a door, revealing a hidden room.

"What the..." Saipha whispers. "How did you know this was here?" She grabs my shoulder and half-turns me, looking me dead in the eyes. "Isola, are you *cheating*?"

49

I freeze, searching for a plausible excuse for how I knew this was here. My friend inspects me. She knows me too well. She'll see through any lie.

"First the food. Now this. Is the vicar giving you an advantage?" she asks, a frown tugging on her lips.

I'm caught between a convenient excuse and a desperate desire to never be seen as relying on that man—but I can't betray Callon. "Yes." The word is as acrid as scourge on my tongue.

"Great. Another thing you couldn't trust me with." Saipha leans away, regarding me with a wary expression.

A flash of pain ignites in my chest. "It's not what you think."

Her gaze darts to Lucan. Ignoring me, she asks him, "Did you know?"

Lucan shakes his head.

"I thought better of both you and the vicar," she says cooly.

"Excuse me?" I say, head spinning.

"The Tribunal is sacred. The vicar has said as much himself."

"Since when do you care about whether or not what the Creed says is sacred?" It's like I don't even recognize her.

"Since when are you willing to take the easy way out?" she fires back. "The Isola I knew didn't want to be handed anything, especially not by the Creed and the vicar. She wanted to earn her rank and title. She was willing to lie and sneak if that's what it took to get in the wall on her own so she could practice for Mercy. Now you're accepting the vicar's help to cheat?" Saipha looks away with a shudder.

I need to fix this. Now. "That's exactly what I did! I got the vicar to mess up and say something he shouldn't."

That pauses her, and I seize my opening. I hate compounding my lies, but I've no other choice. I can't bear to lose my friend.

"I probed and pushed him, Saipha. It's no different than me sneaking into the Creed's library. I wasn't sure if what he told me would even be helpful—or if I read between the lines correctly. But the first thing was helpful. And I think this will be, too."

She chews on this, and I fight holding my breath—fight looking even guiltier.

"Can we talk about this inside?" Lucan gestures toward the opening in the middle of the wall that the crossbow plaque revealed. "Before someone sees the only safe spot we have?"

Saipha gives me a hard look, and for a second I really think she's going to refuse to enter. But, with a sigh, she steps through the opening behind the placard. Lucan meets my eyes and gestures for me to go ahead. At least he doesn't look mad at me…

We close the trick door and make a quick inspection of the room. It appears to be another workshop of some kind. Four open doorways line one main room—two workshops, a bathroom, a laboratory that will serve well as a kitchen. To my relief, I walk over and note it has a running tap. A thick blanket of dust covers all the surfaces, casting everything in a gauzy hue.

"It looks like no one has been in here for a long time," Lucan muses.

"That means no one else knows about it," I say, feeling confident in this at least. "Perfect place to hole up."

"And probably somewhere we're not supposed to be," Saipha murmurs. "Maybe the vicar was testing you to see if you'd cheat and this is a trap."

"There're lots of hidden pathways and rooms throughout the monastery that they only seem to leverage when it's necessary. Maybe they didn't need it this year," I say. "I don't think the vicar knew what I was doing."

Saipha frowns. "Or maybe the inquisitors will come in during the middle of the night and give us hell for being here?"

"It doesn't matter where we go. If the inquisitors want to give us hell, they will." I plant my feet and cross my arms. "This is where I'm staying tonight—and every night we can between now and the next test. I hope you both stay, too. We're stronger together, and this place is hidden—at least from other supplicants. We can be safe here, and all get a good night's sleep without having to take rounds of someone keeping watch."

"I'm in," Lucan says without hesitation.

We both look to Saipha, who turns her attention from us to the window, sighing heavily. "You're sure, Isola?"

"I am."

"Then I trust you." Her words nearly make me tear up. "It's definitely better than sleeping in the open."

I smile, relieved she came around, but not surprised—Saipha always has moved on from things quickly once she understands them. "It'll all be all right."

"I hope so." She rubs her eyes. "Sorry for being snippy, I'm just…tired."

I cross to her and rest a hand on her shoulder. "It's been a long day—many long days—for all of us. It's not like one good meal is going to fix it. How about Lucan and I go and do an initial scout to see if we can find one of the supply caches left by the inquisitors? You take stock here. Maybe clean up a bit?" I imagine simple, mindless tasks will help her calm down. I never realized how much Saipha was the sort of individual who needed a consistent, safe space until she didn't have one. I suppose we're all learning things about others and ourselves in here.

"You're sure you won't need my help?" Her protest is weak. She's never looked frailer.

"Someone should stay to stake our claim, just in case other supplicants manage to find this place."

"That's not a bad idea." She doesn't put up much of a fight. "I'll see what I can do to clean up here."

I toss her a smile, and Lucan and I head out, shutting the panel behind us. With little more conversation than a nod, we strike out. It's the same plan as last time—see what we can find in the obvious places and then expand our search from there. Lucan heads for the greenhouses, still our resident expert on the plants.

I search high and low for a cache left by the inquisitors. But my heart sinks with every corner turned, every shelf looked behind, every piece of furniture peered under. The other supplicants I run into look just as frustrated as me as the hours drag on. Wherever these things are, they're well hidden.

Dragging my feet, I make my way back to our base with some meager supplies I decided to gather from the artificer workshops. Cheesecloth, a hammer, some twine... It probably won't be very useful, but I couldn't bear coming back empty-handed.

With a heavy sigh, I'm about to turn the crossbow when I hear the familiar scrape of boots from down the hall. *I know him by the sound of his gait.* And something about that has me fighting a smile.

"Lucan—" The words are instantly lost. He's holding a drawstring bag stamped with the image of a sword with a dragon curled around it. *Mercy's seal.*

My heart jumps into my throat, and I rush to him. "Where did you find that?"

"It was strung up in the rafters above the second floor of the library. I had to climb the shelves and then jump into the beams to get it." Way over my head, and something only a really tall person might be able to get to.

"The keys on the first day were all hidden in places related to dragons... Maybe the caches are all somewhere high—to mirror Mercy Knights on the wall?" I muse aloud.

"Something to check tomorrow. We should get this inside and wait out the night," he says, but I don't miss the note of approval at my deduction.

We pull open the hidden door to find Saipha's organized the shelves with items she found in the main room and adjoining areas.

"You got one!" Saipha jumps up from one of the chairs around the central table.

"Lucan did," I say.

"Isola helped," he lies and sets the bag on the table and sits.

I glance over at Lucan as he begins to unpack the bag, and something deep in my chest pinches as I sit next to him. Not for the first time, I'm grateful Lucan is my ally. *Our* ally. Just his presence really does make everything feel a bit better.

A few flat loaves of bread and bean cake wrapped in wax vellum are in the muslin bag tied with a ribbon that's *almost* the same shade of red as the robes the curates wear. I doubt they'd waste real dragon's blood on ribbon for the Tribunal.

I take in the room with our added supplies. "Not a lot of creature comforts, but it's sheltered, warm"—just as Callon promised and Saipha wanted—"and hidden."

"We stay here as long as we can," Lucan agrees.

"I can go out tomorrow to look for more supplies," Saipha offers. "I doubt they'll be restocking the bags, so we'll want to get as many as we can upfront."

"Good idea," I agree. Before I can tell her my theory on where they've been hidden, Saipha continues.

"And I can check in any dragon-focused areas, since Isola freezes at the sight of them, and make sure nothing is hidden in those spots—like they did with the keys," she says and stands.

Her words land like a punch to the gut, and my theory is lost. I glance to the window at the far end of the room. Even if Saipha didn't mean to wound me with the remark, my eyes sting. *I've been doing better*, I want to object. I stood up to that dragon on the rooftop, after all.

"Sounds good," I murmur instead. I'll tell her about the caches being in high places in the morning.

Saipha yawns. "Anyone object to me taking that space?" She points to the interior workshop. Lucan and I both shake our heads, and she shuffles to the room, shutting the door behind her.

Lucan and I are left alone, side by side at the table. Suddenly, the whole room feels much smaller. He's close enough that I can hear him slowly inhale, gathering air like Etherlight. I find myself breathing in time with him.

"Don't let what she said bother you," Lucan says quietly. "You're perfectly capable of hunting for resources."

"It's true that I'm lacking in some areas." I drag my nail along the ridge at the table's edge, picking out remnants of long-forgotten dust.

"Not as much as you think."

My attention returns to his, and I settle my chin in my palm, studying him. "Careful, Lucan, or you might give me an inflated ego."

"Inflating the ego of the woman who's hailed as Valor Reborn? Impossible. Your ego is already as big as it gets." His eyes flash with amusement in the evening sunbeams cutting through the slim window.

I laugh. "Now that's how I'm sure you don't know anything about me." The words are hollow now. More like a playful echo of things that I once meant.

"I'd like to think I know much more than you give me credit for." He sounds genuinely offended. Somehow it makes him even more endearing that he missed my joking.

I play along. "Oh?"

"Yes," he insists.

"Like what?"

Lucan leans forward, and somehow, an already small room is now breathlessly tight. The joking leaves me, and in its place is nothing but coiled tension. He's been this close to me before, but it feels…different now. He feels like a man I've never met.

Someone I'm not certain I can trust myself around.

"I've learned that you're quite clever." Lucan answers my question. "That's obvious to anyone remotely paying attention." I allow myself to be a bit arrogant for the sake of provoking him. The brief narrowing of his eyes makes it worth it.

"You're actually a really good shot with a crossbow."

"I'm offended by the use of 'actually.'" I inspect my nails.

He laughs softly. "You *actually* have a bit of a sweet tooth."

"Guilty."

"You have a complicated relationship with your father."

I sit up straighter, muscles tensing, surprised he'd noticed such a personal thing. "What makes you think I have a 'complicated' relationship with my father?" The last time we spoke was good. But, before that, Lucan's right.

Lucan shrugs. "You love him, and he loves you. That isn't in question, but I think beyond that, it's complicated."

"You could say that about a lot of people." I pull away, leaning back in my chair and catching my breath in the space I've reclaimed from him.

Lucan mirrors my movements yet again, sitting back and taking a deep breath, as if showing he's aware of the tension he's created. "But it hits you differently to lack that relationship with him. You want it—something like what you have with your mom. But you can't seem to find it."

"What makes you so sure about that?" I cross my arms over my chest. He's spot-on, frustratingly, and I want to know how. *Well, spot-on before the last talk with my father*, but I didn't tell him or Saipha all the details of that.

Eyes still on mine, he says, "I saw your expression when your father turned you over to the vicar for training. The way you looked back at him in betrayal as you walked away. His beaming pride that never quite seemed to touch you." I stare down at the table, throat tight with emotion. "I also saw how he always deferred to the vicar, and how every platitude killed you inside." Lucan's words are gentle, as if he knows how delicate the topic is. That instinct of his is right. "He's enamored with you being Valor Reborn, and that drives a wedge between you two."

His words make my skin feel tight. They remind me of how just one productive conversation and good intentions can't completely wipe away years of complicated feelings. Even if I want them to.

I stand and cross to the window, leaning against one side of the narrow opening to the outside world. Even with the iron-barred glass, I can peer through and catch a glimpse of Vinguard and the massive wall that perpetually looms beyond. *My world.*

It suddenly seems so small, and a part of me yearns for something more. Something beyond…*this.*

"I would've said you were completely right, if you'd told me this a couple of days ago," I murmur, thinking of the last time I saw my father. There's so much I never understood in how and why he and Mum acted as they did.

"But not now?" Lucan stands as well, crossing to lean against the other side of the window. It's narrow enough that we're mere inches apart, which causes my body to buzz with energy, like every time we're close.

"I feel as though I'm beginning to understand my parents," I say. "There're so many layers to them, to our relationship… Ones I'm just beginning to understand."

He considers this a moment. "It's difficult when you're several people at once, isn't it? When you have different truths depending on who you're with."

I blink up at him in stunned silence. He has an ability to understand my situation as though he has lived it himself. Though I suppose he has, having navigated a life around the vicar, the Creed, and how his position impacts how Vinguard views him.

"Sometimes I wonder if it wouldn't be better to just..." I shift my gaze to stare out at the wall beyond the window, chest aching with longing for something always out of reach.

"Just?" he presses.

"Just live as we want." I whisper the confession. "If that means the scourge or the dragons ultimately get us, then so be it. At least we're not spending our lives tested, fenced in, and cowering. At least we're not living lies."

"Is that what you want?" His question is sincere enough that I realize how long it's been since anyone asked, *truly* asked, what I want, and wanted to hear an honest answer and not just what I've been taught to say. I think the last person was Mum. But even she, after a point, stopped asking.

"I want to stop the scourge," I answer.

"By going to Mercy and killing dragons."

I study him. My pulse quickens as I wonder if I should say more. Any whispers that Valor Reborn doesn't want to be a Mercy Knight and slay dragons mindlessly would be considered absurd and an affront to the Creed.

He studies me like I'm one of the heavy scrolls the curates read for hours on end. "Will you really be content living by their rules for the rest of your life?"

"Of course." I shrug and look away, hoping to end the conversation.

He says nothing for what feels like forever, never taking his eyes off me. My skin flares hot, and I force myself to not fidget. It feels as if he's seeing right through my skin, beneath my scars, straight into my heart.

"You're lying," he says, finally.

My chin jerks back in his direction, brows furrowing. I almost instantly regret it. It's like I'm about to shatter with one look from him. I barely manage an, "Excuse me?"

"You think I don't see it?" He pauses. "You want more than being a Mercy Knight—than being Valor Reborn."

I could deny it. I *should* deny it.

"Isola." His voice is soft. "Trust me, like I trust you."

The words hang in the air between us as I stare into his eyes. I want to trust him, and every instinct in me pushes me to, but a lifetime of guardedness and deception is hard to overcome.

"We're more alike than you think," he says.

"I don't want to kill dragons," I confess.

His eyes widen.

"I don't think killing them is the way to stop the scourge," I say.

"Then why go to Mercy?"

"Because I'm 'Valor Reborn,' and going there will keep me and my family safe."

"So you don't want to kill dragons," he repeats like he's trying to make sense of it.

"If I *had to*, I suppose I would." In a way, I already have, six years ago. But it doesn't feel like it counts—like nothing about that day was real. "But I don't *want* to. I'm so weary of bloodshed and struggle. It shouldn't have to be like this for any of us. There must be a better life than this. I don't think a scourge of death will be solved with more death. I don't think the solution to a curse we don't even understand is killing our fellow citizens."

His eyes shine in the fading light, and his tone is thoughtful. "It does strike me as noteworthy that you, out of all people, are the one who should be destined for Mercy...a woman with no interest in killing dragons."

"Do you think me lesser for that?"

"I should."

"But do you?" I press, not entirely sure why this means so much to me. My heart thunders in my chest as I bite my lip, wait for his answer.

"Not in the slightest. If anything, it makes me admire you more. It requires a lot of bravery to go against what you're taught and told—to venture from the path others have set for you."

His words immediately settle the unease in my shoulders.

But then he adds, "Though Vinguard isn't a place where rebellion does particularly well."

And I stiffen. Is that where my thoughts are leading me? Rebellion?

He stares out the window, over the city, gaze unfocused. It gives me an opportunity to study his profile...the strong bridge of his nose, the fullness of his lips and how they round into the pronounced curve of his chin. The setting sun highlights it all in a fiery orange, and for a moment, I find it hard to breathe. The golden outlines make me think of him at the Font, and my knees nearly give out at the memory.

Vinguard isn't a place... My body feels like it's lit up with Ether, every inch of me heated and alive. *What is wrong with me?* I've never been this distracted by...anyone.

He turns back to me and smiles—not smirks, or grins, or coyly regards me—just...smiles with pure fondness. The same fiery intensity that lights up the sky shines in his eyes. As if they are burning. As if that fire could incinerate me to the point there's nothing left but ash. That same heat that threatened to burn me alive when we were just outside the Font. His hands all over me, holding me up, pressing me into his warmth.

Part of me feels I should be afraid. Terrified, even. My heart is racing...yet it's not from fear.

Touch me, a voice within me whispers; it is entirely my own, yet a voice I've never heard before. It's so sudden and unbidden, it freezes me in place. It's confident. The demand of a woman grown, with desires and needs. *I want him to touch me*, and the second I realize it—admit it—I want it so bad, I ache all over. I want our clothes to be so thin they might as well be nothing. I want to feel my skin fusing with his again.

Fear immediately follows the revelation. But it's not him that I'm afraid of. It's me and what I want. Things I've never wanted before. Things I barely have names for.

Even though this voice of mine is a stranger to me, even though he cannot hear it, it's as if he responds to it. His hands twitch. I can imagine him reaching for me. I can feel the pull of his grip on my hips. Imagine the taste of his lips on mine.

Lucan shifts away from the window, and my heart pounds even

harder. If it keeps beating at this speed, it's going to stop completely.

"You're afraid."

"How can you tell?"

Lucan lifts a hand, and I'm completely undone. There's nothing else in the world but him and this singular movement. I know his touch is coming before it does, and yet it still ignites my entire body when just a few of his fingertips trace my jawline. His thumb rises over my chin, brushing against my lips ever so delicately. All his focus is consumed by me.

"It's your lower lip." His voice has dropped to a whisper, as if it's hard for him to speak, too. "It quivers when you're unsure or afraid. You try so hard to hide it. I don't even know if you realize that you bite it half the time." At the mention of me biting my lips, he licks his own. Never has a movement so small demanded so much attention, nearly to the point of obsession. "What are you afraid of right now?" he murmurs, eyes still locked on my mouth.

I feel like I'm melting. That I might explode like the Font, sending golden stars everywhere. "All of it," I say. "Dragons, the Tribunal, failure, death." His steady gaze never wavers as I fight to keep my breathing even. "But in this moment..." I continue, because I feel like if I stop now, I might never say it again. The words fight their way up from deep inside. "I think...I'm most afraid of you."

"Of me?" Lucan sounds genuinely surprised.

"I don't know what to believe when it comes to you," I admit. My breaths are shallow, chest barely rising and falling. It feels as though the leather and cloth around my breasts have further constricted. Tight enough that all I want is release. Even my heart flutters, but, for once, it feels good. Exciting. I'm utterly lost, and I've no interest in being found.

"What do you want to believe?" he whispers.

"That, no matter what, you won't hurt me—that you're safe." If he were to betray me—hurt me when he's the first person I've ever dared to feel like this around? It would be too much to bear.

His brows furrow, and a shadow passes over his eyes. "I cannot promise I won't hurt you, Isola." The words drive a chill down my spine. "Because I know I already have. I know the person I am, and it's someone who will inevitably hurt you again." His eyes never leave mine. "But I can make you another vow, instead: I will never tire of trying to be worthy of your forgiveness. Even if it takes a hundred years. Even if you ask for me to be your weapon and reduce cities to ash and ruin in your name. Even if it kills me. Were you to ask for my destruction, I would hand you a blade and beg for Mercy."

I am breathless. Staggered. Trapped by his eyes and words and the heat that perpetually radiates off him and holds me ensnared.

We both stand at the precipice of the point of no return. *Who's going to break first?* Is the question that hovers in the air. *Who will give in? Who's weaker? Or perhaps that's not it; perhaps it's who's stronger? Braver?*

He leans forward. I don't move away. My lids become heavy as his hand slides up my jaw, cupping my cheek. The pads of his fingers draw me in closer.

Everything within me wars. Where we are. Who we are. His warnings. How much I still feel like I don't know about him. The fact that all of this is likely nothing more than desperation—wanting to be touched, for once in my life. To be made flesh and blood after years of veneration from afar by the masses. Desperation to feel something among so much death and fear.

Even if I can logic through every desire enough that I could pull away from him, I find that I don't care. *I want him.* I want *this*.

I want to feel his mouth on mine. To have him pull me to him as roughly or as gently as he likes. For so much of my life, I've had to play the part of someone who's strong and in control. Just this once, I want to know what it would feel like to surrender.

"Isola." My name is nothing more than a breath. My own hitches, as he's close enough for me to feel his warmth on my cheeks.

My eyes are nearly closed. "Say it again."

"*Isola.*" His grip tenses, as if he, too, can't decide if he wants to be tender or tear me apart.

Without warning...Lucan releases me. I sway on my feet.

He turns away, not even looking at me. I'm left standing in the faded sunlight with limp, heavy arms. The constriction around my chest vanishes, and my breaths come too quickly, making words difficult.

"What—"

"I can't," he interrupts. "Not with you."

"Not with *me*?" His words hit like a volley of blows, my body aching as if the vicar has tried to coax Ether from me again. My voice comes out hoarse and thin. "What does that mean?"

His back is to me, so I can't even see his face, but his shoulders are stiff and his fists balled at his sides. "I can't," he repeats, as if that's somehow an answer. As if it's the only explanation I should need. "Good night, Isola."

Before I can get in another word, he strides to a side room, giving me the workshop, closing the door behind him. I imagine that if it had a lock, I would hear it engage.

And I'm left just standing here...

Not with *me*. Meaning he'd want it with anyone else, *from* anyone else. How untouchable, undesirable must I be to not even be worth kissing when at any second either of us could die?

I flex my fingers and relax them, then rub the violently aching scar in the center of my chest. I pace to his door, nearly throwing it open, nearly demanding he just kiss me once to be done with it.

I was ready to give you my first kiss! I nearly scream.

Instead, I storm away, disgusted by my desperation for a man who's made his feelings clear.

Back at the window, I stare out at the fading light but can find no comfort in it. Nothing is going to calm me. Not here, not now.

Unable to take the atmosphere of the room for a moment longer, I cross to the door. With a deep breath and a wave of forced conviction, I push the open door to submit myself to the nighttime hallways of the monastery—because nothing out there can hurt me half as much as what happened right here.

51

The monastery feels different tonight. Or maybe *I'm* the one who's different.

I don't walk. I *stalk*. I move fearlessly through the darkened passageways and rooms, almost inviting the inquisitors or anyone else to challenge me, and wishing someone would. Just to give me an outlet for all this frustration. And yet no one bites.

Somehow, this makes me even more agitated.

I stop in the middle of the library and barely suppress a groan of frustration. I know there are other supplicants who've taken residence in the study halls on the second floor. I'm sure there are people watching me right now, yet none of them engage.

An inquisitor observes me from the archway that leads to the central atrium, but he doesn't move. I'm sure this is the start of some new game that will play out over the coming days before the final challenge.

A game I'm already tired of.

I shoot the man a glare and turn. Challenging an inquisitor? I'm not thinking straight. *Pull yourself together.* This is about survival, not hurt feelings. I place my hand over my sternum, to quell not the itch, but the ache deep in my chest.

I should return to the safety of our base.

"*Pssst.*"

The sound comes from the mezzanine off the library. Cindel leans with her arms draped over the railing. Of course, out of everyone I might stumble into, it would be her. *I was looking for someone to give me a challenge.* We lock eyes. She gives me a come-hither motion with a curl of her finger.

Despite my misgivings, my curiosity is too great—or my self-preservation is still too low—to turn down the invitation, and I make my way upstairs. She's hardly moved when I arrive. It's only as I approach that she straightens away from the railing, leaning her hip against it. I can make out two other figures in the shadows of the shelves behind her; I don't get any closer.

"Out for a stroll?" she asks, as if this is a perfectly normal interaction.

I shrug. "Something like that."

"It's fortuitous. I've been meaning to talk to you."

"Have you?" My tone is dry and uninterested. I cross my arms and tap my foot, trying to press her to tell me whatever it is she has to say.

"I wanted to apologize for how I acted after the Font." She grips the railing harder, as though bracing herself. I see the slight tilt in her body as she leans back—away from the idea of apologizing to me. It's only a flash of tiny movements, but I don't miss any of them. "I wasn't in my right mind."

A pang of sympathy has my muscles relaxing slightly. "It's all right. I understand. Consider your apology accepted." I turn to leave.

But she stops me, pushing off the railing. "You don't believe me."

I regard her warily but say nothing.

Cindel smiles. It's as bitter as vinegar. "I have something I want to give you, a gesture of goodwill."

"Go on." Every part of me is still on guard. But grief can change people. Especially grief as profound as losing a parent.

"I discovered a cache. I'm going to let you have it."

"I don't believe you," I blurt.

That bitter smile presses thinner. "I had a feeling you'd say that. Fine, I want half of what's inside, and I'm too much of a coward to get it. But *you* could." Cindel acting in her own interest, I do believe. And if my theory is right about where they've placed the caches, it would be challenging to get to.

"Why have me do it? Why not one of your"—I almost say *lackeys*—"friends?"

She gives a soft snort, as though she doesn't see them as such. "They're too scared, too. But I thought Valor Reborn would be brave enough."

She has me. I either back down and look like a coward, like I'm not Valor Reborn—I can feel the eyes of the inquisitor in the archway below on me—or I follow her into what feels very much like a trap. I glance at the man in the archway. His hooded face is definitely turned our way.

Damn. He's going to know if I back down, and it'll get to the vicar. My father's warnings about obliging Vicar Darius right now more than ever ring in my ears.

Although...there is the slight possibility that Cindel is sincere. One more cache might be all we need. Then we wouldn't have to search for anything else. We could hole up in our little room and play games and tell stories for three days. I'd do anything to see my best friend at ease again.

I suppose it doesn't hurt to look, I think before getting swept away in the fantasy of an easy few days before the final test. "Show me."

"This way." She pushes away from the railing and turns.

I fall into step after her, her two lackeys behind me. I'm very aware of their presence, my guard all the way up. The shadows of the monastery completely envelop us as we leave the faint light of the library.

There are no signs of life around us, even though I know that supplicants and inquisitors are there. Cindel leads us through the corridors, up into the artificer tower. For a second, I think she's going straight for our hiding spot, but she turns into another workshop.

As we enter, I have the distinct sensation of eyes upon me. I glance over my shoulder, past the lackeys, and into the corners were the shadows cling. No one is there.

"It's just out here..." Cindel says, guiding us around a shelf of tools to a narrow window with wind hissing through it. The wall around the window frame is pockmarked with the holes left behind by nails. A tarp that I can only assume had been blocking the opening a short time ago is crumpled on the floor. "Can you see it?" She stands off to the side and points.

I hesitate but ultimately step forward, keeping my hand on the window frame in case she'd dare to give me a shove. There is a narrow ledge outside that runs along the side of the very top of the monastery. Its width is barely the length of my foot. To the right, in the direction that Cindel pointed, is a muslin bag strung up by crimson ribbons that hold it closed. It sways in the wind, hanging from one of the buttresses that prop up the outside of the monastery, showing off its Mercy seal as it rotates. From here, it certainly has the same look of what Lucan found earlier, though it's hard to be sure in the darkness. It hangs over a wider platform, but to get there one would need to side-step on one of the narrowest ledges I've ever seen.

"See why we were all too scared to get it?" Cindel whispers near my ear. She moved closer while I was distracted. Closer than I'd like her to be, and I barely resist the urge to shove her away. "But we all agreed that whatever it is must be very special. If it wasn't, why would they put it somewhere that inaccessible?"

"You raise a good point," I admit. "Which is why I'll come back in the morning to get it." Along with Lucan and Saipha.

"In the morning?" She sounds aghast. "Why would you wait that long?"

"It's hardly safe for me to go outside in the middle of the night."

"Mercy Knights thrive in the night." She smiles thinly.

"Mercy Knights have a wall much thicker than the sole of their boots to patrol."

"You're Valor Reborn, the hope of Vinguard. Surely *this* doesn't intimidate you."

She's trying to pressure me into a corner again, but there's no inquisitor around, and I don't care enough about what Cindel actually thinks of me, so it won't work. Besides, when I glance at the narrow ledge, my whole body tenses, rejecting the notion. But when I bring my gaze back to her, there's something almost…hopeful about her stare. As though she really wants to see me do it.

Then, as if disgusted with herself, she shakes her head and steps away. "Well, if you find the courage, don't forget you owe me half—a finder's fee." She points back at me, now a few paces from the door, collecting Mikel and the other guy whose name I never bothered learning. "I'll know if you got it."

They walk out, and their footsteps slowly disappear. I strain my ears and hear nothing more.

I'll know if you got it. So will the inquisitors. They saw me going here to get this cache. Will they go to the vicar, and if they do, will it turn his ire on me or, worse, the people I love?

I stare at the bag.

Saipha is struggling. She'll never admit it, but she's at her limit. I know her well enough to be certain. I bite my lip. There might be something in the bag to help her regain her steadiness. Still, it would be wiser to return to the room and get Lucan and Saipha.

I glance back at the doorway, and prickles creep up my neck. I have no doubt we were seen coming in here, and like Cindel said, it's only a matter of time before someone else discovers the bag. If it wasn't the inquisitor that overheard us, then another supplicant.

Cursing under my breath, I think of Saipha's shaky hands and step onto the window ledge.

The wind sweeps up the sheer walls of the monastery like a warning, whipping my hair around. With one hand still gripping the inside of the window frame, I lean out ever so slightly to inspect the path. The ledge is maybe a bit bigger than I thought at first, but still too narrow for comfort. But there's a sort of landing created by a bracer from the buttress that extends underneath the bag.

A Mercy Knight would do it. The thought sticks like a thorn. *Don't be a coward. Choose to be unafraid. Your friend needs you.*

Committing myself, I shuffle my feet to the edge of the ledge. I shift my grip on the window, transferring my hands to the outside. I keep my back to the wall and lean into it, using my legs to create tension.

The dark city beneath me seems to stretch farther and farther away as it feels like the monastery rises several stories into the air with each shuffle of my feet. I blink several times, reminding myself it's all in my head. But from out here, it feels like I'm no longer just four floors up; I'm dozens. I'm in the clouds.

You can do this, Isola.

My fingertips tremble and ache as I grip the nooks and crannies in the stone. Every bump of worn and mislaid brick digs into my back as I try to meld myself with the building. One step. Then the next. Little by little...

I keep my focus on the bag. It's almost within reach. A few more steps and...

I slide my right foot onto the small landing under the bag and then practically jump the rest of the way, throwing myself slightly off-balance as I spin my arms. I wobble, try to recover, my stomach pitching as my gaze catches on the ground far below. I nearly tumble off the ledge and have to swallow a scream as I finally steady myself in the last second.

One palm against the wall, I pant softly and catch my breath before loosening the tie that holds the bag onto a hook hammered into the stone above. Luckily, the knot isn't too tight. The inquisitors must've thought they'd made this one hard enough to get to as it was...no need to add more difficulty.

The sack's heavier than I expected. Lumpy, too. I'd been hoping for food...but my gut tells me that's not what's inside. Not with these weird angular edges and curved shapes poking the bag.

Clutching it to me, I slide it down my body, lowering it to the platform at my feet, Fingers trembling with excitement, I undo the ties at the top of the sack and open it wide.

"Scrolls?" I take a deep breath and scowl at the bag. This

doesn't make sense. Unless... I begin to rummage through, looking at titles, heart sinking. They're all basic information. "What good are random scrolls?"

As my confusion mounts, a cackle rings from the window. My eyes meet Cindel's. She grins. "This is how I *know* you're not Valor Reborn. Our savior would never be so stupid."

My cheeks burn instantly, and I straighten. I was right. It was a trap. I knew better, and I walked right into it.

Her expression shadows, becoming positively sinister. "My mother is dead because of your inaction."

Standing on a tiny platform where one slip would mean my death is not the place to have this discussion. I glance over my shoulder, then back at Cindel. The only way inside is through the window where she stands. "Cindel—"

"She died because of you! I demand blood now!" Cindel screeches. She moves so fast, it's almost a blur. She nearly launches herself from the window to throw an artificer's cog at me.

I narrowly dodge, managing to keep my balance on the landing as the heavy metal disc falls and falls to the ground below. I reach for one of the scrolls, readying my own projectile. But another one of her lackeys is there, what looks like the broken leg of a chair in hand. They were both ready—I bet they were the ones to put this damn bag here to begin with. I dodge again, boots scraping to collect my balance.

Cindel is back, and I'm not fast enough this time.

I don't even see what she throws, but something heavy and dull smacks my temple, and I stumble. The world blurs. I blink rapidly, trying to bring it back into focus. Reaching out a hand, I search for the wall, but I can't find it. The world tilts, and my fingers grope the open air.

Shit.

I fall.

52

The world oscillates between a hazy night and complete darkness as my stomach shoots into my throat, blocking my scream.

Howling wind rips at my clothes and stings my eyes, drawing water from them that blurs the world around me. I blink, but it does little good. Part of me is screaming, *I'm going to die*, but another part of me is just...falling. It feels inevitable. Like this was the moment that had been stolen from fate.

I should have died that day... The rogue thought that's haunted me for six years is one of my last. *Why didn't you kill me?*

The question I'll never have answered. The dragon's copper eyes shine in my mind. The warmth of its breath washing over me as the beast just stared at me. As if waiting. The talon. Then the blinding light that changed my eyes and the course of the rest of my life.

My death was stolen from that dragon—from fate itself—that day.

And I always knew fate would catch up to me eventually. But I'm not ready to die.

The thought screams in my head like breaking glass, and then I stop suddenly, my body slamming into *something*. No, not slam into... I'm caught *on* something, and my head snaps against stone as I'm brought to a violent halt. The world spins as pain explodes in my joints. My ribs pop, and I dry heave as the air is knocked completely from my lungs when I double over. I vaguely note that some sort of loop encircles my waist—as though someone is holding me.

I force my eyes open but see nothing. My lids might as well be closed with how blurry and dark everything is. It's as though I've fallen into a cloud of black smoke. *Whatever Cindel hit me with really messed up my vision.*

Like a rag doll, I'm dragged through a broken window. My arms are scraped by the jagged glass, but the pain hardly finds traction. Everything is numb and distant. The floor embraces me, supporting my body, and I gasp in pain. Every beat of my heart says it cannot take much more.

Vaguely, I hear the heavy thrum of wind…no, not wind. Panting. Ragged breathing. Someone who's more out of breath than me.

Two hands on my cheeks.

"Isola?"

Lucan.

"Isola, are you…?" A ragged breath and then, "Please come back to me."

I want to. Really, I do. I want to be able to pull myself out of this state. But the connection points between my mind and body are scattered. My heart continues to flutter and strain.

Sleep…

"Wake up," he growls, grabbing both my cheeks firmly. *"Wake up!"* There's a deep resonance in his voice that I've never heard before. Something almost feral. Raw. It seems to speak to my very soul.

His hands are on me. I feel them yanking at the laces on my jerkin. His fingers brush against my collarbone, warm and familiar. They trace over my scar, the palm of his hand pressing against the sigil etched into my chest.

Heartbeat slowing, warmth returning to my body, I manage to open my eyes. The world is still a bit blurry, but I can now see him looming over me. Lucan is nothing more than a shadow, backlit by the shimmering gold of Ether. He's using his healing sigil.

"Thank you," I rasp.

He hangs his head and draws a shuddering breath. I stare at him in the flickering light of the single sconce.

For a moment, I think he's about to cry. But when he looks back at me, his eyes nearly glow with rage. "How. Dare. You."

"How dare I?" I blink, the world coming back into clarity. *What did I do that would upset him?*

"What were you thinking, going off with them?" Lucan's thumbs brush over my cheeks as he commands the space above me. Between the exhaustion in my body and the weight of his presence, I'd have to struggle to move away if I wanted to. But I don't want to. "You knew whatever she had for you wasn't going to be good."

"You...were there?" The feeling of eyes on me the whole time I walked through the monastery with Cindel. It was him? "Why didn't you say something?"

"And risk them doing something worse because they felt cornered?"

"Worse than knocking me off a ledge?"

"I didn't think you were actually going to go out there!" His voice rises slightly. "If I hadn't..." He scrapes his fingers through his hair, clearly frustrated.

"If you hadn't what?" I probe.

"I was going to attack them, but it happened so fast. When I heard her triumph, I practically threw myself down the stairs to catch you from the window in time..." His voice softens, and he straightens away, looking across the shattered glass that shines like distant stars in the barely-there light.

Now that he's not looming over me, I sit up as well. We're in a study room of some kind with three tables with several chairs each. The window's been ripped open, the iron twisted back, the panes completely gone.

"How did you do that?" I whisper. For a fraction of a second, he tenses, and suddenly, there's an unease in the air. *Something's not right.*

"As I raced down here, I was sorting out what to do," he says calmly. "I combined our sigils. I drew the armor one you found and my healing one to make an aura that defended me enough to break the window and catch you without sustaining too much damage to my own body. I was just in time, too."

Does that explanation make sense? Combining sigils is advanced magic. Doing it in the sundering pits nearly tore me apart. Can Lucan do that?

I touch my temple where Cindel got a direct hit on me, and my fingers come away damp, stained crimson. Or maybe it's from when my head cracked against the outside of the building. His story doesn't feel right...but my head hurts so badly, I'm not thinking straight. *It'll make more sense in the morning,* I tell myself.

My cheeks feel warm as he leans away from me and I lace myself back up. My trembling fingers fumble with the cords as I struggle to pull them taut.

"Let me help you," Lucan says softly, reaching forward slowly enough that I have plenty of time to object.

I don't.

There's something so entrancing about watching his fingers carefully, almost delicately, put my clothing back together that I nearly forget about the pain I'm in. I trace his outline with my eyes. The lines of focus etched around his brows. His strong jaw. Every strand of dark-blond hair.

"There," he murmurs as his fingertips smooth over the leather by my collar. "Now, let's finish healing you." Etherlight swirls around him, rising like a gentle tide. It washes over me, enveloping me. Its warmth sinks into every cut and scrape. A soft golden glow illuminates us both.

A stretch of silence passes between us. I'm mesmerized by the movement of his hands as they hover over me, bathing me in magic. Especially when he brings them close to the side of my face where the thing that Cindel threw hit me. He meets my eyes, and my chest squeezes as my mind takes me back to the moment between the two of us in the window of our hideaway only an hour or so ago. He's nearly done, and I feel like this might be my only chance...

"What did you mean earlier?" It's the least important thing for me to ask right now, but it's the only thing I want answered. "Why couldn't you... With *me*?" The question is half-formed because I'm not quite sure how to phrase it. I'm not quite sure what we were going to do, how far things would have gone. If I was right about what I saw in his eyes at all. I have suspicions, but the last thing I want to do is say it out loud and be wrong.

He doesn't answer. For a second, I think he's not going to—that he's just going to ignore me again.

"You're a difficult person," he says slowly, as if the words themselves are hard to say.

I laugh. "Me? Difficult?"

"I can't be the first person who's told you as much."

"I think you might be."

"Liar." He grins, and I realize the expression mirrors my own. "You are *astoundingly* difficult."

My grin only widens. *This* is the Lucan I've become familiar with in the Tribunal, even grown fond of. "You still haven't answered my question."

"See? Difficult." He pulls his hands away, and the Etherlight fades. I want to tell him to keep going, just so I can see the details of his face more clearly. "How do you feel?"

"Much better." I tilt my head from side to side. There's still some stiffness in my spine, but nothing major. "Thank you."

"Always," he says sincerely. Lucan stands and extends a hand down to me. "We should go. I don't think anyone saw me catch you, but it's hard to be sure." There's a worried edge to his tone. He's no doubt thinking of Cindel and her lackeys tracking us down.

I take his hand and let him help me up, even though I don't really need it. It's an excuse for our fingers to linger intertwined. His skin is almost burning hot. He lifts me up, drawing me closer to him than normal. Closer than people tend to stand—closer than friends.

Neither of us move, fingers linked.

"You *still* haven't answered me." I lock eyes with him, speaking with purpose. I'm not moving until he elaborates.

He groans and runs his free hand through his hair. The movement angles his body in just the right way so the bulk of the muscle in his arm is on display. I can't stop myself from admiring the flare of his shoulders.

Then he turns his gaze fully to mine, and I almost drown in their stormy depths. Brown and gold are warring as much as he seems to be fighting to find his next words.

"I... I don't know how to do *this*," he finally says, giving my hand a squeeze. "I've never been with anyone before. But I know without a doubt that wanting you is the only thing in this fucked-up world that keeps me sane."

The words are so deliberate, said with such intensity in his stare, they puncture a thousand tiny holes in me. And yet, somehow those same words mend them at the same time.

My grip on his hand tightens, and my heart races—my body betraying me by craving something that I'm certain will destroy me.

"What about you?" Lucan turns the question around. "Surely, you must have your own mixed feelings surrounding a man who was adopted by the vicar after all he's done to you."

"You were orphaned. I can't fault you for clinging to the people essential to your survival. Doing so would make me a monster worse than the dragons."

"Worse than the dragons," he echoes under his breath with a small huff of amusement.

I continue, "And besides, it's not as though you have a deep, abiding love or loyalty for the vicar or the Creed."

"Hardly." He scoffs.

"Most of my 'mixed feelings' surrounding you now come from not knowing what *this* is..."

Lucan examines me. His thumb glides over the backs of my knuckles, and I don't know if the movement is entirely conscious. I think...I *hope* it's not. I hope he's as drawn to touch me as I am to him. I take a half step forward. The space between us collapses into a dangerously small distance. Yet so much room still for *anything* to happen. Or nothing.

"I might be inexperienced. But I'm pretty sure I can tell you what *this* is."

"Can you?" My voice is soft.

"You want me."

I swallow thickly. Three words I've only just admitted to myself. So plain. Simple. Obvious.

He continues to study me. "You want me...and that scares you." His eyes narrow slightly. "Why?"

"Because I'm afraid of letting someone in." His brow furrows, and I take a deep, silent breath. *Don't ruin the moment.* "And, I...I don't have very much experience in *this*, either," I admit.

Lucan's expression relaxes, a smile flashing across his face. He leans forward, and the hand not laced with my own cups my cheek, guiding my face upward with a featherlight touch. "We can figure it out, together, if you're willing."

A shiver rips through me from his touch. From the implication. From...suddenly not being so afraid. We're both at a loss. We could both find each other, ourselves in each other. There's a curl of something exciting that collects in my gut at the notion.

"You're sure?" I whisper.

"No." A slight smirk that's somehow even more reassuring despite what he said.

I can't stop the smallest of laughs. "Good. Neither am I."

"I want to kiss you," he says like it's nothing, and I forget how to breathe. The fear that streaks through me is nothing like when I'm facing a dragon or squaring off with the vicar. It's a different sort of fear. One that propels me forward into the unknown. Lucan searches my eyes, oblivious to my pounding heart, as if waiting for me to say no.

I don't say no.

And he leans down more. My eyes dip closed on instinct, even though a part of me wants to watch him. I inhale slowly, my chest nearly brushing against his. The heat within me is as overwhelming as what radiates off his body. It's too much and not enough at the same time. Enough that it would put the sun to shame.

Lucan pauses, lips quivering so close to mine that I can feel our breaths mingling. Time itself changes into something far more nebulous. It fades away with the rest of the world. We stand at the beginning and the end—of what? I don't know yet.

Like the ignition spark of a cannon, like the snap of a crossbow or toll of the bells, he closes the last distance in a rush. His lips meet mine. Timid at first. Just a brush—barely-there contact that's so much softer than I could've imagined.

Lucan pulls away suddenly, and my eyes snap open. He's studying me as though searching for some kind of sign that what he's done is all right. I respond by gripping onto the sides of his jerkin, clinging for stability as the laces of my own are suddenly too tight—so tight my head spins, as I pull him back to me.

I want more. That wasn't enough, not by even a half measure. My body is on fire, and he's the spark... He needs to take responsibility for the blaze.

This second kiss is unyielding and gloriously messy. We've tasted something forbidden and realized we're starving. Now that we know it can be done, we're suddenly trying to find every way our mouths can fit together. Lips shift and move, and teeth hit awkwardly, but it somehow only enhances, rather than has me dying from embarrassment. He tastes of smoke and secrets. He's fire under my hands.

My heart hammers but for once doesn't shudder or skip. My skin tingles but doesn't itch. My mind is blissfully calm, thoughts focused on him and him alone.

It's as if this is what my body was waiting for all along. I respond with a fervor I didn't know I possessed. Moving on instincts I didn't know I had.

He releases my hand, gripping my waist like he's afraid I'll vanish if he doesn't, that this is all some kind of delicious fever dream. He tugs our bodies even closer, like he can't get enough of the shape of me pressed against his hard lines. His other hand ventures from my cheek to the nape of my neck, fingers tangling in my loose hair.

Give yourself to me, his every movement seems to whisper.

And all I can think of in reply is, *Yes*.

With a shift of his mouth and press of his thumb at the edge of my jaw, he guides my lips to part slightly. His tongue gently probes for entry. I grant it and immediately get a jolt akin to Ether as he deepens the kiss.

A growl rises from the back of his throat. Primal. Almost feral. It nearly makes my knees melt, and I'm grateful for the hold he has on me. My jaw relaxes further. His tongue gains full access, and Lucan kisses me fiercely, as though he intends to devour me.

I grip him as tightly as he does me. My body responds to his every touch with goose bumps and soft sighs that have almost become moans. His hands begin to roam—caressing and exploring every curve covered by thick leather as our tongues dance.

Never have I touched or been touched like this and… Dragons above, Font below, it feels *so good*. My whole body is on fire. *I could do this for hours.*

We seek more of each other. All of it. I want to lose myself in the submission, the surrender, to whatever this is. I've spent my whole life being wanted by the world around me for what I could offer, but this feels like the first time anyone has ever needed me for who I really am.

It's as though he's killing me slowly, and I've never felt so alive.

Then, as quickly as the moment began, the kiss comes to an abrupt end. Lucan pulls away slightly, his breathing heavy and eyes shining in the hazy glow of the sconce light with a desire that I can't believe I've caused.

"Isola." My name is a groan—no, a *growl*. It calls out to the primal part of me that I've never even acknowledged before him. Lucan's eyes lock with mine. "I want to devour you."

He means it. Every word. His finger trails down my spine with a gentle caress that promises the opposite.

"I could be consumed by you." I tilt my head back as he leans down like he can't stop himself to place soft kisses along my jawline and down my neck. A gasp escapes me as I realize just how sensitive the skin is there—more than I've ever realized.

"Don't say that." He takes my skin between his teeth, right at the hem of my vest collar. My breath turns into a low moan, and I hold him tighter. "Or else I will. Gladly."

My eyes press closed, and I lean farther into him. Our hips press together, and I feel every glorious part of him and want more.

I'm ready to surrender myself entirely—to tell him to take it all and then some, even as the notion terrifies and thrills me.

Nothing could make me pull away from this man.

Almost nothing.

"Isola Thaz and Lucan Darius." Horror and disgust war in the prelate's tone.

Shock relaxes our grip more than conscious choice. I'm still half leaned back, his face by my neck. My fingers are so knotted with the laces of his jerkin that they don't fall away when they go limp. She and three other inquisitors loom in the archway of the room.

Is she going to tell my father? I hate that the question jumps into my mind with a girl-like panic. Even if she does, what I do when it comes to matters of the heart or body isn't his business. By Vinguard's standards, I'm a woman grown.

But...were she to tell the vicar... Vicar Darius does see himself as having control over anything that relates to me. What would the vicar do if he found out? I shudder even trying to imagine it.

My cheeks flame with raw hate for his prelate ruining the one truly good moment I've had since coming to this abysmal place.

But she's not done. "You both need to come with us for sequestering."

"Sequestering?" Lucan straightens, hands still on my hips. The way he holds me feels protective, and I lean into him slightly.

"Indeed. This way." She half turns, waiting for us to follow.

For a second, neither of us do. We share an uncertain look, as if searching for a way out of this…but there isn't one.

Cheeks burning, I release him, ball my hands into fists, and lead the way. Lucan is close behind; he's the only thing that lends me strength as we descend through the monastery.

We enter the large basement that I suspect is the same one Saipha and I were trapped in on the second night. Except this time, it doesn't have the unnatural aroma of green dragon vapor. And, this time, it's lit.

It's empty, save for three cages.

53

The cages, perfect cubes that are Lucan's height and a half, almost look small in the center of this vast room. The floor is bare rock and compacted soil. The walls are stone and completely devoid of embellishments in the harsh, too-bright lamplight. The entrances to the three cages make a triangle shape, but the corners don't touch.

"In." The prelate opens one of the cages and gestures. We share a look, then both move. "Only one person per cage."

I go first. Lucan is put into the cage to my right. I don't miss how she almost seems to hesitate for a moment, as if reconsidering what she's about to do. *I hope she feels guilty.* Lucan gives her a glare, sharing my hatred for her.

She locks his door and then comes to mine.

"You're very good at locking me behind iron doors," I say under my breath, staring up at her.

The prelate ignores my remark.

"Isola?" Saipha's voice echoes in the room. "Lucan? What's happening?" Two inquisitors escort her over, each with a hand on her elbow.

"Into the cage with you." The prelate gestures to the final cage.

"What?" Saipha takes a step backward. "Why?"

"The three of you are under suspicion of being dragon cursed. You will be kept sequestered until the next challenge."

"Until the next challenge?" I step forward, gripping the bars. "That's days from now."

"We are aware of the length of the Tribunal." The prelate casts me a withering stare over her shoulder, tipping her head up enough that I can see under her hood. This time, one of her eyes is golden. Did I see incorrectly down in the Undercrust? A trick of the light? I certainly wasn't in my right mind...

"Will you feed us? How will we go to the bathroom?" Saipha asks.

"You will be taken out as needed to attend to such matters. Supervised, of course," the prelate says.

"As needed" may not be often if they're not giving us very much food or water. My grip on the bars tightens. "Let my friends go. We both know I'm the one you're suspicious of." I wish I knew what I did to make her hate me so much, but I suspect she's probably just like Cindel and believes I'm not really Valor Reborn.

"No." She smirks slightly.

During our exchange, Saipha is locked in the third and final cage.

"Those keeping watch, stay. The rest of you to your posts," the prelate commands. She follows a group out of the room and up the stairs the way we came, rather than through the secret door Saipha and I found.

Five other inquisitors remain and assume positions along the outer edge of the wall. Their cloaked forms are stark silhouettes against the pale walls turned almost white in the harsh lamplight.

"They can't— You can't really leave us in these cages." Saipha is trembling like a leaf. *How I wish I was able to get her some food.* She goes to the back of her cage, closest to the wall, trying to get an inquisitor's attention. "This is just some kind of test, right? Isola's right: we're not cursed!"

"Saipha," I say firmly.

She ignores me, voice pitching higher. "If we were cursed, you would've seen it by now. Between the challenges and what we've been through here..." She moves from bar to bar, as if testing to see that each one is sturdy, her movements becoming frantic. I've never seen my usually steady friend look so terrified.

A cool unease washes over me. Saipha is the blood of dragon

hunters. She's *destined* for Mercy. She's always been calm under pressure. If this place could break her down, what chance do I have? I need her to be my rock.

"Saipha," I repeat, firmer.

"Talk to us!" Her voice rises to a shout, echoing in the empty room. "We're not animals. We're not cursed. We're people just like you. You can't treat us this way."

"Saipha!" My yell has the crack of a whip behind it. She flinches and turns her wide eyes to me. I immediately soften my expression now that she's paying attention. "It'll be all right."

"But..."

"As you said, if we were cursed, it would've shown by now." My own doubts have been nearly completely silenced with the reassurance of my parents and all I've endured without succumbing to the curse. "This will not be easy, but hard doesn't mean impossible. Don't fear difficult."

She swallows and nods.

I move to the door at the front of my cage and sit. No cage is close enough for us to reach out and touch one another, even at the corners. But I'm at least a little bit closer this way.

Lucan takes the unspoken invitation, moving forward as well and sitting at the front of his cage. We both look to Saipha expectantly. She finally, somewhat begrudgingly joins us. I hold in a sigh of relief. My attention drifts over her shoulder and back to the inquisitors against the wall. None of them have moved.

Her panic can't bode well for her. The sooner we can get her calm, the better. Hopefully, if we hold our composure, they might let us out early.

"Lucan, do you know End-to-Beginning?" I ask, knowing Saipha does.

"The letter game children play?" Lucan's surprised.

I nod. "You both want to play a round?"

"Right now?" Surprise seems to draw Saipha from her terror.

"Sure. We have time," Lucan says.

I force myself to snort in amusement at that, trying to relieve some of the tension.

Saipha was clearly hesitating, but she's drawn in by his enthusiasm. I cast him a warm glance as a thank-you. "What's the theme?"

"Clothing," I say. It's a simple enough topic that it'll be easy to think of many things, but also nothing that could bring us back to dragons or our current predicament. "I'll start: vest."

"Tailor," Lucan says, using the last letter of my word.

"Tailor isn't a type of clothing," Saipha objects.

"She didn't say types of clothing, just 'clothing.' Which means it could encompass all things related," he counters.

She rolls her eyes and relents. "Fine. Rag."

"Rag is *definitely* not clothing related," Lucan says.

Saipha throws her hands up. "It's made of fabric, isn't it?"

"That's the most tenuous connection I've ever heard." Lucan leans back. "You just can't think of a better word."

"Robe." Saipha narrows her eyes at him, instantly looking more like herself.

"Earmuffs," I say after a moment of thought.

We go around like this, saying a word that begins with the last letter of the previous word, until one of us can't think of anything—Lucan is the first one out. Saipha and I continue going until she gets the better of me, letting out a triumphant, *"Ha!"*

The next round, the theme is "building materials."

The one after is "things you'd find in a library."

It's a good time-killer. When we've exhausted that game, we move onto the next one we can think of to play from afar. And then the next one...

Eventually, Saipha lets out a monumental yawn. I'm not far behind. It's impossible to tell how much time has passed in the basement. The lights are just as harsh as they were when we first came in. I'd guess it's somewhere around noon, now? Not that it matters.

"I think I'm going to take a nap," Saipha decides.

"Another round?" Lucan asks me.

I shake my head. "I'm going to get some sleep, too, I think."

"But it's the middle of the day." He seems genuinely disappointed I'm not going to stay up and play games with him.

"Perfect time for a nap." We need to keep our strength up, and we've been up all night, our nerves clearly preventing us from sleep. I doubt they're going to let us sit here and play games for days on end. "I don't suppose we could dim the lights?" I say loud enough for all the inquisitors to hear. None of them move or react. "Yeah... didn't think so."

"By the way"—Saipha sprawls out on the floor, still near the front of her cage—"where were you two last night?"

"I went for a walk." It's not a lie, just not the whole truth.

"I heard her leave, and when she didn't come back immediately, I got worried." Lucan lies back, putting his hands behind his head.

As I stretch out in front of my cage door, resting my cheek on my biceps, I stare at Lucan, thoughts of last night returning to me. *Without him, I would've died...* What really happened when I fell? I try to think back, but everything is a hazy blur or a complete void in my memory. There are two sensations that stand out from the rest:

Foremost, the feeling of his arms enveloping me. Clutching me as though it was both of our lives on the line.

The second is the strange wind and what almost seemed like smoke blotting out the night.

I think harder, trying to remember what happened. And when that fails, I think of Lucan seeing me go out onto the ledge and being afraid of what would happen and running to a room below. I imagine him smashing through the window, a golden aura surrounding him. Then he catches me, and my body doubles over. *What good timing he had...* I yawn. There was the wind as he dragged me in over twisted iron and broken glass. *Does it all make sense?* It doesn't have to. I'm safe, and he saved me. What matters more than that? I'm too tired to think too much on it, especially when the thoughts of what followed are deliciously distracting.

The sensation of safety in his arms carries me off into a light and dreamless sleep.

When I wake, I blink several times, not convinced that I've managed to open my eyes. The whole room is as dark as if they were shut. No. Darker. At least if my eyes were shut, I'd see the faint glow of the harsh lamplight from the other side of my lids. There is nothing.

They killed the lights.

"Saipha. Lucan." I don't know why I whisper their names. I can't get to them. And the inquisitors will know we're awake.

I stand, hearing movement from their cages but no response.

It's then that I realize:

I'm not alone. *Someone is in the cage with me.*

54

Panic has a metallic taste.

After the first shock of being imprisoned, the bars had taken on a new meaning: safety. They were something that, even subconsciously, I'd thought of as keeping the inquisitors *away*.

How did they get in? I was in front of the door the whole time. Unless there's a back door to the cage? I didn't think to check all the seams. I was so focused on the prelate and then my friends, I hardly even looked behind me.

The movement nears. Light footsteps churn over the compacted dirt. Someone's shallow breathing.

"Saipha, Lucan," I say, louder. *Wake up!* I want to scream. But I don't want to alert the person behind me that I know they're there. As I speak, I sink a little deeper into my knees, ready to spring. "You two up?"

"What?" Saipha murmurs groggily.

I hear shifting from Lucan's cage. I hope it's him.

As I open my mouth to call out to them again, a sharp jab comes from my right toward my lower back and side. I hear the soft grunt as the man throws his weight into it.

I dodge on instinct and swing my hand in an arc, throwing the blow off course. It grazes me harmlessly. I use the momentum to spin, swinging and bringing my fist into a jaw. He lets out a noise of surprise and pain. I don't relent.

With my other hand, I swing up, aiming for where his chin should be. I hit nothing but air. Movement at my side. He lands a solid blow this time, straight into my stomach. Pain blooms hot and sharp, radiating out all the way to my fingers and toes. I wheeze, falling back against the bars. I grab the cold metal, then grunt and kick out with my feet. I meet a satisfying resistance and push hard, shoving him away before he can land another blow.

Noises of struggle rise from the other cages, but I can't allow myself to be distracted. There's nothing I can do right now for Saipha or Lucan. I must stay focused.

A breeze alerts me to the presence of someone behind me—on the other side of the bars. I'm jabbed with something sharp, and I cry out in pain as I stagger forward. Someone out there is prodding me like an animal. The man in the cage lands a blow that sends me reeling.

Stars dot the darkness, even behind my eyelids. I'm beaten down with precise, rapid blows I can't keep up with. The only way I'd even managed to hold my own was the initial element of surprise—he hadn't been expecting me to sense him at all. *Damn it…is the fact that I heard him going to be somehow used against me to try and prove I'm cursed?*

The question haunts me as my knees crash into the compacted ground. Another blow sends me sprawling. He must have a sigil that senses where I am.

I barely resist drawing a flame of Etherlight. Would the vicar want me to? Or should I keep it a secret? *Will it be used against me?* That last thought has me concealing my power. It's not worth the risk for any of us.

The sounds of Saipha's and Lucan's struggles and ultimate beatings combine with my own. It becomes hard to tell who's enduring what—where the screams of my agony end and theirs begin.

All at once, it's over. We're left whimpering in our cages. Left to the darkness.

...

THE LIGHTS DON'T come back on for what feels like days on end, even though I know it can't be more than one or two. The only way I know the passage of any time is because—as promised—we are taken out one by one to attend to our physical needs. The prelate has a lantern in hand, and one inquisitor approaches the cage, flanked by others wielding crossbows.

I cannot see Saipha or Lucan clearly in the low light. Their bars cast ominous shadows over them and across the floor. We don't speak when we're taken out of the cages. I think we're all afraid of what they might do to us if given an excuse.

Inky splotches of blood stain the floor—proof of what they've done to us. What they continue to do... All in the name of "pushing us to our limits to ensure we're not cursed."

The prelate *hates* me. It's my only conclusion.

· · ·

TODAY THEY'VE USED sigils to electrify the cages and have placed our food just beyond the bars.

· · ·

TIME HAS BEEN muddled by the all-consuming darkness of the room and the seemingly endless rotation of tortures. *Has anyone ever died before from going too long without seeing any kind of light?*

We're quiet more often than not, now. After the first beating, we tried to keep in communication to keep up our spirits, but it became too difficult. Everything seemed to get worse when we spoke.

It's been so long since I've heard their voices that I wonder if they're even there.

My eyes flutter closed, and I inhale deeply as my mind takes me back. Saipha and I sit on her front stoop at twilight, knowing we'll be called inside soon. Starsight Night is one of the few nights of the year where people dare to risk the dragons...just to see the shining stars. I try to breathe it all in—the fresh, crisp air, the smell of the roast, the baked squash slowly cooking. A complete portrait in scent.

Then...the aroma turns acrid.

What was once beautiful begins to melt before me like too-hot wax. The colors run across my senses. Something wriggles on my tongue, and I rush to spit it out. A long centipede hits the floor. I cough and swear I see another long insect follow.

I let out a scream, but in a blink, they disappear—never real to begin with.

The scent of green dragon vapor crept upon us so slowly that none of us noticed until it was far, far too late.

• • •

WE DROWN IN relentless visions.

And I learn something new.

There are only so many times you can watch ravens pick out the eyes of your loved ones or feel the heat of dragon's breath as it burns you to a husk before you stop screaming.

• • •

I WAKE TO the shuddering breaths and soft weeping coming from Saipha's cage. The room is still devoid of light. I roll onto my side, staring at where I know she is.

Be it fear or exhaustion, I don't call out to her immediately. And I hate myself instantly for it. I can't let them win—let them take me from the people who matter most to me. Let them take my heart and soul and crush it with their fists and unending assault.

"Saipha." My voice is little more than a croak, weak and thin. I don't sound like myself. I try and clear my throat. It does little good for the overall quality, but I manage, louder, "Saipha."

The whimpering pauses. "Isola?"

"Yes. I'm here." Wishing every second that I could be closer, that I could hold my friend's hand.

"How do I know it's you?"

I ache at the question, knowing exactly where it has come from. Exactly how her hallucinations tortured her. There's even a part of me that doubts in this eternal darkness that this moment is real. "It's me."

"How can I know?" she repeats, a little more frantic.

"Even... Even if it's not me. Even if this isn't real. There's a piece of me, then, in you trying to help. There's an Isola alive in your mind trying to defend you."

She lets out a groan that devolves into whimpering and then muffled tears. "I can't do this any longer."

"Yes, you can," I insist. "You're not going to let them win. Because you're going to be invited to Mercy, with me, and then you and I are going to patrol the wall together."

"We're all going together," Lucan chimes in. His voice is gravelly from screaming. "We're going to show them that we're not dragons—we're what the dragons should fear."

I reach my hand through the bars of the cage, even though I know that they're too far to touch. I imagine them reaching back out to me. I haven't heard them move, but in my mind's eye, their fingertips are just beyond my reach.

"It's so cold," Saipha murmurs. She doesn't sound fearful anymore. Merely tired. Somehow, it's worse than the alternative.

Her body is going into shock. Or her mind is retreating from reality. Either way...I can't let her leave.

"Think about the wall, Saipha. Think about walking the ramparts with me," I instruct.

"Is it warm there?" The question is so small.

"I'm sure it is. It's the highest place in Vinguard, never any shade at all."

"That sounds…nice…"

I think I can hear her teeth chattering between her words. "It will be one of the many things we do together. So you must endure, okay?"

There's no response.

"Saipha?"

A long pause that I hold my breath for. Finally, "Yes?"

"Promise me you'll endure?"

"Are you still with me?" she asks.

"Always," I say.

"Will you always stay with me?"

"I will never leave your side," I vow.

"Then I promise."

...

FINALLY, THERE'S LIGHT. We go from what seems like endless night into harsh, blinding, never-ending light. It illuminates our battered bodies, the stained floors of our cages, and the inquisitors that line the walls as they did when the lights were first extinguished.

It's as if it was all a bad dream.

The prelate enters, hood pulled forward, hiding her face. I know her by her gait. I'll never forget anything about her.

She's flanked by two other inquisitors, as usual. I wonder if she's worried about us attacking her the moment she unlocks the cages. If I were her, I'd be worried.

I stand in the center of my confines, saying nothing, locking eyes with where I think hers are in the shadows of her cloak. She doesn't lift her head at all or raise her chin as she turns the key and opens my door. I wonder if she's afraid to meet my stare. *Dragon flames...I hope she is.*

She goes to unlock Lucan's cage next. Then Saipha's. None of us move.

"The residence hall has been reopened," she says simply. "The record shows that none of you succumbed to the curse." Once more, she appears disappointed by that. "There's food in the refectory this evening, and you may return to your rooms at night." She gestures to the distant stairway. "Tomorrow morning is the final test, so I recommend you rest up."

Still, none of us immediately move. It feels like another trap.

I'm the first to take a step forward. I emerge from the cage, and none of the inquisitors move for me.

"Saipha, Lucan, let's go."

The three of us walk out together.

The entire time, my eyes sweep across the inquisitors. Maybe there's more to this place than pushing to draw out the curse. Maybe this place is like a crucible, testing our mettle. Seeing who can stand up to the heat and who collapses. After the sundering pits, the vicar's abuses, the Font, the trial... I am not the girl I was when I entered. I'm something more.

Something so much worse.

After all, it takes monsters to kill monsters. And that is what they have made me.

55

The three of us sleep in Saipha's room together as we had been. Partly habit, partly because I think none of us could bear being alone. Saipha takes her bed, balling in on herself. I take my mattress on the floor.

Lucan curls up behind me, our backs touching. Saipha's hand dangles off the edge of her bed, and I clutch her quivering fingers. That's how I know when she leaves.

The door to the bathroom at the end of the hall is closing as I emerge from the room. I'm not far behind her.

Hand on the door, I pause at the sound of her retching. I'm about to give her privacy. Then I think better of it.

I push open the door. Saipha clings to the latrine with white knuckles. Her body shudders. She chokes back sobs like she chokes back bile, most of her dinner gone.

The moment my hands land on her shoulders, she flinches and turns, half falling back, swinging to strike me. I have no trouble catching her wrists. Our eyes meet.

"It's me," I say.

"Is it?"

"It's me," I repeat, firmer than before.

"How do I know?" The question is as weak and small as she is right now.

"This is real." I pull her to me and throw my arms around her, burying my fingers in her hair. Clutching her in the way I wanted to all those nights we were separated. Tortured. "You're safe now."

She exhales a bitter laugh at that and clutches me back. "You know that's not true. They own this place. They run it. And they can do whatever they want to us."

She's right. It took me coming here to see it, even despite my mother's warnings. Anything—*literally anything* is forgiven, or excused, or permitted in Vinguard if it can be claimed to be a teaching of the Creed, in defense of the city, or an act against the dragons. They commit atrocities against us and teach us it's normal. Tell us to look the other way because the people in power have it under control.

Mum, you were right all along... "It shouldn't be like this," I murmur. My strong and steady friend, reduced to quivering like a leaf. Her skin is clammy and cold. "I'm going to fix it."

"T-too broken... Some things can't be fixed."

I don't know if we're talking about the same thing. I'm talking about the world...but I think she's talking about herself.

"Let's get you cleaned up and back to bed. We have the last test tomorrow, and you should get some sleep before it." I'm certain she's going to object, but she surprises me and doesn't.

I help her up and draw a bath. Thanks to the thermal springs, hot water is common throughout Vinguard, but after our time in the cages, it feels like a luxury. I wait outside while she cleans herself. Then I follow her back to the room.

Lucan doesn't wake up. Or if he does, he gives Saipha privacy. I help my friend into her bed, pulling the blankets up to her chin and running a hand over her hair.

"You don't have to tuck me in like a child, you know." Yet, even as she says it, her eyelids are growing heavy.

"I'm looking after you like a friend, not a child." I'm doing all the things that I wish someone had done for me every night growing up when my skin crawled and I was afraid that the curse was ravaging my body. I'm not afraid of that now. Perhaps that's one good outcome of the Tribunal.

"I feel so weak and pathetic." She laughs. It's a hollow, broken sound filled with self-deprecation and hate. "I thought this place was going to be easy. Maybe not 'easy,' but that it wasn't going to be this hard—at least not for me."

I sit on the edge of her bed, trying to think of the right words to say. I feel like no matter what comes out of my mouth next, I'll always look back on this moment and wish I'd said something more. Different. *Better.*

"You're right; it's harder than we thought." I emphasize *we* so she doesn't feel alone. "But think of how much stronger we're going to be on the other side. We've already faced a dragon head-on. That's something that Mercy Knights don't usually accomplish until the end of their first year of training. Let's break down here, so we don't break up there."

"*If* we make it there."

"Saipha—"

"I overheard them," she interrupts, her eyelids fluttering open. The cold fire of her stare halts what I would've said next. Her words are barely more than a breath, hardly audible over Lucan's soft snores. "The inquisitors—when they took me to the bathroom to bathe, I overheard them talking when they thought I wasn't listening. They said that they had pulled us aside because your father did something with the sensor and they had managed to narrow down that it is one of us who is cursed."

My blood runs cold. My father wouldn't, unless he was forced to. The notion of what the Creed might have done or said to have him put me and my friends at risk of suspicion has me wanting to go into the main atrium and demand answers.

There must be a plan. I trust my parents. There's a plan to this.

"One thing that my father has always told me is that an invention is only ever as good as the artificer behind it or the materials that make it—and not even he is perfect." I lock eyes with her. "If they had a perfect solution—a clear test to identify a dragon cursed—then they wouldn't need to push us so hard. There wouldn't even be a Tribunal. They would know who it was, administer Mercy, and be done with it. Whatever system they're using is not perfect or foolproof."

Saipha looks away, avoiding my stare. She wraps her arms around herself and shivers, then shakes her head.

"It's me." Her words are as soft and small as the ones I always said to myself. Like a hidden confession. No... More like a damnation.

"Don't say that." I grab both her hands.

She looks at me with pure terror and whispers, "But I feel it... moving underneath my skin. Rattling my bones. Warring within me. It's going to rip me apart with claws and teeth, Isola."

Instantly, I'm back on the floor of the sundering pits, the vicar forcing magic through me. That feeling of something, *something* just under my skin, trying to get out.

"We went through every burning level of hell down there. Everything they did was for the sole purpose of breaking us. But here we are. We are stronger than them—*you* are stronger."

"What if I'm not?" Her voice is tiny, trembling with bone-deep fear we both feel.

I'm clenching her hands so tightly my knuckles are white. "If you must shatter, then shatter. But after, you pick up one of those broken, jagged-edged shards of what you once were, and you shove it so far down their throats, they will never find a voice to doubt you ever again."

She looks at me as if she's never seen me before. "You're going to do incredible things in Mercy."

"*We* will," I insist again. A fragile smile curls the corner of her lips, and she nods. It's the best I'm going to get from her, and I know it. "Now, go to sleep."

"I'll try."

I don't release her fingers. I just lie back down and clutch them for the rest of the night.

For as much as I know I should use this time to sleep, I can't shove down the guilt that this level of torture is much, much worse this year because of me.

That the vicar has lied to the inquisitors to justify these more brutal challenges.

What if no one here is dragon cursed and it's a lie? An alternative theory forms. He said as much, forcing my father to put the target on my back with his sensor to justify pushing me. To get me to draw Etherlight without a sigil.

Was the torture in the cages that much worse because I refused? Was it all a test to see just what I could do? If it was, then my friend is breaking because I refrained. I was trying to prevent the torture from getting worse, but what if, by holding back, I convinced them to hit us harder? My father told me to give the vicar what he wanted, but how am I supposed to know what that is when I hardly know the rules of the vicar's game?

I shiver. Each challenge has only gotten worse—and we have one left. The vicar will stop at nothing to break every part of me he can, until I have no will left to fight when he finally comes for my power.

And it will all be my fault if this next one breaks us all.

56

Early in the morning, following a quiet breakfast, the inquisitors guide us across the upper bridges of the Undercrust to our final test. Cold rage has settled between my ribs. If concealing my power was what led to my friends being tortured more, then I am not today. I will do whatever it takes to get through this alive and keep them safe.

I'm done holding back.

We will survive this, and then we'll finally be free of the Tribunal. I can eat a good meal, sleep without keeping one eye open, and maybe…maybe pursue whatever is going on between Lucan and me.

If he still wants to.

Rather than focus on where we're going, I peer over the railings and into the city built into the stalactites as I daydream about everything I'm going to do. That's why I see the procession before I hear it. I've already stopped as the rest of the group slows at a low, somber sound.

A curate stands on a balcony with a strange-looking instrument. I've never seen one outside of a display case. The horn is shaped like a funnel—like the Undercrust itself. I know that inside the instrument, near the mouthpiece, is a tiny bone broken from the base of a dragon's skull that, when blown through, emits an almost ominous hum.

In Vinguard, we use it for one thing: to honor the dead.

Lucan stops by my right side, peering over. "Who do you think it is?"

The procession is coming into view, emerging across one of the bridges beneath us that connects the stalactites. The haze of the

Font deep below shifts around them.

Down on the same level as the terraced farms is where bodies are consigned to the soil. Composted, churned, and tilled, so their nutrients can be returned to the earth and their essence to the Font—to help sustain all of Vinguard for years to come. We are all part of one earth, one flow of Etherlight, a flow we take from and ultimately give back to.

"Someone important." They don't have singing bones for just anyone. That, combined with the length of the procession that marches deeper into the Undercrust, assures me of that much. I lean farther to get a better look.

The Font's haze parts, and I can see the fine embroidery on their ceremonial robes in the vibrant colors that are from rare dyes said to have once come from distant lands. The deep dragon-blood maroon of the curates is interspersed with other finery.

My breath catches, and I grip the railing tighter and lean even farther, nearly doubled over, as if I can somehow get a better view. *It couldn't be...*

I catch every detail of the pennons the people marching behind the curates carry: a crossbow framed by a fan of dragon claws that belongs to the Artificers Guild. The pallbearers wear robes I've only ever seen worn by the high curates. Draped over the shroud-covered body laid on a stretcher are the sashes that are only ever worn by someone high up in the Creed. Sashes I last saw hanging in my father's closet.

"It can't be." I'm amazed I can speak at all. That shock hasn't utterly silenced me.

"What?" Saipha stops at my left side. She squints and sees what I see. "No. It can't... *No.*"

My hands tremble on the railing, my knuckles completely white. All I see is the body. The sashes.

There was only one high curate that belonged to the Artificers Guild. My eyes don't deceive me.

"Keep it moving," one of the inquisitors commands, crossing

over with almost violent intent. We're not the only supplicants who stopped, but I'm certain that we would be the harshest punished.

Yet I don't move. I don't even look when I demand of him, "Who died?"

He ignores me. "Keep. It. Moving."

"Who died?" I repeat, dangerously calm. That wrenching, churning, gut-hardening feeling that I had upon leaving the basement returns in full force.

"I said—"

Something in me snaps. I move faster than the inquisitor can react, as fast as the vicar has spent years training me to be, and the inquisitor clearly wasn't expecting it. I close the distance between us, unlatching the holster for his silver dagger with one hand and drawing it in a fluid movement. With my other hand, I grab his chin and thrust his face upward. Just as his muscles tense and he's about to retaliate, I press the razor-sharp blade more solidly at his throat, and he freezes.

"By this blade I swear, from this breath till my last, all deserving shall know the grace of Mercy, even if it be upon me," I whisper, reciting what I know to be the oath of a Mercy Knight—what the Creed ingrained in me. Just saying the words when you are not a knight is akin to treason. But let him challenge me on being worthy of this vow. Let them all challenge me.

The man's wide eyes are focused only on the knife as the ominous hum of the dragon skull horns resonate in the background.

"Tell. Me. Who. Died." In my periphery, I can see the other inquisitors moving toward us, but my grip doesn't falter. My attention doesn't waver.

"High Curate Kassin Thaz."

Everything stops. My heart, my breathing, the world around me, and for a moment, I think I'm imagining all of this. It's the result of green dragon vapor, or maybe the effects of being hit in the head one too many times in that cage. But then the horn hums its low sound again from the funeral procession below—my father's funeral procession—and reality hits me with a force greater than an inquisitor could inflict. An inquisitor like the one whose life is in my hands.

Kill him. Do it. End it all.

I've never had a murderous bone in my body. I've never delighted in death or destruction. I have only ever wanted to help—whatever that meant. I did not even delight in the murder of the dragons that ravage my city. But now? I am *all* bloodlust.

They tore apart my family.

They took my childhood and made me their savior.

They shamed, blamed, and ostracized my mother.

They have assaulted me and my friends.

And now they've killed my father. I know it as surely as I know my own mind.

What is left for me? What remains if not hate and loathing? I could reduce the world to ash and historians would call it "justice."

The knife is perfectly still. My stance sure.

Lucan's fingertips land lightly on the back of my hand, and I drag my attention to him. He just shakes his head. Saipha stands two steps back, hands covering her lips in horror. She doesn't even dare approach me.

Slowly, I lower the blade. With purposeful movements, I return it to the sheath on the man's hip, even fastening the clip once more. All the while, our eyes stay locked, and he warily regards me as though I'm still holding the knife to his neck.

You should be afraid.

"The other inquisitors are coming," I say under my breath. "Tell them all is well, and I'll say nothing about how you let a supplicant take your dagger."

The man holds my gaze with a scowl. Hate simmers in his eyes. I meet it, welcome it. *Challenge me*, I say without words.

He turns, mumbling something to the other inquisitors as they run up about all being well. The rest of the supplicants regard me with wary looks, staying a few steps away.

Rather than assuaging their fears, I stiffen my spine and keep walking like nothing happened.

Once more, my body doesn't feel like my own. It moves, but the motions are mindless. I stare down at the haze of the city below the entire time we walk, but Father's procession is gone.

Father is gone.

I want to scream, but I can't find sound. Want to weep, but there are no tears. There's just the task ahead and—for the first time in my life—a true hatred for what this city is. What it has made me.

"Isola..." Saipha starts to say something.

"I'm fine." I give her a sharp look. "Let's focus on surviving today."

"You don't have to be—"

I grab her wrist and pull her close. What I say next is harsh, but I can't find it in me to soften the words. "Tonight, in Mercy Spire, you can hold my hair back while I sob until I retch. But I'm not going to give any of them the satisfaction of my pain for a second longer. They want their great slayer, Valor? I'll show them Valor."

Lucan looks at me sideways as I pull away. I expect him to say something about how harshly I spoke to her, but he doesn't. Saipha gives a slight nod and looks forward. I don't miss the shiver that runs down her spine.

I should apologize, but I can't. Right now, I can't allow myself to be tender. Not even to her. If I do, I'll shatter, and I don't have that luxury. I must succeed in this next challenge. Not just for me but for Father.

57

All the supplicants are led up a stairway and ushered out into a massive arena. I've never been here before, but I assume it's a training area for Mercy Knights.

The arena's floor is sunken so that it's surrounded by a tall wall. At least two hundred people are perched in spectator stands that loom above the left and right sides of the long rectangle. A sea of faceless individuals, blocked out by the harsh lights overhead. At the far end is a balcony where the vicar and high curates sit.

Father's chair is empty.

He really is gone...

And I feel...numb. I should be crying, shouldn't I? Maybe something is wrong with me after all. My cheeks are dry. My chest is hollow. For once in my life, I don't even feel my heart beat.

He's gone...

The only thing that's keeping me standing—keeping me pushing forward—is the knowledge that this is it. This is the last test, and then it's over. I will enter Mercy, and there I can uncover the truth of Father's death and find clues for where Mum might have gone into hiding. I'll fight from the inside.

I glance toward Saipha and Lucan, chest tightening with the same pang of guilt I felt last night. I held back, and they might have suffered for it. I won't make the same mistake today. I turn my eyes forward again, resolved. *Play the vicar's game, and we all survive.*

"Welcome, supplicants, to the final day of your Tribunal." The vicar's voice booms. "The past three weeks have pushed you all to grow and to learn. You are coming away stronger—more prepared to live and sacrifice for Vinguard. And with the confidence that you do not bear the dragon curse.

"Today's test will not just be the final hour of ensuring the curse cannot be wrought from your body, but it is also a demonstration for the various guilds and trade masters of our city." He pauses, gesturing to the individuals gathered in the stands. "Following this test, you will receive your gilding and your invitations from them. Will you study under a master craftsman? Will you join one of our city's guilds? It will be determined in part by whose eye you catch during your performance today. But, no matter which path you walk, you will join Vinguard as a full citizen and productive member of our society to further contribute to Vinguard's greatness."

What greatness? The remark sears across my thoughts. None of the people before me are great. They all cower to Vicar Darius, as though he could save them. And the vicar cowers before the dragons. He wouldn't need me if he didn't.

The vicar continues, "For this test, we have constructed three challenges. You will be given one hour to complete as many challenges as you're able. And you may complete any challenge any number of times you wish, as they will adapt as you continue.

"For every challenge completed, you will be awarded with a token. With three tokens in hand, you may pass alone through the doors below, entering Vinguard once more as a full citizen." He gestures under his balcony, where there is a door with three slits in it. Two inquisitors stand on either side like guards. "While those who succeed in completing the three challenges within the hour will be scored more favorably, it is never simply about how quickly you achieve something, but the methodology you use to get there. The way you resolve each problem will indicate to the various guilds and craftsmen here what job you might be best suited for."

While he speaks, I mortar my focus in the present and assess the stadium. Across the stadium are three stations.

One is a rough-hewn cliff face that stands almost as tall as the walls of the arena. Lines of rope stretch down from its top to where they're pinned at the bottom. A table with an assortment of artificer gears, tools, and other supplies is at the cliff's base.

The second station has shelves filled with what look like silver boxes coated in splotches of paint—I'm unable to make out the details from here.

The third station is lowered into the arena's floor—a subterranean ring filled with thin columns of different sizes poking up from a hazy mist. What their purpose is, or what the challenge might be, is impossible to tell.

Then, there are the doors he mentioned with the three slots. Three tokens each are all that stands between us and the end of the Tribunal. I can already taste Callon's home-cooked meals, feel the softness of the pelt Father gifted me. I can challenge the world order after a hot meal and a good night's rest.

One last push, Isola. You're nearly there.

"And, lastly, any supplicants who fail to get three tokens within the hour will be presented with one final challenge to open the doors." Of course there's a catch. "I wish you all the best of luck. Your time begins *now*."

The second he finishes, a large clock lowers from amid the lights above. With a *boom*, the hand clicks forward one notch. After that, it's a steady *thunk* every time the gears turn over, signifying another second has passed.

"Split up?" I suggest to Saipha and Lucan. "We each master one of the challenges and get three tokens and share." The vicar did say we could do them multiple times, and nothing about not being able to share tokens. And none of us are in a state to do a fourth challenge if we don't get the tokens in time.

"Are you sure you can—" Saipha starts to say. I already know what she's hinting at before she can finish her question.

I take a step closer to her, my voice dropping low. "My father is dead, and weeping isn't going to bring him back. Someone murdered him."

"What? How do you know that?" Saipha breathes.

"I can't explain how, but I do." The vicar's hand is in this; I just know it is. Especially after the last conversation I had with Father.

"And no matter what, I'm not getting to the truth of it unless I have a dragon-blood dyed cape on my shoulders. So, I'm doing this, and I'm going to be better than everyone else."

She gives me a nod but says nothing.

"Which challenge do you want?" Lucan asks.

"I'll take…that one, I guess." Saipha points to the foggy pit with the pillars as I release her.

"I'll tackle the cliff, then," Lucan says.

"And I'll do whatever is up with the boxes." That whole setup reminds me of one of the games my father would play with me as a girl, where he'd hide little keys and tokens across the house. Or reward me with them for solving puzzles throughout the week to be able to exchange them for special treats at the end. I'm pretty certain now that he was preparing me for the Tribunal without ever telling me. I swallow the lump in my throat. I wonder if he had a hand in designing this arena and it is the last gift he'll ever give me.

"Meet back here at the center in thirty?" I suggest. Halfway through seems like a good check-in. With any luck, we'll all have tokens by then and can wash our hands of the Tribunal.

They both nod, and we split up, our start a little delayed compared to the other supplicants, but I'd always rather move with purpose and a plan than frantically. I sprint over to the shelves of silver boxes as fast as my legs will carry me. My whole body is still exhausted from my time in the basement. One fretful night in a bed and one solid meal isn't going to fix that.

Compared to all the other supplicants, I'm slower and frailer. Lucan might have been able to mend us with his sigil, but the toll on my body is more than cuts and bruises. But what I lack in physical ability, I'll make up for in skill and sheer determination.

I grab one of the silver boxes off the shelf at random to investigate. Every side is fused together with no apparent opening. The sides have lines painted upon them that don't connect over the edges—each side is different. But as I turn it over in my hands, something inside rattles.

In the center of the shelves is a table with all manner of tools. Cindel and her friends are wasting no time trying to smash into the boxes to see what's rattling around inside. Mikel succeeds, and a plume of noxious gas hisses out from the split seams. He backs away, gagging and wheezing, eyes watering. Blood streams from his nose, and he falls lifelessly to the floor.

Mikel's face is purple. The veins in his throat bulge. But he wheezes, eyes fluttering open.

At least he's alive.

Cindel walks past him without so much as a glance to get to the split box. Raising her shirt over her nose, she pries open his box the rest of the way. Much of the smoke is gone, and from within she produces a small, purple token.

"On to the next!" she declares triumphantly. The rest of her group follow her away even though she's the only one with the token.

Just one from Cindel's pack looks back at Mikel on the ground, still clutching his shirt over his chest. The girl ultimately leaves him behind.

I'm not surprised. Even though I don't like the guy, I go to Mikel. He looks at me, confused but scared. "I just want to see if I can help," I say, loosening the laces of his jerkin. He breathes a bit easier and wheezes thanks. He'll probably survive. The swelling is already going down. But it looks like it's going to be an awful next couple of hours for him.

I turn back to the puzzle boxes on the shelf as other initiates struggle to force them open now that they have confirmation tokens are inside. This is certainly not the way this was intended to be solved. Artificers don't build their creations only to have them smashed to bits.

I stare at the box in my hand, then back at the shelf. There must be some clue here. Some pattern.

A bead of sweat rolls down the back of my neck at the relentless *thunk-thunk-thunk* of the hand moving on the clock above. What

I thought would be a comforting way to check on time is now a distraction.

Think, Isola, think. *What would your father do?*

My father was the master artificer. He could sense Etherlight better than any. He'd make a sigil.

Is that it? Could the lines form a sigil if arranged correctly? No, it's against the law to allow a sigil to be seen. But there could be a sigil hidden on the *insides* of the boxes, since they're hollow. And if the lines match up in a certain way, that sigil is completed.

I rush over to the table, grabbing the remnants of the empty box Mikel left behind. No one stops me. They all must think it's useless. When I glance inside, I see etchings, just as I suspected.

Triumph surges through me, and I look back to the shelves—all the boxes and their different-colored lines. There's some pattern to it, I'm sure. But I'm not going to waste time on it.

Moving off to the side, I set one box on the ground and then grab another. I place the other box around the first, lining up each of the sides. Nothing. I grab another, flipping it three ways until there's a spark of Etherlight between the edges. The sides don't seem to line up perfectly—one box has yellow lines, one blue. But it doesn't matter. I know it's right. I can feel it.

I repeat the process with a third box, then a fourth; the fifth has another spark of Etherlight, and the box pops open harmlessly.

Others take note as I retrieve the purple token. But my focus is on the clock above. Twenty minutes gone. I can get the other two in ten.

I grab another yellow-lined box to start. Then a blue one. But the blue one doesn't work this time. It's a red one that sparks Etherlight. I'm sure there's a pattern here, but figuring it out will be up to the other supplicants.

By the time the clock chimes that we are halfway, I'm back at the center, three tokens in hand. But neither Sipha nor Lucan are here.

Lucan has nearly scaled his wall. He's two thirds of the way up.

I can't see past the haze of the pit to find out what Saipha is doing.

Before I can decide which of them to help, Cindel and her cronies catch my attention once more. The inquisitors on either side of the door gesture for the others to stand back. I can see some heated words flying between them and Cindel, but I can't hear what they are. Cindel just shrugs and approaches the doors, inserting the three tokens into the slots.

The massive doors at the far end of the stadium open just a crack, enough for one person. Daylight on the other side is so blinding that I can't make out what's there. But distant cheers reach my ears, and I imagine all our families right on the other side, waiting for us to emerge. To see us safe and sound after three torturous weeks. Cindel crosses into the light that's so bright it feels like the Font.

The doors close behind her, and her cronies stare at one another like bees at a loss for what to do without their queen.

That's what you get for throwing your lot in with someone like her, I think bitterly. The three of us will be going together.

When I turn back to Lucan, I find him nearly at the top. That'll get one token, but we need two more. I can help.

Running over, I scan the tables of various artificer and renewer tools lined up in front of the ropes pinned before the wall. Lucan chose to climb, but other supplicants had the right of it and made winches—a skill I also possess. There are other supplicants here struggling with the different materials, trying to make heads or tails of them. My hands fly over the gears, springs, and metal with confidence.

I slot the rope into the core of my finished device and grab onto the handles, cranking myself quickly up the wall. I even beat Lucan to the top. Some artificers line the top of the cliff face, each holding a basket of green tokens. The woman closest to me hands me one.

"You can use one of these to rappel down." She motions to a pile of simple, V-shaped devices as she takes my winch.

"See you soon!" I say, and I think I catch a grin before I turn and use the tool to glide back down the rope.

I descend so rapidly, I end up stumbling forward as I reach the ground. I push up from the packed earth of the stadium, relieved to be uninjured, and sprint back to the tables. I suspect the artificers hadn't intended for me to use the V-shaped rappelling device they sent me down with, but I use it anyway. It's an exceptional base to work from. I just need to make a few adjustments so it can be cranked manually.

I have another winch in minutes, and I'm ascending at the same time Lucan is speeding down. Our eyes meet for only a second.

"Welcome back." The woman hands me another token, takes my winch, and gives me another tool to glide down the rope.

Lucan is waiting for me when my feet hit the ground. He grabs my biceps, pulling me up and helping to steady me.

"I thought I was doing this one?" he says, more confused than accusatory or upset.

"You were. You just went about it in the slowest way possible, and I already finished mine." I show him the three purple tokens and two green.

"Have I told you today you're brilliant?" His smile is nearly as bright as the daylight behind the doors.

The sight of it even draws a quirk of my lips. "No."

"Don't let me ever forget to again."

For a second, everything seems hopeful. Until we see Saipha emerging from the pit.

"I got it." Saipha holds up the blue token triumphantly. Her whole body shakes slightly. "It was confusing, and awful, and hard, but I got it."

"You got one…" I try to mask the disappointment and confusion in my voice. *She did her best.*

"I… Yes. Isn't that what we needed?"

"Saipha, we needed three—we each need three, one from each challenge." I fumble over my words, despair crashing on me with every tick of the clock.

She opens her mouth, staring at the token in her shaking palm. I can see her lips tugging down. The knot forming between her brows that might turn into sobs. "I thought— I thought— I misunderstood, Isola. I'm so sorry. I'm so sorry."

I swallow hard and place one purple token and one green token in her hand. Then hand the other purple token to Lucan. He shares a hard look with me, and a slight nod that reassures me what I'm about to do is all right. We both know she's feeling the worst among us. He and I can endure one more challenge to get through the doors, should it come to that.

Leaving the blue token in Saipha's hand, I close her fingers around all three. Her eyes widen as realization dawns on her.

"Take these to the door and go through," I command.

"What? What about both of you? There's less than ten minutes."

"We're going to go get our own blue tokens," I say with more confidence than I feel.

"No... No. Just come with me." Saipha is clearly on the verge of panic. "We can all—"

"We can't, Saipha." I gesture to the door as another supplicant goes through. Saipha sees the inquisitors step forward to ensure it's only one. She's in a worse state than I thought to have missed this. "You need to go."

"If anyone should have this, it's you. Take it, Isola. I already know how to navigate that place. I can do it faster." Saipha tries to thrust her blue token upon me. I refuse to accept it.

"You're not in any condition to go back there." My voice drops to a hush. "You want me to look good, don't you? I can't take charity from someone else as Valor Reborn."

"Of course I want you to impress them." She's aghast I'd even suggest otherwise. Her mouth opens and closes multiple times. "But if you would look bad taking this token, then I would certainly look bad taking two from you."

"Just do it," I snap. The clock overhead continues to tick. "We're running out of time."

I try to move around her. She stops me.

"Whatever is behind the door, don't make me face it alone," she begs, clutching onto me. "We were alone in those cages. I—I can't be alone again. You said you would stay with me. You *promised* to never leave my side."

"The outside world is there, Saipha," I say gently. "It's Vinguard. It's home. It's your sisters and parents and good food and a warm bed."

Her eyes well with unshed tears. "I don't believe it."

"I saw Cindel go through. *I saw the other side.*"

"It's a trick. It has to be." She clutches tighter to me. "Come with me."

"I have to get a token, and I need to know you're safe to focus on doing it. I will be right behind you through the door, I swear it." I grip her hand. Then I pull myself from her grasp.

"Isola, please." She trembles like a leaf. I've never seen her look this scared before. Something in her broke these past three weeks, something that I don't think I can fix, but as soon as we're out of this I'm going to try. Her eyes are wide, tears welling in them. "I can't... I can't do it without you. Don't leave me alone. I—I'll wait until you have yours."

What if it takes me too long? What if I don't get one? I don't trust her to go through on her own in this state. I need to see her go through to know she did. I can't risk her facing whatever "final challenge" the vicar has for not getting through the doors.

"You're stronger than this. It's just a door, Saipha. *Go through the door.*"

"What if I'm not? Isola, you promised me—"

"I need to know you're safe," I say.

"You promised me you wouldn't leave my side," she says weakly.

"Leave, Saipha!" I snap, harsher than I wanted. She leans away, trembling like a leaf. A single tear falls. I reach out and grab her hand, saying gently, "I will be right behind you, I swear." Then I release her.

But...as I start to turn to leave—to put my back to her and walk away—something catches my eyes, and I freeze.

She continues to tremble. She's in a terrible state with multiple scrapes and wounds, ripped clothing, and dirt in her soaked hair. An abnormal amount of sweat covers her body, soaking through the fabric of her shirt. But her eyes are what catch my attention...

Her eyes are normally green. But they're an unnatural shade of blue now. Her circular pupils narrow to slits.

Vicar Darius's voice slithers through my mind, asking a question from our training months and months ago. *What part of a dragon cursed changes first?*

My throat is dry as I stare at my best friend.

The eyes.

59

N o. *"No."* The word escapes as a gasp. I step forward. "Saipha, I didn't mean to—"

I don't get to say anything else.

The eyes. Then the hands, the disembodied voice of the vicar drones in my mind, narrating one of the worst moments of my life.

Saipha's hands stop trembling and go as rigid as the rest of her.

"Saipha." Her name is a gasp and plea. I grab her shoulders, shaking her, as if I could rattle this from her. "Saipha, focus, please. I was wrong. You're right, I promised. I promised, so I will stay with you." I can barely speak the words as emotions choke me. "But I can't do that if *you* don't stay with me. *Stay with me.*"

"Isola." Lucan approaches from behind. I'm sure he learned the signs from the Creed, too. He sees what I see.

"We can go together." I don't say where. It doesn't matter. Let her imagine anywhere. "We'll go somewhere warm and safe."

"Isola…" she whispers. "It hurts."

Her fingers begin to spasm, wrists bending in every possible direction. My hands slide down her arms, trying to lace my fingers with hers to get them to stop. They don't, and all I get is the feeling of crunching and cracking beneath my palms. But I hold them there because I don't want anyone to see. And yet, right now, it feels like the entire world is staring at us.

"I don't want it to hurt anymore," she whispers.

"It won't, I promise." I will promise her the world if that's what it takes.

"Make it stop, please."

"I will do anything, everything in my power to make sure it

stops hurting. So stay with me. *Please*."

She opens her mouth to speak again, but the only thing that escapes is a low, gurgling noise.

"Isola, step back." Lucan's voice is severe. "Now."

I don't have time to object. Saipha's arms violently spasm outward, shaking off my grasp. She lets out a scream. Then she convulses, body thrashing against me with such force, I tumble backward. Lucan catches me and pulls me back against his chest, wraps his arms around my shoulders to hold me still.

"Let me go," I beg.

"You can't help her now; she's already dead." The words are so cruel, even though he says them gently. They're underscored by the toll of bells above. Never have I heard an alarm for a dragon attack from the inside.

Time has run out.

Saipha staggers backward, grabbing her head. Screaming in a way that rakes my bones. Commotion rises in the stands. The other supplicants get as far away as they can. Lucan and I are pushed backward by a flood of what my senses tell me is undeniably Etherlight that spirals from her in a cold tornado. It manifests into a haze of frost.

As if pulled by invisible strings, her arms fly out to either side, as rigid as boards. Her fingers condense into fists and then shoot outward. Where there were once nails are now long claws that look as if they're carved from solid ice. Her hands are already larger, turning blue. Her skin begins to split and jut out, forming the arcs of tiny scales.

"Clear the arena!" inquisitors shout.

"All spectators to the back."

"Supplicants through the door!"

The doors that are set into the wall swing open. The other supplicants waste no time sprinting through them to the safety of the city beyond. Doors that Saipha was so close to going through. *You were so close to being free.* The thought lodges as a sob in my throat. But I still can't move.

"We need to go." Lucan tugs on me.

"I'm not leaving her." My voice shakes, tears streaming down my cheeks, but I will not leave her. Even though I know what this means…what will happen next. I raise my voice. "Saipha, I'm not leaving you! I promised you. I'm sorry. You were right, and I was wrong. So please, come back to me."

The surge of Etherlight continues to grow. It singes the ground beneath Saipha white as permafrost crackles out from her toes, and she rises several inches into the air.

The rest follows faster than you would think. The disembodied voice of the vicar finishes. And it does.

Bones snap and crack. Saipha no longer screams in agony. She doesn't make any noise at all. Her mouth is agape as her jaw unnaturally unhinges and begins to lengthen. Too many teeth fill the space, each the same glittering cut crystal as her talons, each as jagged as the last.

Another scream fills the air, but not from her. It's one of pain—of hurt so deep and raw that there can be no recovering from it. A figure races down the stands, leaping to the stadium floor. The moment the light hits him, I recognize Saipha's father.

Marius stumbles, having landed hard, his expression utterly shattered in its devastation.

I want to save her. Tell me how to save her, I wish I could say, looking from him to her.

What good are you if you can't help us? Why are you even here? Cindel's voice is my reply, echoing within my mind. *You should've saved her.*

Save her. But I don't know how. All this power, all these answers, and all I have is more questions. I'm as worthless as I was when I entered the monastery.

As my friend disappears, replaced scale by scale by a mindless killing machine, my heart feels like it's being split in two, a piece of me forever ripped away. It feels like I'm the one that's being shattered from the inside out. Twisted. I want to scream. To cry. To do *something*.

But I can't. I'm helpless.

So the least I can do is not leave her side until the very end.

Saipha hardly resembles the girl she once was—the girl I've known since we were little kids. The thin sheen of sweat now glistens on arched rows of scales. Her body has become three times its size. A tail grows from the base of her spine. Ice and frost made real by sheer magic hide the most gruesome parts of the transformation as flesh and muscle tear, changing and elongating. Swelling.

Her skin now shimmers with a brilliant blue hue, the color hardening fully into mature scales that gleam under the arena's light.

Arms and legs are still there, though thicker—more powerful—and ending in talon-like claws that could rend metal in two with one determined strike. Wings so vast that they nearly touch the lights above unfurl from her back, the frosty membranes illuminated from behind, casting bony, veined shadows. A chilling gust sweeps across the stadium as they unfurl, forcing the Mercy Knights that had been racing toward her to brace.

Lucan spins us around, shielding me with his body—daring to put his back to her. Even still, frost coats my hair and crusts my eyes. I pry them open to look over his shoulder.

"We need to get farther away," he says.

"I can't leave her." I grab him by the vest and plead with him to understand. I have to save her. What good am I if I can't? I was helpless to save the other supplicants, Cindel's mother, Father... I can't abandon Saipha, too. "She's still in there. I know she is."

He doesn't object. That alone gives me hope that he understands, maybe even agrees.

A roar shakes the very foundations of the arena, followed by the rumbling of the beast landing on all fours. Lucan and I nearly fall over. We're close enough that Saipha could bite us clean through if she wanted.

Crossbows fire. A scream lodges in my throat. Every instinct tells me not to object. This is a dragon before me now. Let the knights do what they've been trained for. But all I can see is my friend. Even in that elongated face that's both terrifying and majestic, I see her still trapped behind those all-blue eyes. Still screaming for me to *do something*.

The swirl of Ether around her deflects the projectiles that aim for her vital organs as she finishes her transformation.

"Close the line! Move in!" a leader shouts from somewhere. More Mercy Knights condense around the upper rim of the stadium floor.

Her father has recovered, and Marius races forward, pulling a crossbow from his hip. The arms fly out automatically as part of his draw. In one fluid motion, he's readied a bolt with sigils etched onto it—a projectile engineered to cause the most harm to a dragon.

"Don't!" I can't stop myself.

He fires.

He shoots at his own daughter. The bolt is deflected by a wave of her wing that's almost followed by a swipe of her claw. But she halts. Saipha's massive head turns to her father, and I can see her draconic eyes widen. For a second, slits are pupils. Blue irises seem greener. He must see it, too, because he stops, frozen to the spot.

Your daughter is still in there, I want to say. But Lucan speaks before I can.

"Isola, pull yourself together." Lucan shakes me, half dragging me back. I fight him. "That's a dragon."

"That's my *friend*."

"You're dead if they hear you say that." The words are harsh. Yet, somehow, I continue to ignore them even when I know he's absolutely right—when for my own good, I should let him pull me away.

"I can't leave her." I lock eyes with his, showing I'm not backing down. "I can't. I made a promise to her—to all of Vinguard! I'm supposed to be everyone's savior, but what good am I if I can't even save my friend?"

"Steady. Aim. Fire!"

The knights unleash another barrage on the dragon. Saipha snarls, spinning, using her frost-covered wings to deflect the attacks. She retaliates with a roar that sprays icy breath on the upper ring of the stadium.

"Bring the rifle!" It's the vicar's voice.

My blood turns as cold as the gusts of wind rolling off her body. I've heard my father speak of this weapon—something he's been working on ever since he had the idea for the cannon. A smaller version that could be wielded in two hands by just one knight. Weaker than a cannon but still *much* stronger than a crossbow. A weapon that he hoped could change the tides of war and let us go fully on the offensive and push into the mountains.

I didn't know he finished it. Is that why he's dead? Did he outlive his usefulness?

"Saipha." I struggle out of Lucan's arms, stepping around him. This time, he lets me go. His eyes are distant and filled with defeat. I ignore them. "Saipha, I know you're in there!" I raise my voice, and her massive, scaled head whips around to me. I hold out my arms in a gesture that hopefully shows I have no weapons—that I mean her no harm. "Don't do this. Come back to us all. We don't want to be without you. *I* don't want to be without you."

I dare to draw Etherlight. It sparks in the air around me and her. No wonder she could see it on the rooftop… She was becoming a dragon herself.

"I'm so sorry I didn't figure it out sooner," I whisper.

"Clear the area!" a knight barks from up along the top of the stadium. I think he's talking to me. But I don't budge.

Saipha has stopped moving; she's focused solely on me. As if acknowledging she's listening—that my instincts are right.

"Fight this." It's too late. I know it is. But if I don't try, I will regret this day even more than I already will. "You're strong enough. If anyone can beat the curse, it's you."

Her head lowers, scaled chin almost touching the ground. This is the closest I've ever been to a dragon's face before—even closer than the attack weeks ago. Closer than the beast that tried to carve out my heart.

But the one similarity she has with those other two encounters is her gaze. She looks at me with the same quizzical eyes that those dragons had. As if it's the first time they've ever even allowed themselves to consider that, maybe, we don't have to fight and kill each other.

I extend my palm with more confidence than I did on that night. I allow more Etherlight to collect. I don't consciously draw it from the Font—I draw it from within myself.

"It's all right," I murmur. "You don't have to do this." I try to make my words as soothing as possible.

The dragon slowly blinks. And I blink back. Its eyes shut once more, and for a heartbeat when they open, they're no longer blue. A familiar shade of green, a stare of recognition.

Saipha. My heart flutters. My palm nearly meets the tip of her nose. Etherlight swells within me, reaching its maximum. I feel it rising like a current. Light begins to glow. *Maybe... Maybe I could reverse the curse.*

There's a flash of light, and a resounding *boom* follows on a second's delay.

The beam of Etherlight is indeed smaller than a cannon's, but it fires straight through Saipha's neck like a lance made of pure light. Then a shock wave shoots out from it as it explodes, decapitating her.

She doesn't even have a chance to make a dying gasp. The dragon's head falls to the ground, followed by its body. Completely limp.

My hand hangs midair. Part of me still wants to touch her. To pry open those giant eyes just to see if I had imagined the flash of green. *She was in there. My friend was in there. And they murdered her...*

I stagger back, trembling. The meager contents of my stomach upturn and splatter across the ground not far from her head. I grip my knees, heaving and gasping for air.

It's me. She told me as much last night. That quiet confession… She knew it. She'd felt the curse overtaking her for who knows how long. Weeks, likely. I see her paranoia in a new light, her snappishness, her exhaustion, her trembling. What I thought was fear and the Tribunal getting the better of her was really the curse ravaging her body.

She fought it for so long.

"You were so strong," I choke out, wiping my mouth with the back of my hand. *You were the strong one, believing in me until the very end, and I let you down.* I want to throw my arms around her massive face and apologize for all the ways I failed her. To mourn for the friend that was far better than I deserved.

But there's no time. At least not for me.

"Apprehend her!" The prelate's voice echoes across the stadium.

Figures race toward me in my periphery. I don't move. There's a second where a rogue instinct tells me to run. But I continue staring at Saipha.

"I'm sorry." My fingers finally land on the tip of her scaled nose. They linger there, only for a second, but long enough to feel nothing left within her—no power, no spark of life.

Then I'm tackled to the ground.

60

My cheek meets the packed earth of the stadium floor—thank goodness it's not where I got sick. I still stare at Saipha through the eye that isn't being forced shut by the weight of bodies and boots upon me. Mercy Knights surround me, followed by the clicking of crossbow bolts being engaged.

Marius staggers to his daughter. He collapses to his knees by the dragon, hanging his head and gripping his thighs. Sobs he does not unleash rack his shoulders. He is allowed to mourn for his daughter now that the Mercy kill has been completed.

He made sure they could take the shot.

Whereas I reached for her as she breathed. I told them all to stop. I committed a cardinal sin of Vinguard: sympathy for a dragon.

"Let her up," the vicar commands, and bile rises in my throat. I'd rather be at the hands of Mercy Knights than accept help from him. "Get her to a room for questioning."

"This way." The high curate from Mercy leads the way.

I'm peeled off the ground by at least three people. Two hands in my armpits, a person grabbing each arm. The hoisting is so violent that my toes leave the ground. There are ten crossbows all pointed at my face.

The vicar looks at me with thinly veiled disdain as we follow the high curate of Mercy. I've never seen the vicar regard me with such contempt so openly. Even if his expression could be mistaken for worry by anyone else, I know better. I know him.

I barely hide my own rage in reply.

Lucan comes to walk at his side, head slightly bowed in his usual stoic statue stance. But, for the first time, I don't resent the sight of it. For the first time ever, seeing him next to the vicar is a balm. Lucan glances my way.

Our eyes meet, and I inhale; I hold my breath and, with it, the sense of safety his arms gave me the other night. It's a fool's hope, I know it, but I have the errant notion that as long as Lucan is near, he'll help. He'll keep me safe.

Mum is gone. Father is gone. Saipha's gone...

As fond as I am of Marie and Callon and they are of me, I wouldn't expect them to stand up for me and risk their own skins. Not after what's happened. I wouldn't blame them in the slightest if they chose to focus on their own self-preservation now.

The high curate opens a hidden door that's flush with the tall walls of the stadium. It unhinges with a push and a hiss of gears, swinging to the side. He takes us within. The inquisitors are rough with me the entire time, but I don't bother fighting.

The little space is barely more than a storeroom, and it quickly becomes cramped with people. I'm forced down onto a crate as they release me, crossbows still locked in my direction. I give the inquisitors a dull look. I'm numb not only physically from all the frost and bitter winter winds, but emotionally from the shock of my friend's death.

"Should I fetch the other high curates?" the man who was leading asks after he shuts the door.

"No. As Valor Reborn, the final decision rests with me."

"She called off our attacks." Of course the first thing the prelate does is try to condemn me.

"Your attacks were not hitting." The vicar regards her warily from the corner of his eyes. There's a sense of betrayal to him, as if he expected more from her. "A dragon freshly changed cannot be stopped by such rudimentary means. The barrier of Etherlight is too thick. Only one with powers such as Valor Reborn could effectively attack in that moment, but none of you heeded her."

I hate that they're talking about me like I'm not here. But I know that anything I could say wouldn't help my case. For right now, it's better to let the vicar spin his lies.

The prelate purses her lips. "Very well, but she cannot be set free into the city, given these circumstances. Why not take her to Mercy for at least a final night of observation?"

"You mean to tell me what to do?" the vicar says coldly.

"You step out of line," the high curate from Mercy scolds the prelate.

She raises her hands in a gesture of submission. "I was giving a suggestion, nothing more. The citizenry will hear of this. Will they not feel more assured knowing she was within Mercy Spire at least for the night immediately following? Could you not say that it is to discuss dragon attack strategies with Valor?"

The vicar strokes his chin in thought. "Very well," he relents. "But before you take her, I would like a moment alone with Valor Reborn, so that I might give her blessings to carry with her into the night ahead."

The prelate looks like she wants to object but doesn't.

"We will be outside," the high curate says.

The prelate and the other inquisitors begrudgingly leave. Even Lucan steps out with them.

The air feels markedly colder as the vicar places all his attention on me and me alone.

"You are Valor Reborn." The words are said as though he could force them to be true with his sheer will. "You will go into Mercy, and you will show them that it is where you are meant to be, not as a prisoner but as our hero."

"I doubt they're going to allow that while I'm in a cage," I say dully.

"Leave that to me." He presses his fingertips together. "All you need to know is that the last thing you want to do, from here on, is disappoint me."

"Or what?" The Tribunal has changed me—maybe not for the better, as it seems my sense of self-preservation has been worn through. The vicar assesses me as though I'm a puzzle that's changed its shape. Seeing the new picture of who I am becoming as I'm simultaneously realizing it myself. I'm not the demure and helpless woman I once was. So afraid. So determined to make everyone around me proud. So desperate to feel normal. *I'm not normal. I'm special, and that threatens you.* A smile slips onto my lips. "I've lost everything. My mum's gone, Father's dead"—his eyes widen; he didn't think I'd know that yet—"my best friend was dragon cursed and was shown Mercy. What else is there for me?"

"You are Valor Reborn," he repeats more firmly. "The savior of Vinguard."

"And what if I'm not? What if you're wrong?"

His eyes widen with shock, which is both gratifying and confusing. Surely, he's known I have my doubts. Why does he look so fearful and desperate?

Did he truly believe his own lies that the girl on the rooftop would change the world?

Or maybe he believed the lie that he'd own that little girl forever.

Without warning, he grabs my chin, jerking my face, nearly pulling me off the box in the process. I don't even flinch. His eyes narrow, and with a snarl, he says, "Valor or not, it doesn't matter. You have what I need. Your power will be *mine*. I will be the savior of this world."

I. Not you. Not we. I.

"You resent me, don't you?" I whisper, thinking of what my father told me. His thumb and fingers press into my cheeks, making it hard to speak. "All that scheming, all that power you consolidated for *years* as you expanded the Creed, and you're still nothing compared to a scared little girl."

He chuckles, low and raspy, like daggers scraping against stone. "You think you have the answers. But you barely have the questions." Stillness overtakes me, and the ground I thought I was gaining slips under my feet. The vicar is still one step ahead—still more powerful with knowledge I don't yet have. "You don't even know what power you possess, and that's why you can't be trusted to keep it."

The vicar releases me and strides for the door, calling through before I can get a word in. "Take her away."

The prelate and the other inquisitors enter eagerly. I stand, calm and composed on the outside, but on the inside, I'm rattled by the vicar's words. Frantically, I covertly scan the room for one person: Lucan. Yet he's nowhere to be found. A pang of hurt strikes me in the chest like a crossbow bolt. I don't blame him for leaving. He was probably freed. But I wanted to see him one last time...

They take me from the room and through back hallways that are crumbling and ancient, yet clearly still well-tended by the endless repairs. It doesn't take long to affirm my initial suspicion of this place—the arena connects to Mercy Spire itself.

I did it, I think dryly as I march forward. *I made it into Mercy after all.*

M ercy is as brutal as its knights.

The walls become perfectly smooth, all cracks plastered over. Sconces in the shape of dragons' maws illuminate the passageways. The Etherlight-fueled lighting casts an eerie glow on just how barren it all is.

I'm taken to a cage similar to the ones that were in the basement of the monastery, in that it's a metal cube of bars in the center of a room—this way, inquisitors can surround me on all sides. The cage door is open and waiting when I arrive.

"Get in." The prelate shoves me harder than necessary. I was already stepping forward. She slams the door shut behind me with a deafening finality. The minute the bars encase me, I taste bile in the back of my throat.

Don't lock me in here. Don't lock me in here. Don't... I want to beg, over and over, but I force myself to maintain composure. I will not give them, or the vicar by proxy, the satisfaction.

"Do I need to worry about people torturing me while I'm inside this cage?" I turn to face her, trying to hide how my chest feels tighter with every ragged breath.

Her lips curl into a wicked smirk. "You'll take whatever comes your way, *traitor*."

"That's for the vicar to decide," I counter, not letting the word hit me the way she wants. "And last I heard, I was still 'Valor Reborn.'"

The prelate tilts her head to the side. Her voice drops. "Only as long as that's useful to him."

I'm reminded of what Father said. It almost...sounds like a warning? But not from the prelate. Surely not.

"Don't worry, Isola. You'll be dealt with soon enough." The prelate steps back and turns. Three inquisitors follow her out, and three remain.

No...not inquisitors. Not here. These are fully trained, veteran Mercy Knights. The way they hold the crossbows is different from any of the inquisitors I've seen. Their stances only suggest that they are relaxed. I'm in a room with hardened killers, and it feels more dangerous than being face-to-face with a dragon.

Sitting in the center of my cage, I wait and focus on controlling my breathing and my wild, racing thoughts. The air is thick. Choking. *What is going to come, will come*, I remind myself. Panic won't suit. If anything, it will be used against me as a sign I'm dragon cursed.

I have one more night to wait, and then this is all over. Then I'm deemed a citizen, whether traitor or not. I will see Lucan and Saipha again and—

My thoughts halt.

Oh, Saipha, you were so close... Her memory has my eyes stinging.

You promised me, Isola, I can almost hear her say from beyond.

I promised I would stay with her, and I failed her. If she'd gone through the door, maybe she would've never transformed. She would've felt safe, and been fed, and it would've bought us time. Maybe I would have found a way to mitigate the curse, like Mum's tinctures.

I could've helped her. Never have I been more sure of anything in my life. Mum's research, my own abilities, *somehow*. I would've somehow gained more knowledge of the power within me, if it's even helpful at all. The thought is heavy in my chest, so heavy it nearly breaks me as much as it sets my blood to boiling—like a hot ball of molten iron.

I could've helped her if this city hadn't stopped me.

I force her from my thoughts. I can't fall apart. Not now. Not here. One day, I'll cry for Father and for Saipha. But today is not that day.

So, instead, I focus on intentionally making my mind as empty as possible. Anything else can wait until I'm free of this predicament... *If* I'm ever free. *No, focus, Isola. There will be a path out.* I just need to find it. But it's hard to imagine my path to freedom when I'm trapped in a cage *inside* a locked room where knights stand guard, with who knows how many more knights on the other side of the door, in a whole tower of knights.

A sconce on the wall by the door changes colors, momentarily breaking my focus. The knights at the perimeter of the room march to the door, each one falling in line and lockstep. The door opens, and three new knights march past them, taking their slots as the old leave.

None of them say anything. I almost wish they would and break me from these endless thoughts. I hang my head, balling my hands into fists and fighting a scream. How did it end up like this? Saipha and I were supposed to go to Mercy. I was going to find a way to help people. I'd learn things outside the wall for Mum. Father...

Father should still be here. My jaw pops as I grit my teeth.

The day drags on, with two more changeovers in my guard the only thing to break the monotony. I keep my head down and guide my thoughts toward what will come next. Tomorrow, they will convene the high curates and vicar to examine my actions, I suspect, probably here in Mercy. I'm already planning what I might say. Already sketching out my case in my mind that will speak to all the things I know the vicar wants to hear.

Make it through tomorrow, and I'm free. Sort of. Mercy will be its own confinement. And I'll still be right in the vicar's hands. But then he'll never suspect me. I will have justice for Father and Saipha.

I'm so focused on my scheming that when the lights in the room flicker, dimming just for a breath before going back to normal, I think I imagined it. Then, all three knights move, racing toward the cage. I leap to my feet.

Two knights move toward the cage door. There's a jingle of keys in one of their hands. I back away, sinking into a crouch, ready to attack.

The third knight throws off his crimson hood, and our gazes lock as the door swings open.

"Lucan?" I breathe in confusion and relief. "How..."

"We're getting you out of here," he says calmly.

"*How* are you here?" I manage to ask. Even if knights invited him to be a page, that wouldn't begin until tomorrow—at the earliest. Saipha's older sister didn't start her duties as a page until four days after her Tribunal. Which, in retrospect, should've been a hint for us as to the extremes we might be pushed to.

But it's easy to gloss over the bad when you're just a girl with big dreams or bigger fears.

"We sneaked in," Lucan answers.

"We?" I repeat. He keeps using that word. *None of this is making any sense.*

The one holding open the cage door lifts her head, and I recognize her as one of the twins who joined the Tribunal late. Something about them is different. They still have the same bruises, of course. But they're standing...taller. More confident. Like it was all an act.

"I'm Myla, and this"—she nods to her twin—"is Ember. Good to see you."

"Is it?" Ember mutters to her twin, lowering her hood as well.

I'm not sure if I'm more shocked that these are more words than I've ever heard them say in the monastery, or by the fact they're here. Definitely the latter. I look between them. "You three have been here for over an hour, and you're *just now* saying something?"

"It wasn't safe before," Lucan says. "We had to wait for the signal."

The signal must've been the flickering of the lights. Someone must've manipulated the artificer sigil that powers the lights. But whoever did it would have to possess an intimate knowledge of Mercy and a confident hand with sigils.

"It's not really safe, even now." Lucan steps inside the cage. "We need to move quickly. The Mercy Knights will be called to prayer soon before the night's patrols. That's our only chance."

Prayer seems an obvious thing that would be done, but the inner workings and schedules of Mercy are a secret to all beyond. Not even Saipha knew. "How do you know that?"

"We have help on the inside."

We. There it is again. Him and who else? Only the twins from the Undercrust? I shake my head slowly.

Lucan must mistake the movement for refusing his offer of freedom. "We're getting you out, Isola."

"You planned this," I whisper, staring at him and only him even as I gesture to Myla and Ember. "How?"

"We're ashborn, from beyond the wall," Myla answers. "So is Dazni."

I shake my head again. Harder this time. There haven't been ashborn in Vinguard in centuries, at least none we've known of, and yet... I stare from one girl to the other. Ashborn are supposed to be monsters. Half-dragon abominations that are one step from walking corpses, according to the sketches and descriptions by the Creed and vicar. Or dead. But these girls are very much alive, and very normal looking. They're a walking contradiction that, despite myself, I couldn't be more curious about.

"We have to go *now*," Lucan says.

I stare at him, eyes wide, heart hammering. Lucan said he was made an orphan during that dragon attack. Did he lie to me?

"You're one of them, aren't you?" I ask, but it comes out more like a statement. Somehow, I already know the answer, as impossible as it is. Lucan is ashborn, too.

His silence screams the truth.

I laugh bitterly. Why is it that, out of everything today, *this* is what makes tears well in my eyes? But I refuse to let them fall. Not for his lies.

"You played me," I whisper.

The remark is so sharp, he leans back as if I've slapped him. "Isola, please—"

"You've clearly been working with them a long time. You lied to me. Over and over. Even as I gave you my secrets." My words are level and as cold as a Mercy dagger.

"Is she always like this?" Ember asks dully.

Lucan gives her a sharp look.

What? she mouths in reply and shrugs.

But I don't take my eyes off Lucan. I study him the whole exchange so that when his gaze returns to mine, I search his eyes for a scrap of the man I thought I knew. But there's something... different. It's like I'm seeing him for the first time.

"What was I supposed to tell you?" he whispers, clearly at a loss.

"I told you everything, Lucan, *everything*. My hopes, my fears, my treason. And you couldn't trust me with just one of your secrets that really mattered."

He opens his mouth to speak again but stiffens as somewhere beyond the main door of the room, a low chime sounds. I can only imagine this is the call to prayer as Myla and Ember shoot glances at the door.

"We have to leave," Lucan says. "We're not getting a second chance."

"And where would we go?" I ask. "Vinguard is controlled by the Creed, and the Mercy Knights will kill us on sight. There's nowhere to hide." Yet, even as I say it, I think of what Father said about Mum going missing. If the vicar had found her, he would've gone out of his way to tell me.

I hate that Lucan still knows me well enough to read my thoughts, because he says, "We're going out of the wall. Your mum is waiting."

Mum. "She's waiting? Outside the wall?" The words are soft, barely a whisper.

"We got her out to keep her safe." Lucan takes a small step closer, and the only reason I allow it is the thought of Mum. "We're going to bring you to her, Isola. We're going to keep you safe, too."

Safe. The one word I've grown to associate with Lucan comes back. The knot of distrust eases some.

"If you stay, they're going to do far worse than kill you," Ember cautions. I give her a wary look. But she turns to Lucan. "Prayer isn't that long. We need to go."

"Vicar Darius is planning on taking your power—" Lucan starts.

"I know," I interrupt. "My father told me. But clearly you could've warned me, too." Anger flares back through me with quickening heartbeats.

"I couldn't risk telling you earlier."

"And *now* seems like a good time?" I gesture at the iron bars.

"Now is the only time—our one chance to leave. You might not like me right now…" He fights a wince as he speaks, and I fight the urge to correct him. "But I'm the best shot you have at getting out of Vinguard." When I say nothing, he continues. "At least stick with us long enough to get out of *this* place. Once we're out, I'll tell you everything. You can speak with your mum and make your choice then."

I can do that much… Mum is beyond the wall. The truth is beyond the wall. And the only thing that's here is a madman vicar who wants to take my power for himself.

Right as I open my mouth to agree, the door opens and a hooded figure steps in.

"Why are you all still here? Is she giving you trouble?" The prelate. My blood turns cold. But she doesn't move or raise an alarm. Which means…

She's in on this.

"Yes," Myla answers.

"A bit," Ember adds.

"Not yet," Lucan says firmly over them both, eyes still locked with mine. "She's fine."

"Then let's get on our way. The Mercy Knights are all in the prayer service. Dazni's keeping a lookout in case it ends early or anyone leaves unexpectedly." The prelate's tone has completely shifted. She approaches slowly, lowering her hood. As she comes to a stop by Lucan, I notice something I haven't before, and I gasp. Maybe I was willfully ignorant. Maybe the notion was too outlandish to really consider. Probably it was that I never really saw her face fully, in proper lighting.

But there's a familiar hollowing of her cheeks. An almost identical shape in her brow as the man standing before me. A similar shading in her hair. The familial resemblance is undeniable.

It can't be... My mind rejects what's right before my eyes. As I behold her, her gold eye fades from existence. Some kind of illusion. I wasn't wrong about what I saw in the Font.

"What in the dragon-burned hells is going on..." I whisper, looking between her and Lucan.

"Lucan, now," she presses. "Make her move, or I will."

"None of you are 'making me' do anything." I take a step forward and give Lucan a pointed look, one in which I try to convey that I'm done with his secrets and scheming. Then I stride past him, as if he's of no concern to me. As if a part of me doesn't want to reach out and grab him.

I look back at the four of them, my hand on the door. "I'm getting out of this city."

62

"And what makes you think you can call the shots?" The prelate hasn't moved, despite my hand being on the door handle. The other three are looking to her for instruction.

I let out a soft sigh and say, "Twenty minutes—probably eighteen now."

"Twenty minutes for what?" It's Ember who asks.

"The prayers. There's the cleansing, beseeching the Font for strength, adoration of Valor, and then the twenty utterances of Mercy. I might not have been a Mercy Knight, but I *know* the Creed's prayers." I glance over my shoulder, looking right at the prelate. Something about being able to look her in the eyes, at last, makes her less terrifying. She's not this unshakable entity. She's just a woman. "But you already knew that, didn't you?"

Her mouth presses into a line, and she strides toward me. Shoving my hand aside, she opens the door. "This way."

We step into a nondescript hallway—the same smooth, bleak walls of Mercy I saw on my way in, punctuated only by dragon sconces crackling with Etherlight. I'm right behind the prelate. Lucan is almost by my side, but I work to stay a half step ahead of him. I am not about to walk shoulder to shoulder with him like we're fine.

I know once I'm fed, rested, bathed, and we can have a good, long talk to get real answers, this might get smoothed over. But right now, I'm not thinking straight, and I'm not inclined to be the bigger person.

The twins take up the back, murmuring to themselves.

"Are there patrols, Pia?" Lucan asks the prelate—Pia.

"Not during prayers. Everyone goes in—at least everyone who's in the spire at the time. Those on the wall stay there. Same with anyone out on a hunt," Pia replies. "So everyone we need to worry about is occupied."

"How did you become a Mercy Knight without your gilding?" I direct the question at Pia. She's not of Vinguard if she's not gilded, so that means, like the others...like Lucan, she's ashborn.

She glances back at me, expression unreadable, never missing a step as we hurry down the hallway. "A small pack of Mercy Knights went out on a hunt into the mountains. Only one managed to survive...or so they thought. A younger woman, new enough that people didn't know her face that well."

So she took someone else's place... "Did you kill her?"

"What's it matter to you? Turning me in, Valor Reborn?" Pia shoots a glare in my direction as we round a corner and quickly pass through an empty armory.

"I want to know what sort of person I'm working with. Because all I know of you so far is that you're not going to hesitate when it comes to beating the shit out of me." My tone is cutting.

"You're really worrying about things as tiny as lies or beatings or murder? The entire world being overrun by the scourge—*that* is the problem."

"You locked me in with the Font!"

"You were better for it." Pia shrugs. I barely resist the urge to slap her.

"Pia," Lucan sighs.

"She's ridiculous, brother," Pia snaps defensively. *Siblings, then.* Pia is undoubtedly older. "Worrying if I killed someone—you know what?" Her eyes shift to me. "I didn't, actually. I didn't kill her. The cold was taking her by the time I tracked them down. But I didn't save her, either. That good enough for the great Valor Reborn to work with me?"

What is your problem with me? I nearly ask as we step through another door. But the pace is brisk, and I'm reserving my breath for what's actually important.

Besides, I can probably guess what some of her problem is with me, given she caught me with her brother's tongue in my mouth recently.

Through another door, and we descend a staircase that extends farther than the light reaches. The air below is markedly cooler. Stale with age. Even the lights down here are dimmer, as if they don't expect people to come often enough to waste too much Ether on lighting the place.

"We have less than ten minutes," I estimate. "If the goal is to escape, why are we going down?"

The twins share a wary look.

"Too much talking, not enough moving." Pia says, ducking to pass through an archway off an ancient, crumbling landing. We're clearly in an unused part of the structure. Through the archway is a long hallway of barely enough light to see by. Every time we pass a glowing sconce, the light sets my mind at ease, sort of. But then we plunge into darkness again as we continue down the long passage with haste.

Seconds tick in the back of my mind like the clock cogs in the arena. Even though we're all in peak fitness, our breathing is labored.

"Pia, we're not going to make it out in time—" Just as Lucan begins to speak, a low chime sounds, the same as before. I was wrong. Prayers in Mercy are shorter than those outside the spire.

We all stop, and our eyes drift upward. Somewhere in the spire above us is where the knights have gathered for prayers. Where those same knights are now emerging from their distraction.

"I know. I didn't expect us to. Fortunately, we didn't have to; our way out is on this level. We have time before anyone wanders from the chapel within Mercy Spire down here." Pia pushes off from the wall she was leaning on, still out of breath, and carries on. The hallway gives way to an old smithy—geared more for larger, simpler weapon creation than the artificer workshops I'm familiar with.

"The way out is underground?" I force myself to avoid distraction and follow closely behind. I hate asking Pia, of all people, but I'm still mostly ignoring Lucan, even if I'm extremely aware of just how close he is. Of how often he looks my way, as if trying to catch my eyes.

"If you are within Vinguard, it's underground. But the exit is at the ground level beyond the wall," Pia answers, still begrudgingly.

But I don't really care if she likes me or not as long as she's answering my questions.

I'd never thought of the ground on the outside of the wall as being lower than what Vinguard's ground level is. But given how built up Vinguard has become over the years, it makes sense.

"We'll connect to the main central passage of Mercy Spire—think of it like a corkscrew. It functions as the primary route up and down. At its base is the way out," she continues as we go through another storeroom, which connects with a nondescript workshop consumed by two long tables and various tools for renewing all manner of objects. "Dazni will meet us there. We're not far now."

"This seems to be going well," Myla says as we leave the workshop through a back door and rush down another hallway. At the end, I can see a sloping passage that I assume is the "corkscrew" Pia mentioned.

"Myla, don't—" Ember is interrupted by the harsh clang of a bell, probably marking the transition of guard shifts. We all halt as heavy footfalls echo to us from the sloping passage beyond. "Tempt fate," Ember finishes by narrowing her eyes at her sister.

"It's fine, keep focused." Pia speaks calmly, but her shoulders are nearly up to her ears. "Like I said, we're lower than most go. The only people who would come this far down are a hunting party, and there's not one scheduled."

"You're sure, Pia?" Lucan's eyes dart to the passage ahead. The footsteps seem to be getting louder.

She sighs in a way that painfully reminds me of Saipha's older sister. But, to her credit, she does seem to take the concern seriously. Pia pauses, opening one of the last doors before the corkscrew passage. It's a small storeroom with a dusty assortment of supplies like waterskins and bedrolls that I imagine a Mercy Knight would need on a hunting mission, lit by a single, flickering sconce. "All right, you four wait in here; I'll go on ahead to make sure no one is actually coming this way."

"Pia." Lucan takes a small step toward her. Worry furrows his brow.

"I'm going to be fine. They haven't suspected me for all these years. They won't now." She grins, but it looks forced, even to me. "Just keep the door shut for anyone but me. If someone tries to open it, they'll think it's locked or barricaded. So much of this place is crumbling and unused."

"Stay safe," Lucan barely manages to say before she leaves.

The moment the door is shut, Ember places her back to it. Myla leans next to her sister, gripping the handle. That leaves Lucan and me, toward the back of a very narrow closet, staring at each other.

"You probably have a lot of questions for me." He rubs the back of his neck as he makes his pathetic attempt at conversation.

"Not really," I reply briskly, glancing his way. We both keep our voices at barely a whisper to avoid anyone beyond the heavy door hearing.

"Isola—"

"I don't care what you have to say, Lucan. You lied to me, over and over."

He sighs. "You know I couldn't tell you the truth. It'd be admitting to high crimes against Vinguard."

"You mean like I admitted to high crimes to you?"

"Ooooh." Ember hums.

"She has him there," Myla adds.

I roll my eyes and suppress a groan. I do not want to have his conversation with an audience. Lucan gives them a pointed look that is about as effective as a practice sword on a silver dragon.

"I know you may never believe a word I say again. Not after all the lies that I told you—that I *had to* tell you to protect myself and my people. But I swear to you, Isola, that what I am about to say is the truth—and this might be the only chance I have to say it. So I'm going to. And you can choose if you want to listen and believe me or not."

Folding my arms and leaning against the back wall, I drag my eyes to him and let my silence be the best encouragement I can offer.

"I was born beyond the wall and spent my childhood there with my mother, my father, and my sister."

I was right. This might be the first time I have ever outright hated being correct. "You said you didn't remember anything from before the attack. That all you knew was your name. Another lie."

"A half-truth," he corrects, somewhat defensively. "When I first woke up following the attack, I didn't remember anything. I swear it. I didn't know who I was or what had happened. There was just a big, vacant spot… But the memories came back in pieces over time."

Do I believe him? Can I after everything?

"As the memories returned to me, they seemed impossible. I didn't believe them at first. I had all these recollections of people and places that were so different from anything that surrounded me—from this place that people were telling me was my home. I thought it was all a dream, I really did. I was just a child then."

"What made you believe it wasn't?" I ask, almost angry at myself for indulging him. Almost. But I want the truth, and I like him enough to see if it changes my feelings about all this.

"Your mother. She found me as she was hunting down information from the day of the attack." It makes sense. Lucan was the only other survivor. Mum would have questioned him for her research—or at least try to see if he saw anything when I unleashed the Etherlight. "And that was the start of me reclaiming my memories. After she was cast out of the Earthwardens and her research halted, it took a couple of years before I saw her again."

My jaw goes slack. "That was how she always seemed to know what the vicar was doing with me." Even if I never told her. She was always way too good at reading between the lines. She wasn't reading at all. She knew.

He nods. "I… I wanted to tell you everything for years. But she made me swear not to."

"You acted like you didn't even know who she was when I asked you to cover for me so I could celebrate her birthday," I breathe, staring off at nothing.

"I knew how remarkable a woman she was. And how much she loved you and would've loved to see you." Lucan takes a half step closer, and the space between us instantly feels intimate enough that my cheeks are flushing. The other two are so close. "But she also wanted nothing more than to protect you, and it was my honor to help then—even if it meant turning you in so we all continued playing our roles—just as it is my honor now."

An ashborn boy in the city. His sister infiltrating the knights to find him, check in on him. Mum figuring it out, and, of course, when she did, she'd naturally want to pick his memories for information on the world beyond.

There's just one thing that still sticks out to me. "If you were born beyond the wall, how did *you* get in?" I know how his sister did. But there was no mention of Lucan.

"Sorry to interrupt," Ember cuts in, "but it's been a while, and Pia still isn't back."

Lucan tenses, as though the time that passed physically struck him. He blinks, staring at the door, as though Pia just left through it. "She told us to wait."

"For how long?" Myla glances at her sister, and they share a look of quiet dread.

Lucan opens his mouth, closes it, then opens it again. "We haven't... It hasn't been *that* long."

"It's been long enough." Myla shoves her hands in her pockets and mumbles, "Probably longer than you think, lover boy."

My cheeks are hot, and I can't tell if it's embarrassment or annoyance.

Ember, in contrast with her sister, stands tall, confident and cool. "Are we supposed to wait here until we're caught? We know the path Pia was talking about—the way out to the other side of the wall. It's the same path she used to get us and Dazni in. We're dressed like their knights. We can easily sneak out."

"You want us to leave Pia and Dazni?" Even Myla is shocked.

"Dazni was meeting us at the tunnel out, and Pia is smart. She'll figure it out." Ember's confidence is unwavering. "Pia might have gone off to find Dazni, anyway. We don't know, but the longer we wait, the more the knights will have a chance to get down into these lower levels."

Lucan shakes his head. "We need to wait for the all-clear. We don't have the gilding or Pia's sigil to fake a golden eye." *So that's how she's doing it.* "Anyone would know we're not proper knights at a glance."

"It won't matter as long as we move quickly and keep our hoods up," Ember counters quickly.

Lucan gestures to me with a flick of his wrist. "She's not dressed as a knight and is the most recognizable person in all of Vinguard, not to mention the fact that she's supposed to be locked up as a dragon sympathizer... That's a much bigger problem than the gilding."

I don't love being called a "bigger problem," but he's absolutely right, so I keep my mouth shut.

"We can scout ahead when needed or lie and say we're escorting her to a new cell," Ember says, impatience hastening her words. "It's better than waiting for who knows how long. They're going to find out she's missing soon, and that will put them on high alert."

Something is off... It's like a chill in the air—a subtle shift that has the hairs on my arms rising. My skin prickles to gooseflesh. I've no reason for it, but it's as though an evil specter just passed through the room.

But they're right. We can't stay. And I've no solid reason to object.

Bracing myself, I gather my courage and say, "Let's go."

Lucan's head turns sharply, searching me. Looking to me as though I am the sole decider of what we do next. "Are you sure?"

I don't flinch. "I want to—*need to* get out of here. Ember is right. We should move before more Mercy Knights spread through the tower or raise the alarm."

Lucan hesitates a second longer and then nods once. He pulls his hood forward, and the other two do the same. The motion has a sense of finality to it, and my heart slams against my ribs. We emerge into the hall, and when the door clicks softly back into place behind us, it somehow feels louder than the ominous toll of dragon bells.

Ember and Myla take the lead, heads down, hoods pulled low. Lucan stays at my side, close enough that I can feel his perpetual warmth. Close enough that I'm fighting grabbing his hand for comfort.

We emerge from the side hall into the vertical heart of Mercy Spire. It's just like Pia said, sloping up and down in a gentle curve—like a corkscrew—with the same plain, plastered walls punctuated with dragon sconces as everywhere else in Mercy Spire. We move deliberately down, every footstep seeming louder than the last. Somehow, the silence is even more deafening.

There aren't any signs of life until heavy footsteps rise from below.

Myla and Ember glance back. There isn't any time to discuss before a Mercy Knight crests the curve of the pathway.

As his chin lifts, Lucan grabs my arm with a firm grip.

The twins nod and tug their hoods forward even more, casting their faces in deeper shadow. Lucan does the same as the Mercy Knight raises his eyes. The shift in him is instant. His jaw drops. There's recognition, then suspicion, but beneath it all is something uglier—something I've never seen from a citizen of Vinguard: hate.

"Look who we've captured," Lucan says triumphantly, squaring his shoulders. "No doubt trying to escape her punishment. Dragon sympathizer *and* a coward." He's a little too good at putting hatred in his voice. It almost stings.

"Excellent. We need to put her somewhere secure before she can manage to slip through our fingers again." The knight's expression shifts as his scowl breaks into a wide grin.

"I couldn't agree more." The chill in Ember's words couldn't feel more real.

"Follow me. There's a room with a good lock just around the bend we can put her in, for now, until we get shackles." He turns and begins starting down the way he came—the direction we were headed.

A series of glances are exchanged as we move. Myla and Ember catch each other's eyes. Then Myla looks back to Lucan, who nods; meanwhile, Ember's head shifts slightly. We're all going along with this for now, but I can sense what's unspoken: they're waiting for the right place to strike.

We've just rounded the bend when there's a flash of silver. The knight lunges for Ember, barely missing her chin. Myla lunges into his side with a grunt, shoving him away. My heart pounds in my throat as I watch the dagger sweep over her head.

The knight recovers, positioning himself ahead of us, down the slope. As though he knows where we're heading. "Don't make another move."

"It's four against one." Myla steps forward, already sinking into a crouch, hands balled into fists. "You think you'll get us all before we take you?"

"And we have Valor's power," Lucan says confidently.

Panic hits me, and I swallow thickly, trying to look confident. Trying to back him up. But I never promised this. I wanted to escape—to get out from under the Creed. Not attack random Mercy Knights.

He could've been Saipha, in another world.

The thought has my throat tightening.

"Put the dagger down and you won't die," Ember says firmly.

The knight just smirks. Footsteps echo from deeper ahead. A voice twice as vile as the acid of a green dragon oozes through the passageway.

"I don't think he will." Vicar Darius steps into view from around the curve of the tower. Robed in blood red, his eyes alight with triumph.

He doesn't come alone. Two Mercy Knights flank him, dragging Dazni and Pia. The ashborn are bloodied, bruised, and barely able to support themselves. Both have blades pressed to their throats. Four more knights are close behind.

"If you value their lives, you will do as I say."

63

Two things happen at once, so quickly I hardly have time to tell which is first.

Lucan's hold on me relaxes, leaving behind cool air in stark contrast to his heat. I recognize his intention before he lurches forward. It's the way he shifts his weight, the power gathering in his legs. Without thinking, I reach for him and manage to snag his wrist.

His wide eyes swing back to me, surprise flashing across his face like the sparks of Etherlight off a yellow dragon's wings. I don't release him, not even when his brow furrows and jaw sets. He strains like a dog at the end of a leash but doesn't yet rip himself free.

"Let them go," he snarls to the vicar. His voice is lower than I've ever heard, almost guttural—almost *inhuman*.

At nearly the same second, I feel the chill of metal underneath my chin. Ember has unsheathed the dagger she wore as part of her disguise as a Mercy Knight. The movement was so fluid I didn't even see it happen, though my focus was on Lucan.

I go stone-still. Every breath is shallow. Is the blade fake and part of a disguise? Or, to make the disguise believable, did they get the real deal? I'm not going to risk a single movement to find out.

"You're not the only one with something to bargain." Ember's voice is clear and unwavering. "Don't move, or something will happen to your precious Valor Reborn."

The knights across from us tense visibly as their eyes dart to the vicar, waiting for his reaction, palms hovering over their daggers. Even the muscles of Lucan's forearm go rigid under my fingers. There's a quiet horror in his expression as he looks at Ember.

She wouldn't, would she? I can feel us both think at the same time.

The vicar lowers his chin, a shadow passing over his eyes. But rather than scowling, his lips curl upward. He smiles, as if utterly delighted by this turn of events, like a man who's just uncovered a particularly fascinating artificer sigil to play with. "Very well, let's arrange some kind of deal."

"Don't listen to him!" Pia urges, stance strong despite her bound wrists and the bruises across her face. "He will not—"

"Shut her up," the vicar snaps, the pleasant facade falling away like a blanket.

The knight holding Pia yanks her back, an arm around her throat. She gasps, hands straining against their bindings to reach for the forearm constricting her throat, her face flushing red as she struggles to breathe.

"Look at how strong your vicar is, afraid of some words from an ashborn," Dazni quips to the other knights.

"One more word from either of you, and it'll be your last." Another knight wields his dagger openly, pointing it at them both. These people aren't going to be swayed from the Creed.

"Don't you dare." Ember shifts her grip on me and presses the dagger more fully into my throat, reminding them who really has control here.

Lucan practically vibrates with barely contained rage. He lets out a low growl, mouth fighting a snarl, eyes sweeping between Ember and the vicar. If I released my hold on him, I'm not sure if he'd lunge for the dagger at my throat or the vicar. Either way, it'd be the end of us.

"Enough." The vicar's gaze returns to me, even though Ember is the one holding the dagger. "This is between me and my Valor Reborn. The rest of you do not matter."

"Excuse me?" Ember lets out a brief and disbelieving laugh. She pulls me a little closer, and I feel the blade kiss my flesh. "I'm the one with the weapon at her throat. Or are your eyes starting to fail you in your years?"

"You have no leverage here; we all know you're not going to kill her." His lips twist past the point of smiling and into a sneer. Pure triumph oozes off him. "You know what she is. Otherwise, why would you risk everything, including your lives, to steal her from me? But I'm afraid I've invested too much in her to let her go now."

He turns his fevered gaze on me, and I shudder. "So, my negotiation is with you, Isola. Don't let them deceive you into believing they have power. Don't even think about summoning your little flames. It is my power that is absolute here. They won't touch you because they need you alive, but we both know I will slaughter them without a second thought." He sweeps his eyes over Lucan and the twins before returning them to mine.

"It's time to fulfill your destiny, your great calling, your birthright." His voice is laced with hunger. "Agree to do as I say, and I will let them go free."

Laughter nearly escapes me. *Let them go free?* He already showed his hand seconds ago. This chaos is clearly throwing him off-balance. I know all too well the vicar will kill them the moment he no longer needs me. But I keep my composure. One crack and they're dead. They're only breathing because he thinks they're leverage over me.

And he's not wrong... I won't let them die if I can prevent it. But that doesn't mean I will merely give up and do as he says.

He still thinks I'm weak. Naive. Pliable. A token in his game. But I'm not that girl anymore.

"All right," I say, allowing some of the genuine worry I have about walking this dagger's edge to inject into my voice to make it crack. I need to sound smaller than I feel if he's going to believe this... "I'll do as you wish, I swear it. Please don't hurt them."

Ember inhales sharply. "What?"

"Fight, you coward," Myla breathes, dripping more venom than a green dragon's fang.

"You can't win." I look at Ember from the corner of my eyes, gambling everything in the hopes that she'll read between the lines. If I manage to convince her, Myla will fall into place. "You're outnumbered and overpowered. Give in and beg for forgiveness from the Creed. The vicar can be a merciful man to a reformed heart."

"If you think I will ever—" Ember starts with a snarl.

But she's interrupted by Lucan. "She's right." Lucan slumps slightly, his posture going slack as if he's seeing defeat. I can feel his tension—his defiance under my grip. But he plays his part. "We can't win."

Not right now. Not like this.

"Lucan?" Ember's voice breaks on his name, equal measures confused and hurt. "What are you saying?"

"Have you lost your mind?" Myla adds with quiet horror.

"They've won. We've lost. It's as simple as that, Ember," he says flatly.

Then his eyes find mine.

Time halts for a breath, the silence between us roaring. He asks a question that I'm not sure I can answer with a heartbeat's worth of staring alone. Do we trust each other? Even after what's happened, can we work together?

I won't let you die, Lucan. I feel it more than think it. As though my heart responds when my mind and my mouth cannot. *I saved you once, and I'll do it again. But you better not make me regret it.*

His attention shifts back to Ember, and time seems to speed back up. "They have more power than you realize."

"Listen to him," the vicar counsels with practiced ease, but I don't miss the edge in his voice. His monster within is clawing against the surface. "Lucan would intimately know our power, after all. Isn't that right, *son*?" The vicar shifts toward the knights. "Take them all to the Grand Chapel."

"Sir? Even the ashborn?"

"*All* of them," the vicar snaps. His patience is wearing thin. "Their presence will ensure she does as she's told."

No one dares question him again.

Ember lowers the dagger at my throat. In the process, she murmurs for me alone, "You better know what you're doing."

So, she did figure out I was trying to send a message.

There's no time for any kind of response. The knights are upon us, disarming the three of them with stunning efficiency and knocking them to their knees. Their arms are wrenched together, rope quickly tied around their wrists in front of them. I press my lips shut to keep from speaking up for them. Anything I could say would only make things worse.

Bound, they're forced back to their feet. Even though their expressions are of reluctant surrender, I can see Lucan's arms flexing against his binding, testing its strength. The Mercy Knights push them ahead, casting me cold, wary stares as they pass.

I'm left with the vicar, who now regards me like a vengeful god who's weighing my fate. He reaches out with a bony hand and cups my cheek. His touch is cold and dry, with little more life than the dragon head in the sundering pits. I fight the urge to flinch and withdraw.

"Come," he whispers. "To meet your destiny."

He grips my elbow like a vile groom might escort an unwilling bride, leading me up and out of Mercy Spire.

64

My stomach lurches at the vicar's touch. Just his hand on me, and I'm nearly sick all over his shoes. Every step is a struggle, his grip never easing on my elbow.

The world around me blurs into a smear of color and shadows and smooth walls and dragon sconces. I can't focus on anything when he's this close. When he's touching me. All I'm aware of is his proximity. His suffocating presence that makes my skin crawl.

Breathe, I tell myself, *breathe and keep your head high*.

We reach a carriage house that opens to Vinguard. It's so strange to see the city from the streets after weeks of looking out upon it from the height of the monastery. Two ornate carriages await, their polished exteriors familiar and as flawless as ever.

These things never show up when anything good is happening.

"Valor Reborn with me," Vicar Darius instructs. "My *son*, too." He says *son* with a note of disgust. "Put the rest in the carriage behind."

The number of Mercy Knights surrounding us has doubled. Now they also wield crossbows. The message is clear: run and die.

The vicar guides me to the carriage door, his hand never leaving my person. "After you." The kindness is a mockery.

I climb in and instantly go for the farthest corner. The relief of breaking physical contact with him is so overwhelming that I practically collapse into the seat, pushing back as far as I can into the plush velvet—the carriage is small, and I want all the distance I can find. To my surprise and delight, the vicar doesn't immediately follow; instead, he barks additional orders, probably to the driver, given how the carriage rocks.

Lucan is pushed in by a knight next.

He slides in beside me, and there is a single moment where it's only the two of us. The vicar is still just on the other side of the half-closed door, along with a small army of Mercy Knights. But I'm not paying attention to them. All I see is Lucan, his gaze holding mine. He shifts slightly to face me.

My heart races, and suddenly all the things I was mad about before evaporate. I don't want to lose *this*. Whatever it is between us. Even if it's messy and confusing…it's real. It's mine. And one of the last things I have.

"I will get us out of here," he breathes, voice so low that even in the confines of the carriage, I strain to hear him. "You saved me once already. Now it's my turn."

"Lucan, please—" I begin, voice catching.

"He cannot have your power. He cannot have *you*." There's a fierce protectiveness to the statement that steals my breath.

I swallow hard, words fighting past the knot in my throat. All I can say in reply is, "I don't want him to hurt you."

"Even though I betrayed you?" He doesn't move. He's so rigid he must be forcing himself not to reach for me. I can almost feel his hand gliding across my cheek as if to smooth over the vicar's offending touch.

Dragon-burned hells, I *wish* he could touch me.

"I am hurt, angry… And I could hate you for it. Maybe I should. But that doesn't mean I want you dead."

"*Do* you hate me?" Desperation creeps into the question.

"Hate you? Of course not." I catalog his face like it's a sigil. I want to remember him perfectly for however much time I have left. "Lucan, I…"

The words evaporate on my tongue. Every notion I can come up with is inadequate or incomplete or both. How can I name this feeling that's sprouted like hope in a scourge-filled wasteland? It's as though my heart has run off the map of everything I've known and straight into uncharted territory.

What is the word for this?

It's not love. Not yet... Love is something *more*. At least I imagine it to be.

This feeling is like a blossom—a possibility. Fragile and precious. It *could be* love one day. It could be love with enough apologies and explanations and forgiveness on both sides... Perhaps, it would be love, if we had time.

"You?" Lucan hangs on my unfinished thought.

My heart aches. It doesn't skip or shudder. It simply hurts in its yearning for him.

But there's no time. The vicar climbs into the carriage, and Lucan leans away and settles into the seat. The door closes, and with a spark of Etherlight, the carriage lurches forward, the only sound the grinding of the wheels on gravel.

The vicar finally breaks the silence with a dramatic sigh. "I must admit, this is...disappointing. I invested so much in both of you." He has the tone of a loving father, not the monster that we both know he is.

I nearly lunge for him. It's almost impossible not to throw my hands around that wiry neck of his and squeeze until he stops breathing.

"You both had so much potential. You, my Valor Reborn"—his eyes shift from me to Lucan—"and you. You were to be my successor. Once I had ascended, you would lead the Creed—my army, as my mortal hand."

"I would rather die." The Lucan I saw in the Tribunal is on full display. *This* is the man who loathes the vicar. Who has bitten his tongue for half a decade. Who has played his part time and again even as he made his own movements in the shadows.

"That will be arranged." The vicar smiles, eyes shining with crazed brutality.

The carriage halts. The ride between Mercy Spire and the Great Chapel is short. The vehicle hasn't even stopped rocking when the door swings open.

The vicar steps out and extends his hand back to me. "Come. It is time to meet your destiny."

The urge to slap his hand away is nearly overwhelming.

"Unless you no longer value their lives?" the vicar chides ominously, voice low.

I glance back to Lucan, who sits unflinching, face unreadable. Minutes ago, he was full of hope, promising to get us out of here. Now, he's as trapped as I am.

I place my hand into the vicar's and fight the bile rising in my throat. He helps me from the carriage, and two lines of waiting curates lead us into the Grand Chapel of Mercy. My head spins as every fiber of my body rejects what's coming—rejects the notion that I am at the whim of Vicar Darius.

Above ground, the chapel is technically just one story tall, but its roof soars daringly high, taller than four stories. Every pointed spire impales a sculpted dragon, their mouths fixed in agonizing snarls. People of stone, dressed in the armor of the Mercy Knights, scale walls, ready crossbows, and skewer dragons with lances of carved lightning and steel.

"I want two daggers on each of them at all times. If they so much as even look the wrong way, kill them," Vicar Darius instructs the Mercy Knights. Pia, Dazni, Myla, and Ember are taken from the other carriage and follow behind as I am escorted past two rows of praying curates in the square in front of the chapel.

Never has the Grand Chapel been so empty. There are none uttering prayers. No curates performing rites. No offering before the statue of Valor.

The late afternoon sun bleeds through the tall windows, stretching long lines of crimson across the empty pews. The statue of Valor at the far altar is emblazoned in golden light, holding a sword aloft—the sword said to be the weapon by which the Elder Dragon will be defeated.

"What are you going to do to me?" Terror makes my voice softer than I want. I am trying so hard to keep my courage even in the face of the twisted man before me. *He needs me, and I will use that against him, somehow*, I remind myself.

"I waited for so long for your power to mature…but I cannot wait any longer. Now it is time to meet your destiny, and that is *not* as Valor Reborn yourself," he says gently, patting my hand as if in condolence. The Mercy Knights stream in with the five ashborn. I try to glance back toward Lucan, but I can't find an opportunity while the vicar's attention is on me alone. "You are the catalyst by which the true Valor Reborn will return to this world."

My heart hammers in my chest with every step closer to the altar—and the statue of Valor. I realize that it is not just the sunlight, but the elegant blade is actually *glowing* with Etherlight. Are there sigils hidden on it? Within it?

The magic dances in the air around it, gnarled and contorted. It's Etherlight, but it moves in ways I've never seen before. Ways that feel unnatural.

That's when I see it. Something else. Magic that vibrates in tight knots of crimson, wrestling against the threads of Etherlight. Magic the same shade as dragon's blood—as the scourge.

Ethershade.

"You were chosen by fate and guided by me." Vicar Darius drops my hand and ascends the altar. His fingers close around the grip of the weapon, and he pulls it down. The Ether seems to revolt at his touch. I can almost imagine it screaming. "Sacrifice is rarely pretty. But it is always necessary."

"What do you want from me?" I refrain from stepping back as he descends with the weapon in hand.

The vicar merely smiles. "For you to die."

Without warning or hesitation, without another word, he plunges the blade into my stomach, impaling me clean through.

65

A scream lodges in my throat. The blade cuts more than flesh; it's as if it tears through a part of my raw essence.

Air leaves my lungs as little more than a gurgle. I can't breathe. I can't even *think*.

In the distance is a dull scream. Lucan? It's so hard to hear. I feel as though I've been plunged underwater.

The sword pulses with power that vibrates against my insides. As though it's alive and pulling itself even deeper—knitting itself into my being. My hands go to the hilt, but I can't find a grip; it's too slick from my own blood.

Then the ground beneath me flares with light.

Etherlight, golden and pure, so brilliant and potent that it lights up the entire cathedral, rushes out in jagged fractures from under my feet. It webs away from me in jagged cracks that seem random until they begin to connect. Until the lines merge and a pattern begins to show.

"Wh—Wh—" There are no words. I keep trying to grab the hilt, but my hands don't have the strength. My fingers tremble violently as my whole body begins to shudder. The only thing keeping me upright is the blade.

The vicar's voice cuts through my terror. "It took me years to assemble the pieces required to activate it again. But assemble I did. Valor's greatest work, the most magnificent artificer sigil ever conceived, will be the foundation by which your power is given to me. There is nothing gained without sacrifice." The vicar looms over me for one moment longer, as though admiring a masterpiece. And then he releases the blade and turns, strolling casually as though I'm not dying and the room isn't awash in the golden light of Ether.

I collapse to my knees. My vision blurs, and when it comes into focus again, he's climbed the altar steps. There, he lies upon the altar before the statue of Valor, a tether of Ether flowing directly from the sword lodged in my body to his supine form. There must be some kind of sigil upon it as well, something to connect it with the sword... I'd figure it out if I wasn't about to die. Distant screams rise—identical to what I heard in the Font.

Straining against the pain, hand still on the bloody sword hilt, I look back. One of the Mercy Knights is wailing, holding his gilded eye. Molten gold drips between his fingers and fades into stardust before it hits the ground. It'd be beautiful if it were not horrifying. More sounds of agony rise from beyond the entry.

The ashborn look on in horror. All except Lucan. He stands perfectly still, eyes on me, shining as though illuminated by their own Ether. Pure terror on my behalf fills his expression.

My lips part, and I want to cry out. To reach for him. But I can't move. I'm going to die, and I don't want to die alone. *Was this how Saipha felt in her final moments when I pushed her away?*

The thought guts me as violently as the sword.

I look back to the vicar, but it's hard to see him now through the surge of Etherlight. The world blurs and fades away as Ether overwhelms my consciousness. It is the same feeling as when the Font exploded, but more complete. As if my body has been taken into a different time and place where the pain has vanished, as has my physical form.

For a moment, there is no beginning and no end. No me. No Ether. Just...sameness.

Slowly, the world comes back into focus, but I am no longer in the Grand Chapel of Mercy.

I stand in a cavernous space that reminds me of the deep thermal pools of the Undercrust. The clear water is a window to a rainbow of luminescent striations that bathes the space in a pale, off-white glow.

A man in his prime, with fair skin, blond hair, blue eyes, and his upper body as naked as the day he was born, wades into the water. His skin is marked with lines like an artificer's sigils. The spring is so clear that I can see countless bones of beasts of all shapes and sizes lining its bottom.

The moment he descends into the water, there's a burst of Etherlight that has me flinching as though a wall of fire assaulted me, bracing like I'm back in the Font. I lift my hands to protect myself, but no pain comes. When I lower them, I'm at the top of one of the snow-capped mountains I've grown up in the shadow of.

The man is there again—clothed this time. His eyes now glow a brilliant gold. He addresses a group of people beneath him with impassioned shouting. For me, the words are muffled and hazy, as if underwater. I can't make out a single one. The people listening cheer in reply.

The man before me turns, golden eyes meeting mine as if he can see me.

One look, and the mountainside beneath me crumbles. I tumble backward, falling. For a second, I hear the beating of thousands of wings. They fade away, rising on an updraft. One remains.

Lucan.

I feel him in my blood. He's right there, next to my heart, where he's been all along. I reach out for a shadow. My feet meet the edge of a wall, and the world twists. I'm no longer falling but standing at the edge of a precipice.

It's a tower that will one day become Vinguard's wall. But the city within is gone. It's a hollow pit that stretches deep, *deep* into the core of the earth—to the last remaining Font in the world. More towers stand tall at the pit's rim. Between them, a crater is filled with…

Bones.

Thousands upon thousands of bones. Bones from what must have been half of humanity piled into this void of nothingness, framing out the depths that will become the Undercrust. The golden-eyed man next to me surveys the work with another, giving direction and input. Once more, the words are lost—swallowed by the wind. But I catch a glimpse of the parchment.

I'm drawn closer to it.

It's not plans for a city... It's a massive artificer sigil. What I know as towers and the roads are all lines to draw Etherlight upon. Even disembodied as I am, my stomach churns.

Etherlight flows within everyone. Humans are the catalyst for it in the world. If one were to pile a bunch of corpses and tie them together with some kind of sigil...

It could make a Font.

"Why?" I think, and the question resonates aloud. The world liquefies at the vibration of my words like a stone thrown into a calm pond.

"To survive," a new voice answers.

I turn, and everything shifts around me, swaying, coming back into place in a vast plain. Tall grasses sway in a wind I can't feel. The sky overhead is a blue more brilliant than I've ever seen in my lifetime. It never occurred to me that the scourge was so thick that it tarnished even the sky.

The man comes into focus once more, this time in simple clothing that is oddly reminiscent of what I've worn for weeks in the Tribunal.

"Who are you?" I ask without speaking. Even though, deep within me, I already know.

Before he can answer, he staggers back, turning his face skyward. Screams turn to roars. A swirl of Etherlight consumes him, and he begins to shift. Massive gray wings protrude from his back.

I stumble two steps, recover, and look up to find myself suddenly face-to-face with the mightiest dragon I've ever beheld. The statue in the monastery didn't do it justice.

Its eye alone is so large that I could lay comfortably in its socket. The silvery hue reminds me of the milky eyes of a great grandparent. Yet, despite it lacking any pupil—even the slitted one of a dragon—I am acutely aware that it sees me. Four large, curling horns protrude from its head. Among slate and silver fans of spikes and jagged scales, long tendrils of white hair extend from its chin, behind where I'd imagine its ears to be, and down its long neck. Its wings are speckled with holes of ancient battles. Scars cross and line its body in angry trellises.

My throat is as barren as scourged earth. The swirl of primeval Ether that radiates off the creature batters me. I'm awed. I'm humbled. Reminded of just how small I am. How grand and wonderful and terrifying the world is all at once. Even though I've never beheld this monstrosity before, I know, beyond all doubt...

It's the Elder Dragon.

I stare into its golden eyes, drowning in the swirl of its Etherlight, the visions continuing to assault me. They batter me like falling stars, too hot and too bright. But they fall into constellations in my mental landscape. Lines connect them to form a word.

I stare into the almost-dead, unseeing eye of the Elder Dragon and whisper a name:

"Valor?"

The dragon leans away. The wind whips up. And the hair on the back of my neck is instantly on edge, as there's a massive swell of power.

The Elder Dragon opens his mouth, revealing three rows of blade-like teeth larger than my entire body. I realize a breath too late that he's going to attack. But as he lunges for me, he disappears into nothing more than a whisper of Etherlight.

I EXHALE, HAND still wrapped around the sword plunged through my gut.

I am back in the Grand Chapel of Mercy. The screams return to my ears—a chorus of agony sung by every citizen of Vinguard. Lines of gold are still etched upon the floor. It feels as if the entirety of the Font has been dredged up to where we all now stand.

But none of that matters now. I know the truth hidden from every citizen.

The Elder Dragon is Valor.

Valor is the Elder Dragon.

He made the Font and then changed himself into the Elder Dragon with this place.

Vinguard wasn't humanity's last stand. It wasn't Valor's fortress. It was never even a city at all.

It was an artificer sigil designed to funnel power into one man. But that power... Something in it was too much. Or twisted. And Valor became the Elder Dragon.

I don't know how the power in the Font was able to show me all of this. Perhaps it was a piece of its artificer still trapped within it, like a maker's mark on an invention. Or could it be that the magic itself was crying out for balance?

And now, if I don't stop this, history will repeat itself. Only worse.

What can you do? The small, doubtful voice of the girl I once was bubbles up to the surface. *You're not Valor Reborn.*

I'm not. In the end, I was nothing but a tool in a plan I don't even fully understand. I thought myself so smart, so capable. But I never had more than half the information while fate mocked me, holding the rest.

I stare at the blade protruding from my stomach. The only reason I'm still alive must be the Etherlight flowing through me. Yet there's even more I don't understand. I press my eyes closed, willing it to change, to be different, to wake up back at the start of the Tribunal and find a way to fix all this.

But when I open my eyes again, the sword is still there. As is the tether of Etherlight that connects me to Vicar Darius. My fingers slip again on the hilt as I reach for it, my eyes now solely focused on the man who's made my life a living hell for years.

"No." I force the word through gritted teeth. Past the crushing agony and endless doubt that's tried to pull me down for the past six years.

He took everything from me. My freedom. My future. My hopes and dreams. My friends and my family. I will not let him have this power.

Maybe you're not Valor. Lucan's words return to me softly, as though he's murmuring them right in my ear. I can almost feel his warmth at my back. *But that doesn't mean you can't save this world. If anyone can find a way, it'd be you.*

Vinguard deserves a hero. But all they have is a scared eighteen-year-old girl.

So I'd damn well better be enough.

I grab the hilt of the blade with purpose, my fingers finally closing around it. Gritting my teeth, I yank on the blade and begin to pull it from my stomach. Skin pulls and grabs and slices with every inch. I grit my teeth past the pain, focusing on the vicar and what I have to do. When it's on the cusp of being too much, my rage holds me together.

Somehow, not even this kills me. It tries—oh, how it tries—but it cannot. Not with this much Etherlight surging through me.

The blade I rip out is not the same as when it entered my body. Gone is the steel, and in its place is a sword seemingly crafted of crimson Ether—as if my blood has condensed into a glowing weapon. Pressing my palm into my stomach, I find my skin has mended. The wound is no longer there, a merely blood-soaked slit in my clothing.

"Isola!" Lucan cries from behind me as I cross to the dais upon which the altar and the vicar rest, my legs shaking. The sound of his voice empowers me like a surge of Ether.

My focus remains on the vicar alone. I ascend the stone steps to the altar where he lies. His eyes flutter open as I loom over him, raising the sword aloft, holding it nearly vertical, pommel to the ceiling, point down toward him. Etherlight no longer connects us. It swells around me alone, and all I see is red.

"What are—" His wide, frantic eyes search me. In his horror, he whispers, "It was supposed to be mine."

"Nothing of mine was ever yours." I bring down the blade, stabbing the point through his throat—all the way to the stone below—and killing him instantly.

66

The moment the vicar dies, the ground groans and shudders. It's as though the earth is revolting. Etherlight sparks and bursts, cracking stone and pocking the sculptures of the Grand Chapel. The screams continue from beyond and from within—the Mercy Knights still howl behind me, holding their faces as gold drips away. Most of them have collapsed to the floor. Some have gone silent.

But all I see is Vicar Darius. His crimson blood that stains the altar and the Ether around us emits a noxious haze like the scourge, as though this whole time he has been rotting from within. He was the real blight that beset our city.

A hand closes around mine, yanking me away from the vicar's corpse. I'm swung around and find myself face-to-face with Lucan. His other hand rises, cupping my cheek.

"Isola…" he breathes.

"It's over… It's finally over," I whisper, even as the world around us crumbles. Even as my knees threaten to give out.

"No." Lucan's eyes are wide enough to encompass all the horrors of the world. "It's only just beginning."

I open my mouth, but no words come. The ground continues to shudder.

"We have to go." Without another word, he shifts to my side and wraps an arm around my waist, supporting me. I might be healed by some miracle, but I am utterly exhausted.

"Go where?" I'm in a daze. The others are waiting with equally panicked expressions.

"Far from here." Lucan pulls me quickly through the chapel, and the others flank us. The Mercy Knights are struggling to stand and can do nothing to stop us. The one on the ground is still breathing, but they're thin, raspy breaths. His cheeks are sunken.

"We must help them." I tug Lucan's hand. "We can't leave. Vinguard needs us."

No sooner have I said as much as than unfamiliar man shouts, "She killed the vicar!"

"She... What's happening came from her! The vicar tried to kill her to save us." One of the Mercy Knights is struggling to her feet.

"No. You don't understand. Vinguard is a sigil. It was Valor who made it—who made the Font."

"Heresy!" Another curate appears in the doorframe. They must be running from the square outside.

"I know what I'm saying is hard to believe, but—"

"Isola Thaz impersonated Valor Reborn to kill the vicar!"

The curate lunges for us. Luckily, he's unarmed, and Lucan deflects him, pulling me away. Ember launches in, Pia not far behind. Myla and Dazni on our sides, regarding the other curates warily.

"Isola, I know you want to help," Lucan says softly but hastily, eyes flicking around, assessing every threat closing in on us as a low rumbling shakes the ground ominously beneath us. "But I don't think they're going to listen."

"We have no other choice." We're backed into a corner. A whole city who is going to see us as the enemy outside. "We must make them believe."

"We have one other choice."

Lucan's words catch Pia's attention. She shifts back, fists still up, and locks eyes with Lucan. "Are you sure?" Her voice is tight with worry.

"I'm not sure about anything. But we don't have any other option." Lucan wears an expression of sheer determination, eyes narrowed and jaw hard.

"Are we getting out how I think we are?" Myla's eyes dart between the other ashborn. She nearly vibrates with excitement. It's far more energy than I have left in my tired bones.

"Myla, now is not the time to sound like you're about to get sugarcane," Ember says dryly. Pia just shoots Myla a look.

"I have been wanting to see this for *years*." Myla gestures to Lucan. "He's the one."

"No. Not me." Lucan leaves no room for doubt as he looks at me. "It's Isola. It's always been Isola. Every credit, every praise, and every hope is her."

I rub my stomach where the wound should be. Where there is mended flesh and not even an ache. I instinctively wielded magic I don't even comprehend.

The ashborn carve us a path through the curates strong enough to stand outside to the courtyard in front of the Grand Chapel. A few punches are thrown. But it's mostly shoving and brandishing of Mercy daggers. There's a reason why the Creed has Mercy Knights to uphold its teachings—the curates hardly put up a fight.

It's easier than I would've expected because most of the curates are on the ground, wailing in pain like the Mercy Knights inside the chapel. They've crawled to the stairs, but one or two didn't make it. A man and a woman lie on the ground, eyes blank, skin shriveled as though all the life has been drained from them.

Lucan pauses to release me, waiting to completely let go until I find my feet. "Wait here."

"What are you going to do?" I nearly grab for him to keep him close.

With a sad smile, he gently tucks a strand of hair behind my ear. He struggles to find words, and all he manages is, "Forgive me."

As he steps away, I reach for him. "Lucan—"

Pia blocks me with a strong arm. "Give him space."

I glare at her, but I don't move. Not because of her command, but because this is clearly what Lucan wanted. Still, it feels as though a part of me is drawn toward him with an invisible string that tugs from my heart to his. Something far more powerful than what flowed between the Vicar and me.

Lucan strides to the far end of the courtyard before the Grand Chapel, far from anyone else. He looks small and almost insignificant amidst the cracking foundation of Vinguard and the glittering haze of Etherlight that seems to flow in reverse from the Font deep below. He shifts his stance and looks back to me one last time before Etherlight collects around him, swirling like a windstorm.

My lips part in a soundless cry, my heart thundering in my chest. I know what's about to happen before it does, because I've seen it before.

"Lucan!" I scream as he is engulfed by thick black smoke and raging fire.

Wings unfurl from the vortex. Small at first, then growing to massive size. The smoke and flame condense back onto his form as scales of fire orange and smoke black. Two horns curl from his head by his temples, just above his ears. His eyes are completely orange, sparking with flame at their edges.

For a second, I can still see the man, even half-coated in scales and clothed in smoke and flame. But then he disappears completely as the fire burns away the remaining flesh. With sparks and embers, claws grow, scales cover, bones snap, and a scream of anguish rends the air as the large form of a dragon fills the square.

The ground feels like it's tilting beneath my feet, and I reach out to hold on to Pia.

It's him... The dragon from all those years ago. The one who attacked me.

Horror hits the back of my throat like bile. This man attacked my city. I think of the bodies and the flames. Of the destruction.

But, then, the copper dragon lowers its massive face to us and stares right at me—right *into* me.

His eyes aren't the blazing orange I remember from six years ago. His pupils are not slits. He stares at me with familiar hazel eyes.

"Lucan?" I whisper.

A dip of his chin. It's him. These are not the vacant eyes of the dragons that attack Vinguard. It's the man within, just in a different shape. It's like the flash I had of Saipha in her dragon but more solid and sustaining.

Lucan said he didn't remember anything for a long time after the day of the attack. What if there is the person *and* the beast?

It'd be one thing the Creed got right. The dragon traps the people within when they transform. But something can bring them back, something I don't yet understand.

One hand on my chest, over the scars against my heart, the other on his muzzle.

"It was you. It was always you." The way he was drawn to me. The way that even when I found him insufferable, I couldn't stop myself from staring at him. The way I was compelled to trust him over, and over, and over again.

The mark on my chest—the *sigil*, my father told me—he gave it to me. Etherlight flows between us like a dance. We are tied together in ways I can barely understand. I breathe, and he does the same, in tandem, as if we share one breath and one body.

"So. Amazing," Myla whispers, breaking the moment.

Ember has dropped to her knees at her sister's side. Tears stream down her face. "It is possible. It is possible," she repeats over and over. "They can be changed back."

"We need to move!" Dazni scans the walls. "A dragon is now in Vinguard."

Pia nods in agreement and grabs my elbow. Dazni helps the twins.

Lucan lowers his belly to the ground and relaxes a wing. Dazni begins to climb the wide, scale-coated muscle and bone that connect the membrane of the wing. Pia is next, and she extends a hand back to me.

I don't hesitate. I take it and begin crawling up the wing. I might not know everything, but I know that even though the body might be the same, this is not the dragon that attacked me six years ago. This is Lucan. *My* Lucan.

Dazni, Ember, and Myla have made it atop his back, and Pia is not far behind when a shift in the Etherlight has my head jerking in the direction of a tower.

"Lucan, go!" I scream. "Go now!"

His monstrous head turns, and he sees what I do. With a mighty flap of his wings, he takes to the skies right as cannon fire shoots across the city, and I am helpless to do anything but cling to him.

I strain with all my might to keep hold of Lucan's thick scales as he launches himself skyward, away from the courtyard of the Grand Chapel of Mercy, but I cannot. Between the wind and swift movement of the wing, I lose my grip and am thrown.

The ashborn scream from Lucan's back as a ribbon of deadly Etherlight from the cannon streaks between us. I stare up at Lucan's dragon form as the Etherlight harmlessly dissipates. *He'll get away. They'll get away*, I think as I fall through the air and brace myself for impact.

But it never comes. With a roar, Lucan reaches a clawed hand down and grabs me right before I hit the ground. My body sags slightly in his grip, hair brushing against the stone where my head would've slammed.

I stare up at him for a breathless second that is nothing more than the time it takes for him to flap his wings once. Then we shoot into the sky. Wind swirls with smoke and sparks as Lucan's powerful wings propel us higher and higher.

Even though I am little more than a rag doll in his talons, I cling to one of the four massive claws that are wrapped around me, as if I'm the one who's holding him and not just along for the ride. The world below shrinks rapidly as we ascend. Cold air whips my cheeks, drawing water from my eyes.

Beneath us, it looks as though someone has dipped a brush into raw Ether and drawn it across Vinguard. Ancient streets illuminate pathways to the original towers, now embedded deep within the modern walls. The Grand Chapel is at its center, streaming Ether into the sky with a column of light.

Cracks split the earth as it rumbles once more. Slivers of Vinguard between the lines of Etherlight slip ever so slightly. Buildings collapse, people streaming out into the city just in time to avoid being crushed. But I know not everyone made it. They couldn't have. And my heart sinks for those that couldn't. Tears burn my eyes—of mourning, and of hate for the man that brought about this destruction for his selfish desires.

Vinguard's greatest danger was never the dragons, not even the scourge, but the greed of men within.

I scream again, this time for Vinguard. The only home I've ever known. There is no right or wrong anymore, no good or bad. Everything has changed in an instant, and I no longer know what to believe.

Everything is out of control.

We soar higher, racing to get away from the chaos and destruction. The blighted lands unfurl beneath us like a quilt of shadowed ruins beyond the walls. The glowing metropolis of Vinguard is in stark contrast to a sea of decay that has left its scars across the earth itself. The walls that had once felt so...secure, so *important*, are reduced to nothing more than thin lines that carve out a city from nature. From this high, it's almost pathetic to think we believed that brick and mortar might have truly kept us safe.

Another boom rattles the clouds around us.

"Left!" Pia shouts from atop Lucan's back, fingers firmly grasping one of his dinner-plate-sized scales.

He banks hard, and another beam of Ether from a cannon punctures the night sky. I scan the towers below. More cannons and ballistae are readying.

Think, Isola. Think about all the times Saipha pointed out where the cannons were stationed. All the times Father mentioned where they were building new supports for the massive weapons.

"Right, Lucan! Next is right!" I shout.

He banks right before another cannon shot.

Tucking his wings, he barrels toward the mountains in the

distance. At this speed, we won't be in range for much longer. The cannon fire can only make it to the steep foothills.

My eyes water as I clutch the scales that line his talons. They're softer than I would've expected, though copper dragons don't have the steely scales of silver dragons.

Lucan is a dragon. The surreal notion races in my mind as I grip him tightly. Wonder dances with hurt in my chest. Anger tries to cut in. Lucan didn't tell me. He knew, and he tried to stop me from saving Saipha.

The distraction has me looking away from the wall for a second too long. A cannon shot bursts from behind, and I barely have time to turn my head. We are nearly out of range—the hills below are turning to the rocky feet of the mountains. So close, and yet...

Lucan tries to dodge by wildly throwing his body. But it's too late. His right wing is punctured clean through, nearly at its base.

We all let out a scream in unison. Lucan's roar echoes off the mountains. The talon holding me unfurls, going limp. I try to cling on, but my fingers can't find purchase. The scales are too slick, and my strength is still sapped. The safety of the dragon's grip leaves me, replaced by open air.

I fall.

68

It's such a surreal sensation that I don't even let out another sound. An odd sense of calm overtakes me as the wind howls in my ears, and the chill of the mountain peaks envelops me.

Pia, Dazni, Myla, and Ember are all thrown as well. They are nothing more than dark shapes against the inky sky. Barely visible beneath Lucan's massive spark-haloed form.

My heart begins to race faster and more erratically than I've ever felt. My skin *ripples*. Every ragged, panicked breath feels like it's tearing my lungs apart.

The world is spinning as we free-fall. What was down is up. Up is down. My skull is going to split apart long before it smashes on the rocks below.

Lucan's roar fills the night, rattling my bones with chilling horror. Another burst of light—this time orange-tinted—explodes around him. As the magic fades, he is left back in a shape similar to the one I know well. Except dragon's wings still protrude from his back—one is broken and hanging at an odd angle. Half his body is coated in blood. The shot hit more of him than I realized.

I have to save them—save him.

I twist in the bitterly cold air. Trying to get to him—to all of them. Not that I know what I'd do if I could.

Copper scales rise along his neck and creep onto his cheeks. His hands are barely human, nails black and sharp. He's completely limp; it's as if his body tried to revert back into its normal, human state, but couldn't completely finish.

The errant thought of the night I fell during the Tribunal comes back to me, the pulsing wind I felt. How he caught me despite all odds. He dared to use this magic then, too, to save me.

He risked everything for me then—and now.

I must do the same for him. We can't die like this. There's too much left for all of us to do. The truth about Valor, Mum's research, the scourge, how to save this world, and the magic within me... None of it can end here.

"This won't be the end," I vow as the wind rushes past my ears, my body still plummeting toward the ground.

Think, Isola. Think. There's so much power within me. I have to be able to use it for myself. *Use it, Isola. Use it!*

I draw on whatever Ether surrounds me. I don't care. It doesn't matter if it could give me the strength to stop them. A cry rips through me as a flood drowns me in a surge of sudden power.

The feeling of Lucan's and my Ether flowing that day in the Tribunal returns, coursing between us, even at this distance.

Smoke fills my nose, trailing off my battered form. Fire sparks around me, snuffing before it can turn the air into an inferno. Trails of gray smoke curl through the air where the pops of Etherlight once were.

As if heated from within, I can feel the scars made when I was twelve. He's been a part of me all this time, carved onto my heart. Changing me into what I've always suspected I was—into what I've always dreaded most.

Stop being so afraid, Isola. The vicar and his Creed were the ones who told you to fear. What if I give in? What if I stop fighting it?

Wrenching, churning, snapping, popping.

I gasp, flailing through the air. My joints ache. My skin is too tight, and I claw at it, drawing blood, as though it's a horrible coat I must shed. Two invisible swords are pushing through my chest, skewering my lungs, slowly protruding from my back. They punch through the skin with a pain so sharp and bright, it's nearly pleasure.

I scream so loud, my voice swells into a roar. Two membranous wings unfurl, outstretching behind me. I see them in the outline of my shadow on the snow below. They catch the wind, slowing my fall. Instinct has me trying to flap them—to save my life—but I've never done such a thing; they're unruly and strange.

My arms and legs grow. Scales coat them, and as they do, the pain begins to vanish. Everything slowly starts to fade away. Things that were just so important are suddenly not so. Vinguard is little more than a distant memory, growing hazier by the second. The pain of Father's loss, of Saipha—

Saipha.

No. I grit too-sharp teeth in a too-long muzzle. I will not forget her. I will not succumb to the beast. I will not let it have me. My magic is my own.

A burst of Ethershade shoots out from me as ribbons of crimson. There is no gold, and there are no orange flames. It is as red as the blood I spilled across the altar of the Grand Chapel of Mercy. I imagine it enveloping the others, catching them like clawed hands.

A breath. And then a shock wave of crimson light and acrid mist. The whole world seems to take a collective gasp and go dark.

I force my eyes open, then blink. I'm on the ground, though I don't remember hitting it. The others are here, too. They roll on the deep snow of the wide cliff we've landed upon, unconscious but moving slightly. Twitching. Breathing. Wounded and blood-covered, but alive.

My chest squeezes tight as I catch sight of Lucan. He's there, just beyond my reach. His one wing still hangs at a sickening angle. But I see the rise and fall of his chest. He's hanging on, but he needs help.

The snow where I've landed has melted in a circle around me. I place my hands on the blackened rock between us, ready to crawl over, but notice something...unnatural. The stone is not blackened like smoke or fire or even the shock wave of Ether. It's a dark gray, just like it was in the Font when my blood dripped upon the stone. Except now it's faintly spotted with red.

Blood? No... More dots appear.

Shifting onto my knees, I tip my head back and stare up at the sky. Tiny motes of what look like bright-red ash fall like snow. The once cloud-dappled night sky is now overcast with an ominous, deep-red haze from which it falls.

Quivering, I reach up and behind and gasp when I catch sight of my hand. My fingers are crimson-scaled—obsidian nails extend from my fingertips, sharpened into points. The wing curves to meet my transformed hands. I see it in my periphery, then by craning my neck for a better look.

The bony structure of the wing is covered with tiny crimson scales in the same shade. The membrane is slate, dappled with swirls of red, as if painted to match the scourge that clouds the sky above us. The wings emit a haze I last saw in the sundering pits.

In horror, I shut my eyes, waiting to wake up, hoping it's nothing more than a vision, like when the power of the Font flowed into me—but it's not, and I know it. I open my eyes and blink at my taloned and scaled hands. Red...

I shake my head. There are copper, green, purple, blue, yellow, and silver dragons. There is the mighty white-and-gray Elder Dragon. But never, in my life, have I ever heard of a red dragon.

What... What am I?

Lucan's words from days ago come back to me, *Like it or not, Isola, you're something special.*

I stare at the blighted ground beneath me. With every inhale I take, the scourge my body emits fills my lungs, sizzling but not painful. It doesn't ravage my body as it does the land. It feels... *powerful.* Tilting my head back, I let out a scream that is part terror and part triumph, one that becomes a roar unlike any have ever heard before.

ACKNOWLEDGMENTS

Each book follows its own, unique path to publication, and *Dragon Cursed* is no exception. Countless people touched this story and made it possible—so many that it's impossible for me to thank everyone by name. While I will try to acknowledge as many as I can, I want to begin with a heartfelt thank-you to every individual who helped bring this book to life. From formatters to proofers, from printers to booksellers whose names I may never know... Thank you.

From the bottom of my heart, *thank you*.

Robert, my love, you must be the first I call out by name. Thank you for the countless hours you gave me to make this book happen. From the late nights to the early mornings, without your steady supply of lattes and all the baby-dragon wrangling you handled so I could focus, this story would still be scattered sentences and half-baked ideas. A special shout-out to Rae and Zoey as well for all your help wrangling the tiny dragon so I could work.

Speaking of people without whom this book would not exist, Liz. Thank you for believing in my storytelling and coming along for the ride with all my wild ideas. I deeply appreciate the ways you pushed and encouraged me to make this story the best it could be. It is an honor not only to be part of Mayhem, but to have been there from the very start.

Hannah and Mary, thank you both for the countless editorial hours you put in. The number of rewrites and last-minute changes could have had many flipping tables, but you pressed on and always brought your best. Even when this manuscript was at its worst.

The entire editorial team and all the people who gave feedback on this story inspired me to do the absolute best I could, and I hope you love the finished product as much as I do.

Speaking of teams, publishers exist because of the collective, tireless effort of incredible individuals. From publicity to promotions and marketing to logistics, thank you to everyone on the Mayhem team who helped make this book real. You are extraordinary. I must give a special shout-out to Elizabeth, without whom this gorgeous package would be far less gorgeous. Thank you for blessing *Dragon Cursed* with such a stunning cover.

Once more, thank you, Jenny, for helping me navigate the publishing process and for always being in my corner. I appreciate not only your advocacy, but your insight.

Emily, thank you for keeping me organized and coordinating so many moving pieces in my world so I can focus on writing.

A special shout-out to some of my closest friends. My safe space, my guides and guardians, where I go to for both reality checks and support. Danielle, I treasure our friendship endlessly. Thank you for always being a text away. Katie, thank you for beta reading and letting me bounce ideas off you. You're one of the best hype-people I know. Gideon, your help has allowed me to grow my business in ways I never imagined; thank you for beta reading and giving honest gut-checks. Michelle and Dominique, I cherish our lunches—you are such earnest and loving friends. Brigid and Sooz, even if we don't talk every day, every time we do, it reminds me how grateful I am to have you in my orbit. Ana, thank you for reminding me to take care of myself and giving me an excuse to do so.

To all my publishing teams around the globe, thank you as well. I am honored that you believe in this story enough to bring it to your readers, in your languages, in your homes. I appreciate all of my translators, editors, publicists, marketers, and everyone across the publishing world who help bring these pages to life.

A special shout-out to my patrons on Patreon...

Ellie T., Ashley B., Briceida R., Bri B., Julia R., SmallLittleMama, Julie L., Ariel J., BG, Jessica H., Katie C., Leslie K., Adele M., Austin L., Helens84, Melis, Shree P., Amber H., Emily B., Lauryn, Mary C.,

Becky M., CAnn K, Cathryn K., Luc L., Tori H., Sandy W., Erica A., Tracey M., Ashley H., Marta S, Matthew, Chelsea M., David A., Gie_are you listening, SWD, Elizabeth H., Megan F., Christina B, Zachary F., Madalyn W., Francesca, Jessica G., Emi C., Lauren B., Courtney, Maryalce B., Allie A., Karin, Amanda H., Christine P., Pippa S., Tiffany H., Zoe B, Courtney, AJ T., Kristyna, Elizabeth H., Dyani S., Jade, Amanda C., Imzadi, Vixie, Caitlyn P., MasterR50, Rebecca R., Anne of Daze, Laura R., Casey S., Sarah T., Mandi S., Melinda H., Karolina N. B., Laura H., Dani W., C Sharp, M Knight, Monique R., Claribel V., Sarah L., Lisa, Sorcha A., Caitlin P., Audrey C W., Mackenzie S., Amanda T., Kayleigh K., Renee, Alisha L., Esther R., Kaylie, Heather F., Andra P., Melisa K., Alli H., Jordan H., Healther E., Mani R., Samantha C., Katrina S., Sara E., Karin B., Eri W., Michael P, Dana A, Alexis P., Sheryl K B., Aemaeth, NaiculS, Lindsay W., Kira M., Charis, Tiffany L., Kassie P., Angela G., Elly M., Amy B., Meagan R., Axel R., Ambermoon86, Tarryn G., Kathleen M., Alexa A., Cassondra A., Emmie V, Emily R., AncientBeing, The Cherry Blossom Sky, Cindaren, Chelsea K., Ashley L., elanur, Javier A., Tomoaki K., Ekaterina O., Heather K., Ashley J., Brooke, Carolyn H., Rose G., Bridget W., Allison S., Nutmeg1422, Jule M., Chelsea S., Charles B., Rhianne, Kaylee C.

...thank you for being part of this adventure and helping ensure these stories are told.

And last, but never least...thank *you*, dear reader. Thank you for picking up this book and taking a chance on it. We may never meet (though I truly hope we do someday). We may be a world apart. But I appreciate you every single hour of the day. I couldn't do what I do without you. Here's to many more fantastical adventures!

ABOUT THE AUTHOR

Elise Kova is a #1 *Sunday Times* and *New York Times* bestselling author. She enjoys telling stories of fantasy worlds filled with magic and deep emotions. She lives in Florida and, when not writing, can be found playing video games, drawing, chatting with readers on social media, or daydreaming about her next story.

HODDERSCAPE

WANT MORE HODDERSCAPE?
JOIN US!

Sign up to our mailing list to get exclusive early sneak peeks and offers:

Follow us on our social channels:

 @hodderscape

Buy our books, find out more, and discover exclusive content:

www.hodderscape.co.uk

RAISING READERS
Books Build Bright Futures

Dear Reader,

We'd love your attention for one more page to tell you about the crisis in children's reading, and what we can all do.

Studies have shown that reading for fun is the **single biggest predictor of a child's future life chances** – more than family circumstance, parents' educational background or income. It improves academic results, mental health, wealth, communication skills, ambition and happiness.[1]

The number of children reading for fun is in rapid decline. Young people have a lot of competition for their time. In 2024, 1 in 10 children and young people in the UK aged 5 to 18 did not own a single book at home.[2]

Hachette works extensively with schools, libraries and literacy charities, but here are some ways we can all raise more readers:

- Reading to children for just 10 minutes a day makes a difference
- Don't give up if children aren't regular readers – there will be books for them!
- Visit bookshops and libraries to get recommendations
- Encourage them to listen to audiobooks
- Support school libraries
- Give books as gifts

There's a lot more information about how to encourage children to read on our website: **www.RaisingReaders.co.uk**

Thank you for reading.

---

[1] OECD, '21st-Century Readers: Developing Literacy Skills in a Digital World', 2021, https://www.oecd.org/en/publications/21st-century-readers_a83d84cb-en.html

[2] National Literacy Trust, 'Book Ownership in 2024', November 2024, https://literacytrust.org.uk/research-services/research-reports/book-ownership-in-2024